MURDER *in a* COUNTRY VILLAGE

BOOKS BY F.L. EVERETT

THE EDIE YORK MYSTERY SERIES

A Report of Murder

MURDER
in a
COUNTRY VILLAGE

F.L. EVERETT

bookouture

Published by Bookouture in 2023

An imprint of Storyfire Ltd.
Carmelite House
50 Victoria Embankment
London EC4Y 0DZ

www.bookouture.com

ISBN: 978-1-83790-467-9
eBook ISBN: 978-1-83790-460-0

For Andy. Who loves the countryside and dogs.

'Life in England is not cheerful, but it is interesting.'

— IVAN TURGENEV

'There is nothing half so green that I know anywhere, as the grass of that churchyard; nothing half so shady as its trees; nothing half so quiet as its tombstones.'

— CHARLES DICKENS, DAVID COPPERFIELD

CHAPTER ONE

FEBRUARY 1941

The offices of the *Manchester Chronicle* were unusually silent. It was early in the day, and the few of us who had already arrived had hung up our coats and hats and were sitting with bent heads over notes and typewriters. The buses were almost back to normal after the Christmas Blitz, and recently I'd started to enjoy the quiet before the workday began in earnest with its ringing telephones and gossip, crime reporter Des shouting about headlines, and the editor's secretary Janet Paulson clacking up and down in her wedge heels, covertly checking on us all.

I was studying the births, marriages and deaths column in yesterday's edition of the *Chronicle*, wondering if *Miss Emilia Berry, 83, retired headmistress of Grange Park Girls' Grammar, taken too soon* would make a good subject for my obituary column, so I jumped when the swing door crashed back against the wall and Basil, the new post boy, burst in. He was clutching a large sack of letters and an even bigger bunch of forced lilies, the cat-like reek of which I could smell from across the office.

'Miss Cooper in?' he called. Ethel Cooper was my friend on the letters desk, though she seldom arrived until just before nine, due to Having a Mother, as she put it; one who lived with her and was widely known to be rather difficult.

'That bloody parrot.' Ethel would say. 'She's besotted with him, he's always clinging to her shoulder while I'm trying to wrestle her into her petticoat.'

Nelson the African grey parrot could say 'Victory for Europe!' and 'Please, stop it, Mother', along with several other choice phrases about Hitler which, if we were invaded, Ethel rather hoped he wouldn't feel compelled to repeat.

'She's not here yet,' I told Basil, and pointed to her desk. 'Just leave the letters there.'

'These are hers too,' he said. He was only about fourteen, and looked nonplussed by the great spray of heavily scented blooms in his arms.

'There's a note,' he added helpfully. He dropped the bouquet onto her blotter as if it were a squalling cat, and waved a square of cardboard.

'It says: *To dearest Ethel, will you be my Valentine? I believe you—*'

'Stop it!' I cried. 'That's private, Basil. She won't want the whole world knowing her romantic business.'

'Oh, righto.' He shrugged. 'Anyway, I've got a bunch of something with very spiky thorns for a Mrs Borrowdale. Where's she?'

I stifled a laugh. Mrs Borrowdale was the morally outraged and permanently bad-tempered widow who ran the newspaper cuttings library.

'Third floor,' I said. 'You can't miss her.'

I assumed the spiky thorns were the reporters' idea of a joke, and hoped she wouldn't be too offended. I'd quite forgotten it was Valentine's Day – it had never brought me anything romantic in the past, and was unlikely to start now – but I was surprised that Annie, my best friend and flatmate, hadn't mentioned it last night. She had just started to step out with our friend Arnold, and he was quite clearly entranced. I imagined him hovering shyly on the steps of the hospital where she was an auxiliary nurse, clutching a wilting bunch of snowdrops, although perhaps that was expecting too much. I hoped he wouldn't forget to send a card at least; Annie set great store by 'romance' – meaning Hollywood melodramas, novels with titles like *How Bright the Stars*, seventy-eight records featuring yearning strings and crooning endearments, and scented letters professing eternal adoration.

Ethel, however, had never mentioned a suitor, so perhaps the flowers were a statement of hopeful intent. I thought how happy I'd be for her if she ended up marrying a lovely man who also liked nineteenth-century literature and country walking, instead of being beholden to Mother and the imperious Nelson night and day. But Ethel always claimed she wasn't the marrying kind.

More colleagues were beginning to arrive now, coming from the trams in little gaggles of damp hats and battered briefcases, joking wearily about their lack of valentines, and scanning the office for any sign of Vi and her tea trolley. You knew when it was coming, thanks to the high, agonising screech of its wheels and the violent, metallic rattling of the urns. It sounded rather like the approach of a ramshackle medieval army, but, in its favour, it occasionally carried buns.

'Crikey,' said Des, who had recently emerged from retirement like an old terrier scenting a rabbit. He threw his hat onto the coat stand, and it wobbled alarmingly. 'Ethel's got herself an admirer.'

'Looks like it,' I said. 'Good for her!'

'Nothing for you, m'dear?' he asked in his avuncular fashion. 'No billets-doux, no declarations of nuptial intent in the postbag?'

'I hope not.'

I shuddered. Horribly recently, my own brief love interest,

Charles Emerson, had turned out to be a murderer, and died under the rubble from an incendiary that scored a direct hit on the flat I shared with Annie. The idea of ever falling for anyone again seemed slightly less pleasant than three hours at the dentist followed by an evening of Chinese opera.

'Ah well,' he said comfortably, tapping his pipe. 'Mrs Des will be enjoying an evening avec moi over a small pork pie from Ferguson's and a milk stout, if I'm not mistaken.'

I laughed, just as Ethel pushed through the door, wrestling with her umbrella.

'Good heavens,' she said, stopping dead. 'What in the Lord's name are those?'

'Valentine's flowers for you,' I said. 'There's a card, apparently.'

She shrugged off her wool coat and hung it carefully, keeping her tartan beret on, and picked it up.

'It doesn't say who it's from,' she said, puzzled. 'It just says, *To dearest Ethel, will you be my Valentine? I believe you appreciate lilies. An admirer.*'

'Gosh,' I said. 'How thrilling! A secret admirer.'

'I don't know...' she murmured. She looked rather pale. 'You get some funny people writing in, you know, Edie. I mostly put the loons straight into the wastepaper bin, but sometimes they get ideas.'

'Anyone you've had your eye on?' I asked.

She shook her head. 'Not really.'

That wasn't quite 'no', and I resolved to probe further at lunchtime. Poking about in my friends' romantic lives was as close as I was prepared to get to love these days.

I had looked up from my typewriter and was flagging down Vi and her wobbling vehicle mid-morning when I noticed that the lilies had disappeared.

'Gone in the bin,' said Janet Paulson, as she passed. 'Smelled like a tomcat's doings, and Miss Cooper says her mother's allergic to them.'

As luck would have it, my lunch break coincided with Ethel's.

'Fancy a bun at the Kardomah?' she called, as we gathered up our coats and handbags. I did, but drew a regretful breath to explain that I was on a penny-pinching drive, as Annie and I now had a new flat with an exorbitant rent.

I had just paid up for the first week, and the money I had left was of the clinking rather than the rustling sort. As we set off, Ethel saw me rummaging in my purse for change.

'I'll stand you a bun, dearie,' she said. 'Perhaps even a small cheese sandwich, if I'm feeling flush.'

I didn't like accepting charity – a childhood spent in a children's home, dressed in hand-me-downs, had offered enough experience of do-gooding to last me a lifetime – but Ethel was kind, and I was eager to know more about her admirer.

'I'll stand you lunch on payday,' I promised.

December's bomb damage had been swept away from the roads and pavements now, and though the old buildings of Manchester still stood broken and twisted, scaffolding had gone up amongst the sandbags; helmeted workers swarmed over it, rebuilding and repairing.

The rain had stopped and there was the merest hint of spring outside, a softness in the atmosphere and an acid green fuzz just beginning on the trees. Perhaps things were on the up. Romance in the air for Annie and Ethel; a new home; and – for the time being, at least – the bombing seemed to have stopped. Now we just had to worry about a coastal invasion.

On the way to the Kardomah, we talked about how to extend the life of our old spring hats.

'Add a jaunty ribbon plucked from around the cat's neck,' suggested Ethel.

'A stained tea towel will readily serve as a cheerful headscarf,' I supplied. Nothing amused us more than mocking the 'wartime housewives' tips' which readers sent in.

Once we were settled at Ethel's usual table behind a pillar, and had ordered from the harassed waitress – cheese on toast for me, and sardines for Ethel – I leaned forward to speak over the clatter of cutlery and the little jazz band which was thumping away in the background.

'Who do you really think your admirer is?' I asked.

Ethel sighed, studying the damask tablecloth as though it contained the answer. 'I really don't know, Edie. To be frank, I'm troubled by those flowers.'

'Why? I can't imagine what they must have cost at this time of year,' I added. 'I didn't know you could still get flowers like that.'

'I think I might have upset somebody,' she said, fiddling with the strap of her green lizard-skin handbag. It had once been Mother's, she'd told me, and Ethel had found a sucked cough sweet stuck to its silk lining the first time she used it. *Beggars can't be choosers*, she'd said philosophically.

'In what way?' My greatest ambition was to be a crime reporter, but directly after that came 'recipient of secret gossip'.

'Oh... it's so silly,' said Ethel, as the waitress banged our plates down in the wrong places. We silently swapped.

'Tell me anyway.'

'Well,' she said. 'As you know, I love country walking. It keeps me sane, what with Mother and Nelson. Years ago, I was part of the mass trespass on Kinder Scout, and it was marvellous, all of us together with our backpacks and boots, and such a feeling of freedom.' She smiled. 'I still go walking around Birchcroft up in the Peaks whenever I can, and I've met quite a few friendly walkers on my travels.'

Ethel forked up some tepid sardine and chewed experimentally. I waited.

'One of the people I met was Joyce Reid,' she said. 'She's an artist, very bohemian, and she inherited a huge, remote farmhouse back in the twenties. She's turned it into a sort of ramshackle set of studios for artists and crafters. Different people come and go, some stay for months or years, and they all go on these great long walks together at weekends, and paint and sketch...'

'But that sounds marvellous,' I said, puzzled. 'Where does your admirer come into it?'

'Well, that's just it,' said Ethel, putting down her empty coffee cup. I wondered if we had time for a cake.

'There are several quite glamorous younger people there, and they tend to drift in and out of each other's rooms... it's rather shocking, but as I said, it's very Bloomsbury Group, nobody belongs to anybody and they're all wildly free with their affections... nothing has ever happened with me and any of the men, of course,' she added hastily. 'Look at me, I'm thirty-four, with a tartan hat. As if they'd look twice.'

I was about to argue – Ethel was terribly pretty, despite her rather firm nose. 'But,' she went on, 'I went for tea the other week, and they were all there – Joyce, Nora, Joan, Sabrina, Theo, Jean-Luc and even Aubrey, who hardly ever comes out of his studio.

'He's a painter,' she added. 'Rather good. Big, angry landscapes and portraits. I believe they sell for quite a lot.'

'They all sound fascinating,' I said. 'But what's this got to do with your flowers?'

'It sounds ludicrous now I'm telling you,' said Ethel worriedly, 'but here goes... We all were talking, eating Joyce's awful sugarless seedcake – honestly, it was like eating a sandbag – and we began to discuss symbolism in art and life, and why big concepts like birth and death are represented by certain images – like storks and rosebuds for babies...' She trailed off.

'And?' I prompted. The waitress was stumping back towards us.

'Somebody mentioned lilies being representative of death,' she said quietly, waving her away. 'I know it's silly, mine are probably nothing to do with it, but... it stayed with me, that's all, and I wondered if someone over there dislikes me, or wants to... well, to warn me off.'

I was silent. It did seem an odd coincidence – weren't roses and violets more in keeping with Valentine's Day? Lilies were certainly not available yet in the flower shops, so whoever sent them must have gone to great efforts.

'Whatever would they need to warn you about?' I asked. 'It's not as if you're part of their odd little set, you're just an occasional visitor. What was the conversation about lilies exactly – can you remember?'

She paused. 'I think I said something about how sinister they could be. How I went to a funeral of a friend who was killed, and all the church smelled of lilies. How evocative a scent it is.'

'Who made the link to death?'

'That's just it,' Ethel said. 'I can't remember. The conversation moved on to something else soon afterwards. The thing is, I haven't met anyone else at all recently – and I can't imagine any of the men at the office being so lavish, can you?'

I considered the *Chronicle*'s current ragtag mob of the very young and very old, and shook my head.

We were silent for a moment.

'Look, Ethel,' I said, 'I do think that's rather odd. I have an idea.'

'Edie, last time you had an idea you brought down a Nazi spying ring,' she said, raising an eyebrow. 'Are you sure you want to have another one quite so soon?'

I laughed. 'It's a thoroughly harmless one this time. Why don't we both go to Birchcroft and say we're going walking in the hills – and perhaps I can meet Joyce and the others and I'll use my best reporter's skills to see if I can find out if anyone's developed a grudge against you? Though why they should, I've no idea. I'm pretty sure a stranger simply likes you. Or perhaps it's Des,' I added, and we both guffawed.

'If there was a bottle of milk stout and a pack of Ogdens' Nut Flake tobacco on my desk, it would definitely be him,' she said. 'Actually, Edie, that's not a bad idea about the trip. I was thinking of going for a ramble this weekend, if the weather improves. Come with. Have you got walking boots?'

I almost laughed at the idea of myself owning anything quite so hearty.

'I'll lend you some,' she said, rolling her eyes. 'Let's meet at nine o'clock tomorrow at Knott Mill station, and bear in mind it'll take ages to get there because they've blacked out all the railway signs so we have to stop and wait for stragglers at every station. Bring sandwiches.'

She signalled for the bill. In all the excitement, we'd missed our chance of a cake.

I'd assumed Annie would be out when I got home – either still at work healing the sick and injured up at Manchester Royal, or leaping into Arnold's shiny black mortuary van for a romantic evening out at the pub. He was well versed in dealing with the dead now he ran the family business – perhaps I should ask him about the symbolism of lilies. When I let myself in, though, I was surprised to find her sitting at our little fold-out dining table, an unopened envelope in front of her.

'Oh, thank goodness you're back,' she said. 'I can't open it, Edie.'

'What do you mean? Is it the grocer's bill? We've been perfectly sensible this month; I haven't even collected all my meat ration—'

'No,' she wailed. Her cup of tea was cooling beside her, which was thoroughly unlike Annie. Normally, she drank tea at a temperature that could strip varnish. 'It's a letter,' she whispered. 'From the War Office.'

My legs were suddenly wet strands of wool, and I sat down heavily. There was only one person Annie knew well enough to warrant an official letter.

'Do you want me to open it for you?' I asked. I took her hand, which was cold and shaking.

'No, I mustn't be cowardly. I'll do it, now you're here.'

She retrieved her hand and slit open the envelope with the butter knife. Inside was a single piece of thin paper. She scanned it, then laid it back down and stared straight ahead. Gently, I reached across and turned it towards me.

With the deepest regret, I must inform you that your fiancé, Private Peter Barker...

A few more words jumped out: *in action... bravery... may you take comfort in knowing...*

'Oh, Annie,' I said. An agonising lump blocked my throat. 'I'm so very sorry.'

'He wasn't even my fiancé any more,' she said in a small, tight voice. 'We agreed it was all over long before Christmas. I just... I suppose I thought I'd see him again.'

Her voice cracked and tears filled her eyes.

'His poor mother,' she said. 'And oh, Edie, his little sister, Kate – she worshipped Pete. She's only sixteen. She...' Her tears turned to sobs, and she laid her head on the tablecloth and howled. I rubbed her narrow back and murmured how sorry I was, and what a horrible shock it must be. I hadn't known Pete well; they had been out together just before the war, and he'd made a hasty proposal to Annie immediately before he was sent abroad to fight.

'I only said yes to cheer him up,' she'd said afterwards. 'In case he goes and cops a bullet.'

Now, it seemed, he had – and Annie was inconsolable.

'I know it was all over and done between us months ago,' she managed through her sobs. 'I didn't even want to marry him really, but I... I strung him along. I was cruel and thoughtless and now he's dead!'

'Annie, you weren't! You were quite clear with him and he wrote back and wished you well, you know he did.'

He just hadn't told anyone they were no longer engaged, I thought. Perhaps he hadn't wanted the other lads feeling sorry for him as they talked about sweethearts back home and showed off their fading photographs. Annie was a prize, and poor Pete knew it.

'I wish I'd been nicer to him,' she said, and I gathered her up and let her sob snail-trails all over the shoulder of my wool suit.

It was a shock when our new landlady, Mrs Turner, tapped on the door and opened it a crack without waiting.

'There's a young man downstairs,' she said, disapproval radiating from every frost-white hair of her head. 'He's asking for Miss Hemmings. Please don't keep the front door open, it chills the hall and depletes the coal ration for all of us. And I'll thank you to remember that I am your landlady, not a butler. In future, I should be grateful if you'd deal with your own callers.'

She bustled off, and Annie looked at me with despair.

'It's Arnold,' she hissed. 'We're supposed to be going to a St Valentine's Day concert by Bram Rogers and his Toe-Tapping Ensemble. What shall I tell him?'

'Are you sure you can't go?' I ventured.

'Look at me!' Annie said, indicating her tear-streaked face. 'I can't be sobbing over one man and going out with another!'

'But it's only Arnold,' I said helplessly. 'He'll surely understand.'

'I don't know what I feel towards him now,' she said dramatically. 'I'm distraught about Pete and I'm going to have to write to his mother and Kate, and I just...' She burst into tears again, and ran into her bedroom. I heard the squeak of bedsprings as she flung herself head first into the pillow.

'I'll tell him myself then, shall I?'

'Please!' came a muffled shout.

Sighing, and heavy-hearted over Pete, I went down to greet Arnold. The blackout began a little later now, and it was still light on the step. He had smartened himself up; he'd shaved, and Brylcreemed his bright red hair, and now he was going to be terribly let down.

'Still prinking is she?' he said, and I noticed he was holding a little bunch of early crocuses.

'Bit hopeless, I know,' he added, seeing my glance. 'Picked them in the garden, but I have got her a nice card. It's got two mice on it, sitting in a watering can, and one's saying to the other—'

'Arnold,' I interrupted. 'I'm so sorry, but I'm afraid tonight's off. She's had bad news.'

'Oh! Not her mum again, I hope?' His kind face crumpled with concern.

'No. It's... well... has she ever mentioned Pete Barker?'

If this was my best attempt at tact and diplomacy, Ethel might be best off taking somebody else to do her probing at Birchcroft.

'Her chap in the army?' said Arnold. 'She told me they'd called it a day, but if that's not the case...'

'Oh no, they did!' I said.

Behind me, I heard footsteps. 'Door!' shouted Mrs Turner.

'Gosh, she's a stickler, isn't she?' said Arnold admiringly.

'An absolute martinet,' I agreed, pulling it to behind me.

'The thing is, Annie's just had a letter from the War Office,' I went on. 'Pete's been killed in action, and as you can imagine, she's horribly shocked. She knew his mum and sister, and she's not quite in the mood for a concert...' I struggled on, unsure why I was downplaying Annie's distress other than from an inbuilt desire not to cause awkwardness – a less than ideal trait for an aspiring crime reporter.

'Oh, how awful.' Arnold looked genuinely shocked. 'Might I nip up and see her?'

'No, you might not!' shouted a disembodied voice from the direction of Mrs Turner's rooms.

'Don't worry,' I said. 'I'll pass on your condolences. But I'm sure she'll be in touch very soon.'

'Gosh, I hope she's all right,' said Arnold. 'That poor chap... when my old man died, Mum didn't come out of their bedroom for a week. And we're in the business, so to speak.'

Aware that cold air was seeping into the hall, I was alert for another shout from Mrs Turner, when he said, 'I don't suppose you'd like to go with Lou, seeing as I've already got the tickets? I know he's at a loose end tonight.'

For a moment, I thought how much I'd like to go and lose myself listening to the Toe-Tapping Ensemble with my most briskly sarcastic friend, but Annie was still crying on her bed, and it seemed particularly heartless to snatch Arnold's tickets on St Valentine's day.

'I can't,' I said. 'But you take Lou. He's not bad at the foxtrot when he puts his mind to it.'

Arnold laughed. 'Give her my love, and these,' he said, and he handed over the card and flowers and wandered off down the path.

I took his gifts to Annie, and she sat up, dishevelled and pink-cheeked.

She opened the card as if she were unsealing a court summons, and barely glanced at the little posy.

'I know it's poorly timed,' I said, 'but he's awfully sweet on you, and I thought perhaps you could...'

'I can't, Edie,' she said, and sank back against the pillows. 'I feel so guilty about Pete. I think I just lead men on for my own amusement, and I don't really mean it, and then they get all hopeful and I don't have the heart to tell them I wasn't serious...'

'But you like Arnold,' I said, shocked. 'I thought you were going to make a go of it, you seem so happy together!'

'It's only been a month,' she muttered. 'I don't know, Edie, I think I'll just hurt his feelings, like I hurt Pete. Maybe I should just become a nun...'

The thought of my bottle-blonde, jitterbugging best friend donning the habit was so unlikely I laughed.

'Oh, it's all right for you,' she said, 'with your proper job, and your ambitions. Girls like me won't have anything to do when the war ends, except get married. And I don't know if I want to marry Arnold.'

'Can't you just go out with him for a bit?' I ventured. 'Have some fun?'

'That's the whole trouble!' she exploded, sitting up. 'I *had some fun* with Pete, and now he's dead!'

There seemed no logic to this, and I tried to say so, but Annie wasn't listening.

'I shall tell Arnold we can only ever be friends,' she said sadly. 'It's best we go no further in case I break his heart, too.'

I picked up the card that she'd discarded. Inside, the printed message read: *May your Valentine's Day be happy and gay, With treats as nice as these wee mice*, which didn't strike me as hopelessly love-struck, but I knew Annie well, and once she'd made her mind up, there was no shifting her.

We spent a gloomy evening together while Annie wept into her fish pie and I tried feebly to cheer her up, then she took herself off to her room again to write to Pete's family. War was so pointlessly miserable, I thought. All these beloved young men being killed and forgotten by the world, when they could have had long, fulfilling lives, good jobs, happy marriages, children... By the time I went to bed, I felt rather heartbroken myself.

I lay awake for a long time, thinking about how I could help Annie. I thought about friendship, too, and how the war had in some ways brought us all closer, despite everything. I had never enjoyed relying on other people, but lately, I'd had no choice. Annie and I had stayed at our friend Clara's family home for two weeks after our own building was bombed; our poor old landlord Mr Benson was killed by the same bomb that did for Charles Emerson. Clara's parents couldn't have been kinder, giving over their spare room to us both, with reading books carefully chosen by Mrs Lafferty placed by our pillows, alongside carafes of water and little etched drinking glasses on the bedside tables.

Like her husband, she was a keen amateur Egyptologist, and the entire house was stuffed to the gills with murky paintings of the Pyramids, sudden displays of scarab beetles round dark corners, broken bits of granite brought back by a globe-trotting great uncle, and tottering piles of books. I had been given *In the Footsteps of Ptolemy*, by Captain W.C. Borwood, and Annie had *The Mysteries of the Tombs*, by the Reverend I. Laird-Porsch, with a withered rook feather marking a chapter entitled 'The Boy King: Death Rituals'.

'Swap?' she'd suggested gloomily, but neither of them greatly appealed to me. We had spent most evenings after work scouring the classifieds for suitable accommodation.

'It has to be near the hospital,' she said, and I added, 'and on the bus route to work.'

'And with a pantry,' Annie said happily. She had long fantasised about having one, and had spent much of our time at Mr Benson's sniffing the milk and prodding the butter, muttering 'gone off again'.

'It'd be nice to have a proper bathroom too,' I added. 'With pipes that don't clank as if a mastodon's having a wash.'

'Why would a mastodon make the pipes clank?' Annie

asked. 'It'd crack the bath of course, but the pipes wouldn't be affected.'

'You and your medical training,' I said, and threw a small, folding map of Cairo at her head.

Ten long days after our search began, we had found Mrs Turner's Lodging House. It was a tall, red-brick Victorian, tucked away in a leafy road behind Alexandra Park. The lodgings were on the second floor and had a view over its grass and trees, so you could almost believe you were in the countryside, if it weren't for the buses rattling past.

'There's a very modern kitchen,' Mrs Turner said. She was very small, at least seventy-five, and wore a large silver cross round her neck. She was rather terrifying.

'I had the oven installed just before the war,' she went on. 'It's got a pantry and a very smart pottery hen you can keep your eggs in. Should eggs ever become available.'

Annie shot me a look of purest longing.

'The bathroom's quite new too,' Mrs Turner said. 'You've got your own drying rack for smalls, a basin with cold running water and a shared indoor lavatory. I've turned the old privy into a bomb shelter.'

Annie mouthed 'let's say yes' to me, and I subtly gave her a thumbs up.

'We'd love to take it,' she said. 'I think we can afford the rent between us, can't we, Edie?'

'Driving a hard bargain' was not in Annie's lexicon, but I nodded. It was so much better than our old flat, I could surely squeeze out a couple more shillings a week from the pittance the *Chronicle* paid me.

'Good,' Mrs Turner said. 'I won't have late payers. And you must understand that this is a suitable and Christian home for single ladies. There must be no male visitors hanging about like tomcats.'

'Oh!' said Annie. 'But Arnold...'

'And Lou,' I added. Lou was not a male visitor, I thought. He was a policeman, and our friend, despite his enormous capacity to irritate me. Nothing would feel the same unless they could drop in for a cup of tea and a regular dispatch on local crimes.

'We have a friend,' I said carefully. 'He's a Detective Inspector with the Manchester City Police. He likes to make sure we're safe.'

'Well, I expect he can walk you both to the gate,' said Mrs Turner firmly. 'Other than that, he could be standing at the Lord's right hand dressed in the fiery plumage of glory, and I still wouldn't allow it.'

Annie and I shared a despairing glance. We knew when we were beaten.

'Pick up the keys Tuesday week,' she said. 'I'll get the rat man round first, just to be sure.'

I was glad to have Annie just across the hall as I lay in the creaking brass bed in my little bedroom, finally allowing sleep to overcome me. I had no family, but perhaps over time, good friends made up for that.

There was a note with the first post on Saturday morning, and when I opened it, I was surprised to see Lou's neat, copperplate handwriting.

Heard about the trouble, he'd written. *Arnold not happy. Telephone me at your earliest convenience. Lou.* (*DI Brennan to you.*)

Annie's rejection had clearly affected Arnold much more than his politeness had suggested. I was dying to hear Lou's version of events. On my way to the bus stop, I took a detour to the nearest telephone box and rang up Lou at work.

'DI Brennan,' he barked. 'Ah, it's you. Look, are you free later on?'

I explained my plan to investigate the provenance of Ethel's flowers and, less enticingly, climb a large hill, and he snorted.

'If you're not back by evening, I'll send in the huskies,' he said. 'Otherwise, I'll pick you up from Mrs Turner's Prison for Young Gentlewomen this evening, at seven thirty.'

'I shall look forward to it,' I said.

By then, I hoped to have something even more interesting to talk about than Arnold's broken heart.

CHAPTER TWO

I met Ethel on the station steps. She was wearing tweed slacks, a huge hand-knitted bottle-green jumper and a warm jacket, and had a woolly hat pulled down over her ears. On her feet were well-used leather walking boots, and she carried an extra pair, which she held up to me as I approached.

'Here are your boots, Cinderella,' she called. 'I've made enough sandwiches to feed half of Lancashire.'

I had a flask of tea and one mouse-trap cheese roll, so I was glad to hear it.

'They eat awfully well up there,' she told me, as we waited for our train to pull in. 'Nobody seems to be on rations at all, they've all got vegetable patches and fresh eggs and chickens.'

'Oh, but do they have to kill them with their bare hands?' I asked, as we climbed aboard. 'I don't think I could stand it.'

There was a young WVS sitting opposite, who gave me a rather disgusted look and pulled her knitting from her bag, determined to ignore us. I didn't know if it was due to our manly slacks, or my choice of conversational topic.

'Well, I don't suppose they kill them by singing them into a pleasant coma,' Ethel said. 'But honestly, the eggs... they're simply wonderful.'

'When did you have the eggs?' I asked, curious.

Ethel smiled. 'Oh, I stayed at Athena House once, when there was a storm and the trains stopped. I slept on a mattress in a little back bedroom full of wet oil paintings and I swear I was hallucinating from turps fumes when I woke up. But Joyce did make me a marvellous boiled egg for breakfast.'

'Athena House?'

'Named after the Greek goddess of creativity,' said Ethel in a deliberately dramatic voice. The WVS rolled her eyes.

'It used to be Netherwood Farm, but Joyce likes the classics. She's awfully clever; she went to Cambridge on a scholarship after the last war. But then she inherited the place from her uncle, and put all her energy into arts and crafts and general bohemianism. She's quite formidable, as you'll see when you meet her.'

The WVS cleared her throat. She was beginning to annoy me.

'Excuse me,' she said, 'are you talking about Joyce Reid?'

'Yes,' said Ethel. 'Do you know her?'

'Well,' she said coldly, 'I know of her. That's enough for me.'

'What do you mean?'

'I'm from up Birchcroft way,' she said. 'Sally Corrin. How d'you do. That lot up at the madhouse – they're all pacifists, you know. *Conscientious objectors*. Cowards, more like. Never mind all our dads and husbands and brothers and sons off to war, getting killed and maimed for the sake of our freedom, never mind the sacrifices and the march of Hitler across Europe, and the bombs that have almost destroyed us all...' She was getting quite poetic. 'Apparently, according to Joyce and her artistic cronies, it's all pointless, and we should just fall down and let the Nazis roll their tanks over us because "all war is bad".'

She drew an outraged breath. 'It's not as though any of us

wants it! But we don't have a choice! You can't just stay out of things!'

Sally only looked about eighteen, but she could argue all right. I felt rather sorry for her parents.

'I know Joyce likes the idea of pursuing a peaceful route where possible...' said Ethel diplomatically.

Sally sniffed so violently she almost choked. 'If that's what you call it. Holding meetings saying all our war efforts are pointless, urging everyone in the village to down tools and drift about painting abstract *responses to conflict* that a child could do better. Making it seem as if our families and friends are risking their lives for nothing.'

'Oh dear,' I murmured. 'I can see why that might be difficult.'

'It's more than difficult,' snapped Sally, 'it's an insult. We all want them to leave, but they won't go. And they've the morals of alley cats, the lot of them. Mum says it was a lovely house before they ruined it with their daubs and turned it into a... a heathen bear garden!'

She threw herself back against the seat and resumed knitting.

'Look, I'm sorry,' she muttered. 'I'm sure you've good reason for knowing her. She just gets my goat, and I'm not the only one.'

Our uncomfortable silence was only broken by the guard flinging the carriage door open and making jocular remarks about ladies in slacks.

The journey took almost two hours. Ethel read *The Times* and I read my crime book, which was rather gripping – *The Fashion in Shrouds*, by Margery Allingham – but as Ethel had warned, whenever I looked up it was strange to see the anonymous stations, with their painted-over signs, sliding by. I had no idea where we were, so when the guard bellowed 'Birchcroft!'

and I looked out of the window to see sage-green hills and huddled stone cottages, it came as a surprise.

'Good luck to you both,' said Sally, as we hastily alighted from the train. We gazed after her stiff, departing back.

'Goodness, that was awkward,' said Ethel.

I smiled weakly. 'Perhaps we won't mention it when we visit later.'

'Oh well, Joyce probably will, regardless,' she said. 'She's very keen on her pacifism campaigning. She was a nurse in France in the Great War, you see, when she was only seventeen, and she said the whole ghastly experience had made her realise that no war can ever be justified.'

'Maybe she has a point,' I said. 'But then again...'

I thought of Charles and his mother Lillian, and their passion for Hitler. I imagined the Nazis goose-stepping into Manchester, rounding people up, hanging their stark scarlet and black banners from our Victorian town hall.

'No,' I said more firmly. 'Everything about war is appalling, but I simply can't see any alternative.'

'Nor can I, ducks,' said Ethel. 'But I suspect you'll like Joyce anyway. Once encountered, never forgotten!'

I was beginning to feel rather intimidated by this forceful woman who lived how she liked, and campaigned for peace in a village full of people who hated what she stood for. I wondered if the whole plan was a terrible idea and we should just have our walk and go straight home, so I could wash off the mud before meeting Lou.

Ethel produced a well-used map and flapped it open on a mossy stone wall.

'I thought we'd go up over Nether Ridge, skirt round Birch Hill, then we can clamber up to the summit,' she said, helpfully tracing her finger along the printed contours, though as far as I was concerned, they could have been darts in a dress pattern.

'It's an easy ramble if we take it slowly, and we can eat our sandwiches looking out over the valley. Then back down, we'll go for a cup of tea at Athena House, and you can do your finest detective work.'

Ethel folded the map and gestured at the hills looming above us.

'Lay on, Macduff,' she said cheerfully.

I had no idea how far we'd be walking, or what we might encounter – I had a sudden image of a charging bull, head lowered, eyes rolling – but Ethel was striding forth up the cobbled lane that led from the station, and I had no choice but to follow her.

Just over an hour later, we were trudging up a muddy hillside. To our right, soft spring sunlight bathed the wide hills, creating a dappled sweep of colour, and below us, Birchcroft's weathered stone glowed as chimney smoke rose into the still blue air. Snowdrops dotted the graves in the old churchyard, and a tiny train chugged over a distant viaduct, a plume of purest white steam dispersing in its wake.

Ethel had been right, it was a glorious day and I was enjoying myself, even if my borrowed boots were slightly too big.

'Isn't... it... beautiful?' she panted. She paused for a moment, to my relief. 'Look.' She put a hand on my shoulder and pointed. 'That long path over there leads to Athena House. You can't see it because of the trees.'

'Might some of them be out walking today?' I asked, bending over with my hands clamped onto my tweedy thighs to draw in breath. I really wasn't terribly healthy for twenty-four.

'Oh, perhaps!' she said. 'I hadn't thought – we could have met up earlier if I'd dropped them a line.'

I was quite relieved she hadn't – I felt a cup of tea with them would be enough bohemianism for one afternoon.

We continued on, pointing out seventeenth-century churches to one another, stopping occasionally to gaze over the valley at lonely farmhouses and distant horses standing patiently in their fields. It was easy to pretend the war wasn't happening up here. Perhaps that was why Joyce was so wedded to her pacifism – because she didn't see the dark chaos of the city's bomb damage, wires spilling from broken houses like tangled wool, beams and joists heaped in a blackened game of spillikins where people had once lived. There were no bombs here, no sandbags, nothing to suggest disarray, other than the small figure of a woman far below, raking over a tidy vegetable patch in her garden, where once, perhaps her husband or son would have done the outdoor jobs.

'Is the summit much further?' I asked Ethel. I felt we'd been walking uphill for several hours, but my watch claimed it was only half past twelve.

'No, I promise,' she said. 'Just round that bend, then a quick scramble and we'll have our lunch as a reward.'

A few minutes later, we pulled ourselves up the last few feet of slithering scree and collapsed onto a small, grassy plateau dotted with rocks. The valley lay spread before us, its soft greens and umbers glowing in the sun. I tried to imprint the scene onto my memory, so when Mr Gorringe was being particularly intransigent at work, or Lou was riling me simply by existing, I could instantly return here and breathe the pure, spring air.

'We won't stay too long,' said Ethel, setting out our picnic on a flat rock. 'The weather can spin on a sixpence in the hills; those clouds on the horizon could turn into something nasty.'

'No wonder you love it here,' I said. I wandered nearer to the edge, with its sheer drop to a wide, grassy shelf below.

'Careful!' Ethel called, as I peered over.

'That's odd,' I said. I leaned further out.

'Edie!' she shouted. 'Whatever are you...'

'Ethel, come here.' My voice sounded high and strange – not like my own at all.

'It's not safe!' She put down the flask and moved nearer. 'Honestly, you need to get back from the edge...'

'Look.' I pointed. Down on the close-cropped grass, where further large rocks had been tumbled by some long-ago geological event, I could see a rectangle of bright red. Whatever it was, the rest was hidden by the way the rock base jutted out. But though it was a fair way down, and perhaps just a piece of discarded clothing, I couldn't help but see it as an arm. The way it was flung followed the natural bend where an elbow would be.

Ethel peered, standing back from the edge.

'There? Isn't it just a blanket or something like that? Perhaps there's somebody sitting beneath us.'

'I don't think so. Crawl forward,' I said. 'You're taller than me.' She held onto my jersey and inched her way to the edge.

'If I go, we all go,' she said, and craned over for a better view. 'Oh! It's a person! I can see long hair – I think she's lying down.'

'Asleep?' I asked, with a quiver of hope.

'I don't think so,' said Ethel. We looked at each other, and there was fear in her hazel eyes.

In a great rush, we scrambled back down the slope, sliding and bumping, and hurried around the sheep-nibbled path of the hill brow. Ethel had been right; vast, billowing clouds were now gathering like Herdwick sheep behind the far hills, and a cold breeze had sprung up.

We rounded the base of the rocks where, moments before, we'd been about to eat our sandwiches, and now it was clear that there were fingers poking from the red sleeve. Ethel reached out, and without speaking, we clasped hands as we stepped forward.

We passed the jutting stone that had blocked our view from

above, and there, like an ancient sacrifice on the rocky hillside, lay a woman.

She was on her back, eyes closed, with one arm flung over her head. Her hair was a wild mass of brown and grey curls, she wore a red Fair Isle jersey, muddy corduroys and walking boots. Her left leg was twisted underneath her right, and it was clear that she'd fallen.

'Is she breathing?' I whispered, but Ethel was staring at the woman's face in horror.

'What is it?' I said. 'Come on, we must check her pulse.'

'My God,' she said faintly. 'It's her. That's Joyce Reid.'

I crouched down, thankful that Annie had practised her auxiliary nurse training on me, and pressed my fingers to Joyce's cold wrist. I could feel nothing, but my hand was trembling, and I had no idea if I was pressing too hard.

'Try her neck,' Ethel urged. I moved my fingers beneath Joyce's thick tangle of hair and felt below her jaw. Annie had done the same to me less than two years ago, muttering 'stop *moving about,* Edie' as she did so.

I tried to slow my breathing, to pour all my concentration into my fingertips, to sense the faint beat of life, but I could feel nothing.

'Here,' Ethel said. She pulled a small powder compact from her knapsack.

'Hold the mirror under her nose. Oh, Joyce, come on...'

She sank to her knees and grasped her other wrist. Joyce's skin was so cold there was no discernible difference in temperature between her body and the grass and stones. She must have been there for some time, I thought, with growing dread.

'I can't feel anything,' Ethel said. 'Can you? Oh, Edie, she can't be dead!'

The mirror was clear. I didn't know if the kiss of life would make any difference now, but it could do no harm. I tipped her head back, pinched the bridge of her nose, and blew gently into her mouth. Nothing. No answering rise of the chest, no sudden warmth in her lips.

'Keep trying,' begged Ethel. 'Please keep trying.'

I did. I tried until it became quite obvious that Joyce was gone, and then I sat back, suddenly light-headed with shock.

Ethel was crying quietly beside me.

'I can't believe it,' she said. She took Joyce's chill hand.

'She was so full of life. The last person you'd ever imagine...'

'I suppose she fell,' I said. 'Perhaps earlier on this morning. If only we'd arrived here sooner.'

Ethel nodded. 'Or if we'd met up with her... oh, it doesn't feel real. We must get help,' she added in sudden panic. 'We can't carry her ourselves.'

She was right. Joyce was a big woman, tall and broad-shouldered, and it was a long way back down.

'We'll go as quickly as we can,' I said. 'It seems awful just to leave her here, but there's nothing to be done.'

We cantered down to Birchcroft, sliding on mud and crashing through streams, holding hands like frightened children, going as fast as we could manage over the rough hillside. It still took us almost half an hour to reach the path above the church.

'Who should we ask?' I gasped.

'Pub,' said Ethel, pointing towards a low, stone building with mullioned windows. 'It's lunchtime, and they'll know everyone.'

We ran.

Inside the Black Horse, gentle bars of light fell across the red-tiled floor and illuminated the brass beer pumps along the old mahogany bar. Farmers and ramblers sat at the wooden tables, snoozing dogs at their boots as they drank their lunchtime pints. Above their heads, wreathed in hovering tobacco smoke, hung a large stuffed pike, and the brass 'last orders' bell stood on the bar. We stood panting, scanning what we could see of the warren of little rooms, but there was no sign of the landlord. Ethel grasped the bell and clanged it violently. Several of the drinkers jumped, and one moustached man wearing a blue neckerchief called, 'Now, look here!'

'We need your help!' Ethel shouted to the room at large. 'There's a body up on Birch Hill, below the summit. We found her – we need strong men to help carry her, and we must tell the police!'

She was excellent in a crisis. All those years of coping with Mother, I assumed.

People were lumbering to their feet, exclaiming, and one man shouted, 'Where's Ned?'

'Changing barrel in't cellar,' another replied. 'I'll get 'im.'

A younger woman in canvas dungarees who had been drinking a lemonade with the blue-neckerchiefed man hurried over.

'Blimey, catch your breath, you poor lasses!' she said. 'Whatever's happened?'

We both tried to talk at once, so I subsided and let Ethel explain.

'Ned, there you are!' cried the woman, as the landlord appeared from a subterranean passage behind the bar. 'These poor creatures have found a body up on the Brow! I don't suppose you know who it is?' she asked us.

'I'm afraid I do,' Ethel replied, and the room fell silent, immediately afraid.

'I'm so sorry to tell you, in case she has friends here, but...' Ethel hesitated, and a man called, 'Spit it out, lass, do!'

'It's Joyce Reid,' said Ethel quietly. 'From Athena House.'

There was uproar. I heard an older man shout, 'I said this

would happen! I said it!' and others shushing him, while Ned, a wizened little man who looked like a pickled walnut, turned to us.

'Who are you, then?' he asked. 'How do you know Miss Reid?'

Ethel explained that she'd met her out walking. 'I don't know her all that well,' she said. 'But my friend and I were going to go and see her for a cup of tea after our ramble. We went up to the summit and we... well... found her.'

Ned gazed intently at the beer pump, as if it were a crystal ball revealing a misty image of the scene.

'Below summit, were she lay?'

We nodded. My legs felt unsteady as I recalled breathing into her cold lips, and I grasped the back of a chair.

'She'd go up there every day,' Ned said. 'Rain or shine, snow or gale. I see her passing by the pub door. I dwell up above,' he added, pointing at the ceiling. His slow, croaking voice was almost hypnotic; it was rather like talking to a creature from a fairy tale. I felt he was about to ask us to solve a riddle.

'Question might be,' he went on, 'how'd she get there?'

'What do you mean?' I asked. 'I think she walked up there...'

'Nay, lass.' He tapped his tobacco-stained finger on the bar.

'How'd she fall? She goes out all weathers, never a trip nor a slip. Then up she walks, sun's out, falls down dead. Peculiar, in't it?'

I wondered if he was accusing us, but he turned to the room and shouted, 'Where's Harold?'

'He was in betimes,' someone yelled back. 'He went up church hall.'

Ethel and I stood helplessly, and the dungaree-wearing girl turned to us.

'Harold's the village fire warden,' she explained. 'Keeps an eye on the blackout and organises the war effort too. I'm not sure how much use he'll be, mind you...' she murmured.

'Run and get 'im then,' shouted Ned. 'And somebody go to phone kiosk and ring up police over Lower Brackenfield.'

A young lad shot out from one of little rooms and through the door, I assumed to fetch Harold.

'I'll ring the police,' said the girl. 'I know Constable Creech. I'm the land girl up at Brackenfield Hall,' she explained, thrusting her hand out. 'Rita Norton. Pleased to meet you. I'll be back in a tick.'

'Need a drink?' Ned asked us, polishing a brass beer pump with a tea towel. 'Brandies on t'house, for shock?'

I nodded. 'Please.'

Ethel was paper-white. 'We must tell the others at Athena House,' she said suddenly. 'Better they hear it from us than the police – they don't trust them,' she added to me. 'The men are scared they'll be conscripted. They'll be distraught when they hear. Oh, dear God...' She downed her brandy in one, and I did the same, in the hope that my legs would stop quivering.

A rush of warmth shot through me, and while the temporary courage was upon me, I said, 'You're right. We should go now, before they hear any gossip.'

'No gossip round here,' said Ned reprovingly. 'You'd best wait for Harold and police.'

'No,' said Ethel firmly. 'We've explained where she is – we have to go and break the news to her friends.' I followed her out, wishing we had a car rather than another distressing trek ahead of us.

As we emerged into the sunshine beyond the shadowed porch, a muddy truck beeped its horn and Rita leaned out of the driver's side. 'I've called the constable, he's on his way,' she called. 'Jump in, I'll give you a lift to Netherwood.'

Gratefully, we scrambled up, transferred a ball of twine and a stack of garden canes to the floor and crammed into the wide leather seat beside Rita. There was a hairy black and white collie in the back, lying on a pile of sacking and panting happily.

'Don't mind Dart,' said Rita. 'He enjoys a drive, don't you, boy?'

She pulled away with a rattling lurch.

'Sorry!' she cried. 'I'm not used to this great beast, but Mr Miller – Brackenfield's head gardener, he's the one I was with – he's using the car today to go over to Lower Burnside for tomato seedlings, though we can't plant them out till next month to avoid the frosts, so I don't know why he's in such a rush for them...' She chatted on, as Ethel and I were flung back and forth on the slippery passenger seat.

'Awful shock about Miss Reid,' Rita added, turning into the long lane that led past the church. 'I didn't know her. But I knew *of* her, of course. Everyone did.'

'I take it she wasn't very popular,' I ventured, as we bounced over potholes. I didn't know much about trucks, but this one seemed to be made from an iron bedframe and rubber bands.

'Ah well,' Rita said. 'It's quite a close-knit village, and she got people's backs up, with all her talks. They're all a bit suspicious of the artists' colony. Think they're slacking, prancing about painting pictures and avoiding the call-up. I don't disagree, I must admit.' She veered heavily onto a hedge-fringed single track, which seemed, to my dismay, to be nothing but craters.

We weaved and swayed up it, Ethel and I clinging together like baby monkeys as Rita said, 'I just think it's not on. We're all working so damned hard. I've had to leave Mum back in Sheffield with the little ones, my brothers are on a ship somewhere, probably about to be blown sky high... ah, here we are.'

She pulled up in a muddy yard, which led to a long, stone farmhouse with mullioned windows. There were several dilapidated outbuildings, and someone had attempted a rather scruffy vegetable patch, though it was too early in the year for anything to show through the clumps of soil. The peeling front porch was a chaotic jumble of muddy galoshes, coats, hats and walking boots, along with a startling scarlet and blue Mexican poncho draped over a withered pot plant, and the green panelled door was ajar.

'I shall have to make haste, I'm afraid,' said Rita. 'I'll go and explain to Harold where you found Miss Reid, before Ned sends him on a wild goose chase.'

We thanked her for the lift, and she accelerated away in an arc of spattered mud as we watched the truck bump and swing into the distance.

'Right,' said Ethel. She gripped my elbow. 'Ready?'

'As I'll ever be.'

I fought my rising dread, and followed her.

'Shouldn't we ring the bell?' I whispered.

'There isn't one.'

Ethel led the way down the hallway, an untidy muddle of dusty antique furniture, half-finished, unglazed sculptures of heads and naked bodies and stacks of fuzzily printed leaflets. The walls were a peculiar mix of Victorian taxidermy – a glass case contained several dull-eyed waterbirds wading artistically amongst faded reeds – and far more modern canvases, most unframed. I glimpsed a series of squares in various shades of brown, and a cubist portrait of a naked, pregnant woman who appeared to be screaming.

'Hello?' Ethel called, and from behind a panelled door at the end of the hall, an answering voice shouted, 'Joyce? Is that you?'

We exchanged an anguished glance.

'It's Ethel.'

'Oh, Ethel! Is Joyce not with you?' We heard quick footsteps and the door opened to reveal a tall, attractive woman in her early twenties, with long, unkempt blonde hair, wearing a green silk kimono printed with dragons and lotus flowers. Her feet were bare, and she was holding an enamel mug of tea.

'She was supposed to be back hours ago, we were to have a house meeting,' she grumbled. 'Anyway, come in, I'll put the spirit-kettle on again, although I warn you, she's a temperamental old beast – Joyce got her from the Mothers' Union, and I don't think she's had a polish since 1915...'

'Sabrina—' Ethel sounded anguished.

'I'm so sorry, how rude of me! I haven't introduced myself to your friend. I'm Sabrina Chattock – I'm not in my right mind today, what with one thing and another...'

She clearly expected us to follow her through to wherever the kettle was, but Ethel now seemed struck dumb with the horror of it all.

'I'm Edie York,' I said. 'And look, I'm so sorry, but you need to sit down – we need to tell you something awful.'

Sabrina turned round and laughed incredulously. 'What on earth's happened? Gosh, the pair of you do look solemn! If it's about Bunty, that damned cat's had it coming for years. She *will* go and sleep on the farm machinery and then pretend she's surprised when it starts up underneath her. Sad, but she's never been what you'd call a quick study...'

She trailed off. 'Not Bunty? What's happened, then?'

'Oh, Sabrina,' said Ethel. 'We've some truly upsetting news, I'm afraid. Are the others here?'

Sabrina's glittering social manner dropped away.

'I'll fetch them.' She ran from the room and we heard her calling. I glanced about. We were in a large, white-walled living area furnished rather like a school common room, with sagging armchairs set in groups of two and three, a large refectory table and bentwood chairs by the windows, and a very long, button-backed brocade sofa supporting a tottering pile of canvases and a stack of hardback books. The fireplace contained a drift of unswept ashes, and in the far corner was an easel with a calico cloth slung over it. The sideboard held a winding sculpture made from straw, great cylinders and poking copper wires all woven together. It was oddly disturbing.

On the walls hung more canvases, nailed up between oil portraits of melancholy early Victorians, some bright landscapes and one huge picture that dominated the room: an abstract of what looked like a battlefield, with rolling eyes and bloodied hands clutching at empty air, and great, slashing ropes of barbed wire. I remembered what Ethel had said, and assumed this was one of Aubrey's, the artist who created 'big, angry' paintings.

I was about to ask Ethel 'will you tell them, or shall I?' but I was interrupted by clattering boots and slamming doors. Sabrina reappeared, and behind her, a cluster of men and women, whose ages ranged from early twenties to mid-forties.

She introduced them: 'Aubrey, Jean-Luc, Joan, Nora and Theo,' though she didn't point out which was which. I longed for the promised cup of tea, ideally sweetened with three sugars for shock, but this was not the moment to remind her.

'Hello, my dears,' said one of the older men. He was luxuriantly bearded, handsome in a louche, large-featured way, and wore a blue sailcloth cap stained with varnish. 'Aubrey Fagan. How d'you do? What's going on? Joyce sprained her ankle?'

He glanced knowingly at the others. 'I'm forever warning her she'll come a cropper up there. She never listens.'

We were all still standing up, like characters in a drawing-room farce.

'Look,' Ethel blurted, 'something absolutely dreadful has happened, so I'm just going to say it. Joyce fell from the summit of Birch Hill this morning, and we... she...' Ethel stopped, her face working frantically to stem the tears.

'We found her body,' I said. 'I'm so dreadfully sorry. I know how much she meant to all of you.'

There was a charged silence, then a furious hubbub of exclamation and disbelief.

'Is this a joke?' asked the tall girl in slacks and a fisherman's jumper. 'Some sort of cruel prank, dreamed up by those village idiots? Have they put you up to this?'

She had short black hair, cut like a boy's, and a face free of make-up. Her dark eyes and brows were striking, her cheekbones sharp as blades. She reminded me of a Tamara de Lempicka painting.

'No! Ethel and I found her, about an hour ago,' I said. It seemed days since our innocent plans for a picnic had been so violently derailed.

'The police are on their way there, Joan,' Ethel added, 'and Harold, the warden, was going too.'

'But what are you doing?' demanded the young man at the back. He was short but muscular, with pale, speedwell-blue eyes fringed by dark lashes and his accent sounded French – he must be Jean-Luc, I thought.

'If she is dead, truly, why do you come here? Why not send the police?'

I wished Rita hadn't left us to it; she seemed to know everyone and would have done a far better job of breaking the news.

'He... Ned at the pub thought it'd be best if the police dealt with the... her...' Ethel took a shuddering breath.

'"Dealt with her"?' Aubrey stepped forward. 'With our own Joyce? No, this isn't real. It is a ghastly opium dream,' he announced. 'She was here just this morning. I was speaking to her while she put her boots on after breakfast, she asked if I wanted to come and I said no, I wanted to finish *Peace Process III*, there's a challenging bit of sky – we agreed we'd see everyone at the house meeting and then she didn't turn up... *Christ*!' he suddenly bellowed, and thumped the sideboard, making me jump and the sculpture skitter across the surface.

'She can't be gone! Joyce is an... an elemental, she's like fire, earth, air! She's part of this place, this land, part of us, and we of her!' He gazed wildly at the group. The slacks girl was now trembling with shock, and the other older man, thin and pale, with a shaved head and a jaundiced gauntness about his face, was holding onto the sideboard and gasping for air.

'Is it your asthma, Theo?' said Sabrina. 'Shall I put the kettle on to steam for you?'

He shook his head and waved his hand, though his breath was coming in rattling gusts. 'Nerves,' I heard him wheeze. Sabrina rubbed his back, as Aubrey took Joan into his arms and let her sob on his shoulder. It seemed very loud, then I realised that he was sobbing too.

The red-haired woman hadn't yet spoken. She was pale and delicately beautiful with waist-length hair, like Millais's portrait of Ophelia. It was easy to imagine her surrounded by reeds and scattered flowers. I thought of Joyce again, and blinked to dispel the image of her still, white face.

'I'm Nora,' she said. She was Irish. 'Is it really true? Joyce has had an accident?'

I nodded. 'It seems she fell,' I said. 'She was lying just below the summit, so I think she must have been admiring the view and slipped. I'm so sorry,' I said again, helplessly. 'We tried everything we could to save her, but it was too late.'

'Accident,' Joan said with bitterness. 'Are we entirely sure about that?'

Nora looked shocked.

'You can't mean it was deliberate?' Ethel said shakily.

'Do you have any idea how much those bloody villagers loathed her?' asked Joan. 'She was hated, you see, for trying to explain that peace is the only answer. They despise the men here, too, for being conscientious objectors, with morals...'

'Well, originally, I was considered an invalid,' put in Theo, who had begun to breathe more normally. 'Gas at Ypres.'

'He was sixteen!' said Joan. 'Boys, broken and ruined, and now it's all happening again, innocents sent to their deaths to make this bloody government seem as though they're doing something, when it's perfectly obvious that the only solution to this ludicrous carnage is peace talks!'

'Joan,' murmured Nora. 'Joyce is...'

'Sorry.' Joan wiped her eyes violently with a rather grubby handkerchief. 'But that's her legacy, surely! We must carry on her mission, spread the word even further.'

I decided she was in shock.

'Aubrey,' I said, 'do you think somebody did this to Joyce? She looked very peaceful,' I added, hoping to reassure them, although Ned the landlord's suspicious questions buzzed in my mind.

'Joyce is – was – the most experienced walker I know,' said Aubrey through his tears. 'It's a perfectly sunny day – why would she fall? And enough people down in that village despised the ground she walked on.'

At this, Jean-Luc began to rock on his heels, his hands over his eyes, keening, 'non, non, non...', while Sabrina simply held her pale hands over her face.

I longed to escape from this ghastly tableau of grief and rage, but Nora whispered, 'Sit down, everybody. I'll put the kettle on,' and crept out. I didn't feel we could throw our fatal grenade into their midst, then run away. Besides, Joan's – and Aubrey's – conviction that Joyce's death was no accident had made me wonder if they could possibly be right. Could anyone in the village hate bold Joyce Reid and her unwelcome opinions enough to murder her on a sunny spring morning? I thought about the furious girl from the train, and what Rita had told us, and a bitter chill ran through me.

CHAPTER THREE

With Joyce gone, Aubrey seemed to be the group's unofficial leader. He guided us all to the long table, pulling out chairs, ushering us to sit as though we were taking part in a council meeting. Joan was still weeping, and Jean-Luc was muttering in distress. I wondered how Constable Creech was getting on, whether Joyce's body had been removed from the hillside yet, and how long it would take to manoeuvre the stretcher back to the village. Where would they take her – would they check her injuries properly, to see if it really was an accident?

Perhaps when we left Athena House, we could go back to the pub and find out. I assumed Constable Creech would want to talk to us, too.

Nora brought out a tray, rattling with mismatched cups and enamel mugs, some of which looked very much as though they'd recently harboured used paintbrushes, and set it down. There were no biscuits – I thought sadly of our abandoned picnic.

'We must make a plan,' said Aubrey resonantly to the group. 'And as none of us are churchgoers, and nor was Joyce, I suggest we choose a suitable way to honour her memory here, perhaps with songs and poetry.'

'But she will be buried in the churchyard, non?' asked Jean-Luc. 'It is the way of things.'

'Unfortunately, I doubt we can simply lay her to rest here, on the land she loved,' said Aubrey heavily. 'But we will keep the truth of Joyce in our hearts.'

'I don't suppose she'd want lilies and all those trappings?' I put in. It was crass, but I was curious as to whether anyone would react. My attempt was futile, however, as nobody responded. A silence fell. Nora clanked her spoon in the enamel mug and whispered an apology for the noise.

'But will *we* stay?' asked Sabrina suddenly. 'Can we, with Joyce gone? Did she have a will?'

'Sabrina!' said Joan. 'Joyce was alive this morning, I hardly think it's appropriate to—'

'Sabrina's right, I'm afraid,' interrupted Theo. 'It all depends who will inherit Athena House, and whether she died intestate.'

'We can't lose our home,' cried Sabrina, appalled. 'We're a community, a family! Where would we go?'

Aubrey gulped tea loudly. He struck me as a man who did everything loudly.

'All in good time,' he said. 'Now is the moment to mourn, to grieve, and eventually, an untrodden path will reveal itself.'

The others were nodding earnestly. Nora murmured, 'I simply can't believe it – and so soon after all the fuss earlier this week.'

'Fuss?'

'Oh, didn't you know?' She turned to me, as the others continued to weep and exclaim over Joyce's death.

'Two of the evacuees up at Wrights' Farm have gone missing,' she said quietly. 'Young Johnny and Maggie, been here since the start of the war, almost eighteen months now. Only Spud is still there.'

'Spud?' said Ethel. 'Like the vegetable?'

'Ah, he's a funny little thing,' Nora said. 'Milk-bottle glasses, and I suppose he does look a bit like a potato, bless him. He's very upset, I heard.'

'But how old are they?' asked Ethel, aghast. 'Children?'

'No, no.' She shook her head. Nora seemed less troubled than the others by Joyce's sudden death, and I wondered why.

'They're fourteen and fifteen,' she said. 'To tell the truth, I think they'd had enough. Herbert Wright is a harsh man, and his wife Martha's no different. They used the wee ones for farm duties, you know. Digging and planting, and feeding the animals. I'd see them out in all weathers, sleet and snow, like something from a fairy tale, slaving away. They didn't send them to school, either. Said they were too old. But Maggie was only thirteen when she came here.'

'Are Johnny and Maggie brother and sister?' I asked. She shook her head.

'No, Spud is Maggie's little brother, but Johnny got billeted there too. Nobody else wanted a big lad, they eat too much. I wondered if they were sweethearts, the two of them, and cooked up a plan to escape. But I can't see how they'd leave Spud all alone.

'What a week,' she sighed. 'I'm very sorry you found Joyce. It must have been horrible for you both.'

She was the first person at Athena House who had acknowledged this, and I warmed to her.

'It was,' I said. 'But worse for Ethel, as she knew her, of course.' I glanced at her pale face. 'And more dreadful still for all of you. I expect the policemen will want to talk to us.'

'There's only one,' said Nora. 'Creech. As much use as a wax fireguard, that one.'

What I'd heard so far didn't fill me with confidence. I longed to tell Lou what had happened and ask his advice. Ethel was talking in a low voice to Sabrina, who looked stricken; Aubrey was still crying on Joan's shoulder; and Theo was murmuring to Jean-Luc, who had his hands clasped together so firmly his knuckles were white and shining. He was nodding, eyes closed against the pain. I wondered how close he'd been to Joyce. He was younger, perhaps around thirty – but these were bohemians, I reminded myself, and presumably, a woman being significantly older than her man-friend was unimportant.

'Nora,' I said quietly, 'I don't suppose... were Jean-Luc and Joyce...' I couldn't work out how to phrase it delicately.

'Lovers?' said Nora, baldly. 'I imagine so. But not serious, you know; we're just quite free of social conventions here. Of course, us younger girls still have to be careful. It's not a place for a baby, it'd be impossible to do our work.'

It took me a moment to digest this, and I tried so hard not to look shocked, I must have inadvertently grimaced.

'Oh, I know it's not for everyone,' she said. 'But we don't get jealous or possessive or anything like that. It's a shared sort of love and respect between us all. A family, like Joan said.'

I nodded. It sounded a funny sort of family to me, but what did I know? I'd been brought up in an orphanage after my parents abandoned me – I was hardly a shining example of tradition.

'Did Joyce know the evacuees?' I asked.

Nora sighed.

'Not very well. She was worried, though, like all of us here.' She emphasised 'here'.

'Were others not?'

'Well,' Nora said, 'nobody round the village seems to think they've come to harm. But what if they have? What if young Johnny has hurt Maggie, or... well, passions run high with the young ones, don't they? Romeo and Juliet, all that,' she added vaguely. 'And I don't trust Herbert Wright,' she went on. 'Nasty piece of work, him. He hates us.'

'Why?'

'Pacifism,' she said. 'Their son was killed in the Great War, and they think we're making a mockery of his death with our campaigning and Joyce's talks. For goodness' sake,' she added. 'Wouldn't you think the opposite? That they'd not want it to happen to anyone else's precious child?'

I nodded. I could see both sides, but I was beginning to wonder uneasily whether the disappearance of the evacuees might somehow be related to Joyce's death – could they be lying dead somewhere in the hills, and with nobody looking for them? Even though, I reminded myself, Joyce's fall was more than likely to have been a terrible accident, and I had a tendency to let my imagination run away with me – not a good trait in someone who hoped to be a crime reporter one day.

Soon after, we left to look for Constable Creech in a flurry of renewed weeping from Joan and impassioned hand-clasping from Aubrey.

'Come back and see us,' said Sabrina to Ethel. 'Joyce was so fond of you. Come for the funeral, too. And you, Edie, if you'd like to.'

We agreed that we would, and said again how sorry we were, and they waved us off from the untidy porch, holding each other upright and looking like a group of motherless evacuees themselves. Without Joyce, what would happen to them?

'It seems as though this day will never end,' said Ethel, as we trudged the long, shadowed lane back to Birchcroft. It was after three, and the pub would be closed. Our planned train back had already left, and there was only one more that day. I sincerely hoped that Constable Creech would conclude matters swiftly.

There was nobody near the Black Horse, and the door was locked. I was about to suggest we could ring up the policeman on Monday and arrange to give our statement, when a short, moustached older man wearing an official armband rounded the corner of the lane.

'Ethel Cooper?' he called.

'That's me,' said Ethel. 'You must be Harold, the warden.'

'*Mister* Harold Walker, Birchcroft ARP Warden, yes,' he said reprovingly. He shook our hands with an iron grip.

'I know Constable Creech has been hoping to track you down,' he added, as though we'd absconded.

'We went to tell them up at Athena House,' explained Ethel. 'We thought they should know.'

'Oh, did you now?' he said, somehow implying that we had wildly overstepped our duties. 'Well, I shall let Constable Creech know you're here at last, and you'd best come along with me to the church hall.'

We followed him obediently, past stone cottages and a small Victorian school with a brass bell hanging from its cupola.

'Where is she – Joyce – now?' I asked him.

'Cottage hospital,' he said. 'But I imagine her earthly remains will eventually be released into the care of her... those people,' he amended. 'Unless we can track down a family member.'

'I doubt it,' Ethel said. 'Her family is dead. It's her friends who will need to know what's happening.'

'Apparently so,' he said stiffly. I wondered how much Walker knew about what Annie would have called 'the goings-on' up at Athena House.

'Did you know her?' I asked him.

He shook his head briskly, as if the very notion was impossible. 'She wasn't a village person. There was some bad blood. I don't get involved in that sort of thing.'

Ethel and I exchanged a disbelieving glance.

'Here we are.' He led us up a small, flag-stoned path beside the church, to a single-storey brick building. Inside, it smelled of old plimsolls and disinfectant. There were large Ministry of

Information posters pinned up reading: SAVE FUEL FOR BATTLE... *Coal is essential to our advancing forces. Your fuel savings in the home will help to keep them supplied...* and AFTER THE RAID, detailing all the problems that people might have if their house was bombed. A quick glance suggested that Annie and I would have had them all, if it hadn't been for Clara and her family.

The hall was colder than our rather dank new pantry. Dusty-looking bunting was pinned to the ceiling, and we faced a small, wooden stage. An easel beside it showed forthcoming events. Chalked beneath 4 March was: MISS JOYCE REID TALK: TOWARDS A PEACEFUL RESOLUTION IN EUROPE. (NO REFRESHMENTS). So she had still been trying, though the audience would have numbered very few – perhaps only the other residents of Athena House.

'Wait here, please,' said Mr Walker, and left us at a wooden table as he strode out.

The late afternoon light cast long shadows across the scuffed parquet floor. There was no food to be had anywhere, and it would be several hours until our next cup of tea. We'd never see my Thermos flask again, either.

'Gosh, Edie,' Ethel said, seeing my expression. 'I'm so very sorry I ever suggested a walk.'

'I'm not,' I said. 'Imagine if you'd been on your own.'

She nodded. 'But you're only here because of my silly wild goose chase about lilies.' She took a shuddering breath. 'It was all for nothing, and now something really tragic has happened. I feel such a fool.'

'Ethel,' I said, 'I know Joan and Aubrey were in shock, but do you agree with them that perhaps Joyce's death wasn't an accident?'

As I spoke, the door opened again, and Harold Walker came in, followed by a very thin, pale policeman in a constable's uniform. He looked about my age, which didn't reassure me greatly. He had small, pink eyes and a long nose and rather reminded me of the baboons at Belle Vue Zoo.

'I shall leave you to it,' Walker said to him. 'I need to have a word with Mrs Hughes on Church Lane about her blackout curtains. Light streaming out like a ruddy celestial visitation every night.'

We introduced ourselves while Creech folded his bony limbs into a chair.

'I'll require a statement from the pair of you,' he said. 'We have removed the body, Harold and I, and I believe the... *friends* have been informed.'

I nodded, and once again told the brief, grim little story of finding Joyce. He wrote it all down, and took our addresses.

'And I'm told you're both lady journalists,' he said doubtfully. 'Can this be right?'

'Well, yes, I work on the *Chronicle*'s letters desk,' said Ethel.

'And I'm the obituarist,' I added.

'Secretaries,' he wrote carefully.

'Constable, do you think foul play could have been involved?' I asked. 'A lot of people didn't like Joyce in the village.'

'Foul play?' he said incredulously. 'It seemed pretty clear to me that the lady slipped and fell. Knock on the head. That can see you off, all right. We had one young lad over to Grazebrook, fell off a ladder when he was washing his mam's windows – bang, lights out.'

'So her injury was consistent with the angle of the fall?'

'Goodness me, you're quite the little copper, aren't you, miss?' he said nastily. 'I think you'll find that Harold and I know our business and I've no reason to suspect anything other than an unfortunate accident. Happy now?'

'No,' I said. He was making Lou look like Hercule Poirot on a winning streak. 'I just wonder how she fell, when she was an experienced walker, and it was a bright, sunny morning.'

'Edie's right,' put in Ethel. 'It does seem odd, and we've met several people who suggested that she might have upset some of the villagers.'

'Oh, I see,' said Constable Creech. 'The locals are murderers now, is that it? You town folks, you spend a morning in the countryside and you think you've found some sort of plot? Let me tell you' – he thrust his weedy shoulders back – 'Birchcroft is one of the most welcoming and friendly places in all of Lancashire. There's no side to folks round here, we take as we find, and—'

'Yes, I'm sure,' I interrupted, 'but all we're saying is that someone might have had a grudge.'

'Plenty of folks have grudges. Doesn't make them murderers.'

If he said 'folks' one more time, I thought I might scream.

'So you won't open an investigation then?'

'Not when I deem it to be entirely unnecessary and a waste of my limited wartime resources, no. Right, I've got all I need,' he said, rising stiffly to his large feet. From the side, he resembled a golf club. 'I shall let you get on your way, and advise you that spreading wild rumours and unsubstantiated theories will be heavily frowned upon.'

I opened my mouth to reply, but he was already marching through the door, allowing it to slam behind him. Ethel and I looked at each other.

'Welcoming and friendly,' she said.

It was long after six when I finally arrived home exhausted. The sunny morning and our train journey to Birchcroft seemed as though it had happened to someone young and innocent, many years ago. It would take me a long time to forget finding Joyce, her chilled, white face and the raw grief of her friends – almost equal in strength to the indifference of the locals.

Annie was out at work when I let myself in, and I realised I was still wearing Ethel's boots. I left them in the hall, and had what my old friend Suki used to call 'a lick and a promise' in the basin because the boiler wasn't on – we had to ask Mrs Turner in advance for anything as decadent as a warm bath. I pulled on my tweed skirt and a clean woollen jumper and, aware that I hadn't eaten anything since breakfast time, I poured out a bowl of Annie's cornflakes and ate them with water, so we'd have milk left for tea in the morning. I was so hungry, they tasted perfectly acceptable.

When Lou rang the bell, I was almost ready, though my hair still looked like a fieldmouse's nest. I shoved a hat on and ran downstairs.

'In a hurry?' he asked, as I flung open the door. His Alsatian, Marple, stood beside him, panting gently. Lou had been looking after him 'temporarily' after his owner's death, but the original plan to find Marple a new home was no longer mentioned, and the pair of them now moved – and often thought, seemingly – as one.

'I thought we'd walk to the pub,' said Lou, and my heart sank. 'Unless your gentle hike has worn out your delicate little feet?' he added, seeing my face.

'Oh, Lou,' I blurted. 'It's been the most horrendous day. We found a body, and the villagers hated her, and I think it might be murder, and some children have disappeared...'

'You found a *body?*'

Marple glanced up at him, enquiringly. I closed the door behind me, and we set off down the road by the light of his torch.

'Yes. Joyce Reid. She was an artist, a friend of Ethel's, and she was just lying on the hillside. I tried to revive her, but...'

'Good God, how awful,' said Lou. He listened as I rambled on, almost sympathetically for him. 'But why on earth do you think it was a murder?'

I explained about the villagers, and Joan's suspicions, and by the time we reached our local, the Fox and Grapes, I'd told him as much as I knew.

It was warm and comforting inside the fuggy saloon bar, and I was grateful for both Marple's giant head on my knee, huffing warm breath, and the brandy Lou put in front of me, alongside his pint. Spirits were in short supply, these days.

'Drink that,' he ordered. 'You're remarkably pale, and frankly, you're hardly rosy-cheeked at the best of times.'

He lit a Woodbine for me and passed it over. At last, I felt a little of the day's horrors dissipate.

'Constable Creech was utterly useless,' I told Lou, sipping the brandy. 'He refused to listen to us and decided we were blaming the villagers.'

'Weren't you?' said Lou, raising an eyebrow. 'I have to say, in their position I'd be on my guard too. Joyce sounds highly antagonistic, and people don't like that in a war. Or at all,' he added. 'It doesn't make them killers.'

'But then, two evacuees have gone missing as well,' I said. I outlined what I knew. 'Look, suppose it's connected?' I asked. 'What if someone in Birchcroft is killing people?'

Lou set his pint down.

'Right,' he said. 'I am prepared to give you greater benefit of the doubt than I've ever extended to most people. You were impressive, admittedly, in the Emerson business – if we discount the part where you fell for his questionable Teutonic charms...'

'Oh, put a sock in it.' The brandy had gone to my head.

'But look, Edie,' he went on, serious now, 'I can't accept that you went for a country walk and came back convinced half the village is being murdered. It's extremely likely – in fact, I'd go so far as to say almost definite – that these evacuee kids have just run back to wherever they're from. Where are they from, in fact?'

'London.'

'There you are then. The London Blitz has eased off, they miss their parents, maybe they think they're in love – did you never do anything stupid at that age?'

I thought back to being fourteen. I went to school, I lived for English lessons, I borrowed all the books I could and read them under the covers. On Sundays, we went to church and sat through interminable sermons about sin, as the stained-glass crucifixion glowed ominously above us. Suki and I used to go for long, boring walks along the River Mersey in the holidays, talking about what we'd do when we escaped.

'I'll live on my own,' she'd say. 'No noise, no big lads, no punishments. And I'll always have hot water for baths and all the food I want, chocolate and buns and the cream off the top of the milk, and I'll wear brand-new clothes every day, and I'll have a big, friendly red setter called Chestnut.'

'I'll be a crime reporter,' I'd counter. 'I'll have an ebony cigarette holder and drive a little MG, and wear a fur cape and bright red lipstick.'

At school, I had Annie, and in the long evenings at the home, I had my detective novels from the lending library to escape into. But no – I hadn't done anything stupid. I was too busy trying to survive.

'It just seems odd,' I said to Lou. 'Maggie left her little brother, Spud, behind, and apparently they're very close. He's terribly upset.'

'Oh, Edie,' sighed Lou, ruffling Marple's ears. 'The world is full of terribly upset children. We can't help all of them.'

'No, but...'

'Look,' he said. 'I agree, Joyce's death should be investigated further, and it doesn't sound as though Constable Screech is up to the job. I might get some time off soon.' He gazed into his beer. 'Actually, that's entirely unlikely, as if it's not the black marketeers on Shudehill popping up like molehills, it's people trying to trace relations who were killed in the Blitz, but they won't believe it.'

He adopted a quavering, elderly voice. '"Oh no, my Stanley wouldn't get himself killed. He's in hospital with amnesia, I know he is..." It's damn tragic, actually, but it all takes up time and money we haven't got...'

'Time off?' I prompted.

'Oh. Yes – so if I do manage to get a few hours away from forging convictions on the anvil of crime, I may come up with you, have a sniff about. That artists' colony sounds criminal in itself.'

I laughed. 'In what way?'

'Self-styled bohemians playing with straw and paint like babies, throwing themselves into each other's arms every five minutes, shouting at the poor villagers slaving away on the home front about *peace talks*.' He shuddered. 'I can't think of anything worse.'

Lou's misanthropy was cheering me up, but I still felt uneasy.

'What if I go back to Birchcroft anyway?' I asked. 'Poke about a bit, see if I can at least find out what's happened to these evacuees? And Ethel says Joyce was originally from Manchester, so I can have her as an obituary. There's my excuse.'

As I said it, I wondered how I'd crow-bar *bed-hopping bohemian pacifist hated by locals* into my column celebrating the great and good of the city, but 'it's all in the writing', as Des often said.

'Fine by me,' said Lou. 'It's not my patch, so do your worst. But don't go getting yourself arrested, for God's sake. I've had enough of bailing you out for one year and it's only February.'

'Talking of which...' I said. 'Arnold. And his not-Valentine's Day.'

Lou sighed heavily and Marple collapsed dramatically to the floor in sympathy.

'He's quite upset,' Lou said. 'You know Arnold, he's a cheery feller, for a mortician. But honestly, he's gone head over heels for Annie.'

'She liked him so very much, too,' I said. 'It was only when she heard about Pete that she decided she couldn't go out with anybody, and ended things.'

'Why?'

'Because she thinks she'll hurt his feelings, the way she did with Pete, and she likes Arnold too much to risk it.'

Lou shook his head. 'Well, that's female logic if ever I heard it,' he muttered. I bristled. 'Besides, *he* might hurt *her* feelings,' he added.

We both contemplated kindly, humorous Arnold hurting anybody.

'Perhaps not,' conceded Lou. 'But for goodness' sake. It's wartime, we should all be enjoying ourselves while we can. Besides, she's a looker, but she's hardly Greta Garbo – why's she so convinced she'll devastate him?'

'I don't know. I suppose she has a glad eye for the fellers, and thinks she might stray.'

Lou finished his drink and stood up to order another. 'Well, you can tell her from me, she's making a mistake. Blokes like our Arnold come along about as often as a sane woman.'

I threw a matchbox at his back as he walked away, and heard him laugh.

Marple trotted after him to the bar, and I stared into the dregs of my brandy, wondering why my life had once again become so complicated.

Back at work the following week, it was difficult to concentrate on the obituaries I was supposed to be working on: a Mr

William P. Robinson, who had died of a stroke while on a visit to his own paint factory ('that'll be a colourful piece,' said Pat, the head secretary, and guffawed); and Vera Snelsby, who had mothered thirteen of her own babies and taken in nine foster children.

'A saint,' said the vicar who had contacted me about her death, as I sat interviewing him in the cold vestry. 'She never took a thing for herself. All she ever cared about was the little ones.'

His fond words made me uncomfortably aware that despite my musings on friendship, I had very few people I cared about – Annie, of course, and her family; and, of late, Lou; and Arnold and Clara – Ethel, too. But mostly, I cared about my job, and my ambitions, and getting through the war without being blown up. How selfish I was. Once again, I thought of Suki, and wondered what had become of her. Had she ended up alone with her friendly dog and her new clothes? I hoped so. It was eight years since I'd seen her and she seemed as incorporeal as someone I'd met in a dream. Perhaps I could track her down... but then I thought of the way we'd parted, the terrible argument we'd had, and I imagined her slamming the door in my face.

'Anything lined up, Miss York?' asked Mr Gorringe, pausing by my desk on his usual morning inspection of the troops. 'We could do with somebody who has lived a genuinely interesting life. The great and good are all very well, but the subjects who were married at eighteen and lived blameless lives of industry are perhaps less fascinating to our readers than those who have enjoyed a more... lively existence.'

I saw my chance. 'There's a woman called Joyce Reid...' I began. I didn't tell him we'd found her body, and nor did I mention that she was a friend of Ethel's – I felt it rather unfair to drag her into it. I explained about Athena House, trying to make it sound artistic and full of passionate intellectuals, rather than the sordid nest of cowardly objectors I was sure he'd instantly dismiss.

He nodded. 'And she was from Manchester?'

'Yes. She grew up in Withington and went to the girls' grammar, served in the Great War before she went up to Cambridge.'

He drew on his pipe. 'Fine,' he said, through a plume of smoke. 'She sounds at least more entertaining than the cat-owning headmistress to whom our readers are being treated this week.'

I lowered my eyes to the blotter.

'Sorry,' I said. 'I tried to find out something more dramatic, but...'

'But she lived a blameless life,' said Mr Gorringe, almost allowing himself a small chuckle. He tapped his pipe twice on the edge of my desk in valediction, and moved on to speak to Gloria, who looked horrified as he loomed beside her.

Pat, though at the next desk to Gloria, remained oblivious to his approach. She had a tendency to pick at the paper's crossword throughout the day, and was attempting seventeen down. '*Husband troubled by sharp-beaked poultry, three, six*', she read aloud. 'What? Chicken bothered? I don't know what on earth...'

'Hen-pecked,' I said.

'Ah!' Pat exclaimed. 'That means fifteen across – HEDGE SPARROW – must be wrong...'

She finally noticed Mr Gorringe and hastily shoved the paper into the top drawer of her desk.

'It's SEDGE WARBLER, if that helps, Pat,' he said, and she blushed.

That man missed nothing.

CHAPTER FOUR

Writing Joyce's obituary meant interviewing her friends – and I could return to Birchcroft on the Thursday of that week, with Mr Gorringe's blessing and Ethel's encouragement. I was also keen to find out more about Maggie's and Johnny's disappearance. I sat on the slow train once again, this time sharing my carriage with a middle-aged woman ostentatiously reading the Bible, and a very young soldier with his arm in a sling.

'Fag, miss?' he asked, offering me a Capstan with his free hand.

I shook my head. 'You keep them.'

'Blimey,' he said, 'something for nothing and you're turning it down? All the more for me, I suppose.'

I smiled politely, and the woman gave him a piercing glare over Ecclesiastes. I stared out of the window as rain-swept fields and dank woods slid by, wondering what would happen if the Germans did invade. Everyone assumed they'd come via the south coast, but supposing they parachuted into somewhere like Birchcroft – how would we know? I wasn't sure the Home Guard was active all night in the countryside. I imagined people would hear aeroplanes and raise the alarm, but the hills were vast. If Ethel and I hadn't found Joyce, she could have lain there for days. What would prevent German soldiers from hiding in the isolated barns and outhouses that dotted the valley? Manchester had wardens and policemen, barrage balloons and searchlights. Anyone parachuting into a city would be likely to impale themselves, if their plane wasn't shot down first, and the beaches along the British coastline were studded with lookouts and barricaded with vicious tangles of barbed wire. But the dark, wooded hills had none of those deterrents.

At work, we'd all been given leaflets entitled 'If The Invader Comes', advising, *You must not be taken by surprise... More detailed instructions will be given to you when the danger comes nearer*. Fat lot of use that was. If we were invaded in the middle of the night, how could we not be taken by surprise? And it would be far too late for instructions then.

It was tempting to think of the Ministry of Information being staffed by experienced, snowy-haired Generals, their chests bristling with medals, but in fact, I suspected it was mostly run by harassed young women like me, underpaid and under pressure. I gazed out of the window as the rain intensified, obscuring the view with sooty, diagonal streaks, and tried to make a plan.

I'd go to Athena House first, and see who was about to share their reminiscences of Joyce. Then I'd ask the way to Wrights' Farm, and see if I could get any sense out of them as to where the evacuees had gone. There was a good chance they'd run off back to London – perhaps Maggie was planning to return for Spud, or had decided he was better off where he was. Or perhaps she was in love, as Nora had suggested, and too young and giddy to make sensible decisions when it came to her little brother.

Surely their parents were worried – did they even know what had happened, or did they think Maggie and Johnny were living happily with the Wrights, saying grace at the farm table before a cheery supper of fresh eggs and a blameless night's sleep?

I needed a reason to speak to them, and I felt they might not take kindly to questions from a stranger. As we rolled interminably through sign-less stations, I decided that I'd say I was writing a report for the *Chronicle* on evacuees running away from their billets and going home. It would be quite in-depth, and I would speak to parents and those *in loco parentis*, as well as billeting officers, to find out whether the British evacuation programme was still necessary. As I pondered, I found that I was very keen to write it in reality, regardless of my white lies. It did seem rather peculiar to have all these children separated from their parents if there were no longer bombs raining down on the bigger cities. It made perfect sense that many children would rather be at home, albeit running to school over broken glass and collapsed roofs, than hundreds of miles away living with strangers. Perhaps, I thought, if there was time, I would research and write the piece and present it to my editor as a fait accompli.

If he didn't want it, I could begin a Mass Observation diary, and include it all in that, for posterity. I was vaguely wondering how I might fit that in alongside my shifts at the WVS canteen and my paying job, when the conductor bellowed 'Birchcroft!' and the Bible-reading woman beside me, who had fallen asleep somewhere around a verse about humanity marching to the grave, gave an enormous snort and startled herself awake.

The lane to Birchcroft seemed even longer in the pouring rain. I had an umbrella, but the water splashed off the rim and dripped into my face. As I trudged on through potholes and churned, reddish mud, I wondered what on earth I was doing. Plenty of people in Manchester had died recently, with most of their relations easily reachable by bus, and in dry shoes. I was worried about the reception I might receive at Athena House – they may not want me to write an obituary, and if they did, it seemed I'd be leaving out more than I put in. I sighed heavily, and looked up to see an imposing figure swathed in waterproofs and galoshes striding towards me, holding a wicker basket covered with an oilcloth. As she approached, I realised it was Joan.

'Hullo?' she called. 'Are you looking for Athena House?'

She peered under the umbrella as she drew nearer.

'Oh, it's you!' she said, surprised. 'Ethel not with you?'

'No – I'll explain, I promise, as soon as I get there,' I said. 'How are you all coping?'

She shrugged. 'All right, I suppose. Considering. We've heard nothing about a will – the funeral won't be for at least a couple of weeks. I'm just off to collect the post,' she added. 'The postman's got a vendetta against us, and he won't bring it up to us, even now Joyce has gone. We have to trek to the post office every day, and it shuts at noon.'

'Isn't that illegal?' I asked.

'I've no idea,' said Joan. 'But it's just the way it is. People round here, they're stubborn as rotten old mules. Anyway, I'll let you get on. I'll see you up there, if you're staying for a while. They're all in.' She lifted her free hand in farewell and tramped onwards to the village.

Nora saw me trudging through the muddy yard past the damp chickens and waved from the window. There was a flurry of frightened clucking as she opened the door. The rain, the noise, the bleak huddle of outbuildings with their dripping gutters all conspired to make me feel that coming here again was a mistake. I was intruding on grief, and I felt my ulterior motives may as well have been written on my damp forehead in indelible ink.

'Edie!' Nora said. 'Come in, out of this downpour. No

Ethel?'

'Ethel's at the office today,' I said. 'I'm here to ask if I can write an obituary of Joyce, for the *Chronicle.*'

'Oh!' She looked startled. 'Well, I don't see why not. It's awful, Edie. She's still at the cottage hospital. It's overflowing with injured soldiers who've been sent home, and the funerals are backed up for weeks. Joyce wasn't a believer, you know, but everyone seems to be assuming she'll have a church funeral and be buried amongst all those great bloody hypocrites in the graveyard...'

She led me through the house, talking over her shoulder, this time bypassing the large living room, and ushering me into the farmhouse kitchen. A speckled brown chicken scratched about on the flagged floor, a crust in its beak, and a large metal teapot stood on a rickety trestle table, surrounded by the remains of breakfast. A painted ceramic toast rack still held a limp slice, and plates smeared with jam and butter lay uncollected. The butler's sink was piled with pots and pans, and one pale green wall was covered in peeling posters from the Russian Revolution, showing hearty-looking maidens with arms full of flaxen wheat sheaves.

'Don't mind the mess,' said Nora. 'The cleaning rota's not been working since Joyce... Well, Aubrey won't come out of his studio until gone ten at night, then he roams about like a bear, eating and drinking by himself and roaring at anyone who tries to speak to him. Jean-Luc's so upset he won't eat at all, and Sabrina's forever vanishing off on her great long walks,' she added. 'Joan's mostly holed up with her paintings, and Theo's feeling even more fragile than usual, so he's been in bed, rereading Hemingway and crying, which sets his asthma off. In fact, all the cooking and cleaning seems to be down to me. Again.'

A look of great bitterness flashed across her face.

'Again?'

'Oh, Nora will do it. Don't mind Nora, she's just a wee oirish bogtrotter, she's got nine brothers and sisters, she's used to cooking and cleaning and mopping everyone up. Never mind her art, it can't be important, she's just a skivvy,' she mimicked, two pink spots flaring on her pale cheeks.

'As if I'm not upset about Joyce! As if I wouldn't like to shut myself up in an enormous studio and chuck paint about to *express my grief,'* she went on. 'God forbid that Aubrey or Jean-Luc or Theo might lift a finger to stop the whole place looking like a midden. They listened to Joyce.' Her voice was weary. 'They don't respect me.'

I nodded. It seemed to me, with my limited experience of such things, that well-meaning communities based on equality and sharing always ended up with someone doing all the cooking and someone else eating all the food.

'I'm so sorry, Nora,' I said. 'Perhaps when things settle down a bit...'

'*If* they settle down,' she said. 'We don't even know if we can stay. Quite honestly, Joyce paid for most of the food and bills, and I'm not sure how we'll manage without her money.'

'I thought Aubrey sold paintings?'

'He does. And he sends all the money to his two abandoned families,' she said. 'One in Bermondsey and one in Paris. Six children – five boys and one girl. Two of them are grown up, but that seems to have made no difference.'

I wondered if Aubrey was keeping his income under his mattress.

'Jean-Luc is estranged from his parents,' she said. 'They were ever so well off, big country house near Lyon, he says. But they wanted him to study for a proper job, like a lawyer or a doctor, and he wanted to sculpt, so... he took a menial day job and sculpted at night.' She shrugged. 'And Theo's never had a bean since the last war. He was living in a dosshouse selling his paintings outside Hyde Park when Joyce found him. Covered in fleas, he was, and coughing his lungs up. He thought she was a saint.'

'And the other women...?' I asked. Nora had not yet offered tea, and it seemed the height of bad manners to ask for a cup, given her domestic rage.

'Oh, Sabrina's a poor little rich girl,' said Nora. 'Ran away from finishing school, then came over here. She met Joyce when she gave a talk in Manchester, in '39, and within a week, she'd moved in. Joyce treated her as a sort of pet, but that turned sour when Jean-Luc...' Nora stopped.

'When...?' I prompted.

'Oh, nothing,' said Nora. 'It's just tricky sometimes, all these people with their enormous personalities living in a house together. Joyce kept us all going, really, but without her, it's turning into chaos.' She sighed. 'Do you know, Edie, I'm not so sure I'll stay on. Goodness knows where I'll go, but perhaps I'll sign up to help injured soldiers and at least I'll be of some use. Nobody wants my straw sculptures, and that's God's honest truth.'

'Aren't you a pacifist too?' I asked, curious.

'I was.' She heaved another sigh. 'But I'm starting to wonder what the point is. Everyone hates us, and now I know how it feels to lose someone close, I don't blame them quite so much. They're not going to win this war gently waving placards, are they?

'Anyway,' she said, 'you're a good listener, that's for sure, and me rattling on won't write Joyce's obituary. I'll take you over to Aubrey and see if he'll speak to you. It's around the time I usually bring him a coffee. Would you like one?'

I felt dreadful asking, but I was desperate for a warm drink.

'I'll make it,' I said.

'Go on with you,' said Nora. 'You'll not have the chance, if Aubrey gets going.'

. . .

Nora made the Camp coffees and led me across the mud-churned yard wearing a knitted tartan shawl and a sou'wester borrowed from the porch. She would have looked comical if her hazel eyes hadn't been so sad.

'Aubrey paints up in the old hayloft,' she shouted over the drumming rain. 'You'll have to go first, and I'll hand up the coffee.'

'Aren't you coming?' I felt rather nervous at the idea of bearding Aubrey in his den alone.

'Not just now,' said Nora. She dragged open a huge blue door, and we entered a dry barn that smelled of the ghosts of summer cows and turpentine and Turkish tobacco. It was oddly pleasant.

'Visitor, Aubrey,' she called.

'I'm working,' he shouted from somewhere above. 'Just leave the coffee by the ladder.'

Nora glanced at me. I hoped my answering look was suitably sympathetic.

'It's Edie York,' she called. 'She's writing an obituary for Joyce.'

There was a rumble overhead, followed by footsteps. I felt like Jack at the foot of the beanstalk as Aubrey's face peered down.

'Up you come, then,' he said. 'I can spare a few minutes. For Joyce.'

I clambered up the ladder and emerged into a large space filled to its rafters with stacked canvases, trestle tables, jugs of brushes, palette knives and squeezed-out tubes of oil paint. On a large easel by the window stood a half-finished canvas, the floor around it spattered with drips and clots of black and red paint. At first glance, it seemed to be an abstract, but as I looked, a face emerged from the wild, slashing paint marks. It looked like a woman with curly hair, screaming.

'Please, don't gawp,' said Aubrey, hurrying to cover it. 'I'm responding to my grief, and at the moment, that's a very private process. We'll sit over here.'

I collected the coffees from Nora's disembodied hands, and followed him over to a pair of paint-encrusted schoolroom chairs. Rain drummed on the roof, and the light was dim and grey.

'What would you like to know?' asked Aubrey, rolling a cigarette. 'Or rather, what do you need to know? Because as I'm sure you're aware, they're not the same thing at all.'

Above the huge beard, his dark eyes were red-rimmed. It was either sleepless nights or tears over Joyce, and I felt briefly sorry for him, despite prickling over the 'gawp' accusation.

'I want to do her justice,' I said. 'The more recollections of Joyce I can gather, the more truthful the obituary will be.'

'Truth!' Aubrey barked. 'What is truth? Mine is not yours. Sabrina's is not Joan's. Even Joyce didn't know the entire truth about herself, for is that not the purpose of art? To discover one's most authentic and agonising truth? Is that not what drives us on, sends us mad, keeps us balanced upon the gleaming knife-edge of hope and despair?'

I counted to five in my head. My sympathy had dissipated very quickly.

'Yes, quite possibly,' I said, and Aubrey made an amused little huffing noise and shook his head. I wondered if everyone would feel quite so sad had it been him found prone at the base of the cliff.

'Perhaps you could just tell me a little bit of the background,' I said. 'How you first met Joyce and came to Athena House. What she meant to you.'

'Meant!' Aubrey gulped his coffee. 'How can one quantify what she meant? She plucked me from the wild, thorny hedgerow and replanted me in her creative garden, she taught me to grow, to love, to exist...'

Lord, give me strength. If this carried on, I'd be throwing myself head first down the ladder.

'What year did you come here?' I asked instead.

'Oh, who knows?' He sighed. 'Time is a capering harlequin, his bag full of trickeries. Nineteen thirty-five? Earlier? Later? I had left Paris, I suppose, and the muffling shroud of the domestic paradigm...'

I assumed he meant his abandoned family.

'Yes, '35,' he decided. 'I remember it was high summer, birdsong piercing as the notes of a wooden flute, sun on my back as I wandered...'

'Where were you wandering?'

'Oh, I don't know, in the Birch Valley, I suppose,' he said crossly. 'I was selling pretty trinkets to scrape a living, while at night I painted my visceral responses to the pain of war, of Paris, of death. I happened upon Joyce. Or perhaps she happened upon me. Swiftly, we became lovers.'

I nodded, as if this vague nonsense stood any chance of running in the *Chronicle*, next to Small Factory Raid Injures Warden and Bright Spring Lipsticks on Sale At Marshall And Snelgrove.

'Joyce was an artiste vraiment,' he went on, 'in her heart, she heard the call of wild things, and she poured her soul onto the canvas.'

I thought of the pretty landscapes I'd seen in the hall.

'I moved to Athena House, and together we walked the paths of creation, of our dreams, which wove together and drew apart.'

'Why did they draw apart?'

'Why?' He took a drag of his tiny roll-up. 'Well, sometimes, mayhap she was drawn to another's vibrational energy – as was I. And we would part, and come back together emboldened, stronger, yet more passionate.'

I assumed he was talking about the bedroom-hopping.

'Who else was she... seeing?' I asked delicately.

'Seeing!' he scoffed. 'There was no "seeing", with its bourgeois connotations of ownership and envy. There has only ever been an eager sharing of joy at Athena House.'

I thought of Nora and the washing-up.

'Jean-Luc, I suppose, occasionally,' said Aubrey. 'Perhaps Joan – she tends to the Bloomsbury in her tastes. Was Theo Joyce's lover once? No. Theo loves only his books and his ideas, like a moth trapped forever within a paper shade...' I sensed that he was wandering off down another ponderous metaphorical byway.

'What will you remember Joyce for?' I asked quickly.

Aubrey sighed. Rain danced and splashed on the glass.

'For her kindness,' he said unexpectedly. 'She was a very kind woman.'

'Do you truly believe anyone could have wanted to harm her?'

'Of course I do! By God, the whole village hated her! For her bravery, her determination to speak out, her immutable core of peace! Joyce was one of nature's Quakers, she spoke with gentleness and honoured our shared humanity – not like those warmongering lunatics! I guarantee, any one of them would have happily seen her dead.'

'You think she was killed?'

'Entirely likely,' he said. 'Though, of course, Creech is convinced it was just *a nasty accident*. I bet he is, with his little bicycle bell and his self-righteous homilies. I wonder sometimes if he sent the letters.'

'What letters?'

'Oh, we've had several since the war began,' said Aubrey. 'Horrid little missives from ignorant little people. *Get out, deviants, You're doing Hitler's work for him, You lot don't deserve any peace*, that sort of thing. And once, *Get Out Sinners* was daubed on the front door. Sabrina was terribly upset.'

'How horrible,' I said. 'Do you have any idea who it was?'

Aubrey snorted. 'Probably all of them. Enfin, I must return to the tender entreaties of my muse, Miss York. Tell Nora I may be down for lunch later if she's making a pie.'

I returned to the porch, unsure who to try next. I had absolutely nothing useful from Aubrey, other than perhaps his certainty that Joyce's death was not an accident. Joan still seemed to be out, Sabrina was nowhere to be seen, and I assumed Nora had retreated to brood in her straw and wire nest, wherever it was. As I turned to leave, wondering if I should leave a note, I heard footsteps on the stairs and looked up to see Jean-Luc peering over the banister.

'Good morning,' he said. He looked wretched. 'Do you 'ave news?'

I explained the reason for my visit.

'I will speak with you,' he said, rather grandly. 'Jean-Luc Arsenault, je suis desolé,' he announced, joining me in the hall. 'We will go to my studio, and I will share my experiences of Joyce Reid. Follow, please.'

He set off through the house at a fair clip – I felt like Alice trotting after the white rabbit. He led me up back stairs, down a series of crooked landings and wooden steps, up a short flight covered with worn flowered carpet, and eventually opened the door to a large, airy attic room. It was painted white, and overlooked the rain-misted hills at the back of the house. In the corner was a high brass bed, with tumbled sheets and a patchwork quilt, but everywhere else, there were tables and dressers entirely covered in tiny sculptures. Delicate heads, small figures, animals, birds, fish, glazed and unglazed, all with distressed or blank expressions, and at the centre, a long trestle table holding a bucket of clay covered by a damp cloth, and a stack of scruffy drawings. It was like being inside a crazed museum, the little objects seething and multiplying wherever I looked.

'Goodness,' I said inadequately. 'You've made so many sculptures.'

'Ah, yes.' He shrugged. 'It is all I can do. All I wish to do.' He fished a bottle of brandy from under the bed and poured a generous tot into a grubby glass tumbler, rather sweetly offering it to me first.

'No, thank you, I'm perfectly fine,' I said, as though the vicar were offering Earl Grey. There were no chairs, so I perched on the bed, hoping he wouldn't somehow interpret my damp, buttoned mackintosh and firmly-pressed woollen-clad knees as an invitation. I retrieved the notebook from my handbag as he lounged against the table, fiddling with a little sculpture of an alarmed-looking fish.

'Monsieur Arsenault, I'd like to know how you first met Joyce,' I began. 'Anything you remember about her.'

'Well...' He gazed out of the window. 'I first come here at twenty-eight, I now am thirty, an old man.'

He waited for me to say 'not at all!', which I did in the hope of moving his recollections along.

'Thank you. I leave my work in France, I come to England, I come to Manchester where I have one cousin. I work at the different jobs, so dull, but always, I make my sculptures. I make friends who are artists also, and they say I should meet Miss Reid, she has a colony of les artistes, and there may be room for me...'

I nodded encouragingly.

'So,' he said, spreading his hands out to indicate his room. 'I come. I love – the quiet, the peace. I do not like war,' he added, as if he were talking about sardines, or tins of spam. 'Here, I do not think of it. I can work, and Joyce, she understands this.'

'Nobody *likes* war...' I said.

He waved a hand irritably.

'I do not get involved in this. War games, little boys with the toy guns. I like Joyce, I like what she tells about le pacifisme.'

'Do you remember anything particular that she said?'

'Ah, she speak of this all of the time,' he said. 'She say many things.' He opened his bedside table drawer and withdrew a crumpled page, smoothing it out to read aloud.

'At a meeting last year, she say: *Patriotism is not real. All countries are one – with the same fields and rivers, the same weather and animals and people, and the seas that lie between us are not barriers but a route towards one another. Let us respond to one another as humans, not citizens, as people, not patriots.* I write it down,' he added proudly. 'She say this, and some make applause, but many, they go...' He made the sound of low booing. 'They do not understand.'

Joyce's rhetoric was rather impressive, I thought, writing it down in my homegrown shorthand, even if I didn't quite see how her idealism would apply to the threatened Nazi occupation.

'Was she frightened by the people who didn't agree?' I asked. 'Aubrey said there'd been letters...'

'Non, non.' Jean-Luc shook his head violently. 'Joyce was not ever frightened. She say that those who write such things, they are afraid and she feels sad for them, that they can never know true peace. Joyce is – was – brave, she knows that many people hate her words, and she becomes even more... déterminée.'

She did sound brave, I thought, and perhaps bull-headed, too. I wasn't sure how to ask the next question, but I didn't need to, as he added, 'Joyce and me were un couple.' He made a balancing motion with his hand, which I took to mean 'on and off'.

'She had thirteen years more than I – but we are as equals, we talk about art, or books, about peace – I admire her,' he said. 'I bring her a cup of tea each morning. She is asleep and I come in and put down the tea, and she say, "What would I do without you, mon chéri?" I love her.'

His eyes filled with tears.

The simple sentiment took me by surprise, and, at last, I had a sense of Joyce as a real person, playful and kind, as well as strident and bold.

'Did you ever feel jealous, when she had other... interests?' I asked.

Jean-Luc shrugged. 'What we have... had... it was a tendresse. An understanding. It was itself when it occur, and other times, not so. I have other interests, also.'

'Sabrina?' I guessed.

'We are a... I don't know how to describe...' He waved his arm, frustrated. 'A circle. Equal. Not Joan. She is... different,' he said delicately.

I had no idea how I was going to get any of this past Mr Gorringe.

'What about Joyce's art?' I pressed. 'Did you admire her work?'

Jean-Luc replaced the fish and picked up a furious-looking little cat, glazed in speckled blue. He made it walk along the table edge with his hand, like a small boy playing with trains.

'It was... competent,' he said eventually. 'Joyce loved to paint, but her real art was in her life. The people she finds, and bring together. Her eyes for talent. The way she speak, her love of nature. Her passion, her interests. She lives her art.'

I scribbled all this down, feeling relief pour through me that I finally had some decent quotes. If I could extract some of her life history, I thought, I'd have the makings of a piece.

'Once,' said Jean-Luc, staring over the hills, 'I have hurt my arm, on some barbed wire. La corde du diable. Did you know, Miss York, that it was invented in France? And then they make to tear young men apart in war.

'Joyce, she bathe the wound. She stay with me, in case it

turns to blood poison. She hold me all the night, and watch over me.' He turned back to look at me. 'She care for us.'

I thought Joyce sounded rather maternal towards Jean-Luc. 'Did she ever want children?' I asked him.

He shook his head firmly. 'She say, we are her family. Her artistes, her people. We are her children, and she is ours.'

They were all terribly poetic at Athena House. I imagined the disgusted face Lou would pull at all this earnest sentiment, and suppressed a smile.

'Will you stay here?'

He gazed around the room. 'I hope so,' he said. 'There is nowhere else for me.'

I picked up my bag and thanked him for his time.

'Jean-Luc,' I said, as I stood, 'Do you think Joyce's death was an accident?'

He looked at me. 'Of course,' he said. 'What else?' He held out the little cat sculpture.

'Take this for Ethel,' he said. He pronounced it 'Essel'. 'I know she has cat – Silence...?'

'Silas Marner.'

'Yes, he. She tell me she like cats. Give it to her from me.'

I wrapped it in a hanky and placed it carefully in my bag. He turned back to the window as I left, and I eventually found my own way out, getting lost in several turning passageways and wandering into a bleak little back bedroom – was this where Ethel had slept? – before locating the stairs again. There was still no sign of anyone else, and judging by the empty kitchen and its cold range, Nora was assuredly not making a pie.

I let myself out, and headed back down the streaming lane, hoping the welcome at the Wrights' would at least provide a chance to take off my soaking wet coat.

CHAPTER FIVE

I stopped at the post office to ask for directions to the farm. There was no sign of Joan – perhaps she'd gone for a quiet drink at the pub. She seemed the type of woman who wouldn't mind going in alone. I felt rather nervous in her presence, and told myself I really didn't have time to go all over the village looking for her. I imagined her saying 'What on earth do you want now?', knitting her eyebrows in puzzled irritation.

Outside the little building, Harold Walker stood on guard in dripping oilcloths, raindrops dinging off his metal helmet. He didn't recognise me.

'Morning,' he said, as I opened the door and a brass bell tinged. I joined a short queue of damp women in headscarves, holding steaming umbrellas.

'And the prices!' one was saying to another. 'You'd be better off digging out a pond and fishing for dinner yourself, it's daylight robbery.'

Her friend added, 'It's George's birthday next week – he's begging for a party, but I've no idea what I'll give them to eat. I've barely enough sugar for a cuppa, never mind a cake.'

The queue shuffled on, and I drifted away, thinking about

Athena House and its residents, when I heard the first woman say, '... and the queerest thing is them leaving little Spud all alone.'

'Excuse me,' I said. 'I'm very sorry to interrupt, but I'm only looking for directions to Wrights' Farm – might you be able to help?'

'You the new land girl, are you?' asked the first woman. 'Good job. With the runaways gone, they need all the help they can get. I know they'd like that Miss Norton,' she added to her friend, 'but she seems to be very much installed at Brackenfield. Feet under the table, cosy as you like.'

Her friend nodded, knowingly.

'I'm not a land girl, I'm afraid,' I explained. 'I'm Miss York, I'm writing about evacuees for the *Manchester Chronicle*, and someone mentioned that they might have run away.'

'No *might have* about it,' said the friend, who wore a blue headscarf tied tightly enough to cut off her air supply.

'I'm Mrs Byrne, and this is Mrs Prewitt. I know Martha from the church committee, and she's beside herself. All the help gone, and now they're stuck with a disturbed child who barely speaks. Running off like that!'

She shook her head in disgust.

'It was very good of Martha to take them,' added Mrs Prewitt. 'Good country food every day, miles from danger, a clean, Christian household, and this is the thanks they get. Herbert went looking all over, he was going to strap them both for their sheer cheek, but he said there was no sign.'

'Out on the first train to London, back to their flea-infested slums, I should think,' said Mrs Byrne. 'Good riddance.'

'But what about the little one?' I asked. 'Will he go back, too?'

She rolled her eyes. 'Well, he's not much use here,' she said. 'The question is, *can* he go back? Nobody can get hold of the parents, I heard.'

'Never known the like,' said Mrs Prewitt. 'I thought I was a woman of the world till this war began. Yet I'm shocked afresh with every day that passes.'

They had almost reached the front of the queue, and more damp people had joined behind me, holding disintegrating parcels and string bags, and I didn't want to get in the way.

'Could you just...' I reminded them.

'Lane past the station, keep going over the bridge, turn left up the path, there's a wooden signpost, past the field with the bull in, don't skirt the gate too close, mind, it's weakened since he leaned on it, up the track and it's the big farm with gables,' said Mrs Byrne. 'Watch out for the sheepdogs – Jess and Fly aren't so good with new folk.'

There seemed to be more terrifying warnings than geography in her instructions, but I thanked her and edged out back into the rain to retrace my steps past the station.

The bull was lurking under a canopy of trees at the far side of the field, minding its own business, but my heart raced as I edged past the 'weakened' gate. I wasn't cut out for the countryside, all these people poking about in each other's business, and terrifying animals leaning on flimsy gates. I liked living in the city where anonymous lives swirled alongside your own, and nobody knew what you were having for tea that night. No wonder the residents of Athena House were considered pariahs – they were near enough to be neighbours, but far enough away in their lives and attitudes to be entirely foreign to the residents of Birchcroft.

As I approached the farmhouse, which had a grim, shuttered air about its grey stone bulk, I heard wild barking, and looked round to see two black and white sheepdogs straining on frayed ropes. I made a dash to the front door, passing inches from their lunging bodies, and wished vehemently that I'd stayed at my desk, listening to Marge's latest complaints about the War Office (largely, that they had failed to keep her updated on her husband's movements overseas. She wouldn't accept that it might be a security risk if the generals wrote to her personally to explain exactly where Vince was fighting. 'I'm his wife!' she always said. 'As if I'd tell anyone!').

There was a hand-painted sign nailed up, reading BEWARE OF THE DOGS in wobbly capitals, and an old-fashioned iron knocker. I tried to tap it gently, but it fell back and made a sound like ten buckets falling down a flight of stone steps.

The door flew open, and I looked up at a tall woman in her fifties, wearing a long apron over her dress. She had dark, greying hair scraped into a tight bun, and a deep crease between her pale blue eyes.

'Are you the new land girl?' she said. 'Because if you are, I may as well tell you now, you'll be coming and going by the back door in future.'

'I'm afraid not,' I said. Behind me, the barking gathered pace and fury.

'I'm Miss Edie York and I'm writing a report for the *Manchester Chronicle* about evacuees and whether it's time for them to go home. I believe you've been having some trouble...'

'Oh!' she said grimly. 'Haven't we just. I only took them in because no folk else would, the great lumps, eating like starving foxes night and day. And just as they're getting the hang of things, making less of a hash of everything they're asked to do, they up and go! Off to bed, normal as you like, then I get up the next day, the range isn't lit, the dogs are still asleep, and there's no sign of the pair of them.'

It was hard to hear her over the frantic barking. Rain was now soaking through my mackintosh, and she eventually noticed because she added, 'You may as well come in. I thought the land girl was coming today, but happen it's next week. They don't tell us anything, and I've had her room ready since Friday.'

I followed her upright figure into the kitchen – presumably, the parlour was only for higher-ranking guests. It was rather stark, with scrubbed flagstones, a long wooden table and ladder-back chairs. There was a portrait of the king on the wall, and a block of Sunlight soap with a scrubbing brush by the sink. Everything gleamed. Mrs Wright was obviously a fan of elbow grease.

'Have a seat,' she said. 'Herbert's up with a cow who's taken bad, she's calving, but nothing's happening.'

She removed a small, hand-rolled cigarette from a battered tin printed with 'Rowntree's Clear Gums', and lit it with a spill from the range.

'Let's have it out then,' she said. 'What information do you want from me? And we'll not have our address in the newspaper, thank you very much.'

As she spoke, there was a heavy thud from the hall and a high voice shouted, 'Ow!'

'Samuel Percival Dawson!' shouted Mrs Wright. 'If you slide down that banister once more, I shall hammer nails into it!'

'Sorry,' said a youthful voice, and a small boy with round glasses, sandy hair and freckles appeared in the doorway.

'Had any news?' he asked, ignoring my presence.

'None. I assume your sister will shift herself to write to you eventually,' said Mrs Wright. 'Though where your mother is, I've no idea. No reply to my letter, she may as well have vanished into thin air.'

The boy's round face crumpled with worry.

'You must be Spud,' I said quickly. 'I'm Edie York, I'm a writer for the *Manchester Chronicle* and I'm researching a piece on evacuees. I'm here to speak to Mrs Wright about your sister, and Johnny.'

'Can you find 'em, Edie?' he said. 'They've been gone for a week or so now, and I don't mind telling you, I'm worried sick.'

I tried not to laugh at his grown-up tone, and Mrs Wright hissed, 'Miss York, to you.'

'Perhaps I could speak to you, too?' I added. 'If you'd like?'

'I flipping well would like, yes,' he said. 'My sister's disappeared, and everyone's acting as if we've lost a teapot. She could be dead!'

'Samuel!' Mrs Wright snapped. 'Don't blaspheme! I have done everything in my power to find them both, and if that's not enough, I don't know what...'

He ducked out of the room, and I heard him mutter, 'One mouldy letter is all.'

'I'll be in the pig pen if you need me, Edie,' he shouted, and the door slammed.

I paused.

'Did he say the pig pen?'

'Oh, for heaven's sake.' Mrs Wright shook her head. 'That child! He's taken to it, because there's no pigs there at the moment. He's turned it into a sort of den, with all manner of clutter – old mugs and books and candles... it's like a beldame's hovel!' she added furiously. 'Though goodness knows, I can't stop him. He doesn't listen to a word either of us says. Maggie was the only one who could make him see sense, and now, well...'

'Perhaps you could tell me what happened,' I said. 'Did Maggie and Johnny seem happy at first?'

'Oh they were love's young dream,' said Mrs Wright bitterly. 'I'll tell you what, Miss York, I'm glad Johnny was sleeping over the stable, because I didn't trust him one inch. I picked them both up from the village hall, because Jane Tither, the billeting officer – she runs the grocer's too, she was rushed off her feet – she said nobody wanted such big evacuees, and Maggie wouldn't be parted from Samuel. We had the room and we needed the labour, so we agreed, much against our better judgement, I might add.'

I was longing for a drink. Water would have been fine, but none was forthcoming. She settled back in her wooden carver chair and lit another cigarette from the tin.

'Well,' she said, 'Maggie and Samuel shared a room – perfectly pleasant, clean as a whistle, though to hear her complain, you'd think it was a dungeon – "Oh, I need a mirror..." "The straw mattress is prickly and it's hurting me..." like the princess and the pea, she was. We rise early on this farm, and she looked like the sunken *Titanic* for the first few weeks, but I'll not have laziness, Miss York. She was expected to earn her keep. Herbert taught her to milk the cows, and once she got over being "scared of them"' – she rolled her eyes – 'she'd do that and then help me in the house.'

'And what was Johnny doing?'

'Helping with Brutus and Blaze, the shire horses,' said Mrs Wright. 'Odd jobs, that sort of thing. Herbert had him digging over the potato patch, and you've never heard such language. Of course it was frozen – what else did he expect in January? They'd enough to eat, a bed to sleep in – more than most folks have these days, and that's for sure and certain,' she added sententiously.

'I believe they... fell in love?' I asked, suddenly nervous of using such flowery language in her presence.

'Youthful folly!' she said, blowing out an irritable stream of smoke. 'Love, indeed. Infatuation, batting their eyelashes over the pig pen, running about all over the countryside, getting up to I-don't-know-what. I very much doubt you could call it love.'

'Were you worried?'

'I was,' she said. 'And Herbert was and all, but they always had one excuse or another, and that one' – she nodded in the direction of the pig pen – 'was at school, so he was no use nor ornament, either, when those two went gallivanting off.'

'Do you think they ran away together, then? Did something happen?'

'Aye, it did that,' said Mrs Wright. She paused.

'Maggie had a letter, t'other week. Said her father had been killed in action. He was a soldier, she should have been proud, like we were of our John, God rest his soul, but she took it very badly.'

'She must have been very upset,' I ventured.

'You can say that again,' said Mrs Wright. 'Weeping and wailing as if the world was ending. And Samuel wouldn't speak a word to us – that's when he took to the pig pen. I tell you what, Miss York, I've tried to do the right thing by those children, but I shan't bother again. My nerves are frayed to shreds.'

I thought Mrs Wright had a rather peculiar view of 'the right thing', but I nodded. 'Do you think she went to see her mother in London after the bad news?'

'We thought so,' said Mrs Wright. 'But it's peculiar that she went without Samuel. They were always together, those two, and she once said, "I'll never let anyone upset my brother again," after he'd had a well-deserved hiding for leaving the farm gate open. Then off she goes, little madam, selfish as you like, not a thought for him.'

'And their mother didn't visit?'

'Apparently, "too busy",' sniffed Mrs Wright. 'Doing war work, driving ambulances I believe. No job for a lady, I can tell you that much.'

I wondered who Mrs Wright thought should be driving the ambulances in the London Blitz – trained monkeys, perhaps.

'What happened the day Maggie and Johnny left?'

Mrs Wright's gaze drifted towards the kettle on the range, and I felt briefly hopeful, but she was only resettling in her chair. It was past lunchtime, and I was hungry. I thought of my jam sandwiches, sitting in a paper bag back at the office. Des had probably eaten them by now; he had a habit of absently scooping up unattended food as he wandered past.

'I was up at five, as usual,' she said. 'It was a frosty day, and I expected that Maggie would have gone down to the milking shed where it's warmer, so I wasn't that surprised when she wasn't in the kitchen and the range was unlit – though normally she'd make some porridge for herself and Samuel.'

'Not for you?'

'Herbert and I generally like a full cooked breakfast to set us up for the day,' she said coolly. 'She made that after the milking.

'Any road, Samuel came down, and said his sister wasn't in her bed. I sent him out to the shed to look for her, and she wasn't there, either. Herbert went to check she'd not sneaked off to the stable block to see Johnny, which was strictly forbidden, of course, and he came back saying Johnny had gone too.'

'Did you think they'd run away?'

'Not at that point. I thought they were playing silly beggars and trying to get out of an honest day's work. But there was no sign of them by noon, when Samuel comes back from school for his dinner, and that was when we started to wonder if they'd run off.'

'What did you do?'

She shrugged. 'What could we do? They're big enough to shift for themselves, and we thought they must have saved up some money and caught a train back home. There's been no sign of them since, and we're stuck with that cheeky little so-and-so out there till his mother can be bothered to come and fetch him.'

'Did they get paid? Would they have had money?'

She sucked her teeth. 'Not that I know of, and I can't say I know of any's gone missing. But I can't be entirely certain.'

I thought how unlikely it was that these indentured slave-children would have been able to scrape any money together to pay for train tickets back to London. And how peculiar that Maggie had left Spud behind, to such a mercilessly unhappy home.

'Did Johnny have a temper?' I asked.

'Why'd you ask that? He did, as it happens. I've seen him roaring at the dogs, demonic he was, just for giving him a little nip. And there was a time last year after Samuel's hiding that Johnny was yelling what-for at Herbert, and waving a metal hoe. They almost came to blows,' she added. 'I was for sending him back there and then, but Herbert said he had a way with the horses and we should keep him. That was the end of his home comforts, though,' she added, with satisfaction.

I leaned forward. 'Do you think he could have hurt Maggie?'

She looked surprised. 'Well. I wouldn't put it past him, now you say it.'

'You don't think we should mention that to the police?'

'Good Lord, what would be the point? The two of them are long gone, and just as soon as I track his flighty mother down, Samuel will be, too. That new land girl can't come soon enough.'

I felt I'd heard enough from Mrs Wright, and I thanked her.

'I hope you'll not be listening to a word Samuel says,' she said, showing me out. 'He makes things up, he's not to be trusted.'

I smiled vaguely, and left the farmhouse with a deep sigh of relief. Outside, the rain had stopped, and a weak sun made the puddles shine like polished half-crowns. The air was scented with fresh earth and the dogs had quietened. I felt surprisingly cheerful, and seeing the pig pen at the farthest corner of the farmyard, I called, 'Spud?'

It was a ramshackle structure, with mossy stone walls and rusting corrugated panels for a roof. It didn't look much of a den, but Spud popped up from behind the wall and shouted, 'Edie! Come and visit me, please.'

Mrs Wright would have reminded him to call me 'Miss York', but I didn't really mind.

I picked my way through the puddles, and he opened the gate with a flourish.

'Welcome to Spud Mansions,' he said. 'The finest views and the most well-appointed suites for entertaining.'

I laughed. He had lined the muddy ground of the sty with wooden pallets and covered them with a tatty rag rug. A small box held two enamel mugs, a half-drunk bottle of lemonade, three well-thumbed adventure books, and a metal canister with holes in the lid, on which somebody – presumably Spud – had painted MICE?

'Are you not sure about the mice?' I asked.

'Ah,' said Spud. 'That's for when I catch any. *She*' – he indicated the house – 'won't let me have a pet, so I thought I could keep some very small mice out here. But I can't say as I've found any so far. Have a seat.'

I sank onto the filthy rug, glad of my still-damp mackintosh.

'Lemonade?' Spud asked.

I was so thirsty, I agreed. He poured some into a mug and handed it to me. It was rather flat, but I didn't mind – he was politer than Mrs Wright.

'Do you mind being called Spud?' I asked.

'No,' he said. 'It's because of my initials. SPD. But sometimes I add Uriah.'

'After Uriah Heep, in *David Copperfield*?'

He looked at me blankly, the sunlight glancing off his spectacles. 'Who? Maggie had a friend called it at school. I liked it.'

I smiled at him. 'I'm so very sorry about your dad.'

Spud nodded. 'I'm very sorry too. I knew he *might* be killed, but I didn't think he really would be.'

I thought of Annie and Pete. That summed it up perfectly.

'Things must be quite difficult for you,' I said. 'Have you written to your mum?'

'Yes. Last week, and then when Maggie went. But the last

time we heard from Mum was when she wrote to tell us about our dad.'

There had been no major raids on London lately, but it was worrying, I thought.

'Did she ask Maggie to go back home?'

'No. She said she was working hard and she'd come and see us as soon as she could. And she said to be good and try not to be too sad, because our dad died a hero.'

I wanted to cry. Instead, I asked, 'Did you like Johnny?'

'Oh yes!' said Spud. 'He stuck up for me. He used to show me the newts in the pond, and tell me about his dad's adventures in the last war. Did you know, he killed seven whole Germans?'

'I did not know that. Do you think Maggie and Johnny ran away together?' I asked.

'I think they must have done,' said Spud seriously. 'But Maggie didn't take her things, that's what's funny. She didn't take any extra clothes – just her coat and her blue hat. And she left her bag, so I don't think she can have taken her diary, either. She wouldn't go far without that, she's always writing in it. So she must be coming back.'

'What about Johnny?'

'He didn't have anything since that old bat took his stuff away. Sorry, but she is,' he added. 'Mr Wright is horrible, too, but at least you know where you are with him. Johnny just took his jacket, I think. He didn't have any letters from home, or anything. He told me his mum and dad couldn't write.'

'Do you know if they had any money?'

'Don't think so. If they did, I didn't know about it. What I'd give for a few shillings! I'd be on a train back to good old London before Mrs Wright could say "Boy!" – he adopted an elderly-sounding screech – "Come and do your impossible jobs, boy!"'

I tried not to laugh. 'I'm sure you'll be able to go home soon.

I would like to help find Maggie and Johnny, though. Was there anyone else she knew in the village, who might have helped them?'

'Maybe Norman,' he said. 'He's the funny old feller who lives on the campsite. Doesn't talk much, but Maggie used to take him eggs sometimes, from the chickens here. She felt sorry for him.'

I would need to track Norman down, whoever he was.

'Nobody else?'

'No. Oh – Miss Reid. That lady from the communism farm, who's died. Maggie went to a talk of hers, and she said they got chatting and Miss Reid asked her for tea. But I don't know if she went – she never said. She could be a bit secretive about things.'

My heart sped up.

'Thank you, Spud,' I said, 'I'll do my best to find your sister, I promise. And I think your dad would be very proud of you.'

Impulsively, I added, 'I was brought up in a children's home, and sometimes I was very unhappy. But I grew up – and now I have a much better time of it. You will, too.'

He gave me a weary half-smile.

'Growing up takes a long time, though, dun't it?' he said. 'I hope you find my sister.'

All the way back to the station for the afternoon train, I thought about what Spud had told me. If Maggie had known Joyce, could somebody have targeted both of them? I thought about Johnny, the 'big lad' with a temper. Perhaps Maggie had wanted to return to London, and he couldn't bear to be without her. Or had Joyce raised his ire with her talk of pacifism? I would have to go back to Athena House, and I'd speak to this Norman, too. Something bad had happened in Birchcroft, I was sure of it.

At the station, I had ten minutes to wait for the train back to

Manchester. A uniformed porter was sitting on the bench in the small waiting room, warming his knees by the fire.

'Not too long to wait, miss,' he said. 'Where are you off to?'

I told him. 'Do any London trains run through Birchcroft?' I asked.

He wheezed with hilarity. 'No, and we don't go to New York nor Paris, neither.'

'So if anyone wants to travel to London...?'

'These days?' He puffed out his cheeks and scratched his chin, as if I'd said, 'How might I get to Wonderland?'

'I reckon you'd have to change at Manchester, then you'd be looking at another change and a long wait at Rugby, and after that, it'd depend on the day, you might not manage it in one go...' he said. 'What's up in the Smoke for a little lass like you? Young man, is it?'

'Nothing, I just wondered,' I said. 'Look, do you work from this station often? Would you remember seeing a pair of youngsters early on the eleventh? A Tuesday.'

'We see a lot of youngsters.'

'A boy and a girl, about fifteen?' I pressed. 'It would have been very early.'

'First train to Manchester's at seven ten, unless you're talking about the milk train, but that doesn't take on passengers. I can't say I saw any young couples like that, as I recall.'

He creaked to his feet, and hummed a bit of 'I'll Be Seeing You'.

'Train's coming, miss.' There was a piercing whistle and a blast of steam. I boarded, feeling that any mystery had only deepened over the course of what had proven to be a thoroughly unsatisfactory trip.

CHAPTER SIX

Back at the office, my jam sandwiches had indeed vanished, though Des pointed the finger at Bobo the messenger boy, and Bobo suggested that Vi the tea lady might have thought them finished, and thrown them away on her tidying-up rounds. There was no point feeling aggrieved, so I fixed my mind on the spam fritters we were having for tea later, and went over to Ethel's desk.

'Can you talk?' I said in a low voice, aware that Mr Gorringe often popped out at four to check what everyone was doing.

'Briefly,' said Ethel. 'I'm editing a letter from someone who thinks the *Chronicle* should be covering top-secret military campaigns in exhaustive detail. It's like knitting with Scotch mist. Anyway, tell me quickly – how were things in Birchcroft, and what have you found out?'

'Well, Aubrey talked in dramatic poetic couplets, and didn't really say much, and Jean-Luc was sad, and didn't really say much,' I said. 'Nora seems terribly fed up, Theo was ill in bed, and Joan was out. I don't know where Sabrina was.'

'That all sounds about right,' said Ethel.

'Aubrey thinks it wasn't an accident, and Jean-Luc thinks it was,' I added.

'What did Nora think?'

'I'm not sure. But then I went to see the Wrights, and I found out something interesting...'

I explained the connection between Maggie and Joyce.

'I didn't know about that,' Ethel said. 'But it's a small village, I suppose everyone knows everybody a little bit, at least. What's more worrying is how many strangers wander through, on the way for a ramble. In summer, it can be like Piccadilly Circus.'

'Do you think Joyce may have been killed by a lunatic?'

'Oh, Edie, I wish I knew.' Ethel sighed. 'It all goes round and round in my head, and now the bloody parrot's started saying "what a disaster" because I said it when I came home from us finding her, and Mother's neighbour brought some left-over cake round the other day and Nelson said it to her...'

I burst out laughing.

'Oh, I know it's funny,' said Ethel, giving a reluctant grin. 'But Mother didn't think so. The cake *was* rather squashed, too.'

That reminded me, and I hurried back to my bag and extracted the little sculpture, fortunately unbroken after its trip round the pig pen.

'Jean-Luc sent you a present,' I told her. 'He said you should have it, because he knows you like cats. I thought that was rather sweet of him.'

'Jean-Luc?' She took the cat and weighed it in her hand. 'It looks quite cross, doesn't it?' Her expression was troubled. 'Look, Edie,' she whispered, 'I haven't been entirely honest with you. It's nothing bad, but...'

I heard a door click and the unmistakable footsteps of Mr Gorringe treading the worn parquet.

'I assume Miss Cooper is vouchsafing the details of an urgent obituary, Miss York?'

He came to a halt beside us, and Ethel deftly dropped the cat sculpture into her lap.

'I was just asking her about Joyce Reid, Mr Gorringe,' I said. 'Ethel had met her, you see.'

'In that case,' he said, 'I shall expect nothing less than a spellbinding torrent of nostalgic recollection. Good afternoon to you both.'

He nodded, and moved on to terrify the typing pool. Ethel and I exchanged a glance.

'Kardomah tomorrow, twelve thirty,' she whispered. 'I'll explain then.'

That evening, Annie was on the night shift, so our paths only crossed over the spam fritters.

'I think this batter tastes a bit odd,' she said. 'Maybe the lard's getting old.'

'There *is* a faint aftertaste of ancient cod, I agree,' I said. 'It's all right if you imagine it's fish.'

'I'm so tired of not having anything nice to eat,' she groaned. 'What with Pete and rations and prices going up, and everywhere still a bombsite, and worrying about an invasion, I'm feeling extremely gloomy.'

'Can't you reconsider Arnold?' I asked, forking up her discarded fritter. 'He's awfully sad, according to Lou, and it might cheer you up to chum about with him a bit.'

'No, I've made my mind up,' Annie said. 'I'm in no fit state to be getting involved. Pete's death has made me sit up. I'm twenty-four, I need to take life more seriously. I'll devote myself selflessly to nursing, and when the war ends, I'll look for a husband.'

'This doesn't sound like you.'

'That's exactly my point,' said Annie, pouring herself another cup of weak tea. 'I don't want to be like me. I want to be serious, and impressive and dedicated. Like that famous nurse, Edith Cavell.'

'Annie, she was shot.'

'I know!' cried Annie. 'She was noble, and a wonderful nurse, and she sacrificed herself for her country!'

'Please don't,' I said. 'I need you here, not sacrificing yourself all over the place. If you won't contemplate Arnold, why don't we plan a bit of fun at the weekend?'

'What kind of fun?' She perked up slightly.

'Let's go for a proper dance, at the Astoria on Plymouth Grove,' I said. 'After last weekend, I need something to take my mind off death and despair. I'll see if Clara's about, and we can ask Lou.'

'What about Arnold? We can hardly leave him out.'

'But you're...'

'Honestly, I'd like to be friends with him,' said Annie. 'At least let's ask, he can always turn us down. We could do with another girl, though – make it less awkward.'

'I'll ask Ethel,' I said. 'You'll like her, she's good fun.'

I told her about the parrot and the cake, and Annie guffawed.

'It's funny, save for Clara, I haven't really known you to have close woman friends – apart from me, of course. I'm glad you've got a nice work pal. But I'm your *best* friend,' she said, 'never forget that.'

'As if I could.' I squeezed her arm. 'You saved my life, you know.'

'With help. Anyway,' – she collected our plates and took them to the sink – 'I don't suppose Edith Cavell went dancing much, but still. I'm noble, I'm not a saint.'

After she'd left, I got out my mending basket and set to replacing the buttons on a summer skirt that had seen better days. It wasn't yet March, but our cheerful plans had made me think of warmer evenings to come, and a reprieve from the relentless winter blackouts.

I put the wireless on, and listened to the BBC Home Service, which was playing a Brahms concerto. I might have felt quite peaceful, but for the questions tugging at my mind like a caught thread.

I tried to imagine how Joyce could have fallen. If she had seen something in the distance, and gone right to the edge to peer over, and slipped. Or if someone had pushed her.

There had been nothing unusual in the landscape that Joyce wouldn't have seen before. Unlike me, she was entirely familiar with the summit of Birch Hill, and went up there frequently – there was no need for her to lean out and risk the drop. Had she gone to speak to somebody beneath and fallen? But in that case, why wouldn't they have raised the alarm?

There were enough people who hated her nearby, but was anyone angry enough to murder her? Perhaps a stranger, as Ethel had suggested – but why?

Things were clearly unhappy at Athena House, but without speaking to everyone there, it was hard to get any sense of who was angry with whom. The politics of a close gang of people was a mystery to me. Was falling out normal, or was the trouble at Athena House down to their unique arrangements, and their bohemian attempts to live beyond the usual rules?

I found it tricky to understand the ebb and flow of a group. I had spent my childhood years isolated, with just two close friends – Suki, at the home, who did not get into the Grammar with me, and Annie at school. Somehow, I had never wanted them to meet – at the home (although it was never truly a home to me) I was always quiet, horrified by the idea of drawing attention to myself, or invoking the rage of Mr and Mrs Pugh. At school was when I relaxed. With Annie, I could be silly and young, giggling about the teachers, and I could learn and breathe out, without the big boys calling me 'stupid swot' and grabbing my books to throw between themselves, shrieking like monkeys.

At the home, Suki was my family. Out in the world, I had Annie. Nobody else mattered. Most of the time, I was simply surviving, hiding in crime stories which always worked out neatly at the end, unlike real life.

Perhaps I had been pig-headed, I thought now. Seeing Joyce's body, all that life and passion reduced to a tumble of hair and limbs, had brought me up short, particularly in the wake of Pete's death. Life was brief, the summer of a dormouse, according to Lord Byron, and I had never pursued my lost friendship with Suki. Now I was eight years older, I had lived long enough to be more forgiving and less judgemental. I remembered what Annie had said about my women friends, and it struck me that perhaps my falling-out with Suki all those years ago had made me frightened of female friendship, disheartened that one could invest so much, and love so furiously and have it all end one rainy afternoon, after a terrible row.

I wondered if it might be possible to track her down and see if we could at least shake hands and wish each other well. I didn't want to live with recrimination and regret; the war reminded us daily that life was fragile, and people you loved could be here one moment and gone the next.

By the time the wireless programme ended, I had made up my mind. I would track Suki down and apologise, and I would strengthen my existing friendships. I may not be the marrying kind – after all, I was deep into 'marriageable age' and so far, I'd had no offers – besides, I'd met nobody I'd want to marry. But even if lifelong spinsterhood beckoned, I could be somebody sociable, like Ethel, somebody, perhaps, who people liked and enjoyed spending time with.

. . .

The following day, I yawned my way through the morning. I hadn't slept well, thinking about Suki and going over our old argument, wondering what I'd say if I found her.

'Will you be joining us, Sleeping Beauty?' Pat asked, as I sank my head into my hands and briefly closed my eyes.

'Probably not,' I said. 'I'm still waiting for my prince.'

'He's over there, by the copying machine,' she said, nodding at Des, and I laughed.

'How's your sister?' I asked, in my new guise of 'friendly and likeable person'.

Pat seemed surprised by my interest.

'She's all right, but she's worried about her youngest, Monica – she's off flying planes, can you imagine? Like flaming Biggles, and she was such a pretty girl. She's a lovely dancer, she was going to teach at Cadman's Academy of Music and Movement, and now she's in some Nissen hut eating bully beef.'

I thought of Clara.

'But she's doing a great thing for the war effort,' I said. 'We need women who can fly as much as we need men.'

'So they claim,' Pat said. 'But I just wonder what'll happen to the young lasses when the war's over. All these new skills and excitements, then they'll be back home again, washing some bloke's smalls.'

'Annie says, "You start off sinking into his arms, and end up with your arms in his sink".'

Pat barked a rare laugh. 'If I were younger, I might be off to war myself,' she admitted, unfolding the crossword. 'It beats knitting for the troops, doesn't it?'

Just after noon, I set off for the Kardomah. Ethel had errands to do beforehand, involving queuing for a bit of mackerel for Mother's tea (and, I suspected, for Silas Marner's). I was burning with curiosity about what she had to tell me as I passed the piles of sandbags covering the windows and entered the heaving restaurant. I had been shown to a table by the time she arrived.

'I had to get tinned herring, she'll be furious,' she said, sitting down. 'The queue was all down Shudehill, it's getting ridiculous. They'll be rationing bread next.'

'Oh, don't say that,' I groaned. 'Toast is the only thing that keeps me going.'

I ordered a Welsh rarebit while I still could, and Ethel rather wickedly decided on a mackerel salad, which made me like her even more.

The band was slightly more muted today, and there was less need to shout, which turned out to be a blessing.

'First of all, would you like to come to a dance at the Astoria tomorrow evening?' I asked. 'A few of us are going, and it should be great fun. Billy Wainwright and the Starlight Orchestra are playing.'

'Oh!' Ethel looked quite overcome. 'Edie, that's so very kind of you. I can't remember the last time I went dancing.' She hesitated. 'But I'm rather old you know – I may be a fly in your youthful ointment, as an ageing spinster.'

'Don't be daft,' I said. 'You're not too old to dance, are you?'

'Well... if you're certain your friends won't laugh at me,' she said. 'I'd love to come.'

'I promise they won't. They're more likely to laugh at my attempts at the tango,' I assured her. 'Now, what is it that you wanted to tell me? Say it quickly, and perhaps we'll have time for a cake.'

She smiled, then dropped her eyes. 'I think I'll have to say it very quickly, I'm so embarrassed. I'm telling you because I don't know if it changes anything about Joyce's death. I desperately hope it doesn't, but I can't sleep for worrying about it.'

I put my cutlery down. 'Whatever is it? It can't be too terrible, surely?'

'Oh Lord...' She ran her hands over her face, as if she was wiping a blackboard clean. 'I'll just say it. The night I stayed at Athena House, when I'd missed the train, I stayed up chatting with some of them. They gradually went off to bed, but I was having fun, and I was so relieved to have a proper break from Mother that I drank some brandy and it went straight to my head.'

'Jean-Luc's brandy?'

'Yes, however did you know?'

'He seems quite fond of it,' I said. 'Go on.'

'It got terribly late, about one o'clock I think, and I said I must go to bed, too. Only Jean-Luc was left by then, we were talking nonsense about art and poetry, and then, he suddenly...' She paused.

'Suddenly what? Do tell!'

'Must I really? Well... he leaned forwards and kissed me.'

A rush of blood stained Ethel's pale cheeks the shade of pink gardenias.

I had been expecting a far more dramatic revelation. 'That's not so dreadful, is it?'

'Oh, I suppose not, but... he's younger than me, and their arrangements are so avant-garde – I felt rather foolish, like a deluded old woman flirting with a handsome young man, and thought perhaps he felt sorry for me.'

'Of course he didn't!' I said. 'He thought you were lovely, because you are! Though he is rather free with his affections, and I suppose there's a worry he was leading you on.'

'Well, it's not as if I wanted to marry him,' said Ethel. 'I jumped up and scuttled off to bed, and thankfully, he didn't follow me. Neither of us has mentioned it since, so I think we both put it down to the brandy.'

'Then what's your concern?'

The waitress appeared to clear the plates, and I ordered two steamed jam puddings before the moment passed.

'I won't fit into the *Chronicle*'s Spring Modes at this rate,' said Ethel.

'I'll run you something up from a crashed parachute,' I said, and she laughed.

'My concern is,' Ethel went on, 'that as I was leaving, he said something like "please keep this a secret between us." I said I would, but asked him why. And he said – you see, I was a bit tight, so it's hard to recall exactly – he said something like "somebody here might be jealous."'

'You didn't ask who?'

'I was embarrassed, I didn't want to look as though I was setting up some sort of silly rivalry.' She sighed. 'And besides, why would I have told anybody? It's not the sort of thing I'd advertise in the classifieds, is it?'

'Do you think he meant Joyce?'

'I don't know. I've thought about it every which way. Perhaps he meant Joyce, or Sabrina, or Nora.'

'Ethel,' I said, lowering my voice, 'what if he meant Theo, or Aubrey? I know it's illegal, but...'

'I hadn't considered that,' she admitted. 'Would they really do that sort of thing? I know about Oscar Wilde, of course, but it seems so terribly peculiar.'

'I don't know,' I said. 'But it's worth bearing in mind. Everyone seems to be connected to everyone else at Athena House – it must be quite a tiring way to live. Ethel, do you think whoever is jealous sent you the lilies?'

She nodded wearily. 'That's what I'm assuming.'

'It could have been Jean-Luc, in good faith – he sent the little cat for you. Perhaps he truly hopes for something more.'

'Odd, though, after our discussion about death. Edie, I know you're researching the obituary, and I'd be so grateful if you can get to the bottom of it. It's bothering me dreadfully, and I feel somehow it might be my fault that Joyce has died.'

'Oh, Ethel!' I broke off as our puddings arrived, reluctantly delaying my first bite of hot, sweet sponge. 'Of course it's not! If somebody did kill her, it was probably someone from the village – and besides, how would anybody know what had happened between you and Jean-Luc?'

Ethel stared miserably at her untouched plate. I thought of the 4*d* it was costing.

'I'm such a fool,' she said quietly. 'I did tell somebody. In the morning, when Joyce was cooking eggs and it was sunny and the night before felt like a strange dream, she asked me if I was quite all right. I suppose I must have looked a bit shell-shocked, and I blurted out what had happened.'

'What did she say?'

'She was perfectly lovely about it. She said everyone was equal at Athena House and that included valued guests, too, and that it was all a way of showing affection, and there was nothing wrong with it. Then I asked if we could change the subject, and we discussed the talk she was planning, and that was it.'

I nodded, my mouth finally full of sponge. 'It doesn't sound as though Joyce was jealous.'

'No,' said Ethel. She looked up at me. 'But who did she tell? Because somebody sent me those lilies. And perhaps whoever did was jealous enough to kill Joyce, too.'

I resolved to go back to Birchcroft the following week, to find out more from Sabrina and Theo, and see if I could persuade Spud to let me read Maggie's diary. Perhaps he would have heard from his mother by then, and there would be a simple explanation – *Yes, Maggie and Johnny are both here, so sorry you were worried...* – though I doubted it.

In the meantime, I busied myself writing the smaller obituary for my section – a steeplejack, whose wife fondly recalled that 'he was like a cat, he was only happy when he was high up'.

I was no longer struggling to find enough letters asking for obituaries of loved ones; since the Emersons had been exposed, news of the column had spread. If anything, I now had too many letters to wade through. I divided them into 'no' – they were the ones who said their dad had been a lovely, churchgoing, ordinary man – and 'maybe' – the ones which alluded to something interesting but were too vague to convince, and needed following up. One said: *Mam loved the zoo* and I nearly rejected it (who didn't love it?) until Pat recognised her name and pointed out that she'd been a lion keeper at Belle Vue during the Great War. I was looking forward to meeting her children, assuming they hadn't been eaten.

The 'definitely yes' pile was always the smallest. Late on Friday afternoon, I was sorting through the 'maybe' pile, putting them in order of date so I could reply promptly, when a name caught my eye.

Dear Miss York, I read.

Our father, Bertram Sullivan, was a bare-knuckle boxer. He passed on last week, and we would all wish to see him commemorated in the Chronicle, *our newspaper of choice. He won nearly all of his fights and the boxing club lads in Cheetham Hill got up a collection for him when he took ill. He did not suffer fools, but he went to church and was a faithful husband and provided for all seven of us in difficult times. If you would like to put in something about him, please write to:*

Miss Ada Sullivan

42 Linn Street

Cheetham Hill

I read it again. The name was right, and so was the number of grown children. I wasn't sure Mr Gorringe would appreciate Bert the bare-knuckle boxer taking up valuable space in his paper, but now I had an address, I couldn't let it pass.

. . .

After breakfast on Saturday, I caught the tram and looked out of the window as we passed empty spaces where buildings had been. Weeds were already growing in the rubble. How quickly nature rushed into the cracks we left. I thought of the lonely hills around Birchcroft, and found myself imagining a pair of young lovers, cold and still, moss and bracken creeping over their bodies until there was nothing left of them.

I consulted my pocket map, and was relieved to find Linn Street only a short walk away. The houses were small red-brick terraces, well-kept, for the most part, some with Anderson shelters hastily erected in the front gardens – at the back, there would be small stone yards and an alley running behind, full of rubbish bins and cats. I heard the cooing of pigeons as I approached number forty-two, and my heart sped up. She wouldn't know me, I reassured myself.

A net curtain twitched in the window in response to my knock, and a moment later, a small, middle-aged woman opened the door. Her eyes were tired, and her stockings sagged at her ankles. Ada Sullivan looked as though she'd had a hard life.

'Good morning,' I said, 'I'm Miss Edie York, from the *Chronicle*. You wrote to me about your father.'

'I thought you'd write back,' she said, in a smoker's rasp. 'I didn't expect a visitor. The house isn't fit for it. I was just with the birds out the back.'

I imagined her holding her arms aloft like St Francis, as messengers of the air fluttered around her.

'Me pigeons,' she clarified.

'I didn't realise you were a pigeon fancier,' I said, idiotically.

'Why would you realise? Started at it when our Jim died. No one to take them on, so I said I would. Beautiful birds, they are. Come on through, then.'

She led me down an old-fashioned hallway, with gas lamps still fitted to the walls, and out through a small, tiled kitchen. The little yard had been turned into a sort of coop, with corrugated iron sheets serving as a roof. The noise of cooing and flapping from the stacked wooden crates was overwhelming.

'Here,' she said, lifting a white pigeon with mouse-red eyes towards me. 'This is Fleet. She's my best girl, aren't you?' She made kissing noises and let Fleet touch her mouth with her beak.

'She's very pretty,' I said. 'I'm sorry about your father.'

'Ah well. He were getting on. Eighty-one. Went a bit doolally towards the end. Could barely tell his kids apart.'

'And there are seven of you?' I felt like a barrister leading the jury.

'Aye. Me, Jim, as was – he died of the thrombus five year' back – our Ivy, Bill, Ken, Francis and Rose.'

Francis. Frank Sullivan. There it was. Suki's husband, the man who had come between us all those years ago.

'I think I might have come across Francis,' I said. 'A long time ago. Is he still married? Do they have any children?'

'Did you?' She eyed me suspiciously. 'Yes, he is, and no, they haven't been blessed in that department.'

'I knew his wife,' I said. A pigeon burst from its opened crate in a whirr of feathers, making me jump, and landed on my shoulder.

'Don't mind Soar,' she said. 'He's right friendly.'

I wondered how I would explain a streak of pigeon droppings down my coat back at the office.

'She's a funny one, his wife,' said Ada. 'Quiet as you like, wouldn't say boo to a mouse, never mind a goose.'

For the first time, I wondered if I'd made a mistake.

'Do you have their address, by any chance?' I asked. 'I'd love to pay a visit.'

'Not far from here, as it happens,' said Ada. 'Number twenty-three, Station Road.' She gave me directions.

'Frank'll be out at work, mind,' she said. 'He's a mechanic at the garage up on Lansdown Road.'

I could hardly believe it had been so simple.

'I'll drop in on my way back.'

She nodded. 'Small world. Now, what do you want to know about my dad?'

An hour later, now fully in possession of everything Bert Sullivan had ever done or said, I bid goodbye to Ada and her pigeons. Station Road was very close, and I was shaking with nerves by the time I reached the corner. The worst that could happen was a slammed door, I told myself, and I'd had worse than that over the years. Or perhaps she'd be out, or Frank would be in, after all... but I couldn't pass by without at least trying. I would not be a coward.

The houses on the long, treeless road were Victorian terraces with front doors that opened to the street. This was not a well-off area. A group of scruffy children were rolling an orange-box go-kart along and arguing, while one girl of about six lugged a sobbing, red-faced baby with her. Number twenty-three stood out for its neatness. The front step shone white, and the net curtains were so clean they were blinding, compared to the yellowing hammocks at number twenty-five next door. The letter box and knocker were polished to a brassy gleam. I wondered if Ada had got the house number wrong.

I took a deep breath, and knocked. After a moment, I heard the sound of a bolt being drawn back, and the door opened. Suki was standing in front of me.

CHAPTER SEVEN

Eight years ago, I had only just left the home, the day after my sixteenth birthday. I had found a job as an assistant undersecretary with the council, and was living in a boarding house for girls, sharing a room with three equally broke sixteen-year-olds. Suki was a few months younger than me, and her own leaving date was looming. I had always assumed she'd come and share a room with me at the boarding house, bleak as it was, while we planned the rest of our lives. I hadn't expected her to meet Frank Sullivan in the queue for the pictures to see Madeleine Carroll in *I Was a Spy*.

He had got chatting to her, dazzling Suki with his double-breasted suit and snap-brim trilby, and after the film he took her to Lyons Corner House for ice cream. Frank told her that she was 'a stunner' and said he was looking for models to show off the cars at the garage he owned.

'How old is Frank?' I asked Suki, as she was breathlessly detailing all this to me.

'Oh, I don't know,' she said airily. 'Perhaps about thirty?'

It transpired that Frank was thirty-five, well over twice Suki's age, and very much what Pat would call a 'spiv'. They saw each other every Saturday afternoon for six weeks, and then he asked her to marry him.

'He went down on one knee in Mr Pugh's parlour,' Suki told me.

'He asked him for my hand. Isn't that romantic?'

I thought Mr Pugh would be delighted to welcome another starving orphan to mistreat in her place, but I smiled queasily. I knew, even at sixteen, with no experience of grown men beyond the holy trinity of Hercule Poirot, Sherlock Holmes and Lord Peter Wimsey, that Frank was bad news. When I saw Suki after the third time he took her out, she was flushed and giddy.

'He says he loves me,' she whispered. 'We went for a walk in the park and he told me.' I noticed her jumper was on inside out, and there were leaves and twigs in her smooth black hair.

'I hope he isn't taking advantage of you,' I said.

She bristled. 'I don't need you to protect me, Edie,' she said. 'Frank says he'll do that from now on.'

'Does he?'

I felt a cold stone sink inside me. The fourth time, I saw her two days later and she had a livid bruise on her arm.

'Oh, it was my fault,' Suki said. 'I was chatting away, not looking where I was going. I was about to step in front of a horse and cart and Frank pulled me back.'

'Quite a hard pull.'

'Well, he thought I was in danger!' she said. 'He called me a "damned little idiot", it was just like a film.'

The next time, he took her to the dog track, at White City.

'He bet so much money,' Suki told me, awestruck. 'Bundles of pound notes! I asked him how he had so much, and he said "ask no questions and I'll tell you no lies." What do you think that means?'

'I think it means he's doing something he shouldn't be,' I said. 'Are you sure he owns a garage?'

'Edie, you're like a headmistress sometimes,' Suki said. 'I'm perfectly able to look after myself. I love Frank.'

'You haven't known him five minutes, and he's old enough to be your father.'

'You've never been in love,' said Suki. 'How would you know how it feels?'

She was like my sister – all through our cold, miserable childhoods in the home, we had cared for each other and laughed and bickered over silly things, knowing our bond was unbreakable. Until now, when Frank Sullivan had spotted beautiful, naïve, love-starved Suki in the picture queue, and scooped her up like a handful of toffees, simply because he could.

When she told me about the proposal, she had a red mark on her cheek.

'I was stupid,' she said. 'I asked him a silly question when he was driving, and nearly caused an accident.'

'And he hit you?'

'Oh, but he didn't mean to!' she cried. 'He swerved, and his hand caught me.'

I tried hard to imagine how someone would accidentally whack their passenger's face while swerving.

'So you're marrying him?'

'I thought you'd be pleased for me.'

It was the day after Suki's sixteenth birthday, the same day she was due to leave the home, and we were walking to the bus stop from the steamy café where we'd shared a sticky bun and her news. A late autumn afternoon, it was raining and we were huddled under my umbrella, our feet sliding on wet, yellow leaves. The air smelled of wood smoke, church bells rang for evensong in the distance, and I felt as melancholy as I had done on the interminable Sunday afternoons of my childhood.

'You don't have to get married,' I said. 'You're barely sixteen, and he's so much older than you...'

'What does it matter if he is?' Suki's huge brown eyes flashed fury. 'What's so wonderful about living in a boarding house with a pack of other penniless girls? It's no different from the bloody home. Frank thinks I'm grown up enough to marry him, and I love him.'

'Do you?' I said. 'Or do you love having someone who takes you out, and has money in his pocket, and pretends you're a grown-up?'

'Oh, shut up!' shouted Suki. 'You think you're so superior because you're clever and all you care about is your stupid books. You might be able to earn a living, Edie York, but some of us can't waltz straight into a decent job, and having someone well off and handsome who wants to marry us is our best hope of happiness. You wouldn't understand that,' she added, halting outside a smart, suburban villa called Sunnydene. 'I want to live somewhere like this, and have children and look after my husband.' She was trembling with rage. 'To you, happiness is a made-up person solving a made-up crime. Well, I'm living in the real world, and I'm going to marry Frank.'

'Fine,' I said. I felt cold all over, and the iciness entered my voice. 'You do that, Suki, and don't come crying to me when he treats you like a punchbag, and is out spending his ill-gotten gains on some other star-struck idiot while you're holding a crying baby.'

'Bugger off!' yelled Suki. 'If that's what you think, I've nothing more to say to you.'

She pulled her hat down over her ears and marched off through the misty drizzle with her suitcase, as one by one, the gas lamps lit up along the street. I stood for a while, looking after her, then I turned and walked away.

I wrote to her, care of the home. I sent a present for her wedding and I posted a card to apologise, but Suki had made her mind up. I heard that they'd married at St Saviour's, and moved to the other side of Manchester to be nearer Frank's family. Not a day had passed since then when I hadn't thought about her.

'Edie York,' she said.

'Suki Sullivan.'

We stepped towards each other at the same time, and embraced. I remembered every notch of her back.

'I thought I'd never see you again,' she said, and when she pulled away, her eyes were wet.

'I tried to get in touch, but...'

'I know. I wanted to reply, but I... well, there were reasons why I couldn't.' Suki looked me up and down.

'You look just the same,' she said. 'Well, more grown up and elegant, and not quite so bony – but you're Edie! It's really you. Lord's sake, I've missed you.'

I was flooded with relief and the joy of having made the right decision to call on her, of having taken a risk that worked out well.

She looked so different. Her hair was pinned into a complicated roll, and she wore scarlet lipstick and a smart olive-green dress and heels that seemed more 'evening out' than 'busy housewife'.

'Ada gave me your address. May I come in?' I asked. 'I'd love to see where you live, and we could reacquaint ourselves...'

Suki glanced up and down the street. The children were now busily tying belts to a lamp post, about to attempt some kind of life-threatening swinging game, and the other front doors were closed.

'Go on then,' she said. 'But Frank sometimes nips home for lunch, so we've only got an hour or so.'

I followed her into a two-up two-down house so clean it felt almost oppressive. The rug on the hall floor was free of dust, and when she opened the door to the parlour, it was like looking at a stage set. Two hard, brown armchairs faced one another like warring chessmen, flanking an empty fireplace whose tiles gleamed. There was no clutter, no books, just a small table with a lamp and a whisky decanter, a sideboard holding a wireless and a large, framed wedding photograph, and a brass coalscuttle by the well-swept hearth. The room smelled strongly of beeswax polish and Brasso.

'You're so terribly tidy! What's happened? I used to have to search for you under piles of mess if I wanted a chat.'

She smiled awkwardly. 'Frank doesn't like untidiness.'

'No, but all the same...'

'I'll make us a cup of tea,' said Suki. 'I usually brew a pot for Frank at one o' clock, but I don't think he'll notice if the tea caddy's a bit down.'

I looked up at her. 'Suki, is everything quite all right?'

'Shan't be a minute,' she said, with a hostess's quick smile, and her neat form disappeared into the hall.

I felt uneasy, alone amongst the gleaming polish and deadening neatness.

'I can come into the kitchen,' I shouted. 'I don't mind!'

'No, no, stay there,' she called. 'I'm just coming.'

She was several minutes, and when she reappeared, she was carrying a tray with a full tea set, sugar lumps in a bowl, milk in a little jug and a plate of Dundee cake.

'Gosh, Suki,' I said. 'A cuppa at the kitchen table would have been fine!'

'But you're a guest,' she said. 'Frank doesn't like me to entertain people in the kitchen – he says it's common. Anyway, I've seen your articles!' She smiled genuinely this time. 'I can't believe I know a real journalist, Edie. You've done so well. But the Emersons! I followed the whole story. Tell me exactly what happened...'

I filled her in on my involvement with the art-dealing spies during the Blitz, and she looked thrilled, as if she was a child and I was telling her a bedtime story – which I had done, long ago, on particularly bad nights at the home.

'What are you working on now?' she asked eventually, and I told her about Birchcroft and Joyce Reid and the missing evacuees.

'Gosh!' she said. 'It sounds so exciting, Edie. What do you think happened?'

'I don't know,' I said, 'but Maggie knew Joyce a bit, and I can't help feeling that the two cases must be related.'

'Why?' Suki asked, leaning forward. 'Maybe a madman killed Joyce, and the evacuees have just run away together.'

'Yes, maybe,' I said. 'But it seems odd to have two sudden mysteries in one village, doesn't it?'

'Perhaps,' said Suki, cutting me a large piece of cake, and herself a tiny sliver. 'But there's a lot of bad men in the world.'

'Suki...' I said. 'I don't mean to intrude, but are things all right with Frank? Are you happy?'

'As happy as anyone is after eight years of marriage,' she said stiffly. 'I did hope for a little baby to love, but... well, I lost two early on in my pregnancies, and we've not been blessed.'

'I'm so sorry,' I said. 'You're still young, so perhaps one day?'

'Frank says not. He says it was my fault, and if a horse shies twice, you stop betting on it.'

'My God, Suki! That's an awful thing for him to say.'

She shrugged, and lifted the pot to pour more tea into my cup. As she did so, her cuff fell back, and I caught a glimpse of the purple bruise on her wrist.

'Is that from him?' I asked her. 'Does he hit you?'

'Only if I give him no choice,' she said flatly. 'That's why I keep things nice. He's very particular.'

I was aware that our last meeting had ended in disaster due to my feelings about Frank, and my hopeless inability to keep them to myself. But I was now a grown woman, and so was Suki, and I could not stay silent.

'Suki, I know lots of men do,' I said, 'but it's not right for a man to hit his wife, you know that, don't you?'

'Yes, of course I do,' she said. 'But it's too late now. We're married, and I've no money and I can't leave him. Besides, I'm afraid he'd come after me.'

Suki's marriage was even worse than I'd feared, and I took no pleasure in having been right. She must have seen the horror on my face, because in a moment, all her proud little formalities fell away. She physically sagged, as if her strings had been cut.

'Edie, it's awful,' she said in a low voice. 'I'm not allowed friends, he thinks they'll "give me ideas", so I'm on my own day and night, unless his blasted sister comes round to run her finger along the shelves and check for dust. Now his dad's died it's even worse, he's talking about her moving in with us...' She shuddered.

'Ada?'

'No, Ivy. She's much worse. They all live round here, and they say they're such a big, happy family, but it's a lie. Bert was a horrible man, violent and cruel, though none of them'll hear a word against him, and Frank's just the same. We went to Llandudno on our honeymoon for two days – we stayed at St George's Hotel on the front and he was quite nice to me. I so wanted to be a good wife, but the minute we moved in here, he started beating me.'

I shook my head, about to speak, but she was unleashed.

'Didn't matter if I'd spent all day cleaning, he'd find the one spot I'd missed. If I'd slaved over his dinner, he'd say I'd put too much salt in on purpose – it's all just reasons to knock me about because it makes him feel better. Now with rationing it's even worse, he's got all these black-market contacts and he keeps bringing home stupid things like a pig's head, or a whole trout – I don't know how to fillet a bloody trout! Then he says I'm useless and nobody but him would put up with me.'

She pressed her hands against her eyes.

'He lost all his money on the dogs, and he never owned a garage, he was just a mechanic who worked there. Edie, it's been like this since I met him. You were right, I was stupid and love-struck and a child, and I should never have married him. I could have been taken on as an apprentice hairdresser at Madame Faye's, and I'd probably have my own salon by now.' She swallowed. 'I'll never be free of him, and I've no idea what to do.'

I knelt next to her chair and held her familiar, birdlike frame to me. It was as if centuries had passed since our last meeting, or perhaps no time at all.

'You'll have to go now,' she said, raising her head. 'I'm so sorry, but I can't risk him coming back. I'll get it even worse if he sees it's you.'

'I'll go,' I agreed. 'But Suki, look, you can't stay. He might end up killing you.'

'He probably will,' she said. 'But where can I go?'

'You can come to me.' I told her the address. 'Remember it,' I said. 'Don't write it down.'

'If I can find a way, I will.' She checked the street, where a rather substantial child was lying on the pavement shouting 'it was your flipping belt that broke!', then shut the door quickly behind me. She had infected me with her fear, too, and all the way back to the bus stop, I felt certain that Frank would somehow sense she'd had a visitor and brutally punish Suki. How I loathed him.

I thought of Lou and Arnold, and Annie's brothers – even Des and Mr Gorringe, both born in the last century. I couldn't imagine any of them raising their fist to a woman. Although Herbert Wright certainly didn't hold back. As for the men of Athena House... perhaps at least one of them had committed an act of violence from which there was no turning back.

. . .

Saturday night came as a great relief. I set my worry over Suki aside as Annie and I got ready for our evening out.

'If there's an air raid, we'll look very silly dressed up to the nines in the public shelter,' she observed.

'We shan't, because the band will have to come as well,' I said. 'So they can keep playing down there while we do the foxtrot.'

Annie laughed, then sighed. 'I hope seeing Arnold isn't a mistake.'

She dabbed on bright red lipstick.

'That's nice,' I said. 'Is it new?'

'Victory Red. Just come out. A gift from a grateful patient.'

'Male, I assume.'

'Yes. He was a dear. But he told me he had a girl overseas and he wanted to go back to her if he could.'

'I suppose there'll be lots of that during the war.' I shoved pins into my hair. 'Falling in love with people far away, I mean.'

'Chance'd be a fine thing,' said Annie. 'Can you do my back button?'

As I fiddled with the loop, I noticed a thin chain around her neck.

'New necklace?'

'Oh – no, it was something Pete once gave me. A St Christopher, to keep travellers safe. I never wore it because I never went anywhere. He should have kept it for himself,' she added.

'Are you still very sad?'

'Oh, I don't know,' she said. 'Yes. No. But I felt I should honour his memory and put it on.'

I had been going to mention Suki, but the doorbell rang and I flew down to answer it before Mrs Turner could complain.

Clara greeted me enthusiastically. 'How are you, old girl?' she asked. 'I've got some rather jolly news, but no champagne, I'm afraid.'

'We can toast with a cup of tea upstairs,' I said.

She followed me up and Annie came out of her bedroom. Clara always seemed rather flustered in Annie's presence, and there was some awkwardness over chairs and milk jugs.

'Well, then,' said Annie, once we were all seated. 'Do tell!'

'I'm going to fly aeroplanes!' said Clara. Her open face was suffused with happiness. 'I applied to the WAAF months ago, and it took an age for the letter to come, and of course Mummy and Daddy are dead against it, but I'm going to be a pilot! I start my training at Barton Aerodrome, Monday week,' she went on. 'I'll be test-piloting new monoplanes called Fairey Barracudas. They're starting production this week.'

'That's wonderful,' I said. I raised my teacup. 'To the skies!'

'I'm happy for you,' said Annie. 'But oh, Clara, you will be careful, won't you? I couldn't bear it if something happened to you as well.'

'I'll be as safe as houses,' said Clara. 'And I don't mean your last address. Chin-chin!'

We drank to her new role, and peppered her with questions about what she'd do, and where she'd live, and how she'd appease Mrs Lafferty, and by the time we got to the steps of the Astoria where we'd arranged to meet the others, we were rather late.

Ethel was hovering on the steps alone, wearing the most glorious blue shot-silk dress and a matching jacket.

'You look marvellous,' I told her.

'I ran it up myself before the war, on Mother's old Singer,' she said. 'I don't often get the chance to wear it.'

Lou and Arnold arrived in their best suits, and we all went in together. It was such a joy to forget about the war and Joyce and Maggie, and even Suki's troubles. We commandeered a table along the side of the huge dance floor, ordered our drinks, and then Billy Wainwright and his Starlight Orchestra trooped onto the stage and opened the dance with a blast of trumpets and timpani.

Annie and I did a foxtrot together, then I danced a rather heavy-footed jitterbug with Clara, though we were laughing too much to manage much in the way of steps. The hall was packed, and a miasma of perspiration and cigarette smoke hung over the dance floor like sea mist.

I'd just returned to our table for a gulp of lemonade when Lou appeared at my side.

'Dance?'

'Why not?'

I let him lead me back to the floor as the next tune began, which rather ludicrously turned out to be a tango.

'Just follow me and don't tread on my feet,' said Lou. We stalked and swooped round the floor, weaving between a mass of other dipping, prancing couples. I saw our table flash by. Ethel was chatting to Arnold, and Annie to Clara.

'Have you found anything out?' Lou asked, as he expertly tipped me backwards.

'At Birchcroft?'

'No, I thought you might have parachuted into the Reichstag,' he shouted over the music. 'Yes, Birchcroft.'

'Yes, I have,' I yelled back. 'I'll tell you when we're sitting down. Where's Marple?'

'My next-door neighbour's looking after him,' Lou said. 'She's got a cocker spaniel and they seem to have formed a passionate friendship over the fence.'

The music reached a romantic crescendo, and several couples maintained a dramatic clasp with their noses an inch apart. Lou snapped me back to an upright position as if he was folding up a deckchair on the prom, and led me to our seats. I filled him in on what I'd discovered in Birchcroft.

'I should have pulled rank straight away,' said Lou, lighting a cigarette. I pinched one from his case, and he lit it for me without argument.

'Based on the complexity of the relationships around Joyce,

and the time you found her body, I think it certainly deserved a visit from the county pathologist. But it's a bit bloody late now, thanks to our trusty Constable Creech.'

'Why is the time important?'

'A body cools within an eight-hour period,' he said, hailing a waiter for more drinks. 'And rigor mortis sets in after two to three hours,' he announced into the alarmed waiter's face.

The band was beginning a rather dull waltz, and I saw Arnold offer his arm to Ethel. I was certain he was simply being gentlemanly, but it didn't go unnoticed by Annie, who inadvertently made a face as they clasped each other and set off in a stately clinch. I wanted to comfort her, but I needed to know more about rigor mortis.

'Which means,' Lou resumed, leaning in to shout over the band, 'Joyce probably died more than two but less than three hours before you found her, because she was already cold, but you tried the kiss of life and were able to administer it easily. If rigor had set in...'

'You two look very romantic,' Annie suddenly shouted into my other ear. 'Am I interrupting?'

'We're discussing rigor mortis. You're welcome to join us.'

'I'm quite all right, thanks,' she said. 'I think I'll go to the ladies' and reapply my lipstick. Not that anyone will be kissing it off.'

She glanced across at Arnold, swinging Ethel round the floor as her silk skirt flared out becomingly. She had very good ankles, I noticed.

'Annie, you were the one who...'

'Ended things, yes, I know,' she said, snatching up her bag and hurrying off.

A tall, uniformed Wren stopped by our table.

'Clara Lafferty!' she cried, delighted. 'Fancy seeing you here!'

Clara shouted, 'Connie Platt! My old dear!' and leapt up.

They disappeared onto the dance floor arm in arm, chattering like reunited sisters.

'As I was saying,' said Lou, 'if Joyce died between around nine and eleven a.m., it suggests that there may have been other ramblers about – who would have seen someone rushing down the hillside, ideally holding a large rock and looking guilty.'

'We didn't see anyone else, though,' I sighed. 'It's too early in the season.'

'Didn't you say that the other artists liked to tramp about too, though? Why were none of the Merry Bohemians out with her?'

'Or perhaps they were,' I said, and we looked at each other significantly.

'I don't suppose you asked any of them what they were up to that morning?'

'No,' I said. 'I'm supposed to be writing a fond obituary, not a police report.'

'Well,' he said. 'If you still intend to become a crime reporter, perhaps now's the time to do both.'

'What do you mean?'

Arnold and Ethel trotted past. Ethel seemed to be laughing with carefree joy, and I felt relieved that Annie had not yet returned from the powder room.

'I can't just steam in, with no evidence,' said Lou. 'It's not my area, for a start. But if there seems to have been foul play – and given the circumstances, I'm of a mind to consider it – I could make a case for getting involved. Can you go back, ask a few more probing questions?'

'Of course,' I said, pleased. 'And while I'm there, I'm going to ask Spud to find Maggie's diary. I can't help feeling it's connected.'

'Why?'

I was glad I wasn't in the interview room as a suspect. Lou's dark blue eyes were focussed as a cat sensing rustling in the undergrowth.

'Because she knew Joyce. And I can't see how she'd leave Spud.'

'Half the village knew Joyce,' he said. 'And he does sound a bit of an odd lad.'

'He's a darling,' I said crossly.

'Well, back to the pig pen then, Miss York,' he said, and patted my knee in avuncular fashion.

'I shall report back,' I said. 'And if it turns out I'm right, you can make me an honorary detective.'

'Horribly defective, more like,' he said, and was guffawing at his own joke when Arnold and Ethel returned, swiftly followed by Annie. Clara and Connie were still charging about together to the Jealousy Tango, and I felt the choice of music was rather awkward, given Annie's situation. Even if she had brought it on herself.

CHAPTER EIGHT

I couldn't get back up to Birchcroft until the following Tuesday. This must surely be my last official visit as an obituarist, or Mr Gorringe would soon begin to ask questions about my lengthy absences from the office. I'd spent Sunday working in the WVS canteen, and my arms ached from carrying trays of sandwiches and filling hundreds of cups. The immediate trauma of the newly bombed-out was easing, but we had a steady stream of people who were in temporary accommodation, or had lost their ID cards and papers and were waiting for an appointment with someone who could help.

Annie and I had also lost most of our things when the bomb fell on Violet Bank Terrace. We'd been back a few days later to try and salvage anything we could, but though I'd found the powder compact she'd given me for Christmas under a mangled bathroom tap, and she'd managed to drag her favourite coat from the rubble and have it cleaned, we were now largely reliant on hand-me-downs posted from Annie's cousin Helen in Bath, and whatever the WVS second-hand shop could provide. Clara had sweetly offered us the use of her wardrobe, but she was a giantess compared to me and Annie, and we'd have looked like circus clowns in her clothes. I had at least replaced my vanished cosmetics, and was thankful that, unlike some of the visitors to the canteen, I had no precious photographs of my parents to be destroyed. In fact, I had no idea what they looked like or who they were, and it seemed likely to remain that way.

Knowing how the bombed-out people felt was useful sometimes, and if it wasn't, a strong cup of tea was often all they wanted. That didn't stop me feeling terribly weary of it all. Working at the *Chronicle* meant we were constantly aware of the latest developments overseas and the growing threat of invasion, while Ethel's postbag overflowed with grief and outrage at prices, rationing, bomb damage, the government, the council, public transport and 'women taking men's jobs on the home front'.

My worries were now compounded by Suki, and what I knew was happening to her. I almost wished I'd never found out, but now I had, I felt I must try and help her. Then there was poor little Spud – and it was the thought of him, hiding from Mrs Wright in his elegantly appointed pig pen, that dragged me out of bed early on Tuesday morning, and sent me off to catch the train north.

I emerged from the smoky carriage into a chilly, early spring day, with snowdrops shining from beneath the mossy stone walls and churchyard graves. Pale sunlight made the slate cottage roofs gleam silver, and I felt incongruously optimistic as I walked up the cobbled lane to the village. I intended to have a cup of tea at the Singing Kettle, the little café opposite the post office, and work out my questions before I returned, yet again, to Athena House. Spud would be at school all morning, and I needed to bolster my courage before I went to look for Norman, the shell-shocked old soldier at the campsite, who sounded both strange and unfriendly.

The brass bell jangled violently as I pushed open the door, but I waited several long minutes for the young waitress to notice me and show me to a seat. There were only five tables, and four were occupied, though I didn't recognise anyone. As the waitress pointed rather gracelessly to the spare table, the bell tinkled again and I turned to see Rita Norton, the land girl from Brackenfield, wearing a jaunty red headscarf tied into a knot on top of her head, and Oxford bags with rather muddy hems.

'Crikey, hullo again!' she said. 'I'm having a beast of a morning, so I've come for a cuppa while the chemist sorts out Lady B's prescriptions. I haven't long, though, I don't want to be late for Her Ladyship – shan't make that mistake twice, I can tell you.'

I was pleased to see her. 'Share my table,' I offered.

'Thanks.' She slid into the spare chair. 'No hope of a biscuit here, more's the pity. One slice of toast each if you're starving, with a scrape of Mrs Hooper's pre-war gooseberry jam.' She lowered her voice. 'I warn you, it tastes like Jeyes Fluid.'

We ordered tea for two, without toast.

'I didn't think we'd see you back here so soon after your nasty shock,' she said.

I explained that I was writing an obituary of Joyce, and she nodded solemnly. 'Folk round here couldn't stand her, and I can't say I agreed with her views. But it was a nasty way for anyone to go.'

'Have you seen anyone from Athena House lately?'

'No, not really,' said Rita. 'Even if I wanted to, they don't encourage us to mingle at Brackenfield.'

She rolled her eyes up to the horse brasses that decorated the café's low beams. 'Work till you drop, go to bed, do it all again,' she grumbled. 'I can hardly feel my hands some nights, and I've got arm muscles like a navvy. I only get any gossip at all when I have a quick ciggie with Bessie from the kitchen.'

'Anything interesting?' I asked, as casually as I could manage.

'Not much. Oh!' Rita exclaimed. 'Now you come to ask, there's been a development with the missing evacuees. I heard it from Bessie, who said Ned at the pub told Mr Magellan, the butler at Brackenfield, and he'd heard it direct from Mr Walker—'

I blinked. This was like a game of 'I went to market and I bought...'

'What did you hear?' I interrupted.

'Well,' she leaned forward, 'apparently, they've found a hat.'

'Whose?'

'Maggie's,' hissed Rita. 'It was blue wool and she wore it all the time – she was wearing it on the day they vanished, according to her brother. He said it'd gone from the peg. Though how an eleven-year-old boy would notice such a thing, I don't know.'

I wondered if Spud had read Maggie's diary yet. He must be so worried, my heart ached for him.

'Where did they find it?'

'That's just it, it's awfully peculiar,' said Rita. 'Gosh, I could murder a decent cake or a sticky bun, couldn't you? Shame they're like hens' teeth these days...'

'What's just it?'

I was beginning to see why Lou found interviewing witnesses so frustrating.

'Oh, the hat – someone from the Home Guard found it miles away. There's a great long valley between Birchcroft and Grazebrook, about six miles of rivers and woods and not much else,' she explained. 'According to Bessie, it was just lying by a stream up the valley, soaked through.'

'Do the police know?'

'Creech? I imagine so, but he doesn't seem to have found

out much. I saw him in the pub the other night, and he looked thoroughly glum.'

'Have the Wrights been told? Has Spud?'

'Goodness, I don't know, I'm sure,' said Rita, draining her teacup. 'I suppose they must have been. What do you think – reckon young Johnny's done her in?'

'I certainly hope not,' I said primly. The idea made me feel cold to the core. 'But now the hat's been discovered, surely the idea that she ran away is redundant? I mean, why would it be there, unless she was forced to go that way?'

'The valley does lead to a road, eventually,' said Rita. 'So if they wanted to make sure nobody caught them, maybe they hitchhiked if there were any cars passing that way. It doesn't seem likely, mind you, does it? It's a long journey to London, and it's nothing but miles of stones and trees and bog that way.'

I thought about tiny Maggie, just fourteen, walking alone through a wild, rain-swept valley, then hitching a lift for well over two hundred miles. It seemed profoundly unlikely.

'The police must be looking for her by now,' I said, with more hope than conviction.

Rita nodded and glanced towards the clock above the empty cake display.

'Lawks!' she said. 'Look at the time! They'll have a search party out for me, never mind Maggie. I'm off to chit my early potatoes, duckie. Good luck, let me know how you get on.'

She threw twopence on the table and hurried out, the bell clanging behind her.

As I made my way up the small street, a girl bumped into me with her basket. There was something familiar about her neat WVS uniform and wide cheekbones.

'Sorry!' she said automatically, then turned back. 'You're the woman from the train,' she said. 'I remember, because of what's happened to Joyce. Sorry for what I said, if she was your friend,' she muttered.

'Edie York,' I said. 'I'm writing a piece for the *Manchester Chronicle*. You're Sally Corrin, I remember now. It's all right,' I added awkwardly. 'I know you're not keen on the Athena House lot.' I turned to go, but she stood in front of me.

'I just... look, I have reason not to trust them,' she said. 'You've heard about the evacuees?'

'Yes,' I began. 'In fact, I need to ask the Wrights...'

'I doubt that pair have a clue where they've got to,' Sally said. She glanced behind her. 'Miss York, can I tell you something? It's been playing on my mind, and I haven't known what to do about it. It might sound silly, but maybe you can look into it...'

'Of course,' I said. We ducked into a small gap between the butcher's and the chemist, out of the way of passers-by, and I tipped my umbrella to shield us from view, feeling rather spy-like.

'What is it?' I whispered.

'Well,' Sally leaned in. 'It was a few weeks before she went missing, and I don't know what's happened to the lad, but I saw that Mr Fagan with Maggie.'

'Aubrey?'

'If you like. I was going to meet Rita for a half in the Black Horse on her afternoon off – Ned's all right, he doesn't mind serving girls – but she was late, and I went down to the lane to look out for her. I couldn't see Rita, but I did see Mr Fagan and Maggie coming back down the hill path.' She glanced towards the butcher's nervously, as if there were hordes of German spies lurking next to the board reading PORK SOSSAGE'S AVAILABLE TODAY.

'They looked thick as thieves huddled together, right deep in conversation they were, and she was saying something like "no, really, I can't", as if he was trying to persuade her into something.'

'Huddled together?'

'He had his arm round her,' said Sally. 'It struck me as very peculiar. In fact, I'd not like to say exactly how it struck me, Miss York, but I'm sure you can imagine.'

'But she's fourteen! What would a man in his forties want with a young girl?'

Sally looked at me.

'You don't think...?'

'I don't think anything,' she said. 'I'm just telling you what I saw.'

'Did you tell anybody?'

Sally shrugged. 'Why would I have? It's not as though anything happened to her. I saw her at church the next morning.'

'Unless something did,' I said, fear rushing through me like rainwater in the gutters overhead.

My route up to Athena House took me past a lane marked by a weathered signpost. A newer arrow had been tacked on, with CAMPSITE written in white paint. It pointed up a grassy track with a five-barred gate at the end. I considered my fear of Norman and my relatively flimsy shoes, but it wasn't raining and I had promised both myself and Lou that I'd find some answers while I was here. I heaved a sigh, and crunched my way up to the gate. I could see a wide field, bordered by rough stone walls and on one side, dense woodland. Beyond it were the hills, and presumably, the valley where Maggie's hat had been found.

In the far left corner of the field was a small, buff-coloured canvas tent secured with guy ropes. A circle of stones around a blackened area showed the site of a regular fire, and something that looked from a distance like a ragged shirt was draped over a branch, drying in the weak sunlight.

I felt sick with nerves. What if Norman had killed both Joyce and Maggie? I knew nothing about him, other than that he was 'a bit odd' – but what did that mean? Someone who lived in a tent and sang to himself, or someone who could be a murderer? Yet somehow, I was opening the gate, picking my way over tussocks and withered bracken, and approaching the closed tent flap.

'Hullo?' I called, my heart racing. For a moment, I thought with a rush of relief that he must be out, shooting rabbits or catching trout, but then there was a rustle, the canvas billowed and parted, and a face stared out through the gap.

'Excuse me,' I said. 'Are you Norman?'

He was in his fifties, leathery and grey-haired, with a wild beard like something out of an Edward Lear poem. He could very easily have had two larks and a wren nesting in it. He narrowed his pale gaze against the daylight and said, 'Yes.'

I expected him to add 'what's it to you?' or 'who's asking?' or any number of other irritable queries, but he remained sitting in the tent and waited for me to speak.

'I'm sorry to bother you,' I said, as if I were standing on the vicarage step, rather than in a field. 'I'm helping to look for Maggie Dawson and Johnny...' I realised I didn't know his surname.

'Why?'

'The evacuees have gone missing from Wrights' Farm,' I explained. 'Maggie's hat was found and...' I tailed off. I wondered if I should be here at all; if Norman had killed Maggie, he was hardly going to welcome my probing questions, and there was nobody about to witness me being dragged into a tent and strangled.

'Nothing to do with me,' he said.

'No, indeed, but I wondered if perhaps you'd seen them –

they left very early in the morning two weeks ago and nobody knows where they've gone.'

'I don't see so much,' he said. 'These days.'

I looked at his face, and saw the dull, immobile sheen of a glass eye, contrasting unnervingly with the brightness of the other.

'Oh, I see,' I said and wanted immediately to die of embarrassment. He didn't seem to notice.

'I can't help you,' he said, after a pause. 'Not my business.'

'But something might have happened to Maggie, you see,' I persisted. 'Everyone's terribly worried about her. So if you...'

'She's not my daughter,' he said. 'And you're not my mother. So if you'll excuse me.'

He pulled the tent flap back into place and vanished, leaving me standing foolishly in the empty field.

I paused for a moment, cross and nonplussed.

'If you do hear of her...' I called.

'I won't,' he said. 'You can go now.'

I went.

As I walked up the long lane to Athena House, I felt discombobulated by my brief audience with Norman. He hadn't been unfriendly or angry, so much as absent and indifferent. He hadn't actually denied seeing Maggie, either. Was he trustworthy? I wondered. Did a man with shell shock twenty-three years after the last war see things the way the rest of us did? Or had he simply opted out of society, not just physically but morally, too? It would be easy enough to snatch a slight young girl, and drag her off somewhere remote. I imagined his wiry arm around her throat, her hat lost in the struggle.

The way from Wrights' Farm to the valley would probably go past the campsite – though Maggie could have gone the other way, past the bull field. Or perhaps, I reminded myself, she was safely back in London, and so was Johnny. I needed that diary, whether Spud was willing to hand it over or not.

The yard of Athena House was familiar to me now, and I greeted the scrappy chickens like old friends. The porch door was open, and as I approached, I heard someone calling, 'See you later'.

To my surprise, Theo appeared, dressed for the outdoors in tweeds. A wide-brimmed hat covered his close-shaved head and he had added a sparkling paste brooch to his jacket which gave him the rakish air of a pantomime baron.

'Hullo!' he said cheerfully. He seemed altogether a different man to the wheezing invalid I'd last seen.

'Theo! Are you feeling better?'

'Much, thank you, Edie,' he said. 'Still awfully sad over Joyce, of course, but my health trouble has eased up, now it's not so damp. I'm just off to meet the vicar to discuss the funeral plans. Although' – he lowered his voice, leaning towards me – 'Aubrey won't have anything to do with traditional religion. He's furious about it, so I'd avoid his studio. He was throwing chairs about earlier. What brings you here?'

I explained about the obituary. 'I hoped to speak to you and a couple of the others, so I can include everyone's recollections of Joyce.' *And find out whether any of you killed her*, I added silently.

'Of course,' said Theo. 'I'd be delighted, as soon as I'm back – should only be an hour or so. I might cycle, as it's sunny.'

'Can you?' I asked. 'With your asthma?'

'Oh yes. Doctor Wilson in the village says exercise is good for me. It's just damp weather and being upset that isn't.'

He raised a hand and hurried over the yard to what I presumed was the bicycle shed.

Once again, I walked down the cluttered hallway, and emerged into the kitchen. It was empty, breakfast things standing in the sink, and I turned and went back to the huge drawing room in the hope of finding someone. As I pushed the door open, calling, 'Hullo?', I heard a muffled exclamation, and two people on the couch sprang apart as I entered. It was Jean-Luc and Nora, who was hastily tucking her cotton blouse into her slacks, and gathering her escaped red hair back into its bun.

'Oh, it's you!' Nora looked relieved. 'Morning, Edie – I thought you were Sabrina.'

'Don't mind me,' I said, idiotically. 'I'm so sorry to barge in – I'm just hoping to speak to the others about Joyce, for the newspaper.'

'Yes, of course,' said Nora. She stood up. Jean-Luc remained on the couch, lighting a cigarette. It hadn't taken him long to move on, I thought. If indeed he had ever moved off Nora or Sabrina in favour of Joyce. I really had no idea how these things worked in bohemian circles, and a vague awareness of Virginia Woolf and Vita Sackville-West didn't qualify me to judge.

'I'll fetch Joan,' said Nora. 'She's working, but I'm sure she'll want to speak to you.'

I braced myself for Joan's bark, but when she appeared, she smiled at me. 'Hullo! We must stop meeting like this. Come across to my studio, we'll talk there.' She was wearing men's overalls and a scarf tied over her short hair. It rather suited her. I thought of Suki and her frightened, flawless appearance and wished Joan could have a word with Frank. I couldn't imagine anyone not quailing before her when she was angry.

I followed Joan out of the back door and across to another shed. It was less well-appointed than Aubrey's, and the window was much smaller, but she had whitewashed the walls and added a few bits of bamboo furniture with bright tapestry cushions. A kettle sat on a tiny Calor gas stove in the corner alongside two enamel cups and a battered cake tin. It reminded me of the dens children make in garden sheds, and I thought how much Spud would like it.

'Have a pew,' she said. I looked for her art amongst the

cosy furnishings, and realised I'd walked straight past an enormous canvas the size of a hearthrug that was lying on the floor. The painting was abstract, in yellows and blues, but it was clearly a seascape, with cliffs and clouds rendered in unconventional squares and oblongs. I found I liked it very much and said so.

'Thanks,' said Joan. 'I've a London gallerist on Cork Street, but that's shut down for the duration, so I'm trying to get some work done for a new exhibition when the war's over. Rather harder without a strict deadline, though.'

I was impressed – even I had heard of Cork Street, home to chi-chi art dealers. I wondered what was she doing up here in Birchcroft.

'I like the country air,' she said, as if I'd spoken out loud. 'And I did like Joyce, we were good pals. I could live without the rest, mostly, though Theo's all right when he's not being a hypochondriac.'

'But his asthma...' I began.

'Oh, pish,' said Joan, sparking up a hand-rolled ciggie. 'He just likes to have a fuss made of him. And he's nowhere near as shell-shocked as poor old Norman, whatever he claims. Have you met our local loony?'

'Just now,' I said, thinking that 'loony' was rather cruel. Norman was certainly taciturn, but he didn't seem mad.

'Get anything useful out of him?' She put her booted feet up on a little table.

'I'm afraid not—'

'Bugger off!' Joan bellowed suddenly. I jumped, and turned to see that a large cockerel with plumage like an Ascot hat had wandered in, and was strolling across her canvas. It stalked out again, and she returned to a normal volume and said, 'Actually, I don't mind old Norman. At least he doesn't gossip, unlike the rest of this godforsaken village. Golly, sometimes I wish I lived on an island in the middle of a misty loch. I'd be perfectly happy, and I'd never have to deal with other peoples' ridiculous dramatics.'

'What kind of dramatics?'

'Well, you've met them all,' said Joan, dragging hard on her cigarette. She spluttered a laugh. 'Aubrey's, for a start. He's a one-man show. Never happier than when he's the centre of attention. He agrees that Joyce was murdered, and he simply won't shut up about it, though Creech won't listen. Aubrey and Sab had a row last night over it, and she threw Nora's mutton stew at the wall. Nora was furious, and now there's a grease stain in the shape of Italy there.'

'So Sabrina thinks it was an accident?'

'She does,' said Joan. 'She said' – she adopted a rather accurate high-pitched, upper-class twang – '"Honestly, do people really imagine that the postman or the butcher was so upset that they were creeping round the hillside planning to kill her off, just for giving a couple of talks? It's absurd." I don't think it's absurd,' added Joan. 'It seems perfectly likely to me.'

'People do seem angry,' I said. 'But surely angry and murderous are very different beasts?'

'Not always. Although unless she bumped into someone, how would they know where she was?' Joan said, more to herself than me. 'I saw her that morning at about eight, and I asked where she was going. I remember her exact words: "I'll see where the fancy takes me today." So how would anyone have known in advance where she'd be? It was pure luck that you found her.'

'Unless she'd arranged to meet someone she didn't want to tell you about,' I observed, and Joan nodded.

'Possible, I suppose. But she wasn't the type for secrets.'

'Might one of the others have gone with her – or caught up with her later on?'

Joan shook her head. 'They were all here, as far as I remember.'

Could somebody have followed her, then? But on the route Ethel and I had taken, there were long stretches where it was possible to see far into the distance in every direction. Perhaps someone she knew, or thought was a friend? Pushing someone off a hill, though, was not in any way guaranteed to kill them – Joyce may have simply rolled to a sitting position and run away. An accidental killing? But why would anyone... *Oh, for goodness' sake.* I thought. *I need Lou to make sense of all this.*

'Joan,' I said, 'I don't suppose you know much about the missing evacuees? I was just chatting to Rita Norton about the hat that's been found.'

'As a matter of fact, Maggie came for tea here a while ago,' said Joan. 'I was in and out, but I do remember her blue hat. Quite a little, breathless sort of girl, she seemed to take everything terribly seriously. She was quite awestruck by Athena House, I think.'

'In what way?'

'Oh you know, lots of admiration about art, and general astonishment that we all live here together. She was very taken with Aubrey – he showed her round his studio and she came out looking quite dazed.'

'I see...' I said uneasily. 'Do you know if they spent any further time alone together?'

'I doubt it. What would Maggie want with that old showboater? No, Joyce was her big schoolgirl crush, I think. Maggie couldn't hear enough about the quest for peace, she was full of questions.'

'Did she come back again after that?'

'I don't think so. We were busy, and Joyce was preparing talks and so on – I don't remember anyone mentioning another visit. I imagine the poor child ran away, with that great lunk of a farmhand.'

'Johnny?'

'Is that his name? The horse lad. Ten feet tall and slightly less intelligent than a rugby ball.'

'I think they were in love,' I said.

'Young love,' snorted Joan. 'My first love was Miss Mortimer, the gym mistress, and look where that got me.'

I laughed. 'Tell me more about Joyce, then.'

She sat back. 'Well, Joyce was just... different. No judgement, no creaking Edwardian moral codes based on fear of God or what the neighbours might think. I suppose that's why she attracted similar people – those of us who don't quite fit into the world. Artists, poets... people who live differently and don't always love each other in Noah's Ark pairs. Oddballs, you'd call us, really.' She got up to light the gas stove. 'Tea? I don't drink it much, so my ration awaits you.'

'Yes please,' I said. 'Joan, were you and Joyce... did you ever...'

'Were we *close*?' asked Joan, in a deliberately mocking tone. 'Yes, we were for a while,' she said, more softly. 'I loved her a great deal. But she wasn't quite as single-minded as I was. She adored the beginnings of things, the passion at the start – she wasn't so keen on sticking around when things became a bit boring or day-to-day. She had huge feelings and she always needed somewhere new to direct them.'

I nodded, interested.

'Joyce had... fascinations, I suppose you'd call them,' Joan went on, looking at the smoke curling from her cigarette into a shaft of sunlight. I thought of blood spreading through water.

'She'd collect people. Some perfectly ordinary person would suddenly be the most intriguing human being alive, and she'd court them – drinks and teas and long walks and great philosophical conversations into the night. Sometimes, she'd go to bed with them. But then it was as though she'd squeezed all the interest out, like wringing a wet cloth, and she discarded them. I think she assumed they felt the same way, that they were equally sated by her. But I don't think they always were.'

This was the most articulate description of Joyce I'd so far heard, and explained why people had felt so hurt by her sudden lack of interest.

'Did she do that to you?'

The kettle emitted a violent whistle like a passing train, and Joan used a folded tea towel to pour it. 'I don't have a tea strainer, so we'll have to read our tea leaves,' she said. 'Oh cripes, no milk either.'

'It's all right,' I said. I didn't want her distracted.

'Did she... not really. Yes and no,' said Joan. 'I think she always thought we were friends, sometimes in that more passionate way, and sometimes not. It didn't occur to her that I might feel hurt or jealous.'

'Did you?'

She sighed. 'I'm human. And I miss her.' Joan's face crumpled, and I reached out a hand to comfort her.

'I'm all right,' she said brusquely, blotting her eyes with her sleeve. 'There's nothing to be done. But there won't be many more like Joyce in the world. She was a one-off.'

CHAPTER NINE

I found Sabrina in the front porch, hurling handfuls of bran and boiled cabbage towards the chickens.

'Oh, Nora said you were here,' she greeted me. 'I think I've told you everything I know.'

'I'm just after a few more personal recollections,' I said, as she threw the last fistful and dusted her hands. 'It won't take long.'

'Fine,' she said. 'But I warn you, I'm in a dreadful mood. Theo should be back soon, and he'll be much nicer.'

The sun felt warmer in the shelter of the house, and she put the bucket down and leaned against the porch with folded arms.

'Are you sure you feel like chatting?' I asked. 'When I'm in a terrible mood, I generally want to pull the blankets over my head.'

Sabrina smiled, which lit up her rather doleful face. With the sunlight making a halo of her blonde hair, she reminded me of an angel in a Renaissance painting – but perhaps the avenging kind.

'I'm all right,' she said. 'It's just all the chaos at the moment, trying to sort out the funeral, and Aubrey's being perfectly ludicrous, as usual.'

'In what way?'

'Oh, convinced it's all some dastardly plot, won't listen to reason. Of course Joyce slipped – why are he and Joan so convinced she was killed by some angry villager? It's like a cheap novelette, for goodness' sake.'

'What makes you certain he's wrong?' I asked.

Sabrina glanced at me irritably.

'Because there's no reason to think she was killed. She may have been an experienced walker, but anyone can have an accident and hit their head. It was just terrible luck. I mean, you were there, did it look like a murder scene?'

'I don't know.'

'Well, there you are, then.' She picked up the bucket. 'If we're going to have a chat, let's go into the kitchen. It's warmer.'

Installed at the kitchen table, Sabrina seemed to relax slightly.

'Sorry I'm so bad-tempered today,' she said. 'Aubrey really is a devil for setting people off.'

'Is he...' I paused. Sabrina looked curiously at me. 'Do you think he could be dangerous?' I asked eventually.

'No!' she said immediately. 'He's a hot-air balloon, all wind and whoosh, then he crashes down to earth again. I can't imagine him ever hurting Joyce, he adored her.'

'Did he know Maggie?'

'Maggie?'

'The evacuee who's missing. Maggie Dawson. I believe she came here once or twice.'

She stood up and went to fill the kettle. 'Joyce had a habit of collecting waifs and strays. There were always people in and out.'

'Might Aubrey have known her?'

She looked startled.

'I don't think so. Why would he?'

'I heard they'd been seen together.'

'Well, they may have bumped into one another, I suppose.' She shrugged. 'Nothing more than that, though. Let's just say Aubrey's tastes don't run in that direction – he prefers a tigress to a tittle-mouse.'

I wondered if Sally had got it wrong, and perhaps she had simply witnessed a brief, passing chat between them – she had been distracted, looking out for Rita. Perhaps it hadn't even been Maggie... though Sally had seemed quite certain.

'Did you see Joyce go out, that last day?' I asked.

'No, I was still in bed,' said Sabrina. 'I got up at about nine, chatted to Nora, started a new piece, and then I just remember you and Ethel arriving, and how awful it was.'

She seemed agitated, and I was reluctant to push much further, given that I was only supposed to be writing an obituary.

'What will you all do now?' I asked. 'Can you stay here?'

She sighed. 'We don't know. We've written to Joyce's solicitors in Manchester, but so far, we've heard nothing. We can only hope she left us the house. Otherwise, I don't know what I'll do – it's not as if I can go back to France at the moment.'

'France?'

'Yes, didn't you know? Jean-Luc and I met in France just before the war. I was at finishing school – I know, perfectly ridiculous – being taught how to walk with books on my head and make a lemon syllabub. I was supposed to be a deb when I came home, being presented to the queen, and attending every ball in London until I found a chinless wonder with a vast estate to marry me.

'But Jean-Luc was working as a handyman at the finir l'école, and doing his sculptures at night, and we fell in love. I escaped from the dorm window one night, he waited for me in the woods – and then we came back to England before the war began.'

'But I thought he went to stay with his cousin in Manchester. He said that was how he met Joyce,' I said.

'It was,' said Sabrina. 'But perhaps he didn't mention that I was with him, too.'

I was astonished. Jean-Luc had implied that he and Joyce had begun their tendresse almost immediately.

'Did you part ways... romantically, then?' I asked, in an attempt to be delicate. 'Because he said...'

'Not exactly,' said Sabrina. 'Jean-Luc explained that we'd be moving into a bohemian sort of colony, and I thought it sounded rather exciting.'

'Was it still exciting when he and Joyce...'

'Well, I was free, too,' said Sabrina irritably. 'I wasn't crying in my moonlit truckle bed, waiting for my white knight to return.'

'And you became friends with Joyce?'

'Of course,' said Sabrina. 'She gave us a home, space to work, friendship. She taught us about speaking up for your beliefs, and I was delighted to stand alongside her in the cause of pacifism.'

'Even though France has been invaded since you left?'

'I'm not French,' said Sabrina shortly. 'And even if I were, I'm not sure what use killing people is, and neither is Jean-Luc.'

I nodded.

'What will you remember Joyce for?' I asked. I heard Mr Gorringe in my head, correcting my grammar. *For what will you remember Joyce?*

'All sorts,' said Sabrina. 'Her kindness. Her convictions. Her intelligence.'

It was rather a glib answer. I waited.

'She could be hard work, you know,' Sabrina suddenly said, as the kettle shrieked. 'Saints often are, I've found. I don't think any of us ever quite lived up to her standards.'

'Standards of what?'

She handed me a cup of tea so weak it barely deserved the name.

'Sorry, rations are getting low,' she said. 'Standards of living "truthfully and beautifully", as Joyce used to say. Being free, living through art, not caring about what other people think.' She paused. 'That's quite difficult, sometimes.'

'Did she get cross if you did care?' I asked.

'No, never. It was more a sort of disappointment. A sadness, as if you were too provincial and intellectually limited to meet her hopes. She felt like that about the people in Birchcroft – she was never angry. She just kept trying to make them understand.'

'Do you miss her?'

'Oh yes.' Sabrina sank into the wooden chair and cupped her enamel mug as if it were a precious artefact. 'I'll miss her till the day I die.'

The front door slammed and a moment later, Theo came into the kitchen. He seemed full of bonhomie; the wan, sickly mourner I'd met previously had vanished.

He took off his hat and threw it onto the table, where it skittered into the milk bottle.

'Am I interrupting?' he asked, in his soft, patrician voice.

'Not at all, darling,' said Sabrina. She seemed fond of him. 'I'm off to my studio, I need to strip those vole bones.'

I thought I must have misheard, but after she'd gone, Theo laughed. 'It does sound rather odd to the uninitiated, doesn't it?'

I agreed that it did.

'Sab paints beautiful watercolours,' he said. 'Then she twines together dried flowers and feathers and bones around them, and turns them into little symbols of nature and life and death.'

Symbols. I remembered the lilies.

'Do people buy them?'

'Some,' Theo said. 'But Joyce had plans to introduce her to a Cork Street dealer, once the war was over.'

'Joan's gallerist?'

He looked startled. 'Yes, I believe so. But Joan was rather less keen. She can be very protective about her work, an approach which isn't quite in the spirit of Athena House. Still,' he went on hastily, as if he'd overstepped the mark, 'you want to know about Joyce. We wouldn't all be here if it weren't for her, of course.'

'Do you think Aubrey's right?' I asked quickly. 'That it wasn't an accident?' I felt I needed to know urgently which members of Athena House believed Joyce had been killed.

'No. I think he's being rather hysterical. He loved her, you know.'

Perhaps much more than the others had, I thought.

'He simply can't accept that his perfect muse had an accident, like an ordinary mortal.'

'Why not, do you think?'

'Because Aubrey thought Joyce was a sort of goddess. They were always talking about the classics and Greek myths, sharing poetry, discussing art... sometimes, one felt one was interrupting a true meeting of minds.'

'Theo, you don't think Aubrey might have... harmed Joyce? In a temper?'

'Goodness, no.' Theo looked quite shocked. 'I can't imagine... surely he wouldn't...'

'Has he ever been violent?'

'Only with furniture, as far as I know. No, hold on – he once punched Jean-Luc, actually.'

'What for?'

'I don't know, I'm afraid. Everyone had been drinking wine, it was late, I'd gone to bed. The next day, as far as I know, he apologised and things were back to normal. Nasty bruise, though, for Jean-Luc.'

What an exhausting way to live, I thought. I felt upset for days if Annie and I mildly disagreed about anything, never mind all the thumping and wailing and plate-throwing they seemed to indulge in at Athena House.

'How did Jean-Luc feel about it?'

'He told me privately that he wasn't too fond of Aubrey,' said Theo, leaning closer.

'Do you know why?' I encouraged.

'Well.' Theo pursed his lips thoughtfully. 'I think it was mostly because Aubrey was terribly protective of Sabrina. He's always seen her as a sort of little sister, I think, and he thought Jean-Luc was rather a cad towards her.'

'Because of Joyce?'

'One imagines so,' said Theo. 'But of course, Jean-Luc didn't see it that way at all. He believes in the true tenets of bohemianism – he doesn't think people belong to one another.'

'Do you?' I asked boldly.

Theo sighed. 'Yes and no,' he said. 'When one loves truly, it can be awfully difficult to see the beloved loving someone else. Particularly when...'

He stopped.

'When...' I prompted, but he shook his head.

'Nothing you need to be putting in the newspaper,' he said. 'I think we at Athena House tend to forget quite how viciously conservative the average person is. Never mind the law itself.'

He seemed unwilling to say more.

'Do you recall any particular anecdotes about Joyce?' I asked, to steer the conversation onto a more solid footing.

Theo smiled. His hazel eyes misted with recollection, softening his rather haggard face. 'Oh, lots, I expect. I did enjoy walking with her – she was so fond of plants and flowers, she knew everything about them. And she used to read poetry to us all some nights – before the war, we'd gather round the fire and she'd read aloud in her lovely, throaty voice,' he went on. 'I remember once, she said a poem was warmongering, and she got up, right away, and she threw the book onto the fire. We were all so shocked,' he said, laughing as if she'd done something endearing. 'She was a very principled woman. Except when it came to lovers, perhaps.'

'In what way?'

'I imagine it's pretty clear,' said Theo. 'She didn't care if someone loved someone else, or even if somebody was married. She simply took them away if she wanted them, and then she gave them back. But not everyone was quite so free with their affections.'

'Do you mean people here?'

'Well, Aubrey's wife in Paris, for a start. And his children, I expect. And... others.'

He stopped again, and I didn't think he'd tell me any more.

'Did you manage to sort things out with the vicar?' I asked.

'More or less. Rather a heated discussion over the flowers, though.'

'Surely funeral flowers are fairly straightforward?'

'Oh, you'd be surprised,' said Theo bitterly. 'I suggested local wildflowers to reflect Joyce's great passion for nature and the area. I know it's March, but snowdrops, perhaps some early croci. But no, Reverend Shawcross thinks we should have something "seemly" for church. He suggested lilies of all things.'

I looked up from my notebook. 'Don't you like lilies?'

Theo tutted. 'It's not about whether I like them, dear,' he said. 'We should be celebrating Joyce's life – and everyone knows lilies are a symbol of death.'

. . .

I was intending to give Aubrey a wide berth – I felt horribly unsettled about what Sally had told me, and I knew Aubrey had a temper. Could he really have done something to Maggie – perhaps to Johnny and Joyce too? As I crossed the yard, I heard a door bang, and saw his ragged, imposing figure setting off towards Joan's shed..He hadn't seen me. I had promised Lou I'd investigate, I reminded myself, and so far, all I had was some fond recollections and several confusing snippets of bohemian morality to sift through.

As Aubrey called, 'Joan?' and disappeared into her studio, I slipped into the barn and scrambled up the ladder. If he caught me, I had no cover story beyond 'I was waiting to speak to you.'

I guessed Aubrey was a talker, who would happily interrupt Joan's day for several minutes. I scanned the large studio, unsure what I was looking for – an incriminating note? There was nothing but brushes, stacked canvases, an empty mug that reeked of brandy. I checked the courtyard again, and bent to rifle quickly through the canvases leaning against the wall. More angry landscapes, more cubist, shrieking women – one slipped and a small photograph fluttered down. It was a slightly blurred picture of a very young, pretty girl, taken in the summer – she seemed to be sitting in a hayfield. She was smiling guile-lessly at the photographer, her dark hair lifting in the breeze. On the back, someone – Aubrey? – had written *Mon amour*.

In the distance, I heard Joan call, 'See you at tea, then,' and Aubrey's rumbling reply. I stuck the photograph back between the canvases, hurled myself down the ladder, and ran, slowing to a walk as Aubrey turned back towards his studio.

'Morning,' he called.

I waved cheerfully – though in my heart, my suspicions were growing ever darker.

. . .

As I walked up to Wrights' Farm again, skirting the bull field, I put my concerns about Aubrey aside until I could speak to Lou, and instead wondered whether to tell Ethel what Theo had said about the lilies. It seemed too much of a coincidence, but I couldn't imagine why Theo would send Ethel lilies for noble reasons. His interests did not lie in her direction, I felt sure, so perhaps he viewed her as a love rival. Jean-Luc, I thought. The handsome young man who seemed to have enraptured almost everyone at Athena House, who had hurt Sabrina by choosing Joyce, kissed Ethel, and was now dallying with Nora. Perhaps Theo, too, had developed feelings towards him – or perhaps he was simply intending to protect his friend Sabrina, by warning off her rivals. I was thinking so intently about their tangled connections that I almost crashed into a tall, upright figure coming the other way.

'Miss York!'

It was Mrs Wright herself, wearing a brown felt hat rammed down over her eyebrows, and carrying a wicker basket. 'Jaunty' was not a word that sprang to mind.

'What brings you back here?'

'I'm researching Miss Reid's obituary for the paper,' I said, 'and I thought I'd just pop up and see if you'd had any news on the evacuees.'

'Good heavens, you'd think you were related to them,' she said. 'No, not a word. I know about Margaret's hat, by the way,' she added. 'Before you start getting ideas about kidnappings and what-have-you, she was always wandering about in the hills. She could have lost it at any time, it doesn't mean she went that way when she scuttled off.'

She fixed me with a glare.

'Spud said...'

'Spud! Samuel Dawson is a little fibber, Miss York, and I'm surprised a grown woman like you can't see it. He lives in a world of his own. I don't doubt that a silly goose like Margaret took it into her head to run off with Johnny and they're both back in London, having a good old laugh at the Wrights who were kind enough to take them in when nobody else would.'

I had no idea what to say in response to this tirade, but she clutched her basket to her and added, 'If you want to check for yourself, Herbert's up in the sheep field, and he'll back up every word I say. I'll bid you good day, Miss York. I need to speak to Mrs Tither. Her new girl's slicing my cheese ration short.'

She nodded sharply, and passed me with a rustle of her stiff coat. Unpleasant though the encounter had been, I now had a brief window of time in which to find Maggie's diary.

I looked at my watch. Spud would be back from school in about half an hour, I had at least an hour before Mrs Wright returned, and Mr Wright could, of course, appear at any moment, but my scant knowledge of farming suggested that he would stick to a fairly strict meal schedule and return only when Mrs Wright had prepared his dinner. I hurried on, stones sliding under my shoes on the rough track, wishing that Lou, or at the very least, Spud, was at my side.

The farm appeared no less bleak. Its windows were white in the sunlight, reminding me of Norman's dull, glass eye. I thought longingly of Manchester, its cinemas and shows, dance halls and cafés, throngs of people everywhere, packed trams and buses lumbering past like benevolent dinosaurs. Why would anyone exchange all that verve and excitement for a life in the middle of nowhere, with nothing to look at but cows and mud and rain-swept hills? Poor Maggie, a child of glittering London, uprooted by the gales of war and dropped here, in this cold, grey place. Perhaps Mrs Wright was correct, and she and Johnny had taken the first opportunity to get out. But Spud... I felt certain something was wrong. She would at least have left him a note, or written to him to reassure him that she was safe after a fortnight.

I looked across the farmyard, up the side of the hill. In the distance, a tall figure tramped across a field, followed by two minuscule black and white dogs. They seemed to be heading away from the house, and I calculated I had at least ten minutes, unless Herbert Wright was an Olympic athlete. I edged past the pig pen, noting that Spud had added a cardboard box marked TRESHUR and a ragged tartan horse blanket to his den, and, glancing over my shoulder to mark Mr Wright's slow progress, I darted into the shadow of the porch.

I pressed the iron latch and the door swung open. My heart had been cantering since I'd bumped into Mrs Wright, and now it sped to a jolting gallop. All I had to do, I told myself, was get up the stairs, find Maggie's room and locate her diary – then I'd get out as if the hounds of hell were after me. The house smelled of fried eggs (eggs! How lucky chicken-keepers were) and there was a comfort to it that propelled me up the shadowy wooden stairs. The walls were papered in a dark floral pattern, and there was only one picture above the stairs, a Victorian lithograph of Christ opening his arms to little children.

Four rooms led from the landing, and all had their doors shut. I tried the first, which opened onto a rather stark bedroom containing two tightly-made single beds and a willow-patterned chamber pot – thankfully, clean. Beside one bed was a small, leather-bound Bible, and next to the other, a packet of Craven A cigarettes and a racy-looking Western novel. A mahogany clothes-press blocked part of the window, and a tall dressing table held an age-spotted mirror, a hairbrush and a framed photograph of a young man in uniform. On the wall was another religious picture, this time a print of the Virgin with St Anne, holding a rather simpering, curly-haired infant who looked far too large for her lap.

I quickly closed the door of the Wrights' marital chamber

and opened the one opposite – this was evidently Herbert's work room, full of dog-eared binders labelled LIVESTOCK RECORDS and an oak desk piled with accounting books and pre-war feed catalogues. Leaning shelves on the back wall contained heavy-looking books with titles like *Internal Parasites and Infestation in the Common Ovine Breeds* and *A New Study of Mechanisation in Modern British Ploughing Techniques*. No wonder Herbert enjoyed reading a racy Western at night.

I turned to the next room. Inside, two single beds faced the window. One was neatly made, with a firmly tucked-in white candlewick bedspread. The other looked as though a stray incendiary had dropped on it. An old dressing table held a ewer and bowl, and the scratched wood was spattered with water droplets, as though an enthusiastic dog had shaken itself. Other than that, there was nothing to suggest that a child slept here – the room was as austere as a church vestry. Between the beds was a single cabinet. Quickly, I crossed the wooden floor and opened the little cupboard. A small tower of library books fell out with a heart-stopping clatter – *Swallows and Amazons*, *The Family from One End Street*, *The Great Book for Boys*... I stuffed them back in. On the top shelf was a copy of *Jane Eyre* and a small leather pouch holding a cheap manicure set. My heart ached for Maggie.

I turned to her bed and pushed my hand under the mattress. I encountered nothing but prickly straw poking through the sheet and wooden slats. Frustration was building in me – I didn't have long. Perhaps she'd taken her diary with her, which, of course, she would have done if she'd run away. I ought to be delighted that it was missing, welcome it as a sign that she was safe. But as a final check, I opened the sticking drawer of the dressing table, which was half-full of tangled grey socks, vests and a spare school shirt, and ran my hand along the underside, a trick I'd perfected in the home. If you didn't want the boys to find something precious, you'd stick it under a drawer with stamp glue.

My fingers touched something small and hard, and I dropped to my knees to look up at it. A slim, cloth-covered book was wedged into a corner. I pulled it away as gently as I could, then closed the drawer and slid it into my bag, feeling a queasy combination of triumph and betrayal.

As I let myself silently out of the room, preparing to hurry away, I heard a noise from the direction of the porch. I froze. The sound came again – a heavy thump. Perhaps it was just the second post, I reassured myself – parcels thudding through the letter box onto the hall floor.

But now, the latch rattled and the door was opening. I wanted to scream with fear. There was no possible way of explaining my presence on the upstairs landing, whoever was coming in. I hovered in the doorway. From downstairs came a short, deep cough. Herbert.

I backed into the children's bedroom again, inching the door closed, alert for the slightest squeak. *Please go into the kitchen*, I thought. *Please don't come upstairs.*

From the yard came a volley of barking – the dogs were back, too, and I stood no chance of escape without driving them into a frenzy. I heard Herbert open the door again, and presumably he spoke a magical farming incantation, as they quietened immediately. The sound I'd heard was him removing his heavy work boots – and as for how he'd returned so quickly, one glance out of the window behind me showed the muddy, ancient tractor parked by the gate, and I cursed my own stupidity. The stairs creaked. My prayer had not been answered, and Herbert was now heading in my direction, breathing heavily with exertion. I thought about the vicious spankings he'd given the children, and considered what he might do to me if he were to fling open the door and find me here.

Slowly, I lowered myself to the floor behind Maggie's bed and wriggled into a prone position. If he looked in briefly, I stood a chance, I hoped, of not being seen. I heard his footsteps pass the door, and his own bedroom door opened. There was the flicking sound of a lighter, followed by prolonged coughing as he drew on the cigarette, then he crossed the landing and entered his study, shutting the door behind him.

Slowly, I let my breath out, with a sound like a deflating bicycle tyre. I had one chance to get away, before he finished whatever he was doing and emerged again. I hurried to the door and opened it a crack. The landing was empty. I pulled off my shoes and tiptoed out. A noise broke the silence and my heart leapt into my throat until I realised Herbert was singing, in a tuneless baritone – it seemed to be a half-remembered version of 'Bobby Shaftoe'. Almost vibrating with fear, I scurried silently down the stairs, my shoes in my hand. But where were the dogs? They weren't barking. If I took a chance, they might spot me and alert Herbert, but if I didn't, he might emerge and come downstairs to find me standing in the hall, pulling on my shoes in a ferment of panic.

I pulled the latch, prayed hard, and stepped into the porch. All was quiet, apart from the singing upstairs. I scanned the yard, preparing to make a dash for it, when I heard a snappish, warning bark. Jess and Fly appeared, barrelling along the side of the house. They barked in hysterical duet, as though the entire German army had parachuted into the farmyard, hurling grenades. Though their stiff bodies and flat ears suggested that attack was imminent, so far they were simply pinning me on the step with terror. Upstairs, the singing stopped abruptly. I had no choice. I turned side-on to the furious dogs and knocked on the door. When Herbert opened it, I forced my terrified face into a smile and said: 'Ah, good morning. I'm Edie York, from the *Manchester Chronicle*. You must be Mr Wright.'

CHAPTER TEN

'I see you've set the dogs off,' he said. 'Jess! Fly! Quiet!'

The dogs immediately subsided and lay down, still watching me. It was a great relief to be able to think straight.

'What is it you're wanting?' Herbert asked.

'I'm writing a report on evacuees,' I began, 'and...'

'Oh that's right, Martha said you'd been round, asking Samuel all sorts of nonsense,' he said. 'I believe she's told you everything we know. Want my opinion, they're a pair of good-for-nothings, never done a day's hard work in their lives, and couldn't wait to run off back to the Smoke given half a chance. Good riddance.'

'What about Samuel?'

'He'll be joining them, soon as we can get hold of his mother,' said Mr Wright. 'No doubt she's swanking round the capital, taking taxis to dances while we look after her useless offspring.'

It struck me that Mr and Mrs Wright seemed very well-suited.

'You didn't see Maggie or Johnny the morning they left?'

'I did not,' he said. 'I'm up at dawn, and they were gone in the middle of the night, if you ask me. I count myself lucky they haven't stolen any money.'

I felt the diary burning through the leather of my bag, and I nodded.

I scribbled the *Chronicle*'s number on my notepad and handed the page to him. 'If you do hear from them,' I said, 'please get in touch.'

'Aye, and if a flock of pigs flaps past the barn, I'll drop you a line and all,' he said. 'I'll bid you good day now, Miss York. My wife will be home shortly and she'll not want to be disturbed while she's cooking my dinner.'

He closed the door, and the latch fell back into place with a decisive clatter.

Jess and Fly remained silent and watchful as I hurried from the farm. It was only when I was several hundred yards down the lane that I stopped glancing fearfully behind me. I was so relieved to have escaped, I barely noticed the bull, looming ominously beside his weak gate. I almost ran back into the village, and reached the railway station just as the twelve forty was pulling in through a rainbow mist of sunlit steam. I threw myself into a carriage, took a deep and grateful breath, and extracted the diary from my handbag. As I opened it, a photograph fluttered to the floor and I bent to retrieve it.

May, 1938 – Daddy, Mum, Maggie and little Sam was written on the back, and it bore the stamp of Mr Lyle Mitchell *esq*, Photographic Portraits, Fitzroy Square NW1. I turned it over.

The Dawsons looked happy and loving. Spud was a smaller version of his indomitable self – and Maggie, with her big, dark eyes and long plaited hair, was almost certainly the same girl who had smiled out of Aubrey's photograph at me less than an hour before.

With a chill of dread, I tucked the photograph into my handbag and turned back to the diary.

Maggie's account began last summer.

16 June 1940

Awful bombing in London. So worried about Mum and Dad. Heard on wireless that lots of people have been killed – will count the hours till we hear if they're safe. Haven't told Spud, don't want to worry him. He tries so hard to like it here, but we both know it's ~~blooming~~ truly awful. Can't wait to go home, & see Nanna and Mum and Pouncer again. I wonder if he's getting enough food now it's the war? Are there still mice or have they all been bombed? Getting a toothache.

20 June

*Letter from Mum! Another raid. She says they're all right, but Mrs Banerjee who works at the drapers on Mile End Road has a broken leg. Wish I was there with them all, I'd shout 'stuff Hitler' and march up and down Pall Mall in protest at the bl**dy Germans if I could. Spud says he's building a plane with the bits left over from the Wrights' Anderson shelter and he'll fly us back to London. I wish he would. Not sure how I'd manage without him – he drives me mad, but I like hearing him breathing in the other bed. It's like having a bit of home here with me. Mum made me promise to look after him, and I will.*

15 July

Saw Johnny again after we finished all our work. The Wrights are like slave owners – my fingers hurt from all the washing and sewing that old trout makes me do. He said it's just as bad for him, and Mr Wright said, 'Johnny Rawnsley, I'll tan your hide' just because he was late finishing grooming Blaze. He said, 'I'm fifteen, I'd like to see you try.' Johnny is braver than me, and he looks a bit like Robert Donat around the eyes. I'm glad he's here, he's quite easy to talk to. I can't tell if he likes me too.

There were several more entries in this vein between late July and early October. Johnny emerged as a paragon of young manhood, and the Wrights as even crueller than I'd imagined. Fascinated, I turned the pages, skim-reading entries about Spud's optimistic building projects and Maggie's failed attempt to buy lipstick in the village with the half-crown postal order she was sent for her birthday.

17 September

More bad news. Mum said in her last letter that Dad's definitely fighting abroad now. Why couldn't he just join the Home Guard like other men his age? Then he'd be safe. Johnny says when he turns sixteen, he's going to say he's eighteen and join up right away. He says he can't wait to give the Hun what-for, and he won't feel at all guilty about killing German soldiers because they don't care about us, so why should we care about them. Spud says he likes Johnny because he makes him laugh. I don't know what Nanna would think of him. I don't know if she'd call him a gentleman, which she says Grandad always was, no matter what. But I like him – I can't help it.

25 September

Horrible day, raining and cold. Mrs W made me go back to the village three times for things she'd forgotten, I think she does it on purpose. I write to Mum every week but don't ever say how bad it is because she's got enough to worry about. She says she might get some leave in a few weeks and will come and visit. Spud has got a cough, and Mrs Wright won't give me money for cough syrup, she says a mustard poultice will do.

Poor Spud, covered in mustard like a roast potato. I suppose it suits his name.

I have been going to meet Johnny before tea most days, when it isn't raining. We sit on the wall and talk about our plans, and the other day he said to come and see a friend of his. I followed him down to the village, and then it turned out he meant Loopy Norman! Everyone says he's mad because of the shell shock, but Johnny says he's all right and sometimes he sneaks off and goes fishing with him in the valley. So we went to his tent and Johnny called 'hullo' and Norman came out. He looked a bit angry when he saw me, but J explained who I was, and he said we could stay and have a bit of his rabbit stew. It was very nice, and he said there were nettles in it that gave it flavour. He didn't seem mad really, just quiet and not very fond of people. Johnny says Norman is against the war and I said 'aren't we all?' but Johnny said he meant N was a pacifist and explained what it was. I don't think I agree, but I can see why N would feel like that after last time. I haven't told Spud – don't want him bothering Norman with his daft chat when he's better.

20 October

I walked round the village after church for something to do, but of course, it was as boring as ever. I lie in bed just thinking about the shops and picture palaces and Piccadilly Circus with the lit-up advertisements and buses and the Underground and all the people in London. Their cockney accents are like home. I miss Bill, the flower seller outside the Tube station. He used to give me a flower sometimes for my lovely smile, he said it cheered him up to see it. And I miss Mum and Dad and Nanna and Pouncer.

Had a chat with Johnny. He said he saw a poster and there's a lady giving a talk in the village hall about Norman's beliefs – pacifism – and we should go. I said 'how can we go, they'd never let us.' And he said 'leave it to me.'

I sat up in my train seat – this had happened months ago. Not only had Norman known Maggie, it also seemed that she'd known Joyce for much longer than I'd thought. Heart pounding, I read on.

26 *October*

I can hardly believe the evening I've had! Some excitement for the first time in so long I can't remember, and it's all thanks to Johnny. He told the Wrights that his brother was coming to visit and staying in the village pub, and that he must visit him – and he asked if I could come as I was interested in being a secretary next year, and his brother knew somebody at the Ministry of Food who might give me a job. Well, that was just a stroke of genius, because the Wrights are so greedy they immediately heard 'food' and hoped it might mean more for them. So they said yes! Johnny took the torch, and we walked to the church hall where Miss Reid was giving her talk. I said 'have you really got a brother?' and he said 'no'.

When we got there, lots of people were pouring in, all saying things like 'let's see what she has to say for herself', and looking quite cross.

Miss Reid got up on the little stage and she thanked everyone for coming to hear her. She said after the last war, people said it must never happen again, and yet now our brothers and dads and sons and uncles were once again sent to be killed. She said they were just 'cannon fodder' for the government, and that the people in charge didn't care about our little, precious lives, they only cared about economics and made-up national boundaries. She said 'imagine living in a world with no boundaries – where anyone could go anywhere, and be welcomed,' and she talked about the futility and destruction of war – 'lives, societies, cities, homes, businesses, hopes, all in ruins, and for what?' She said 'look at you all, doing the government's bidding due to nothing more than fear' and laughed at the 'pettifogging uniforms and invented rules' that kept everyone in their places. I wanted to hear more but that was when a riot—

There was a gap here and I turned the page quickly.

... Mrs W came up and blew the candle out and said I was straining my eyes. No wonder when I spend all day doing her stupid sewing! Now it was all yesterday that it happened. Anyway, when Miss Reid said about the uniforms and rules, Mr Walker, the warden, shouted 'now look here!' and some people at the back began to call out 'for shame,' and 'go back to your brothel!' I asked Johnny what they meant and he said, 'You don't want to know, Mags.' The arguing spread through the hall just like a fire eating up paper, and very quickly, everybody was shouting, at Miss Reid and each other. Miss Reid rushed off the stage and out through the back of the hall, and Johnny took my hand and pulled me round to where Miss Reid was still outside, talking to her friends. One, a posh blonde lady with a long face, said, 'What are you two after?' as if we'd come to rob them. I felt I should be brave and I said, 'We've come to tell Miss Reid how much we enjoyed her talk, and sorry about the other people.' Miss Reid stepped forward and shook our hands and said she was glad we'd come, and what did we think of pacifism. I said, 'My dad's away fighting and I want him back safely, so the less war, the better for me.' But Johnny said, 'I would fight. But not for a government. For my pals.'

She said, 'But if it weren't for the governments, there wouldn't be any fighting. Imagine that.'

We chatted a bit more and then she said, 'You seem inter-

esting young people, would you like to come for tea next Tuesday?' I said we would if we could get away.

Johnny and I argued about pacifism all the way back, but then – I don't know if I should write this down. Spud, if you are ever reading this because I am dead, DO NOT READ ANY FURTHER and stop SPYING on your sister because I will haunt you – (pause for Spud to stop reading and feel ashamed) – well, here goes – Johnny took my hand again. It was very dark, even with the torch, and he said, 'Maggie, I like your gumption. Not many girls are willing to argue with a man, you know.'

I said 'or a boy, like what you are,' and he laughed – and then he put his arm round me and kissed me. It didn't go on very long, and an owl hooted and made me jump and ruined it, but – he kissed me! I feel quite swoony, like a film star. Now I can't wait to get back to good old London, where Johnny can take me out and we can go for walks in the park and there isn't mud everywhere. I wonder if Johnny loves me?

I looked up, and was surprised to see that we were already sliding into London Road station, back in Manchester. Flustered, I gathered my things, stuffed the diary into my bag and hurried to the office via a kiosk still standing amid the rubble, where I bought a very dry ham sandwich. But while the buildings stood broken around me, and crowds jostled my elbows as I walked past the fire service reservoir ponds and fenced-off allotments in Piccadilly, I thought how much Maggie would love the teeming life of the city. With a sickening jolt, it struck me that she may no longer be alive to enjoy anything. If she was, I promised myself, I would find her – and if Norman or Johnny or Mr Wright had done any harm to her, I'd hunt them down, too, while I was at it.

. . .

That evening, the doorbell rang as we were clearing away the tea things.

'Probably another suitor for Miss Beamish on the top floor,' said Annie with a smirk. Miss Agnes Beamish was a widow in her fifties who played in a light classical quartet and looked rather like a blinking, bespectacled Mole from *The Wind in the Willows*. She was blessedly quiet, and perfectly polite when we passed on the stairs, but she did not seem the type to attract skeins of suitors.

It rang again – evidently, Mrs Turner was not crouching, spider-like, in her usual spot.

'She's gone to see her sister in Broadheath,' said Annie. 'I'll go.'

Lou swiftly appeared in the doorway, followed by Marple, who trotted in happily and came to lick my hand, before collapsing to the floor with a huff of relief.

'We walked,' said Lou. 'He prefers driving. Thought I'd come by and see what you've found out in Birchcroft, Edie. As for you,' he said to Annie, 'I wouldn't normally pass on romantic messages, but here it is: Arnold says, can you please meet him at Lyons Corner House tomorrow evening at six p.m., because he has things he wants to say.'

Annie looked alarmed.

'What kind of things?'

'I've no idea. Perhaps he'd like to discuss spring fashions and what sort of flowers are being worn on the chicest hats this season. If you go, you'll find out.'

'I'm not going,' she said irritably. 'I've made my position quite clear.'

'Up to you,' said Lou, throwing himself nimbly into an armchair. He looked annoyingly handsome and relaxed. 'Not my department, young love.'

I filled Lou in on my day – I was about to mention the diary, then I stopped. Lou would insist that I handed it over, and probably cross-examine me about stealing evidence while he was at it. I needed to read more, and if it seemed significant, I'd tell him.

Finally, I told him about Aubrey, hinting only that I'd seen a picture of Maggie at the farmhouse. 'Aubrey's snapshot said "mon amour",' I told him. '*My love* in Fre—'

'I know what it means, York,' said Lou.

He shook his head and I thought he was going to say 'you're imagining things again, Edie', but he didn't. He sat very still, staring into his weak tea, until Marple hefted himself upright and came to rest his head on the arm of the chair, like a clerk ready to take notes.

'Well,' said Lou. 'You don't leave a pebble unturned, do you?' He looked up at me, his dark blue eyes narrowed, and added, 'I think you're right. I think Joyce was murdered. And I don't feel too certain that Maggie's still alive, either.'

Now he agreed with me, I suddenly felt like a child whose imaginary game had spun out of control. Perhaps I was exaggerating, perhaps I'd put two and two together and made nine... after my last run-in with the police, the idea of once again being witness to a crime, and potentially in danger myself, made me feel quite sick.

'Why?' I said, a quaver in my voice. I covered it by adding, 'What makes you think so?'

'Same reasons you do,' he said shortly. 'The bohemian, shameless nonsense they all indulge in, leaping between beds like mad frogs, pretending nobody feels hurt or jealous. For God's sake, it's not decent and it's not human nature to share people like that. I'm amazed they haven't got sixteen little unwanted bohemians running about by now. Then there's the fact that half the village hated Joyce and her acolytes, yet she wouldn't stop telling them that they were wrong to risk losing their men in the name of freedom – I can't imagine what an insult that must have been to them all,' he added furiously.

'When I went to fight in Spain, my mother said, "Louis, I will never get over it if something happens to you, but we both know you're doing the right thing." And I was.'

I had never seen Lou so serious, or so angry. It seemed that he, too, would have been in the queue to off Joyce, given half a chance.

'Added to that,' he went on, scratching Marple's head, 'is the fact that she was a very experienced walker. If it had been raining, or blowing a gale, yes, perhaps she could have slipped and fallen. But according to you, the edge of the brow was mostly dry grass, with a few stones, and the sun was shining?'

'Yes, it was.'

'Were either of her laces undone, or broken?'

'Do you mean she could have stumbled?'

'No, I'm worried she wasn't looking fashionable when she fell to her death. Yes, of course that's what I mean.'

I rolled my eyes, and thought back. Joyce had been lying with one leg under the other, but I remembered her boot sticking out, how large it looked on her collapsed body. I'd have noticed a trailing lace – and the other foot... no, both laces had been firmly tied, I felt sure.

'No,' I said. 'I'm fairly sure they weren't.'

He nodded. 'Was her head bleeding – or had it been?'

'No.'

'So just one swift blow to the head, in the right place to kill her,' said Lou. 'How unfortunate. And you say Maggie knew her?'

I thought guiltily of the diary.

'Yes. But I don't know how well. What about Aubrey?'

'That lot seem to be drifting constantly around the hills like unquiet wraiths,' said Lou. 'Perhaps Maggie did just bump into him – young Sally sounds quite the gossip. But I don't like this business with the photograph. I'm struggling to think of an innocent explanation, and I'd like to hear his.'

'Or perhaps she was with Johnny all along,' I suggested. 'I just can't see how she'd leave Spud to face the music all alone.'

'I agree that she wouldn't leave her little brother for long,' said Lou. 'She sounds quite a sane young woman. Unlike that bunch of straw-weaving loons.'

'What do you think about Norman?'

'I think he needs looking at,' said Lou. 'I've no wish to interfere with the old lad's peace and quiet, but a quick visit from HM Police might not go amiss.'

'Do you mean Constable Creech?'

Lou snorted violently, and made Marple start.

'Creech is a reserve constable, some young shaver who fancied a bit of authority over his neighbours rather than actually risk fighting,' said Lou. 'I doubt he'd know a truncheon from his luncheon. No wonder he didn't want to raise the alarm, he'd be so far out of his depth with this, he'd be halfway to Dublin with waves breaking over his head. No, he'll just tell everyone it was an accident, assume the kids went home to London, and back he goes to his cosy station for toasted crumpets till the war's over. Idiot.'

It was pleasing to hear Lou dismiss the irritating Creech so contemptuously, but I said, 'Then what can we do? Nobody will listen to me.'

'I can have a word with the district commissioner and ask him to let me have a look at how things are being run over there,' said Lou. 'Which I shall do. And you and I will return to Birchcroft very soon, and make further inquiries. I don't believe Maggie ran off. I think it's very likely that something's happened to her.'

A chill ran through me. Suspecting it myself was one thing, but Lou confirming it was far worse.

'Look, York, are you free on Sunday?'

'I think so. Why?'

'We could go then,' he said. 'Have a poke around and organise a proper search for Maggie.'

I nodded. 'What about Johnny, though?'

'He's either harmed her, or something's happened to him, too, most likely,' said Lou. 'Let me think what we can do about finding him. And in the meantime, I've several uncomfortable questions for the prancing poets of *Athena House*.' He said the name with such disdain that I laughed, though I felt rather glad he didn't know about my earlier attempt at burglary.

CHAPTER ELEVEN

At work the following day, I intended to begin my obituary of Joyce. It had been well over a week since we'd found her body, and more than a fortnight since the evacuees had gone missing. Time was galloping by, but I was achieving nothing – partly because I was so tired. There had been an air-raid warning the previous night, and Annie and I had been forced to straggle along to the public shelter at one in the morning, due to the fact that Mrs Turner's Anderson shelter only offered enough room for herself and Miss Beamish. It was packed with exhausted, whey-faced people, and when some young man attempted to start a sing-song, he was violently shushed by angry mothers who were trying to get their babies back to sleep. Annie and I leaned on each other, struggling to tune out the crying infants and general grumbling. The smell of unwashed hair and old woollen coats mingled with the dankness of underground, and it was a great relief when the all-clear sounded just an hour later, and we were able to go home to bed.

'Busy as ever?' said Pat, nodding at my silent typewriter.

'Just thinking about how to begin,' I told her. 'Tricky subject.'

'Everyone's tricky,' she said. 'Show me a straightforward person and I'll show you a liar.'

I thought of Charles Emerson.

'You're probably right,' I said. 'How's your Billy getting on in the Home Guard?'

'Oh, he loves it,' said Pat. 'Nowt to do but wander about in the hills, having a smoke. Tell you a queer thing, though.' She lowered her voice, and I leaned in, interested. 'Probably top secret,' she said, glancing between the desks. Gloria was shrieking with laughter at something Peggy, the junior secretary, had said; Des was wreathed in smoke, bashing at his ancient typewriter; and, thankfully, Mr Gorringe was out at a meeting – I'd seen him hurrying past with his bowler hat on. Ethel, too, had her head down, and I reminded myself to tell her what Theo had said about the lilies.

'Well,' Pat breathed, on a waft of floral breath cachous, 'he said they were on manoeuvres last night – manoeuvres!' She scoffed. 'Milling about aimlessly, more like. Anyway, him and another bloke went a bit further away than the others, just strolling along, checking on sheds and things – and he said that in the distance they saw what looked like a town on fire, whole buildings up in flames. Of course, they panicked – my Billy'd panic at a moth in the bedroom, mind you – and they thought there'd been a bomb a few miles away and people had been killed. They ran at top speed, so about as fast as the average tortoise, back to the sergeant, and he told them, strictly in confidence' – she glanced about again, as if spies were lurking in the fireplace – 'he said, they've built a decoy city in the hills out of water towers and bricks, and when there's a raid they set them on fire, so the Germans think they've hit a town and fly straight over the real ones. Clever, I call it.'

I stared at her. 'Who built them?'

'Dunno. The Ministry of something or other, I s'pose,' she said. 'Good idea, though, isn't it? Billy and the lads aren't meant to know, but could be the sarge thought he had to say something, what with them so worried. Though he's a drinker, too, Billy says, always has his hipflask, so happen he didn't mean to divulge.'

At the cinema, they now showed Ministry of Information films before the main picture. I'd recently seen one with John Mills as a sailor, where he told his sweetheart about his ship, and the café manageress overheard and passed on the details, so the vessel was torpedoed. It was rather well done – and after my experience with the Emersons, I found it perfectly believable.

'Gosh,' I said to Pat. 'You probably shouldn't mention it to anyone else, though.'

Pat looked offended. 'I shall keep mum, of course,' she said haughtily, 'and I trust you will, too.'

She turned back to her desk.

'Don't suppose that obituary will write itself,' she muttered.

I had hoped to catch Ethel at lunchtime, but she was up to her eyes in letters. 'I need to tell you about the lilies,' I whispered, as Jan glanced suspiciously over at us.

'Look, I've no time now, but can you come round after work?' she said. 'I think it's on your way home, and I'm dying to know all. I'm leaving early for the dentist or we'd go together.'

After work, I made my way to Ethel's house – or strictly speaking, Mother's. They lived in a rather imposing semi-detached near Victoria Park, though its yellow bricks were blackened with soot, and instead of flowers in the pot on the porch, a large silver tabby cat appeared to be growing.

'You must be Silas Marner,' I said, and rang the bell as he stretched and slithered to the step, revealing himself to be simply enormous. He was butting his head repeatedly against my knee when Ethel answered the door.

'Oh Silas, let her alone, do,' she said. 'Come in, quickly, and we'll go to the kitchen,' she hissed, but I'd barely taken a step into the hall when a querulous shriek broke the silence.

'Ethel! Come here at once!'

'Gosh,' I murmured, shocked by the fury, but Ethel was laughing.

'So sorry. That's Nelson. Clearly, he learned that one from Mother. She's upstairs – oh...'

As she spoke, I heard halting footsteps, and Mother herself appeared. I'd heard so much about her, it was like a character from a book coming to life. She was tiny, no more than five feet tall, with rigid steel-grey curls set in a style last fashionable in 1923, and she wore a stiff black silk dress that rustled like dead leaves.

'A friend?' she said to Ethel, ignoring me.

'A colleague, Mother,' said Ethel. 'Miss York.'

'Stop it now, Mother!' shrieked Nelson from the drawing room. He repeated himself several times in a frenzy, to the accompaniment of wild feathery noises and some alarming banging.

'Has he got his beak stuck in the bars again?' Mother snapped. 'Ethel, I thought you were keeping an eye on him.'

'I was! But the doorbell rang...'

'I shall never understand why Lizzie took it into her head to abandon us,' said Mother. 'Years of dedicated domestic service, then gone like a thief in the night, without a by-your-leave.'

'She's working in intelligence!' Ethel said helplessly.

'I suppose you'd better come through,' Mother said, turning towards the drawing room.

'Oh no, Mother, Edie has something she needs to tell me about work...'

'I see.' Mother compressed her lips into a horizontal line. 'You're away from me all day, and yet now at teatime, when I finally have your company, suddenly it's time for a "work meeting". How very convenient.'

'I'll be very brief,' I said weakly.

'We'll just go to the kitchen...' Ethel said quickly, and I hurried downstairs after her into a cheerful basement room with an Aga and an oak table. There were colourful pictures on the walls, and an ornate sewing machine shoved into a corner.

'Mother doesn't come down here,' whispered Ethel. 'So I've made it my HQ.' As she spoke, Silas slinked in and leapt through the open bottom door of the Aga. I screamed in horror.

'Oh, don't worry!' Ethel tried not to smile. 'It's not hot, just warm. It's the bread-proving oven.' Indeed, Silas was now sitting inside like a risen loaf, purring loudly.

'He does bring me comfort,' she sighed. 'Look, sorry about...' She cast her eyes to the ceiling, where various thumps and exhortations floated from above.

'Now,' she said, 'who sent the lilies? I'm agog to find out.'

'Ethel, it was Theo.'

'Theo?'

'Yes, I think it must have been Theo who told you they were a symbol of death. He said it to me when we were talking about Joyce's funeral.'

Ethel's eyes widened.

'Oh my Lord, you're right, it was. I remember now – we were all sitting round, and Joyce had said something about symbolic flowers in myths, and he'd just come into the room – that's why I didn't remember, because he was standing behind me and I didn't see him. But I heard him say it.'

'Why would Theo send you flowers?' I asked slowly. 'I don't think he... well...'

Ethel nodded. 'Not interested in the fair sex.'

'But,' I went on, 'he may well like Jean-Luc. And if he found out...'

'Joyce must have told Theo about the... you know, our kiss,' said Ethel, embarrassed. 'She wouldn't have thought anything of it, it was all just part of life's rich tapestry to her. But perhaps he wanted to warn me off.'

'Although it's not as if you're Jean-Luc's only love interest...' I murmured, thinking of his clinch with Nora, his initial arrival with Sabrina.

'No. And not even a love interest. Just a regrettable drunken moment. But if Theo did that in a jealous fury, what else might he have done?'

'What might he do to someone who lived in his home; a person he relied on for food and lodging,' I thought aloud, 'if he felt that person had betrayed his trust by snatching Jean-Luc from under his nose?'

'Joyce,' she said quietly.

'Yes,' I said. 'And, Ethel – if anyone finds out about Jean-Luc's latest dalliance, I'm afraid Nora might be next.'

Overhead, Nelson screamed, 'Down with Hitler!' accompanied by the sound of something fragile breaking and Mother bellowing, 'Why must it always be my Paragon china, you stupid, destructive bird!'

'I'd better go and see...' Ethel murmured, and I stood hastily.

It was a blessing to be outside on the cold street, and as I made my way home by torchlight, for once I felt greatly relieved that I had no parents of my own to worry about.

By eleven, I was finally in bed after another exhausting evening shift at the WVS canteen, and I'd rushed through bedtime ablutions with a sketchy top and tail so I could read more of Maggie's diary before sleep overtook me.

19 November

What a day! Mrs Wright said I could go out after I'd finished my tasks, and I sewed extra hard and washed all the *dirty crockery Mr b****y Wright had left after his enormous breakfast.*

I told S where I was going and swore him to secrecy with a blood vow (but we didn't have a pin upstairs, so we just said it three times), and of course he wanted to come, but as he hadn't really been invited, I said he could next time and off I went.

I had no idea what to expect. Of course I've heard the funny gossip (which I don't really understand) about Athena House, but I like Joyce and it was kind of her to ask me, so I decided to be very grown-up about it. I pretended to be Jane Eyre going to Thornfield Hall for the first time, nervous but determined, which I suppose makes Johnny Mr Rochester (and he is a bit like him, he can be so bad-tempered and you don't know what you've done wrong, but then he can be so romantic – the other day he said he could look at my eyes forever and a day, because they were so green. I think they're a sort of muddy hazel, but it was a lovely thing to say). Anyway, I got to Athena House and the posh blonde lady, who is called Sabrina (I have never heard that name before, I think it's beautiful), let me in. It's the strangest house I've ever been to, I think.

'Me too, Maggie,' I murmured.

Sabrina led me into the big parlour and there were so many people I felt a bit overcome, but then I saw Joyce and she was very smiling and kind and she poured me some tea and offered me a scone with Nora's blackberry jam, it was wonderful. They didn't seem like grown-ups at all, the artists. Mr Aubrey showed me his studio and his big paintings, and I thought they were marvellous, though I didn't really understand them. He said he was a pacifist like the rest of them and that killing could never be justified. He got quite shouty about it. Later on, Joyce showed me round the other studios, and she talked about peace, too, and asked how I feel about the war. I said it was awful and I worry about Dad and miss Mum and Nanna. She said 'the wisdom of youth' and she told me that lots of people think fighting is justified for a good cause, but all the people on the other side think that, too, and it just ends up with innocents being killed. I said, 'I do think my dad is fighting for a good cause,' and she said, 'Yes, but an eye for an eye makes the whole world blind.' I am going to tell Johnny all about it tomorrow and see what he thinks. I liked Sabrina best. I'm going to stop now because S keeps asking me questions and I can't write and answer them at the same time.

It was almost midnight, but I wasn't going to stop reading now.

Oh Maggie, I thought, *where have you gone?*

I skipped forward through some mooning about Johnny, and a couple of entries around the Christmas Blitz in London. Maggie was, of course, terribly worried about her mother, but a week later she reported that a letter had arrived saying her family was safe (as was Pouncer the cat, thankfully – I was feeling rather concerned myself), and her normal life resumed.

11 Jan

I've had a horrible argument with Johnny. He said at Christmas that I was his girl, and today I said, 'Well, if I am your girl, we can still see each other when we're back in London.' And he said, 'Let's see what happens.' I don't know what he means by that! He has been kissing me for months and saying nice things about me, and all of a sudden he's not sure. I think he has seen that Rita going about in Birchcroft and had his head turned, but I know for a fact she is nineteen and much too old for Johnny. He turned sixteen last week and I used my half-crown that I'd saved up to get him a shaving brush from the chemist. Mr Allan behind the counter said 'it's real badger, that' and I thought Johnny would be thrilled to bits, but he said 'thanks, Mags', and that was all. It's not as though the Wrights got him anything. S made him a model tank out of some wood he found, and it was quite good, Johnny seemed more pleased with it than my present.

Anyway, I said, 'Have you gone off me?' and he said, 'Don't be silly, but you're still a kid, there are some things I wouldn't ask you to do', and I think he means you-know-what. I said nobody should be doing that till they're married anyway, and he said, 'That doesn't stop your friends at Athena House.' I don't know what he meant, but I said, 'Don't talk about Joyce like that', and he said, 'Oh Mags, you're such a baby,' as if I'm six. I said, 'If that's what you think, Johnny Rawnsley, you can get yourself another girl', and he said, 'Fine, shouldn't be any trouble.' And then I ran back to the house and I've been crying for ages, but I don't want S to see me upset so will go and have a wash. I am going to go up to AH tomorrow to see Joyce and Sabrina because at least they treat me like a grown-up. My heart is broken.

12 Jan

Thank goodness for Athena House. I went at lunchtime, I told Mrs W I had to post a letter. It was freezing cold and raining cats and dogs, but it was worth the walk. Joyce was in and she gave me tea in the kitchen with Aubrey and I told them about J and they were both so nice to me. I almost asked if I could move in to AH, but I don't want to annoy them and I don't know what Mum would think about that. Then the one called Theo came in and we discussed Joyce's next talk and my plans when I go back to London. I said I'd like to be a writer and nobody laughed or poked fun. I want to write books about children like Spud and how they deal with horrible things like war and being taken away from people they love. Aubrey said that sounded an excellent idea, and I asked if he had any children and he looked very strange for a moment. But then Sabrina came in and I was so pleased to see her. The rain stopped and she took me to feed the chickens and said that men came and went, and I mustn't mind too much about Johnny because one day I'd do much better. I asked if she'd ever had her heart broken, and she said 'oh yes,' but she wouldn't say who did it.

The French one, Jean-Luc, came down for a bit. He's very handsome but seems quite sulky and old. Not sure if I like him, but Sabrina does. She kept throwing her head back laughing whenever he said anything, though nothing was very funny.

Before I went, Joyce asked me to come to her next talk, and she said that it was young people like me who could help to end all wars for good. Aubrey asked me if I'd like to go on a long walk with them next weekend and I said I'd love to. I still feel heartbroken about Johnny, but it's very nice to have some friends at last, even if they are all so much older than me. I suppose I'll catch up one day.

There were not many pages of writing left – this had all happened just a few weeks ago, and I was by now feeling terribly protective of Maggie, as if she were my little sister. In some ways, with her innocence and determination, she reminded me of Suki – another worry I'd shoved to the back of my mind.

I turned the page, feeling furious with Johnny.

18 Jan

It was a wonderful walk! Everyone came except Jean-Luc and Nora who said they would carry on working in their studios. We went right up to the top of Nether Brow, and Joyce pointed out all the places you could see, it was like being at the top of the world. She said she comes here often when she wants to think. Joan brought sandwiches and we all sat on rugs and had a picnic, and she and Aubrey did some sketching, I felt sure he was drawing me, but when I asked he hid the page and said it was 'a silly scribble'. They discussed some more about the talk Joyce is giving, she said 'this time it's gloves off', and Sabrina said 'are you sure, Joyce?'

Joyce said 'I will speak the truth, Sabrina, no matter who objects', and Aubrey said, 'hear, hear'. Theo looked a bit worried, but perhaps that's just how his face is.

We came back down and I went to see Norman without Johnny this time. He didn't seem to mind me visiting, he's quite peaceful because he doesn't talk much. He said he'd tell me a secret that he knew, but I mustn't tell anyone. It's quite a big one, and I'm not even going to write it down in case anybody finds this diary.

Still not speaking to JR. Heart is still broken.

25 *Jan*

I went up to AH, and Aubrey was there by himself, the others had gone for a full day of rambling, but he had a painting to finish. He asked if I'd like a 'stroll' over the tops with him, and I thought I might as well. It was very cold, and he gave me his big scarf and put his arm round me, but it was like walking in a three-legged race so he stopped. On the way back down, he asked me for a favour, but he said not to tell anyone – I haven't decided if I'll say yes, yet. He said he'd pay me a bit of money for my time, but it feels awkward being alone with him. I'm not sure about what he wants me to wear, either. I'll make my mind up this week.

I sat up in bed, my heart racing. What had Aubrey asked Maggie to do? I thought of his rackety past, his abandoned families. Was he so far from the moral path that asking a young girl to be secretly alone with him seemed normal? As for what he wanted her to wear... my mind stalled with horror. Had she said no, and signed her own death warrant? I stifled a groan, and turned the page.

7 Feb

The worst, worst, worst day of my life. I can hardly bear to write it down and S has finally cried himself to sleep. Today, we heard that our Dad has been killed by the Germans. Mum said in her letter that there were no details yet, but he was a hero and never to think his death wasn't worthwhile, because it would help the world to be free. She's coming up here as soon as she can, and Nanna put in a special postcard with a kitten on it and said she loves us and is sorry and can't wait for us to come home. But even when we do go home, Dad won't be there and nothing will ever be the same. He was so brave.

I blinked back tears. My poor little Maggie, and poor Spud. It was so recent, too. Surely that might have prompted Maggie to try and return to London? It was now horribly late, but nothing would stop me reading on.

8 Feb

I still can't believe it's true. I keep crying and Mrs Wright said, 'You're not the only person ever to have lost somebody, Margaret.' I hate her with all my heart. S is so quiet, it's not like him at all.

I saw Johnny in the yard, and he said, 'Sorry about your father.' I didn't know what to say, and I hoped he might at least cuddle me, but he didn't, he just went back to the stable. He's a mean, hateful boy.

10 Feb 10

Went to the talk. I said I was going to bed early and climbed down the drainpipe.

Later on, we had an argument and I hate JR and I'm going to say so. I'm not a kid.

I flipped the pages frantically back and forth, but there was nothing else, not even a doodle in the rest of the book. That was where it ended, and Maggie and Johnny had vanished the following day – or perhaps that night.

It was after one, but I couldn't sleep. It was now obvious that she had not gone willingly with Johnny, and any hopeful ideas I'd had about him protecting her all the way to London died away. She was so fiery and bold – if she'd told Johnny she hated him, could he have lost his temper and harmed her? Or had she run away and he'd taken the opportunity to go after her?

As for Maggie's putative agreement with Aubrey, there was no further mention of it. Perhaps he had asked her to meet him, up in the hills, and she had tried to repel his advances... worry fluttered in my mind like Ada's pigeons, but no matter how hard I tried to make sense of what I knew, my thoughts circled and criss-crossed, refusing to form any sort of pattern.

I needed to tell Lou first thing, and we needed to visit Birchcroft again, quite urgently.

'You did what?'

Lou in a temper was never my favourite person, but on the telephone, he somehow conveyed an extra layer of contemptuous rage which crackled down the line like electricity.

'I just thought we needed to know if—'

'*We?*' he said, as I pressed the receiver to my ear to try and contain the explosive noise. That was an error – it was even less pleasant. Around me, people clacked at typewriters and readied themselves for Mr Gorringe's morning meeting. I longed to join them, but I was far too junior to enter the daily symposium of ideas in the conference room. Occasionally, I'd hear his voice floating out: '... and Mr Timms, don't overlook the question of funding when you come to conduct the interview...'

I longed to be ushered within, to sit at the vast oak conference table armed with a list of ideas for exposing the city's criminals as editors nodded, impressed, but that was about as likely as Arnold parachuting through the skylight with a carnation between his teeth.

I tuned back in to Lou's rage.

'I suppose you do realise you've committed a criminal act now?' he was saying. 'Removing potential evidence from the possible scene of a crime. Your fingerprints all over key documents. If she has been murdered, it'll be you first in the dock, York, you bloody little idiot.'

I hadn't wanted to tell him about Maggie's diary, but given the abrupt and alarming way it ended, I'd felt certain there was no choice. I was swiftly revising that opinion.

'And you could very easily have been caught!' he went on. 'Wright would have been well within his rights to call the police there and then, given that you were intruding on his property with absolutely no legal remit to do so! I cannot fathom, Edie, what goes through your mind. You're a perfectly intelligent woman, but sometimes you appear to have the brain of a cabbage. In fact, that's far too insulting to cruciferous vegetables—'

'But Lou,' I interrupted, 'without the diary we'd never have known what happened with Maggie and Johnny, or—'

'We still don't know! According to you, it says nothing of note whatsoever!'

'It does, it says—'

'For heaven's sake,' Lou snapped. 'Bring it to me at lunchtime, I'm at Newton Street Station, and I'm calling it in now as evidence.'

'But it's not a criminal investigation!'

'It soon might be,' he said furiously. 'Don't be late.' He rang off.

I was left holding the slightly damp Bakelite receiver and breathing as if I'd run for a bus. He really could be quite terrifying.

To my relief, when I arrived at Newton Street, Lou was already on the steps beneath the extinguished blue lamp, shrugging his coat on.

'We'll get a quick bite to eat,' he said. 'And then you can tell me what in hell's name you were thinking.'

He seemed to have calmed down slightly, although I was not looking forward to this brief lunch. We hurried through the garment district, past the bombed buildings of Oldham Street, cracked signs still rattling in the wind, and newsstands with boys shouting 'cargo ship torpedoed!' until, eventually, Lou darted down a back alley, led me round a sooty corner and opened the door to a café so small it could serve no more than three people without them all catching the same cold.

'Lou!' bellowed the owner, an ancient Mancunian in a grease-stained apron. 'A treat to see you! Is this your young lady?'

'No,' said Lou, and I said, 'Hardly' at the same time. The owner gave us a sceptical look and seated us at a tiny Formica table, so we were practically on each other's laps. It felt cosy to be out of the wind, with steam billowing from the back kitchen and the menu chalked on a board above the counter.

I looked, hopefully, to see what I might choose, but it read TODAY'S SPECIAL, *5d* with no further information.

Lou ordered two specials and a pot of tea and turned to me.

'Right then,' he said. 'Let's have it. And I'll have to trust that you haven't tampered with it in any way since it came into your possession.'

'*Tampered?* What you do think I am?'

'Extremely fond of taking unnecessary risks. Wouldn't you agree?' he asked coldly.

I handed it over silently, and Lou flicked through the pages.

'I'll say one thing, she can spell,' he said, running his eyes down a long paragraph. 'Though I'm not sure her future as a writer lies in romance novels. *An owl hooted and made me jump.*' He snorted gently.

The special turned out to be steaming bowls of oxtail stew, which I had to admit tasted wonderful.

'Bob's the best cook in Manchester,' said Lou. 'I'd like to see The French at the Midland perform the miracles he does with weekly rations.'

I sighed at his little dig – The French was where Charles Emerson had taken me, and thoroughly turned my head. I really didn't need reminding of what an easily flattered goose I'd been.

'Where's Marple?' I asked, to change the subject.

'Sergeant O'Carroll's taken him on patrol,' said Lou. 'He's very helpful when it comes to encouraging suspects to cough up their misdeeds. They don't need to know he'll do anything for a head scratch.'

He read on. 'Aubrey asking her for a secret favour,' he muttered. 'This sounds as dodgy as a three-bob note. What could he possibly want with her, apart from the obvious? Revolting old goat.'

'Surely we need to try and find out whether she agreed to whatever sordid...'

Lou wasn't listening, he was poring over the final entry.

'*I hate JR,*' he read aloud. 'Interesting.'

'Yes – and knowing this does help, in fact,' I added mutinously, through a mouthful of oxtail. 'Because now we know she and Johnny had a big row the night before she went, doesn't it make it more likely that he hurt her, or worse?'

Lou drummed his fingers on the open page. He seemed to have stopped worrying about fingerprints.

'It might,' he said. 'But she may not be referring to Johnny Rawnsley at all.'

'What do you mean?'

'Keep up, York,' he said. 'Who else did Maggie know with those initials?'

I put my fork down.

'JR...' I said. 'Joyce Reid.'

CHAPTER TWELVE

By lunchtime the following day, I had finished my obituary of Joyce, skirting around her many entanglements, and concentrating on her skills as a classicist and artist. I felt I must mention the pacifism, and wrote:

> *Reid was horrified by the suffering she witnessed as a nurse during the Great War, and became determined that the world must never suffer such destruction in future. She was boldly outspoken in her beliefs, sometimes to the detriment of her popularity locally, but friends and fellow artists would regularly support her impassioned talks...*

I felt that glossed neatly over the near-riots at the church hall. I dropped it in Mr Gorringe's in-tray and felt a weight lift away from me. It swiftly returned, however, as my thoughts drifted back to Birchcroft, and the troubled lives of its residents.

That afternoon, after a deeply unpleasant pork pie from the kiosk – it was more sawdust than sausage – I extracted two sheets of writing paper from my desk and picked up a fountain pen.

'They come as a boon and a blessing to men, The Pickwick, the Owl, and the Waverley pen,' chanted Pat, returning to her desk. 'Always thought that was such a clever advertisement for pens, used to have it on the side of the trolley-buses.'

Huffing at my puzzlement ('you youngsters, you've no idea, have you?'), she retreated, and I turned back to my task. It struck me as ridiculous that Mrs Dawson remained unaware that her daughter was missing. Equally, that Mrs Rawnsley thought her son was safe and sound in Birchcroft. Nobody seemed to be taking charge, or pulling the threads together.

I asked Sally on the switchboard to find a number for the Birchcroft grocer's – they were likely to have a telephone to ring through their orders to the suppliers. It was remarkably easy to speak to Jane Tither, it transpired, and she was both concerned and helpful.

'Hold on a moment, let me swap my hats from overworked grocer's wife to overworked billeting officer...' she murmured. 'I'll just have a look... ah! Mrs A. Dawson, SW1... and Mrs D. Rawnsley, NW1. Camden, I think,' and she read out the addresses.

'I should have written to them myself, but I hadn't realised how long they'd been gone... oh dear.' She sighed helplessly. 'I do hope they turn up.'

I felt that many people should have written to the oblivious parents, beginning with the Wrights themselves. But so far, nobody had bothered – and as more and more time passed since their disappearance, and it remained unclear whether or not they were somehow back in London, enjoying life in the rubble-filled Smoke, I decided somebody had to step in. In the absence of anyone else, that person appeared to be me.

It took me a long time to craft letters that were accurate without being terrifying, crossing out *I'm afraid the Wrights are not quite sure where they have gone...* and *everyone is very worried*, and finally settling on simple facts, and a heartfelt wish that they get in touch with either me or Detective Inspector Brennan on receipt of the letters.

Bobo the messenger boy collected them, and I felt a thrill of horror as they disappeared into the postbag. I imaged two anguished mothers unfolding the paper, running their eyes over the unexpected letter, clutching the arm of a chair and collapsing into it... I had no idea whether I had done the right thing.

It was in this spirit of melancholy that I caught the bus home and trudged up our street in the early evening, looking forward to tea and toast, and hoping Annie would be in so I could tell her all about my trip. As I approached our building, I could just make out a dark shape huddled on the step. I squinted in the fading light and realised it was a person, sitting down, with a large suitcase beside them. Perhaps Miss Beamish had a visitor, or had locked herself out.

I hurried towards our gate, fumbling for my key, but as I approached, the shape stood, and resolved itself into a woman wearing a stylish hat and a fur tippet and looking at me with a combination of anguish and relief.

'Suki!'

I ran up the path and embraced her, dropping my handbag. 'What on earth are you doing here?'

'I'm so glad you're back,' she said into my neck. Her skin was scented with a heavy, floral perfume, but her curled black hair smelled clean and cold, the way it always had. It was like having my sister back after a long, dangerous voyage.

'I waited for hours, I thought you might not be coming home at all today,' she said, still clinging to me.

'I was at work!' I said. 'And Annie will be at the hospital.'

She nodded. 'An old lady came in and I asked her, but she said I had no proof I was a friend of yours and I must wait here.'

'Damn Mrs Turner,' I said. 'I'm so sorry, Suki, come up at once, and tell me everything.'

She followed me up to the flat, and exclaimed at how lovely it was: 'Your view of the park! And is this Annie's room?' She peered in. 'Look at all your books!' She ran her gloved finger along the shelf beside her. 'Still, you were always the clever one.'

'Suki, it's wonderful to see you,' I said, 'but what's happened? Why are you here?'

'Why do you think? I left Frank. You said I could always come here, so I did.'

'I'm so glad,' I said. Even as I felt the wash of relief that Suki was out of danger for now, a part of me was imagining Annie's reaction to our unexpected guest. For some reason, I suspected they wouldn't get on, though I struggled to pinpoint why.

'So can I stay? Is it all right?' asked Suki, still standing by her case, looking like an evacuee herself.

'Of course,' I said. 'I can take the couch and you can have my bed.'

'Absolutely not,' she said. 'I'll take the couch, I'm not having you giving up your beauty sleep for me.'

We tussled gently, and eventually, I gave in.

'Just not having Frank snoring in my ear will be good enough for me,' she said. 'I'd sleep in an orange crate if I could be on my own.'

'Oh, Suki,' I said again. 'I'm truly sorry. Tell me what's happened.'

I made us both tea and toast with the last of the butter, and lit the fire.

She eventually took off her outdoor things and hung them neatly on the hatstand, then she sank into in Annie's usual armchair and heaved a great sigh.

'Oh, Edie,' she said. 'I made such a mistake.'

'You were so young. You couldn't have known.'

'I could,' she said bitterly. 'If I'd only listened to you, and not had my silly, babyish little head turned by all his lies.'

It was nice to be vindicated after all these years of guilt – but I wished it had never happened.

'Does he know where you've gone?' I asked. It occurred to me that a raging Frank Sullivan on the doorstep would not go down well with Mrs Turner. Or me, for that matter.

'Heavens, no. He'd kill me.'

'Do you mean that?'

'I think I do,' she said. Her hair was trained over one eye like Veronica Lake's. Stupidly, I'd thought it fashionable styling, a look Annie called 'all the go'. Now she lifted it away and turned towards the lamp. 'Look,' she said.

Her left eye was swollen and half-closed, a violent bloom of purple staining the skin around it.

'Oh, Suki!' I said. 'We must call for a doctor.'

'No, I won't do that. You don't know who knows each other, with men. One word in the wrong ear, and Frank will know where to find me. I need to stay out of sight.'

I saw the truth in what she said.

'Was this what made you leave?' I asked.

'Not really.' She sipped her tea. 'It was everything. Seeing you so calm and elegant made me realise the sort of life I was putting up with. Being a punchbag for years on end. Never knowing if he'd come home drunk or violent or both. Tiptoeing about, scared to sit down in my own home in case I moved a cushion and set him off. No friends, no company, could never say the right thing. The truth is, Edie,' she said, looking up at my horrified expression, 'some men are just bastards.'

I nodded. 'But Suki, you can't hide away forever – you're not a prisoner.'

'I have been,' she said darkly. 'I know, of course I can't. But for a while I need to lie low, get a job and save up enough money to try and get a divorce, though I know he'll fight me. It's all I can do, and you're the only person I know who'd let me stay with them. Edie, I'm so grateful,' she went on. 'I can never thank you enough.'

'Of course, it's the very least I can offer,' I said. 'Suki, does anybody know where you are?'

'Nobody. I left a note to say I'd had enough, and don't come looking. He'll be beyond furious, but I don't see how he'd find me.'

'Good,' I said, but a chill ran through me all the same.

We were still talking when a key rattled in the lock and Annie came in. 'Oh, Edie, what a day I've had!' she called from the hallway, kicking off her shoes. 'I've got us a bit of cod for tea, it was – oh!'

She stopped, seeing Suki in her armchair.

'Annie!' I said. 'This is Suki. She's... had some trouble, and she's come to stay for a bit. I hope that's all right.'

'Suki?' Annie said. 'You're Suki from the home?'

'I am,' said Suki. Strangely, my two friends had never met – at the grammar school, Annie was my best friend, but Suki had gone to what she called 'the local slum' and left at thirteen to 'help', unpaid, with the younger children at the home. When I saw Annie outside school, I'd gone to her house for tea with her kind parents and funny brothers. It was a haven, and, selfishly, I hadn't wanted to share it with anyone – even Suki.

'Goodness!' said Annie. 'I've heard so much about you, I can't fathom that you're real.'

'Well, I am, I think.' Suki laughed awkwardly. I wondered how much to reveal about her reasons for being here, but she said tremulously, 'I'm very sorry to barge in like this, Annie, but... well, I've run away from my husband. He hits me, and I think he might kill me if I stay.'

'Oh, how utterly dreadful,' Annie cried. 'Of course you must stay here. You can have my bed, if you like.'

We had another debate which ended up once again with Suki on the couch.

Annie said, 'I'll see if the cod will stretch,' and went into the kitchen. I showed Suki where the bathroom was, and hurried after Annie.

'I know it's a bit tricky,' I whispered. 'But I didn't know what else to do.'

'No, of course she must stay,' she hissed back. 'But look, Edie, is this madman going to come after her? Because I don't fancy fighting some lunatic who wants to murder her on the doorstep.'

'She swears he doesn't know where she's gone,' I said. 'But she can't hide forever, can she? She needs an address to use her ration book, for one thing. She can't go back to her local grocer.'

'Rations,' groaned Annie. 'Edie, I don't think we can make ours go round three people, we'll starve.'

Suki peered round the door. 'Is everything all right?'

'Fine!' Annie and I chorused, two tiny pieces of cod spitting in the pan.

By Saturday evening, I was exhausted. I'd taken a double shift at the WVS canteen so Moira could meet her brother who was home on leave, and my arms ached from hefting giant teapots. Annie was working again, and Suki had promised she would 'try to sort out her ration book'.

By the time I let myself in, I was thinking about nothing but what we might have in the pantry that I could cook quickly in the household's remaining teaspoon of lard. I opened the door to find Suki sitting in Annie's armchair, talking to Arnold, while Annie perched stiffly at the table. My heart sank. All I wanted was something to eat and a cup of tea with the wireless on, but I seemed to have walked into a drawing room farce.

'Hullo all,' I said, and Arnold leapt to his feet.

'Edie!' he said, sounding relieved. 'I was just passing, thought I'd drop by, but I had no idea you were out...'

'Mrs Turner's back with her sister – she's "taken bad with gout" – so I thought it safe for Arnold to come up,' Annie explained.

Annie got up to put the kettle on. 'There's no pie left,' she added, with a bitter glance at Suki. 'I can do you some bread and cheese, though.'

I nodded gratefully.

'Gosh, it's so lovely not to have to cook for Frank,' said Suki dreamily. She looked very pretty in the firelight, though her hair was still teased over her bruise. 'Pie I haven't made myself! Like being a lady of the manor.'

'I don't think I'd suit being a lord of the manor,' said Arnold, 'all that riding round the estate, barking at serfs. Tiring business.'

Suki shrieked with laughter. 'You're so funny, Arnold,' she said, and he smiled at her.

Annie clattered loudly in the pantry, and came back carrying a cup of tea and a plate of bread and cheese for me.

'Is there any spare cheese?' Suki asked hopefully.

'No,' Annie said shortly. 'Afraid not.'

It was clear that her nose was entirely out of joint, though Arnold seemed oblivious to any tension.

'I'll need to get a job, I suppose,' said Suki, stretching and showing off her tiny, belted waist.

'Well, we all need to pay our way these days,' said Annie, offering Arnold a cigarette and lighting it for him. I noticed she didn't extend the pack to Suki.

'What sort of thing might you look for?' I asked, through a

dense mouthful of bread. I was glad I didn't feel the need to flirt with Arnold.

'Well, I don't fancy factory work much,' said Suki, wrinkling her nose. 'And I don't think I'd be much good as a nurse...'

'No, probably not,' muttered Annie. I shot her a quelling look.

'So I wondered, Edie,' Suki said, 'whether you might ask at the *Chronicle* for me? I could do filing, or even be a secretary, or answer calls on the switchboard...' She adopted a posh, high-pitched voice: 'Good afternoon, the *Manchester Chronicle*? An obituary for your tabby cat, Miss Mousington? Certainly sir, connecting you to Miss York now...' She pressed imaginary buttons on the arm of the chair.

Arnold was laughing.

'You'd be very good at it,' he said, and she beamed.

I felt rather taken aback. 'I'm not sure there are any jobs going,' I said. 'The pages are reduced because of the war, you see, and Mr Gorringe is a stickler for budgets.'

Annie gave a small smile and blew a perfect smoke ring.

'Gosh, that's clever,' said Arnold admiringly, as it spun lazily towards the ceiling.

'I taught myself to blow one inside another,' said Suki. 'Would you like to see?'

'Oh yes, do carry on,' said Arnold politely, and she borrowed his cigarette and performed her trick, handing it back tipped scarlet from her lipstick.

If this little battle of wiles was set to carry on, I'd be moving out myself.

'*Will* you ask, though, Edie?' Suki asked, and I found myself agreeing that I would, much against my better judgement. Suki was my oldest friend, and I was so glad she'd escaped her violent husband. I just wished her safety didn't have to come at the expense of Annie's happiness.

'Oh, Edie, I forgot,' said Annie. 'A couple of letters came for you, they're on the sideboard.'

I leapt up – they had both arrived by the third post, postmarked NW1 and SW1.

The first was written in capitals, misspelled and blotted, and as I took in its few lines, I gasped.

Dear Miss Edie York,

My mam showed me your letter. I am Johnny Rawnsley and I am back home when I shud of been all along. The Rights are a rotten pare of old slave drivers and I am glad I run away. I took the munney for the train out off the church cleckshun plate, but it was Herbert who had put it in haha so I think he owd it me annyway.

I dunt no where Maggie is. She stopped torking to me after her dad was killed. I have a gud job now dellivring for the Habberdashers on our street and I will join the Army when I can. Good riddense to Birchcroft!

Yours

Johnny Rawnsley, Esq.

Johnny was safe! My vision of the babes in the wood was wrong, thank God – but if he was in London, where was Maggie? Now I knew for sure that she had most likely been alone when she met – who? Aubrey? Theo? Norman? A stranger, who saw her pretty face and bedraggled appearance and decided to hurt her? Unless Johnny was lying – but somehow, I didn't think he was.

With a shaking hand, I opened the second envelope.

'What is it, Edie? You look quite pale,' said Suki, but I held up a hand while I read the letter from Mrs Dawson.

Dear Miss York,

Thank you for your letter which arrived this morning. Needless to say, I am horrified to hear that my daughter is missing. I thought she would be safe in Birchcroft; I never dreamed that she would be unhappy enough to run away – or that worse things may have befallen her. I have cancelled my shifts for the London Auxiliary Ambulance Service, and I will arrive in Birchcroft by the first train north to find Maggie.

I am very glad that you wrote to me, and distraught that the Wrights did not.

I hope you will join me in prayers for my missing daughter,

Yours sincerely,

Mrs Antoinette (Netta) Dawson.

Tears stood in my eyes when I had finished reading.

'Oh, Edie!' said Annie, hurrying over. 'Whatever is it?'

I told her, and Suki listened intently as I spoke about what had happened to Joyce, and my fears for Maggie after reading her diary.

'Interesting, isn't it, that Maggie writes about "JR" in her last entry?' said Suki. 'If she really hadn't spoken to Johnny, she must mean Joyce. Why would she go from such admiration to hating her?'

'If we assume Johnny was telling the truth,' I said.

'Did you believe him?'

'I think I did,' I said. 'He wasn't in danger of cutting himself on his intellect.'

'You sound just like Lou,' Arnold said. 'He doesn't suffer fools, our pal, does he?'

I laughed. 'That's something of an understatement.'

'Yes, I know he can be a bit abrasive,' Arnold agreed. 'But I don't think he means to cause upset – he's always been so keen on getting to the bottom of things, I don't think he can bear it when he feels people are lying, or keeping secrets.'

'I don't blame him,' said Suki. 'I never knew if Frank was telling me the truth, but I didn't dare to ask.' She gazed into the fire.

'Edie, I think you must find out what Joyce said in that final talk,' Suki said. 'Maybe the key to all this lies with Joyce. If Maggie is alive, I bet somebody at Athena House would know where she's gone.'

'What makes you think that?' I asked, my tea forgotten.

'Who else?' said Suki. 'The Wrights wouldn't have said she'd gone missing if they'd hurt her, they'd have said she told everyone she was going back to London. The village sounds too small for someone to commit a murder and get home without anyone noticing something. And besides, that warden seems to be a right nosy parker. If she was staying with somebody, again, someone would notice. And her hat was found in the valley so she must have been walking somewhere. And who did she go walking with?'

I was impressed by my old friend's reasoning powers – I wondered if living in fear for so long had sharpened her ability to read people.

'Artists from Athena House,' I said. 'Aubrey, for one.'

'But if someone killed Joyce...' said Arnold, leaning forward.

'Could they also have killed Maggie?' I supplied.

'When you've quite finished with your "I've gathered you all to the library" carry-on,' said Annie. She was joking, but I could see how put out she was by Suki's enthusiasm and charm. I suddenly remembered her saying *But I'm your best friend... never forget that.*

. . .

I thought I'd go out like a light, but with Suki on the couch, I'd lain awake, imagining every small creak and rustle to be Frank Sullivan breaking in, armed with a carving knife.

'You look as if you could do with a charabanc seaside outing,' Lou greeted me, as Marple jumped obediently into the back seat, paws slithering on the leather. 'Crypt not as comfy as it used to be?'

It was still horribly early on Sunday morning, and I didn't feel like telling him all about Suki just yet. Perhaps later on, I'd ask his advice.

He pulled smoothly away from the kerb. Lou loved driving. I'd barely ever been in a car until recently, but now I appreciated what a godsend it was not to be waiting for buses and trains.

'Hold on!' I said. 'What about your petrol ration?'

'The police have a certain allowance,' he said. 'So I wouldn't worry, as long as I don't mention to anyone that I've been driving all over Lancashire on my day off.'

As we motored through the edge of Manchester towards Birchcroft, families in their Sunday best hurried along, pulling small, reluctant children with scrubbed faces.

'Were you ever a churchgoer?' I asked Lou.

'Me?' he said. 'The spire would burst into flames.'

'Annie goes sometimes,' I said. 'But I'd had enough when I was little. Sunday school seemed to be nothing but angry stories about terrible things happening to people. I liked some hymns, I suppose.'

Lou began to sing 'Dear Lord and Father of Mankind' in a pleasantly tuneful baritone, and I joined in with the bits I remembered.

'To hear us, you'd think we were missionaries on our way to save souls,' Lou said.

'Perhaps we are. Maggie's, at any rate.'

'Let's hope so,' he said. 'Though I think our intervention may be too late for the residents of Athena House.'

As we turned down the long lane to Birchcroft, Lou said, 'Who would you say is in charge round here?'

'In charge? I suppose Constable Creech...'

'No, not that idiot,' he said. 'I mean, who do the villagers listen to? Who organises the bring and buy, who oversees the village fete, that sort of thing.'

'Are you hoping to win a coconut?'

'Only to crack on your head,' said Lou. 'I'm serious, come on, York.'

'Well, I suppose it would be Lady Brackenfield,' I said. 'She lives up at Brackenfield Hall, the big stately home overlooking the valley opposite Wrights' Farm.'

'Perfect,' said Lou.

'Why?'

'Why do you think?' he asked, gliding to a halt outside the church as singing floated from within, and coming to open my door, although I noticed he opened Marple's first. The dog immediately ran to christen a venerable-looking gravestone.

'Because we need her help to form a search party. If Maggie's died of exposure, she'll be out there somewhere in the valley. And if even worse has happened... well. We've got help now, at least,' he added, indicating Marple, who was sniffing ecstatically at the grassy base of GREGORY JOSIAH BAILEY, BELOVED HUSBAND.

'You'll need something of hers, though, won't you?'

Lou raised an eyebrow. He produced Maggie's diary from his inside coat pocket and brandished it.

'I calculate this is the last hymn,' he said, as the voices inside rose for 'O God Our Help in Ages Past', and the organ crashed and boomed.

'We'll intercept Lady B, explain what we need, and persuade her to help get up a search party while it's light,' Lou went on.

'In the meantime, we'll have a word with Norman, then head along to Degenerate Towers and I'll ask a few probing questions. And if there's time, we'll see the Wrights before we go home. If we get nowhere, tomorrow, I'll ring Creech and give him a rocket.'

'I need to speak to Ned at the pub,' I said. 'Netta Dawson might need somewhere to stay.'

'Not so sure her coming here is a wonderful idea,' said Lou grimly. 'If we do find anything...'

It struck me that Lou was excellent at detective work, but his understanding of women was, at best, patchy.

'Mrs Dawson will want to collect Spud and take him back to London,' I explained. 'And I think she'll feel she'd like to be close to wherever Maggie is.'

'Ah!' said Lou. 'Here come the worshippers.'

The vicar had emerged from the vestibule, and a slow stream of people was trickling out, shaking his hand.

'Wonderful sermon,' said one man, and another well-spoken woman added, 'Yes, as you said, I do feel strength of purpose is so important. Would you care to come for a sherry before lunch, Vicar?'

'That's her, I think,' whispered Lou, and I turned to see a large, middle-aged woman in high-heeled shoes and a fur coat. She wore three strands of what Annie called 'gobstopper pearls', and a hat trimmed with an entire parrot's wing. I thought how much Ethel would like it.

'Thank you very much, Lady Brackenfield,' said the vicar, confirming Lou's guess, 'I'd be delighted, I shall cycle up at noon if I may,' and she nodded, graciously.

'Watch out for the soldiers,' she added. 'Some of them like to take a turn in the grounds on Sundays.'

'Soldiers?' I mouthed at Lou, puzzled.

'Convalescing,' he muttered.

Lady Brackenfield was now striding down the worn flagstone path, lifting a hand to various people, nodding at others. She was like a galleon, pennants fluttering in the breeze.

Lou stepped forward, Marple at his side.

'Lady Brackenfield?'

'Yes?' she said imperiously.

'Detective Inspector Louis Brennan.' His voice was much posher than usual. 'Manchester City Police. I'm afraid I need your help on a matter of great importance.'

'Good Lord,' she said. 'Do you really? Is it the cows again? They *will* escape from the top field, and I simply cannot persuade the wretched girl to close the gates.'

I stifled a smile.

'No, it's about the missing girl from Wrights' Farm,' he said. 'We have reason to believe she may have come to harm, and we need your help in getting up a search party amongst the villagers.'

'Oh, I see,' she said doubtfully. 'Dreadful. But the vicar's coming for lunch and I'm not sure...'

'Your Ladyship,' said Lou. 'Maggie Dawson is fourteen. And she may have been a victim of something unspeakable. I'm afraid it must be now.'

'I see,' she said again. 'I do understand, yes.'

She turned to the path, where knots of people were milling and chatting, respectfully waiting for her to give the signal that they could politely leave.

'Men of Birchcroft!' she bellowed, and every person in the vicinity spun round and stood to attention.

'Your help is required!' she went on. 'A young girl has gone missing, and the police now believe she may have come to harm. We are forming a search party. Please present yourselves at the church hall in two hours' time, dressed in stout boots for walking, with sticks if you have them, and the Detective Inspector will give you further instructions. Thank you.'

She turned to Lou.

'There,' she said. 'That should do it.'

Behind her came a rabble of shocked voices – 'police' and 'missing' and 'but the Sunday roast' floated out. I saw the Wrights stepping from the porch – they were immediately surrounded by villagers shouting questions, like a press huddle at a disaster.

'I'd think it best if you were to follow me up to Brackenfield,' Lady Brackenfield said, bending to pat Marple's head with a kid-gloved hand. 'Then perhaps you can explain everything in detail, over a civilised sherry.'

I had never seen anywhere quite so impressive. Brackenfield was a great red-brick pile at the end of a long, straight drive. It reminded me of Manderley in the film of *Rebecca*, although there were no servants standing on the steps to welcome us.

'Where on earth do I park?' Lou wondered, braking beside a trickling fountain whose jets of water spouted unnervingly from cherubic stone mouths. As he spoke, a uniformed valet with a noticeable limp appeared and murmured, 'If you'll allow me, sir.'

Lou handed over the car with Marple still in the back, to the valet's obvious discomfort. I heard him whisper a nervous 'Good lad,' as he climbed in.

A butler – Mr Magellan, I assumed – swung open the oak door and ushered us into a wide, square hall with a ceiling like a wedding cake. There was so much plaster moulding, swags and wreaths and – was that a rearing sea serpent? – I was afraid the whole thing would come crashing down on our heads.

The walls were half-panelled in oak, and grave, ancestral portraits loomed from above, while the enormous stone fireplace stood empty. A carved banister swept up from the centre, crimson-carpeted stairs presumably leading to locked chambers where imprisoned maidens screamed all night.

Lou and I exchanged a glance expressing an eloquent 'blimey', as the butler led us to the drawing room. Threadbare tapestries of hunting scenes in faded silks covered the walls, and a pair of Victorian couches that looked as though various Brontës had died on them faced one another across the acres of priceless Persian rug. Lady Brackenfield, now hatless and with two Pomeranian dogs flanking her calves, greeted us.

'Do sit,' she said, adding, 'down you get, Pyramus,' and sweeping another surprised dog off the couch. I felt grateful that Marple had been left in the car for once, 'to keep an eye on things,' as Lou put it.

'Sherry please, Magellan,' she said to the butler.

'One's servants are almost all off fighting, I'm afraid,' she said, turning back to us. 'The east wing is entirely overflowing with convalescing soldiers, and of course, one has explained time and again that the lake is out of bounds, but they seem constantly to be drawn down there like buffalo to the watering hole, puffing away on those ghastly little pipes they all favour. Do you know, I found one of them in the library the other day, sitting looking at a hand-illustrated encyclopaedia of entomology that belonged to my grandfather!'

'I suppose he was looking for something to read,' observed Lou mildly.

'Indeed, but surely that class has cheap crime novels to entertain them,' she said. I tried not to glare.

'Now – get off, Thisbe! – what's all this about the missing girl?'

I let Lou explain, and when he reached the part about Joyce, Lady Brackenfield shuddered theatrically.

'That appalling little den of vice,' she said. 'One doesn't like to recount gossip, but goodness me, things do reach one from the servants. I don't doubt her death was an accident,' she added, 'but to hear some of the village talk...'

'What are they saying?' Lou asked.

'Oh heavens, I don't wish to pass on unsubstantiated rumour,' she said.

Lou smiled approvingly at her and she twinkled back.

'But I suppose as you're with the police... well, they're claiming she was killed because of what she'd been saying about the war. You know' – she looked disgusted – 'this *pacifism* idea. They're all so-called Marxists and communists up there, they'd have the likes of you and me lined up and shot, I don't doubt, given half a chance.'

'Has anyone in particular been saying this?' Lou asked, taking a sherry from Magellan, who was holding out a wobbling tray with an arm crooked painfully behind his back. The rules of the aristocracy struck me as entirely mad.

'Oh well, one struggles to remember quite who said what,' demurred Lady Brackenfield, sipping from her tiny glass. 'But I do recall Bessie saying something about the landlord at the public house telling her that Norman had been seen wandering about up near Netherwood lately. He's an odd fish.'

'But we found Joyce up on the hill,' I interrupted. 'Surely that doesn't mean he did anything?'

'I am not suggesting for a moment that it does,' she said haughtily. 'I am merely reporting to the Detective Inspector what I have heard, as he requested. There was also some trouble at the church hall when some of the village families attended one of her *talks*. They were highly insulted, and quite rightly so. As for the last one she gave...'

The one Maggie had attended, the night she disappeared. Lou obviously shared my interest because he said, 'Delicious sherry. I'd be very grateful if you could tell us anything you recall about that evening, Lady Brackenfield.'

I was going to tease him later mercilessly about his smarming. But now, I listened as she glanced about, gathered a reluctant Thisbe onto her lap, and said, in hushed tones, 'Well... I wasn't there, of course, but I believe several of the soldiers here attended, perhaps to argue with her points afterwards. Or perhaps some agreed, I've no idea. Apparently, I hear those village types who did attend largely went to try and stop her speaking. They felt her stance to be an insult to their efforts on the home front, and someone shouted' – she drew a shocked breath, and whispered – '"you're no better than Hitler."

'That was when Harold stepped in – Harold Walker, do you know him? Darling little man.' Lou caught my eye and I turned my snort of laughter into a sneeze.

'He brought a halt to proceedings and told Miss Reid she was no longer welcome in the village, and that she was causing real trouble at a time when we should all be pulling together. Apparently, she stormed off, but a young girl ran after her, and I don't know if this is true, but...'

I waited, intent on her next words.

'I heard,' she went on, 'that they had an argument – shouting in the street, I believe, can you imagine? – and one of the soldiers said he saw the girl hand Joyce a white feather.'

In the Great War, some girls had handed white feathers to men they deemed 'cowards' – often simply because they weren't away fighting. I saw Lou wince at Lady Brackenfield's words, and I remembered the injury which had stopped him joining this war.

'I believe that was Maggie Dawson,' said Lou. 'If we may, we'd like to speak to the soldier who witnessed this exchange.'

'Oh!' she exclaimed. 'Goodness. Well, as I told you, it's only idle gossip, but I suppose...' She pulled a bell cord by the door.

When a pink-faced maid appeared, Lady Brackenfield explained, adding, 'Could you perhaps find out which soldier was in attendance?'

'Certainly, Lady Brackenfield,' she said, and while we

waited, we made awkward small talk about the estate's glasshouses.

'All entirely given over to muddy onions and sprouts now,' she said crossly. 'My glorious orange trees, all gone. I insisted on keeping one glasshouse for flowers, though. Or however would we decorate the rooms?'

I followed her glance, and noticed a vast arrangement of unseasonal blooms on a table in the window. *Lilies.*

'Do you ever let people buy the flowers?' I asked.

She looked at me. 'I believe Mr Miller occasionally sells some to those who require a bouquet, yes. All proceeds go to the war effort, of course.'

'Do you know if anyone from Athena House might have...'

I was interrupted by Magellan clearing his throat.

'Your Ladyship, may I introduce Private Carr,' he said, and a young man came in. For some reason I had expected to see him in uniform, but he was wearing a white shirt and tweed slacks, and his left arm was in a sling.

'Have a seat,' said Lou, and Lady Brackenfield raised an eyebrow as Magellan efficiently lifted one of the dogs from an armchair and gave the cushion a brisk brush.

'Now, Private Carr,' said Lou, 'could you tell me exactly what you saw on the night of the talk, after Miss Reid had left the Hall?'

'Of course, sir,' he said. His accent wasn't local – from the Borders, perhaps. It had a lovely sing-song quality.

'Some of the other fellows had left early, in disgust, you might say,' he began. 'But Private Dodds and I stayed till the end, we wanted to ask questions – not to cause trouble, just to explain our own position on the matter to her – and then we were all chucked out, and we saw her outside.'

'Can you describe the girl to whom she was speaking?'

'Well.' He puffed out his cheeks. 'It was the blackout, you know, so I only had my wee torch. But I could see she was a tiny thing. Dark hair, I'd say no older than fourteen, fifteen. She was screaming blue murder.'

'What was she saying? Can you remember?'

He gazed into the distance. 'They were arguing, and I heard her shout something about her old man. Something like "how dare you say my dad died for nothing?" I remember she definitely said "how dare you" because it seemed funny coming from such a young kid to a grown woman.'

'What did Miss Reid do?'

'She tried to take her arm, then the girl pulled a feather – I think – out of her coat pocket and sort of shoved it at her and Miss Reid shouted to someone – Serena? Seraphina? An unusual name, anyway, and this other woman came hurrying round the corner to see if she was all right and they bugg— scuttled off. The girl ran off, too, in the other direction, and Private Dodds and me walked back up here to Back in Blighty Hall – I mean, Brackenfield Hall,' he added, embarrassed. Lou smiled at him.

'Thank you very much, Private Carr,' he said. 'You've been a great help.'

On the way back down the drive, I saw the glasshouses shimmering in the distance.

'Do you think Mr Miller might be at work on a Sunday?' I asked Lou.

'Unlikely,' he said. 'Besides, Marple could do with a walk.'

'I need to ask him something,' I said. 'I bet he'll be at home now after church. Could we quickly drive round to the kitchen gardens? I saw a cottage out of the window, I'm sure that's where he lives.'

'I doubt the man in charge of brassicas holds the key to this mystery,' said Lou irritably.

'He might do,' I said. 'Look, I'll explain afterwards, but please can we just...'

'Fine,' he said, and performed a brisk turn, roaring back up the drive. 'But you'd better have good reason, York. And you owe Marple a thorough scratching.'

Lou parked near the duck pond that faced the kitchen garden, and got out for a cigarette and a look at the geese. I approached the red-brick cottage – which looked more like a well-appointed, gabled house, used as I was to our tiny flat – and knocked on its smart, green door. To my surprise, Rita opened it.

'Edie!'

'Rita! Whatever are you doing here?'

She flushed, and I noticed she was wearing a smart striped frock and red lipstick.

'I'm just visiting Bert – I mean, Mr Miller– he's done a roast chicken and he very kindly offered...'

'Who is it, dear?' called a voice, and Rita stood back, as the man I'd seen her with in the pub appeared in the hall behind her.

'I'm so sorry to interrupt your Sunday dinner,' I said. 'I have one very quick question and I'll leave you to it.'

He looked puzzled. 'I'll do my best.'

'Mr Miller, did anyone from Athena House buy flowers from you just before Valentine's Day? Would you happen to remember?'

'Now,' he said. 'I did sell a few bunches around then, as I recall. Folks like to be a bit romantic, don't they? With all the lads away, not so many as in the past, though a few of the young soldiers up here did ask me...'

'Perhaps lilies?' I added, rather desperately. I could see Lou's cigarette smoke rising beyond the garden wall, and almost feel his simmering irritation.

'Ah! Now, it's funny you should say that,' Mr Miller said.

'Somebody did request them. I said "That's a strange choice for a young lady, sir. You'd want orange blossom, or maybe something trailing." Lilies are a bit stiff for my taste, but Lady B. likes them.'

'Do you remember who it was?' I held my breath.

'I do, now you've reminded me,' he said. 'And he was most insistent about it being just lilies. He said it was very important. It was that Mr Glenn, the little, nervy one.' He snapped his fingers. 'That's it. Theodore Glenn.'

CHAPTER THIRTEEN

We drove quickly to Athena House, Lou cursing the potholes and ditches that pocked the long lane.

'They'll reveal more to you,' he said, as we approached the farmhouse. 'They sense the wafting bohemian within that buttoned-up exterior, York.'

'Don't be ridiculous.'

'Well, they're more likely to talk to a sympathetic woman than a policeman asking questions,' observed Lou. 'So I'll let them know why this matters, in no uncertain terms, then you take over.'

I felt rather nervous about what sort of welcome we'd get as, once again, I crossed the untidy yard, this time with Lou beside me.

'I'll be jiggered,' he breathed, looking at the cluttered porch. 'Are they going on a voyage to the South Seas? Gathering all their worldly goods before setting sail?'

I smiled. 'Wait till you see inside.'

I pushed the door and called, 'Hullo?'

The now-familiar scent of linseed oil, turps and damp greeted us.

'Hullo?' came a shriek from upstairs. 'Let me get my dressing gown on... Coming!'

Nora appeared wrapped in a fringed kimono, breathless and with her long red hair tangled like tide-tossed seaweed.

'Oh, Edie, hullo!' she said, then as her eyes fell on Lou, 'Is this your young man?'

'No,' Lou and I said simultaneously.

'Detective Inspector Brennan,' he said, holding his hand out to shake hers, but she shrank against the banister, gazing at me as if I'd ordered her execution.

'Why have you brought the police here?' she asked me, her voice shaking.

'He's a friend, Nora,' I said, 'and it's not about Joyce – this is about Maggie.'

'Maggie ran away, though,' she said.

'That looks less likely now a few more facts have emerged,' said Lou. 'There's a search party going out at two. I just need to ask you all a few questions. Could you call the others?'

'I suppose so,' said Nora, who now seemed to have recovered from her fright. 'I'll get dressed, hold on a mo.'

She ran back upstairs, shouting to Theo and Sabrina.

'We'll be in the living room,' I called, and led Lou through to the main area, where he glanced around once, shook his head wearily and subsided into an armchair.

Gradually, they trickled in. Jean-Luc first, followed by Nora, then Sabrina, Joan, Theo and, lastly, Aubrey, audibly grumbling.

'I was in flow,' I heard him saying. 'I cannot fathom why people assume one can simply switch on and off like a wireless, any more than a tumbling brook in spate may be turned off like a tap... Oh, hullo, Edie. Nora, dear, could you make us some tea?' he asked, but she bristled.

'It's always me,' she said. 'Perhaps somebody else can make it for a change.'

'I 'ave some brandy?' offered Jean-Luc, but I'd already had Lady Brackenfield's sherry, and didn't feel I wanted to get roaring drunk at Sunday lunchtime.

'Really, don't bother on our account,' said Lou. 'We shan't take much of your afternoon. Or morning,' he added, glancing at Nora, who had dressed hastily in a blue siren suit and remained barefooted. 'But I would like to know how much time Maggie spent here before her disappearance.'

'Barely any,' said Sabrina, just as Theo said, 'She came up a few times.'

'Well, not many,' Sabrina added, and Aubrey said, 'I don't think I ever met the girl.'

I opened my mouth, about to challenge him, but Joan got there first.

'You did,' she said. 'You showed her round your studio the first time Joyce invited her.'

He shrugged, as if showing young women his masterpieces was all part of his calling.

'The first time?' Lou said. 'How many times would you say she visited?'

They glanced at each other. It was clear that they had all lied about not knowing Maggie.

'Why didn't you say you knew her to begin with?' I asked. I tried not to sound accusing.

Nora groaned. 'We didn't want anyone to think we were involved in her running away. The villagers already hate us, and...' She blinked back tears.

'Nora's right,' said Sabrina. 'With Joyce's death, it would have brought us even more unwanted attention, nasty letters... We all knew we had nothing to do with it, so we agreed to fib a bit. I realise now it was rather shabby of us.'

That was one way of putting it, I thought.

'So how well did you really know her?' Lou asked, his face impassive.

'Well, she mainly joined us on our walks,' offered Joan.

'I believe you took her on a walk back in January?' I said to Aubrey.

He shrugged and shook his head, as though I was asking him to recall something that had happened many years ago. 'Perhaps,' he said, unhelpfully.

'She came a few times at the weekends, but of course, it was winter so sometimes only Joyce would go,' said Nora.

'Joyce loved the silver rain,' said Jean-Luc poetically. 'And the howling winds. They were her always companions.'

'And did Maggie go with Joyce on those occasions?' Lou asked, pointedly ignoring him.

'I believe she sometimes did,' put in Theo. I found myself glancing at him more than the others. I now felt certain it was he who had sent Ethel the lilies – a thoroughly nasty and rather cowardly warning – but why?

'Now and again,' agreed Sabrina, who was standing by the door, smoking a cigarette. 'But she didn't often come back here, as I think Mrs Wright was rather strict. She gave Maggie Saturday mornings off, but then she was expected to do her jobs round the farm.'

I looked at Lou. A Saturday morning was when we had found Joyce – but of course, I realised, that was days after Maggie had disappeared.

'Do you remember the last time you saw her?' Lou asked Sabrina.

'Yes,' she said quietly. 'It was the night of Joyce's last talk. I didn't hear all that was said, but Maggie's father had been killed, and she was very angry with Joyce. I saw her running off.'

'Why was she angry? What had Joyce said?' Lou asked.

Joan stepped in. 'She went a bit further than she usually did,' she said. 'She was frustrated by the villagers, what she saw as their "bovine willingness to obey their masters and go unquestioningly to war..."'

'Did she think we should let Hitler invade?' asked Lou icily.

'Well, no, but like all of us, she felt that peace talks would be—'

'You can't talk to a lunatic!' Lou snapped. 'For God's sake, he's not going to shake hands and agree to back down just because we ask him nicely, can't you see that? Our entire country hovers on the brink of invasion, and you people...'

'Lou,' I hissed.

He drew a sharp breath through his nose, and closed his eyes for a moment. 'Anyway,' he said, 'tell me what Joyce said that night, as clearly as you can remember.'

Joan spoke up. 'That evening, I'd said I wasn't going – I'd been to so many of her talks, and I just felt she was fighting a losing battle – sorry for the choice of words,' she said, 'but you know what I mean. People here simply weren't interested. I said she should go back to Manchester, or even London, where there were more people who might agree, but talking to Birchcroft was a waste of time – people would only come to cause trouble.'

'Had that happened before?'

'Yes,' said Joan. 'People shouting rude things at her, jostling us as we left – it was horrid, actually, but we felt we had to go, Joyce had a bit of a three-line whip on it.'

'Did you go?' I asked.

'I did in the end, but I said it would be the last time.' Joan sighed. 'I felt her insistence was becoming quite wilful – she knew people hated her and what she stood for, but she just kept at it.'

'She was very brave,' said Aubrey admonishingly.

'Brave or bull-headed,' said Lou. 'Go on.'

'Well,' Joan said, 'she was fired up that night – she'd been reading about the African invasion, and she felt the war's tentacles were reaching across the whole world. She said "It'll be America soon." Aubrey and Theo disagreed, but she was certain of it. So when she started speaking, instead of talking about the effects of war on the victims – our families and friends – as she usually did, she said, "Our enemies are people too. Those towns and cities, homes and hospitals we bomb so indiscriminately – they contain people just like us, with the same hopes and dreams..."'

'I'm sure they do,' said Lou grimly. 'Go on.'

'She said that by participating in what she called "the war machine", we all had blood on our hands. And then she said that anyone fighting for victory in Europe is just as much to blame as those who would seek to conquer us.'

Even I gaped at that.

'I'm only telling you what she said,' Joan went on, seeing my face.

'The last thing she said was that we venerate our own soldiers and sailors and pilots, but they're murderers, too, and just as culpable as the so-called enemy. That was when the trouble broke out and Harold Walker called a halt.'

'I'm not bloody surprised,' said Lou.

'She did perhaps go a bit too far on that occasion,' murmured Theo. 'One tried to have a word, but by golly, she was so certain of herself.'

'Well, now it's clear why Maggie was so upset,' said Lou. 'Joyce had just publicly called her father, killed serving his country, a murderer.'

The group fell silent.

'And none of you heard from her after that?'

Heads shook.

'Nobody thought to look in on her, see if she was all right? A child, far from home, bereaved and maltreated? No?'

'I now have regret of this, oui,' murmured Jean-Luc.

'Well yes, I'm sure we all do, but Maggie was Joyce's project, really,' said Nora.

'Project?' I said.

'Oh, you know. I think she hoped Maggie would blossom

under her wing, explore her literary side – I remember her saying, "Maggie has so much potential, it's a crime to keep her locked up with those awful people."'

'What did Joyce do when Maggie ran off?' I asked Sabrina.

She looked at her nails and stubbed out her cigarette in a heavy silver ashtray. Another thing that had belonged to Joyce. It occurred to me what parasites they had all been, and I realised that for all her bold confidence, Joyce might have truly feared being alone.

'She was quite hurt, I think,' Sabrina said.

'Hurt?'

'Well yes, she had hopes for Maggie, and Joyce thought she was being rather silly.'

'Yes, thoroughly silly not to want your heroic dead father publicly traduced,' muttered Lou.

'Did Joyce try to contact her after that?' I asked Sabrina.

'Not as far as I know.'

Lou rallied. 'Have any of you seen this Norman bloke hanging about round Netherwood?'

'Round Athena House?' said Theo, round-eyed. 'Good Lord, no. Why do you ask?'

'Somebody mentioned it.'

'Who?'

'I'm not at liberty to say,' said Lou irritably. 'Have you seen him?'

'No,' said Theo and Sabrina, to general agreement.

'He doesn't come up here,' said Joan. 'He keeps to himself. He's got shell shock, he's quite mad.'

'Not everybody with shell shock is mad,' said Theo testily.

'I didn't mean you.' Joan sounded weary. I didn't blame her.

'Could Norman have heard about what Joyce said?' I asked.

'Don't see how,' said Aubrey. 'Besides, even if he had, he'd probably have agreed with her.'

Lou glanced at me, a signal to move. We stood up, and I

thanked them. As we were leaving, Sabrina beckoned me back into the room, where the others were chatting and Jean-Luc was leaning against the wall, lighting a cigarette.

'I say,' she said rather loudly, 'sorry to ask, but is your DI Brennan taken? Because he's awfully handsome, and I wondered...'

'No,' I said shortly. I felt annoyed, I supposed because she had apparently been unmoved by Maggie's vanishing, but was perfectly happy to steam in on a visiting detective inspector.

'He's not available. His fiancée died, and since then...'

Since then, what? I realised I didn't know. I had never asked him if he 'saw' girls. He had never mentioned anyone. If anything, he seemed married to his job, but I didn't like the idea of pretty, flighty Sabrina getting her claws in.

'Since then it's just him and his dog,' I finished.

'Oh, I love dogs,' she said, following me into the hall. 'I grew up with King Charles spaniels, perhaps I could...' The front door was open, and we could see Lou, opening the car door for Marple to relieve himself again. He leapt out and barked violently at a passing chicken, booming echoes vibrating through the yard. Sabrina's chirping voice died away.

'He's quite a large dog, isn't he?' she said eventually.

'Yes,' I said firmly. 'Very.'

People were already gathering at the church hall when we arrived. Lou had finally stopped ranting about the selfish, venal idiots of Athena House and seemed relieved to speak to some ordinary people. He attached Marple's lead to his collar, and was immediately accosted by Harold Walker.

'Fine dog you have there, Detective Inspector.'

'Yes, he is,' said Lou. 'I'm hoping he'll help us find some trace of Maggie.' He surveyed the growing crowd. More people were arriving carrying walking sticks, some with dogs, others with torches. I noticed that out of the city, few bothered with gas masks. The search for Maggie felt very real now, and I thought with dread of what we might discover. Mrs Dawson hadn't yet arrived in Birchcroft, and I was grateful.

Rita appeared, with Mr Miller. She had changed into voluminous slacks and laced boots and was talking to Ned, the pub landlord. She saw me and waved violently, as if we were at a funfair. Nobody from Athena House was here, though Joan had suggested they'd join us 'after lunch', and the vicar was presumably still sawing his way through Lady Brackenfield's Sunday roast. I was starving. I couldn't see the Wrights, either, but as I scanned the crowd, I spotted a small figure darting through knots of people.

'Spud!' I called, and he hurried over, holding a garden hoe and a hessian sack.

'Edie!' he said. 'I'm relieved to see you, I must say. I've been beside myself with worry.'

'I've got good news for you,' I said. 'Your mum's arriving soon and she's taking you back with her.'

'Mum! How do you know?'

'She wrote to me,' I said.

His pinched little face softened as though the sun had burst through a bank of cloud.

'Does she know where Maggie is?'

'I'm afraid not.' I indicated the crowd. 'But we're all going to try and find out.'

'I'm very worried that she's dead,' said Spud.

Lou leaned down to him.

'I'm Detective Inspector Brennan,' he said. Spud looked bedazzled.

'I don't want you to worry about that,' Lou went on. 'The police are in charge now, and I promise we'll do all we can to find your sister.'

'But if she...'

'No ifs, no buts, no sugared nuts,' said Lou. 'Trust in Marple. He'll find her if anyone can.'

Spud reached out tentatively and scratched Marple's quivering nose.

'I expect that's true,' Spud said. 'He looks a very clever dog.'

'Spud, why have you got a hoe and a sack?' I added.

'In case I find clues and need to dig,' he said, as though it was obvious. Tears filled my eyes and I turned my head away. I hoped, so desperately, that he wouldn't.

It was now well after two, and the stream of people arriving had died to a trickle. Lou mounted the steps of the hall and addressed the milling crowd.

'Thank you all for coming,' he shouted. 'I'd like you to fan out – those to my left, take the woods behind the campsite, those to my right, take the hill behind the village. Those in front of me, follow the stream up, which should take you past Nether Brow, and please study the ground and any tree branches as you walk for clothing or any signs that somebody has passed that way,' he went on. The crowd was rapt.

'Every group must have an experienced walker leading, so please nominate yourselves if you know the area well, and if you do find anything, each leader will get a silver police whistle.' He produced several from his coat pocket and held them up. 'Make sure you blow it as hard as you can, and in case I don't hear it, we'll have a gathering point outside the pub, where you can meet me at four o' clock, and lead me to the spot. Is everyone clear?'

There was general assent; people were eager to get started, straining like greyhounds in their traps.

'If you do find anything,' Lou added, 'leave it exactly where it is. Do not attempt to move it.'

'Even if it's a body?' shouted one man in a flat cap.

Lou glared, and I saw Spud close his eyes.

'*Especially* if it is,' Lou said. 'But we very much hope it won't be. Good luck, stay with your friends, and take good care.'

He handed out whistles, and then he produced the diary from his pocket and held it out to Marple.

'Hey!' said Spud. 'That's Maggie's...'

'Shh,' said Lou. 'Secret police business.' Spud nodded solemnly, before trudging off after Rita, clutching his garden hoe.

As Marple huffed at the little book, rubbery nostrils flaring, I spotted a man on a bicycle, pedalling hard up the road. I assumed it was another helper, but as he approached, he shouted, 'Oi!' and I realised with horror that it was Constable Creech.

He leapt from the saddle while the bike was still moving, and ran several wavering steps, somewhat undermining his rage.

'What's going on?' he bellowed. 'You can't just come here, organising searches on my patch!'

'I think you'll find I can,' said Lou. He strolled down the path. 'Detective Inspector Brennan, with dispensation from the district commissioner to look into the case of a missing child in the North Lancashire area. Apparently, you've done nothing about finding her.'

'She went back to London!' Creech spat. 'That's what I was told.'

'Told,' said Lou. 'That's good police work, is it, in your eyes? Being *told* things? I suppose if a bloke in a stripy jumper with a bag marked SWAG *tells* you he isn't a burglar, you wish him well and let him on his way, do you?'

Creech was pale with rage and fright.

'Look, Detective Inspector,' he said, 'I appreciate that you have a job to do...'

'As do you, Constable,' said Lou. 'Hard though that may be to grasp. I suggest you join the men heading up to Nether Brow, and get on with it.'

He pointed at their retreating backs, and Creech reluctantly turned to follow.

'Trickiest route,' Lou said to me, with satisfaction.

'Right. Come on, Marple, Edie.' I noticed I came second on the list.

'Where are we going?'

'To the valley where they found Maggie's hat,' he said. 'With a quick detour to see Norman on the way.'

I was glad it wasn't raining. There was a chill in the air, but it had been dry for the past few days, and for once, I wasn't sliding on mud as we approached the campsite.

'Poor chap,' Lou remarked, as Norman's little tent came into view.

'Not if he killed her,' I said, and he gave me a look.

'Open mind, please, York,' he said. 'First rule of detective work. And journalism, not that you'd know it sometimes.'

I didn't reply to that. We trudged over the field, Marple straining on his lead. Lou called out for Norman.

There was silence. 'He might be afraid,' I whispered, as though Norman were a woodland creature.

Lou approached the tent, and called again. 'Detective Inspector Brennan from Manchester City Police. I need to speak to you, can you come out please, sir?'

There was no sound but the chill breeze across the grass and the flapping of the tent's canvas sides.

'He might be out, fishing or...' I began, but Lou was deftly unknotting the ties and peering inside.

'Edie, come here,' he said. Heart thumping, expecting to see Norman's stiff, curled body, I peered over Lou's shoulder into the tent.

It took me a moment to make sense of it. The cooking pots, the blankets, the little stove, the basin – all Norman's things had disappeared. There was nothing but a patch of dry, yellowed grass where a whole life had been.

'He's gone,' I said blankly.

'Looks like it,' said Lou. Marple whined gently, eager to be off.

'The question we now need to answer,' Lou said, 'is why?'

We began in the valley, tracking the stream as Marple trotted ahead, nose low to the ground. Occasionally, Lou would give him the diary to sniff again, but for the first hour, there was nothing of interest. It was chilly and grey, mist suspended between the trees, and though I scanned constantly for signs of human life, there was very little to see but winter grass and rotting leaves, with distant glimpses of mossy barns with dark slits for windows up on the hills.

'Perhaps she's hiding in one of them,' I suggested.

'Living on what? Mice?' asked Lou. 'She's not a sniper in the jungle, she's a child from the city. She wouldn't have a clue how to survive.'

I sighed. 'Then she must be dead,' I said. 'She can't have vanished into thin air.'

As I spoke, Marple lunged towards a copse of trees, sniffing urgently. He strained on his lead and pulled Lou towards it, away from the stream.

'I think he's found the scent,' Lou said, as I hurried after them. 'Though it could be an otter, I suppose – he's never smelled one of those before.'

Marple was hurrying now, zigzagging up the side of the valley, as we panted after him. We climbed fast for a good twenty minutes, scrambling and slipping over stones, through a small, mossy oak wood, and out the other side.

'If this turns out to be some form of wildlife tracking, I'll be having words,' said Lou, reaching out a hand to yank me over a rockfall.

'Did I ever mention how much I like the city?' I asked, gasping for breath. 'Everything's flat.'

'Everything's flattened, more like,' said Lou. 'They've done almost nothing about rehoming people so far. It's appalling, they're all still crammed into bunk beds in every spare nook and cranny.'

I was about to reply when Marple leapt up a little incline, skidded to a halt and barked, just once. It echoed through the valley like a shot from a cannon.

I scrambled up after Lou, heart racing from both exertion and fear, but there was no small body lying before us. Instead, Marple was standing in front of a high barbed-wire fence, which towered a good three feet over Lou's head. It stretched into the distance with no visible point of entry, then disappeared into the trees.

Several feet along the wire, a sign read:

DANGER
KEEP OUT
PRIVATE PROPERTY OF THE AIR MINISTRY

I stared hopelessly at the tangled metal.

'Well, that's it,' I said. 'We may as well go home.'

Lou was scanning the fence, presumably looking for a weak link. I was about to say, 'I'm not risking my life breaking into a firing range,' when he said, 'Look at this.'

He was pointing to the base of the fence, where a post had been dug deeply into the ground. Half-hidden in the grass, and just visible in the falling light, was a small thread of bottle-green wool.

'Marple,' said Lou. 'You clever boy.'

Marple panted in a gratified fashion as Lou scratched his ears.

'It's from Maggie's coat,' he said. 'It must be.'

He dropped to his knees and felt along the bottom of the fence.

'Look, it's sagging here,' he said, pointing to a spot where the wire was very slightly less taut. 'This is where she must have climbed in.'

Beyond the fence was a dense scrub of bushes which made it impossible to see into the compound. Lou peered through, with the advantage of height.

'I can see something white,' he said. 'It seems to have some kind of metal legs – it's enormous. It could be a water tower.'

I thought of Pat, telling me what Billy had discovered.

'Lou,' I said, 'I think I know what this is.'

'I'd forgotten you were a decorated pilot. Do tell.'

'I think it's a decoy city,' I said. 'They build them in remote places, and set fire to them when there's a raid. So that...'

'... the bombers think it's a real city and they don't need to bother,' said Lou. 'How on earth did you know about this?'

I ignored his question. 'Maggie climbed into Air Ministry property. Why would she do anything so demented?' I was feeling both frustrated and afraid. 'She could very easily have been shot.'

'Well, she ran away at night,' Lou said, 'so it's likely she didn't see the sign. Perhaps she assumed this fence was to keep animals in or out.'

'It's the height of a house!'

'She's not a country girl,' said Lou. 'Unlike you, with your vast rural knowledge. Look, don't you see, Edie – if she came all the way up here, it means she almost certainly came of her own accord. It looks as though she really was running away, rather than anyone harming her.'

'But it could be fenced off for miles,' I said. I thought of leaping flames, shouting men. 'And perhaps she did get hurt.'

Lou looked at his watch.

'We need to get back down before it gets dark,' he said. 'If Maggie is in there, she could be anywhere. We'll need permission to search properly.'

We were a few minutes late to the rendezvous outside the pub. I was scratched, exhausted, and a curious mixture of relieved and worried. Once everyone had returned, reporting nothing but a courting couple discovered in a barn – 'Gave 'em a right turn!' shouted one lad, and several people guffawed – Lou thanked them and promised to let them know of any developments. Creech was at the back, dusting down his bicycle clips and I heard him say, 'Of course, I shall be continuing to pursue the case in Detective Inspector Brennan's absence.'

As people began to disperse, Lou beckoned to Harold Walker, who came bustling over.

'A waste of time, I'm afraid, sir...' he began.

'Not at all,' said Lou. 'In fact, we've found something very interesting. Could you fetch the Home Guard captain and sergeant, please? We need to speak urgently.'

'Sir. Of course, of course.' Walker was rose-pink with the excitement of a sudden development.

There was no sign of anyone from Athena House. Perhaps they had gone straight back home, I thought. Or more likely, their fragile togetherness and optimism destroyed, they hadn't come at all.

'Edie,' said Lou, 'can you ask Ned to open up and get Marple some water? I need to speak to these men in private.'

'What?' I was outraged. 'Why?'

'Because it very likely comes under the Official Secrets Act,

1911, Section One,' said Lou, 'and if they do know anything, they're hardly going to tell a journalist.'

'But I could just...'

'No,' he said. 'Sorry, York. Nothing to be done. And Marple's thirsty.'

Thwarted and irritated, I found Ned and explained.

'Should be all right,' he said. 'But don't let that lot see me opening the saloon door on a Sunday.'

He found a large earthenware bowl and filled it for Marple, who gulped the cold water down like celestial nectar, while I arranged Mrs Dawson's accommodation for the following day.

'I'll give her me best room,' Ned promised. 'Not far from the bathroom, and it contains the brass bed me Auntie Pearl died in. Very comfortable. She said she could hear the angels singing just before she passed on. You look like you could do with a drink yourself,' he added. 'Little tot, on the house?'

'Go on, then,' I said, sinking onto a stool. 'Thanks.'

He pushed the brandy over to me.

'Ned,' I said, as he packed his pipe with tobacco, 'do you know where Norman's gone?'

CHAPTER FOURTEEN

By the time Lou came to retrieve me and Marple, who was lying on the flagstones, tail thumping gently, I had extracted all Ned knew. I thanked him, and saw with surprise that it was already night outside. Everyone had gone home, and blackout curtains and blinds were drawn, plunging the village into a disconcerting darkness.

'I've got something to tell you,' I began, just as he said, 'Do you want to hear what I've found out?'

'You first,' we both said, and Lou sighed.

'Stop talking over me, and I'll tell you,' he said. I mimed buttoning my lip.

'I spoke to the Home Guard captain, Robert Potter, and David Bale, his sergeant,' he said. 'They confirmed your idea about the Air Ministry place, but nobody's allowed to know, so if I see one single word about this in the blasted *Chronicle*, I'll have you hung for treason,' he said, not entirely joking.

'As if I'd put that in the paper!' I said indignantly. 'I might as well write to Hitler.'

'Well, indeed,' said Lou. 'And the strangest thing, they told me, is that they were fire-watching from the hill one night recently – at some point during the last week – and Potter swore he saw a small ground fire in that area, at around one in the morning. He said it was extinguished very quickly, but he's quite certain.'

'Do you think it was Maggie?'

He nodded.

'But it sounds terribly dangerous!' I said. 'Raging fires and soldiers creeping about at night...'

'Yes,' agreed Lou. 'Very. We need to find her – but as it's restricted government property, I'm going to have to get special permission to search the area.'

'Can't the Home Guard help?'

'Not without orders.'

'Oh, for heaven's sake,' I said. 'Her mother's coming tomorrow, what's she going to think?'

'Look,' said Lou, 'I've been thinking about it and I reckon I can justify a couple of days here. There's clearly something to investigate, between Joyce's death and Maggie's disappearance, and Creech isn't up to the job. I'll need to get direct permission from the chief superintendent to breach the Ministry fence too,' he went on. 'I'll let O'Carroll know first thing, then if they need me, I'll have to drive back. But I agree Maggie's in real danger. Look, York...' He rubbed his nose and looked away. Lou seemed embarrassed – not a state I'd seen him in before. It made me warm to him somewhat.

'Yes?'

'I hate to ask this, but is there a chance you could stay up here for a day or so, too? I need someone I can trust, who's good with people...'

I looked up at him, surprised and touched.

'But seeing as I can't find anyone like that, you'll have to do,' he finished, grinning at my expression.

'I'm due at work tomorrow,' I said. 'I can't just vanish.'

'Supposing I telephone Mr Gorringe and explain that

you're vital to my inquiries?' he asked. 'Your editor may be a stickler, but he's got great respect for the Manchester City Police.'

'Oh... very well then,' I said. 'But where can we stay? Ned only has one room available, and Netta's arriving tomorrow...'

Nor did I fancy sleeping alongside the restless ghost of Auntie Pearl, but Lou didn't need to know that.

'Leave it to me,' he said. 'You stay here with Marple, I'll be back shortly.'

As the door closed behind him, it occurred to me that he might be assuming we could bunk down in Norman's tent. I was still crafting my response to that suggestion when he reappeared, beaming.

'All organised,' he said. 'I think you'll be happy with our accommodation.'

'I am not sleeping in an abandoned canvas tent,' I blurted. 'If you think I'm cramming into a damp little tepee with you, with no chaperone or even blankets, you've another think coming, because I'm not that sort of...'

'Tent?' said Lou. 'Whatever are you talking about, York?'

'I thought Norman's tent...'

He bellowed a laugh. 'I may not be a suave Parisian charmer, my dear, but I can do marginally better than a filthy tent. We're joining the aristocracy, for one night only. I do hope you have a tiara in your handbag.'

Brackenfield Hall was shrouded in darkness. The blackout made the busiest places look abandoned, and as we approached, I somehow expected the looming building to be derelict inside, with peeling wallpaper and dried leaves massing in unswept corners. It was a great relief when Mr Magellan opened the door and ushered us into the entrance hall, where a fire was now springing in the vast grate, and light gleamed on the polished panelling.

'Lady Brackenfield has requested that you join her in the drawing room for drinks before dinner,' he intoned, sweeping us across the hallway.

'My dog...' Lou began. Marple was still in the car.

'Sturridge will ensure the hound is suitably kennelled for the night, with the larger dogs of the estate,' said Magellan implacably. 'They're kept down at the stables, sir.'

Lou nodded, though I could see he was unhappy. Marple normally slept on his bed.

Lady Brackenfield rose to her feet as Magellan announced us.

'Welcome back,' she said. 'I've put you in the Rose room, Miss York, and Detective Inspector, I've given you the Prince Edward room, which overlooks the lake.'

'The *Prince Edward...?*' Lou looked baffled, perhaps partly because Thisbe (or was it Pyramus?) had taken a sudden shine to his trousers.

'Yes.' Lady Brackenfield smiled graciously. 'I believe the prince stayed here briefly in 1893. Of course, that was long before Lord Brackenfield welcomed me as his bride,' she added hastily.

'Your Ladyship, we're so grateful,' I said. I sounded like a grovelling medieval serf, but it couldn't be helped. 'We really can't thank you enough for your kindness.'

'Oh, not at all,' she said, patting another dog who had jumped into her lap. 'It's delightful to have the company of young people.'

It occurred to me that half of Brackenfield Hall was filled with soldiers who were undoubtedly both young and people, but it seemed they were strictly confined to quarters.

'Such a dreadful business,' Lady Brackenfield murmured,

waving her empty glass towards Magellan. She seemed to run on Oloroso sherry.

'Runaway children and dead objectors all over our dear little village. Tell me, Inspector, how do you plan to find the girl?' She pronounced it 'gel'.

'We have some idea of where to search,' said Lou, 'but I'm afraid I'm unable to divulge any details, even to you, Lady Brackenfield.'

She twinkled at him, and I felt quite the gooseberry. The conversation moved on to the problems of finding suitable staff during the war. 'One simply cannot find a decent groom anywhere in the county,' she announced. 'Tell me, do you have similar difficulties over in Manchester?'

Lou smiled. 'The police grooms are very good,' he said. 'But of course, there are fewer now. It's a tricky business – one can't have unkempt horses on duty!'

She laughed, delightedly. 'Goodness, no!' she cried, and I wished devoutly that I was back home with Annie, chatting and listening to the wireless, instead of watching a queasy flirtation develop between Lou and Lady Brackenfield, and trying to think of something intelligent to say about horses.

It was a relief when Magellan ushered us to the dining room, where Lady Brackenfield was seated at the head of a long mahogany table, and Lou and I flanked her on either side. There was another leaping conflagration in the grate – I thought with horror of the coal they must get through – and gold-rimmed crystal and crockery sparkled in the firelight. The only concession to the war was, as Lady Brackenfield sighed, 'No footmen – I'm afraid we must serve ourselves, in these barbaric times.'

She waxed lyrical for a while about the glory of the twenties. 'Oh, the parties, goodness me, they carried on for days! Do you know, I once found my sister Augusta dancing the Black

Bottom down by the lake with Lord Beaverbrook. They'd been going all night, and simply hadn't realised it was breakfast time.'

As Magellan staggered in with a silver tureen of leek and potato soup, however, she turned her hooded blue eyes towards me.

'Forgive me, Miss York,' she said, 'I'm afraid I'm a little vague as to your own role in all of this.'

'I work for the *Chronicle*,' I said. 'My friend Miss Cooper and I discovered Miss Reid's body, and so I...' I faltered. It was very hard to explain that a combination of concern, friendship and pure nosiness had propelled me here.

'Miss York is helping me with my inquiries,' said Lou. 'She has a way with people.'

'Oh, I see,' said Lady Brackenfield. 'How lovely.'

'Your Ladyship, have you ever come across the artists from Athena House?' I asked her. Lou shot me a warning glance, but I ignored him – it was my only chance to find out.

Her soup spoon hovered in her hand.

'Goodness me,' she said. 'I very much doubt it. As I told you earlier, they're considered rather *personae non gratae* up here. Not quite the sort one would welcome to Brackenfield.' She ripped off a piece of her bread roll and tossed it to Pyramus, who caught it with a joyful yap. I thought of Marple, in his lonely kennel.

'Although...' she said, 'I do remember a few months ago, one of them – a Dickensian sort of name, I can't remember... Copperfield? Twist?'

'Fagan?' Lou asked, and she nodded gratefully.

'Yes! Mr Fagan, that's right. He was part of a wartime art exhibition, in the church hall. I went along to open it, as one must in my position. Dreadful, abstract things – give me a nice portrait or a vase of flowers,' she went on. 'I do like a painting that *makes sense*, don't you, Detective Inspector?'

'Of course,' said Lou. I could tell he was impatient for her to get to the point, but I was enjoying the soup too much to help him out.

'Did you speak to him?' Lou asked.

'I did, I believe.' She scattered more bread on the floor, as though she were feeding ducks on the lake, and the little dogs dived to reach it.

'I remember he was with an awfully pretty, terribly young girl. I thought she was his daughter at first. Rather shocking,' she added.

'Was she an artist at Athena House?' I asked.

'I don't think so,' said Lady Brackenfield. 'I seem to remember he introduced her as his "muse", something silly like that. She couldn't have been more than sixteen, if that. Of course, girls are so foolish at that age. I expect she imagined he might marry her. Though what a penniless artist old enough to be her father could offer, I can't imagine.'

Lou and I looked at each other.

'Thank you, Lady Brackenfield,' he said, as Magellan balanced our empty soup plates up an arm trembling with effort. 'You've been very helpful.'

'Oh, well, one tries. It's all so dreadfully *sordid*,' she added crossly. 'These people should be helping us to win the war, not drifting about like nymphs and shepherds all over the hills. The people of Birchcroft don't like it, and frankly, nor do I.'

'I don't think anyone does,' Lou said, as a very young maid appeared clutching a vast platter.

'Pigeon with forcemeat balls and champignons à la crème,' she announced, as if she were listing the bus timetable. I thought it sounded wonderful, and Lou clearly did, too, as once we'd been served by Lady Brackenfield, he didn't speak again for several minutes.

On top of the sherry, I had drunk some wine, which I wasn't used to – the last time had been at The French with Charles Emerson – and I already felt rather drunk.

Lou was talking to Lady Brackenfield about evacuees. 'Most went home after the summer Blitz, of course,' he was saying. 'It's rather odd that Maggie and Johnny stayed on.'

'Oh, I believe the Wrights were willing to keep them, to work on the farm,' she said. 'Lovely fresh air, and plenty of eggs. Who wouldn't prefer that to London? One only goes down to see one's friends during the Season, and perhaps for a show... but really, I far prefer our simple little life in the countryside.'

She forked up another slice of cream-soaked pigeon breast, and her golden wine glowed in the candlelight beneath the ancestral portraits. I decided, for once, to say nothing.

After dinner, Lady Brackenfield excused herself briefly, and Lou turned to me.

'Aubrey Fagan,' he said quietly. 'I believe he knows what's happened to Maggie. I'm beginning to think he's responsible for her disappearance, too.'

'It sounds as though he was obsessed with her,' I agreed. 'And he knows the hills almost as well as Joyce did.'

Lou nodded. 'Tomorrow, I'll question him properly. I should have done it the moment I met him.'

Lady Brackenfield returned. 'Brandy in the drawing room, I think,' she said, and once again, I thought of Maggie, her innocence, and Aubrey's hidden photograph. *Mon amour*. Perhaps she was no longer his love – and we had been searching in all the wrong places.

I was briefly confused when I woke at dawn the following morning to find that I wasn't in my narrow bed at home, with the eiderdown that always slipped to the floor in a heap during the night. Instead, I was lying in a huge mahogany bed, with carvings of flowers and leaves looping along the headboard. Light filtered through the rose damask curtains, turning the gleaming wooden floor to sunrise pink. As I struggled to sit up, there was a knock on the door.

'Come in,' I called weakly, and a maid appeared.

'Good morning, miss,' she said, opening the curtains so light flooded into the room. 'Would you like a bath? Breakfast will be served in the morning room in an hour's time. The housekeeper, Mrs Greene, has sent up some toiletries, as your stay was unplanned.'

She placed a little basket on the bedside table, containing wrapped Bronnley's bath soap and a comb and flannel. I hadn't seen soap like that since before the war, and wondered whether anyone would notice if I took it home to use in place of Annie's pilfered hospital carbolic.

'I shall draw your bath,' she said, 'second door along to the left. If that's all, miss?'

I nodded dumbly. I had no idea how to speak to servants – she was a young woman just like me, and all the deference was making me feel terribly uneasy.

The bath was far deeper than any I'd had since long before the war – perhaps ever. The maid had shaken rose bath salts into the hot water, and I felt like a film star as I lay in the vast, steaming Victorian tub. My thoughts turned to Maggie again. Perhaps she had been seduced, or coerced by Aubrey, and Joyce had found out – and he had killed Joyce rather than risk discovery. But as a bohemian, would Joyce or the others have been against such a union? Maggie was fourteen, a schoolgirl with inky fingers who had barely had her first kiss – surely, I decided, even they would have objected to someone Aubrey's age taking up with her.

Or worse, what if someone had viewed Maggie as a love rival – and decided to get her out of the picture altogether? Aubrey Fagan was a man who broke hearts, abandoned families, took up with horribly young 'muses'. Would it be so surprising if one of the women he supposedly adored at Athena House had objected to the pretty younger girl's eager visits? By the time I emerged, I was lobster pink and had raisins for fingertips. I wrapped myself in the bath sheet the maid had left, and went to dress in yesterday's clothes.

I arrived at breakfast to find Lady Brackenfield fondly pouring tea through a silver strainer for Lou, and dishes of poached eggs and cured bacon dotted across the cloth.

'Now, I do hate to leave my guests,' she said, as I sat down, 'but I have a meeting with Cook shortly, to discuss menus for the week. We always meet first thing on a Monday morning – I find it saves time in the long run, don't you?'

I wasn't sure how to respond, not having my own cook with whom to discuss menus, but I smiled vaguely and buttered my toast, glazing over while she chatted about the state of the church – '... falling to pieces, the Georgian font could be in trouble soon, it seems the lime in the water is quite wearing away the carvings...'

I felt Lou and I had a great deal more to worry about than the Georgian font.

'I shall bid you farewell,' she said finally, rising to her feet. Her ropes of pearls swung violently as she gathered the dogs and swept out, our profuse thanks following her.

Lou looked up from his piles of bacon – clearly, he was making the most of it.

'Eat up, York,' he said. 'We've a busy day ahead.'

'Have you spoken to Mr Go—'

'I have spoken to your editor, my boss, someone bad-tempered from the Air Ministry and a very excitable Harold Walker,' he said. 'While you were enjoying your beauty sleep in the Rose Room, Marple and I were down at the telephone box.'

'Oh, is he all right?'

'Never better, apparently,' said Lou. 'Took a liking to the

smallest horse and spent the night curled up next to Puzzle the piebald cob. What Puzzle thought is not recorded.'

I laughed – though it occurred to me, surveying the remains of our lavish breakfast, that it might be a while before I felt so relaxed again.

As we crunched over gravel to collect the car from the garages, Lou lit a cigarette and said, 'Tell me what you found out from Ned last night – I didn't have a chance to ask you.'

'Norman was bullied,' I said. 'Ned told me that some village men think Norman's "peculiar", and a few nights ago, they surrounded his tent and threatened him, told him he wasn't wanted in the village...'

I blinked back sudden tears, which was ridiculous given that Norman could still be a murderer.

'What prompted this, do you know?'

'Ned told me... but I think it's just a nasty rumour...'

'Spit it out, York.'

'He told me that someone said they saw him talking to Maggie just before she disappeared.'

Lou whistled. 'Maybe that's why he was lurking about near Athena House,' he said. 'Looking for a new hidey-hole, further from the village. Do you think he might have harmed her? You've met him.'

I closed my eyes and thought about Norman's frightened gaze, his long silence. He had been kind to her and Johnny, and it was hard to imagine him hurting anyone. But if he'd feared that Maggie meant him harm... could he have lashed out, in panic?

'I hope not,' I said eventually.

. . .

On the short drive back to the village, Lou and I debated our theories. If Theo had killed Joyce, might he have harmed Maggie too? If Norman had taken Maggie, what was his connection to Joyce? Say 'JR' was Johnny after all, and he'd killed Maggie then caught the train? Supposing Joyce's death really was an accident? But what if Aubrey had harmed Maggie...?

My head ached with all the supposition by the time we reached Birchcroft. It was still very early, but there were already a few people about, walking dogs and queuing outside the grocer's.

Lou had decided we'd go to Athena House first, before commencing the search of the Air Ministry grounds.

'Can we get the men out to help us look for her again?' I asked Lou. 'It seems such a vast area...'

'I'm afraid not,' he said. 'Our Air Ministry chum was most insistent that nobody but me needs to know about the place. I may not, in fact, have mentioned you at all.'

'So I'll be the one who's shot dead, then. Thanks.'

'Ah well. Go out with a bang,' said Lou, as we rattled up the lane to Netherwood again. 'I suggest I speak to Mr Glenn, with his shell shock and lilies, and extract some answers about where he was when Joyce died. Meanwhile, you talk to Jean-Luc and Nora separately, and ask who knows about their affair, or their Gallic affirmation of life, or whatever they choose to call it. If I think there's enough evidence to bring Mr Glenn in for questioning, I might caution a couple of the others while I'm at it, too. I don't trust a single one of them, quite honestly, and nor does Marple.'

'Even Joan? I like her.'

'Even Joan,' said Lou, as he parked behind the hen house. 'I've liked plenty of suspects in my time, and at least half of them turned out to be stone-cold murderers.'

I wasn't entirely sure if I was here as a go-between, an

honorary police officer or a nosy obituarist, but Athena House was by now so familiar, I felt quite calm as I pushed open the door and called a gentle 'Hullo?', aware that most of the residents would still be asleep.

It was Aubrey who staggered downstairs in his dressing gown this time, violently towelling his hair, and calling, 'If that's a parcel for me, do not upend it, I beg of you – it contains expensive pigment!'

He stopped short when he saw us.

'Whatever brings you back here?' he asked, in a less than friendly tone.

'I'm here on police business,' said Lou. 'Given the uncertainty around Joyce's death, I'd like another chat with all of you.'

'Good Lord,' said Aubrey. 'Are you *arresting* us?'

'No,' said Lou, 'not unless I find cause to do so. Perhaps you could fetch Mr Glenn for me – I'll wait in the living room, if I may. And Miss York would like a word with Jean-Luc.'

'Would she now?' said Aubrey. 'Well, I'll admit she's not the first woman to demand such a thing. He'll never hear me yelling from down here, so if you know the way, Edie, I suggest you go up to his studio and find him yourself.'

'He might be in bed,' objected Lou, like a maiden aunt.

'I'll knock and make sure he isn't,' I promised. 'Let me know when you've finished with Theo.'

'I shall be working in my studio, while you both ride roughshod over our peaceful morning,' said Aubrey haughtily. 'You know where to find me.'

I passed him, hoping I could remember the way through the farmhouse's labyrinths of back stairs and odd little corridors.

After a few wrong turns, I eventually found my way to the top of the silent house, down the cold, dusty little landing with its moth-eaten Persian rug, and to Jean-Luc's studio door. I wasn't sure how I was going to frame my questions without appearing appallingly rude. I took a steadying breath, and knocked. There was no reply, and it occurred to me that Nora might be in bed with him, hastily pulling on her dressing gown, but I could hear no rustling or sounds of movement from within.

'Jean-Luc?' I called. I knocked again, more loudly this time, and waited.

I expected him to call 'oui?' or throw the door open, dishevelled and irritated, but after a few moments, it was clear he either wasn't coming or hadn't heard. Was he in a particularly deep sleep, after too much brandy? I turned the knob as quietly as possible, and creaked the door open an inch. The room was dim, the blackout curtains still drawn. A small, red-shaded lamp burned in the corner, revealing the empty bed. I glanced beyond, a reflexive check to make sure he wasn't at work or reading, and my eye fell on his work table. It was cleared. All the little sculptures, the clay, the tools, had been swept away and I stepped into the room fully, puzzled. I could now see more. On the floor beyond the table was an ocean of smashed china, broken sculptures and smeared clay – and in the centre of it all, blood pooled beneath his neck, lay Jean-Luc.

CHAPTER FIFTEEN

I don't know how long passed before I screamed for help. I must have been in shock, and my voice emerged in a shaking wail, but it did the job.

Lou made it upstairs first, shouting, 'Edie, are you all right? What's happened?' followed swiftly by Aubrey, Nora and Joan.

Lou took in the scene and barked, 'Stay there, all of you.' He fell to his knees beside Jean-Luc's body and leaned in to see if he could detect breathing, felt for a pulse, then he gently lifted the head slightly and examined his face, lifting and releasing an eyelid. He sat up, and bleakly shook his head. 'I'm very sorry,' he said.

'No, come on, man.' Aubrey pushed past me as Joan whispered, 'Oh, God, no' and Nora sank to the floor, sobbing.

'Theo, don't come up,' shouted Joan, but of course he ignored her and gave an unearthly wail of grief, before running blindly back down the stairs.

'Let me look,' Aubrey shouted at Lou, who was now standing by the body, studying the pottery that was strewn over the floor. 'He can't be gone!'

'I'm afraid I can't let you touch him,' said Lou. 'I'm going to stand guard while Edie takes my car and drives to the nearest phone box...'

'I can't drive,' I whispered in horror.

'I can,' said Joan. 'I'll take you.'

'Ring up this number and tell them it's a murder scene,' said Lou. 'They need to come quickly, on my orders.'

'What if they don't belie—'

'Just tell them I sent you, and hurry,' he said. 'And I want everyone who was here last night in the living room downstairs. Rest assured, I'll need a full account from every single one of you.'

'Now look here...' Aubrey began.

'Oh, shut up, Aubrey,' Nora shouted. 'You're not helping. Jesus, you great fool, show some respect!'

She shoved past us, her ragged sobs audible as she ran down the stairs. Joan and I looked at each other, as Aubrey sagged dramatically against the doorframe. Theo's howls were audible from two floors down.

'Come on then,' Joan said shakily. 'May as well make ourselves useful.'

In the car, with Marple panting between us, Joan's bravado crumbled.

'I can't believe it,' she said. Her skin was pale as rice paper, the blue veins visible on her forehead. Her large, capable hands trembled on the wheel.

'Who would hate Jean-Luc enough to do that? Surely none of us,' she murmured, swinging the car into the lane. 'I can't imagine... we all trusted each other.'

I noticed her use of the past tense.

'Could an intruder have come in?' I asked. 'I mean, you don't lock the door...'

She looked anguished. 'Nobody does in the countryside. We've never thought it was necessary.'

'Or perhaps he had a visitor?' I was feeling very unsteady myself, but trying to make sense of what had happened was, for me, the only route back to sanity. The blood had sprayed everywhere, splashing the broken china. I remembered Nora telling me that Sabrina had thrown her dinner at the wall during a row, and I had to suppress a violent jolt of nausea as we bumped over the potholes.

'I don't think so,' Joan said. 'Last night, Nora made the dinner, then all six of us sat around talking till about midnight, just discussing what we're working on, making suggestions, that kind of thing – all perfectly amicable – and as far as I know, we all went off to bed.' Her voice broke, and she blinked furiously.

'After Joyce...' she added. 'My God. We're cursed.'

'Who was still there when you went up?'

'Let's see,' she said. 'Aubrey had gone up... and Nora seemed to be a bit out of sorts, and said she was going to her room to read. So it was Theo, Jean-Luc and Sabrina.'

Nora, I thought, who had had enough of being treated like a skivvy. With whom Jean-Luc was currently involved. And Theo, who was in love with him. Sabrina, who had been his girl and was cast aside in favour of Jean-Luc's bohemian ideals.

'Here we are,' Joan said, pulling up with a violent jerk of the brakes that threw Marple into my lap. I untangled myself from his vast, flailing paws, spat out a mouthful of dog hair, and ran to the telephone box at the top of the lane, clutching the piece of paper Lou had given me.

Whatever I gabbled, at whoever it was, to my great relief they believed me.

'We'll be there as soon as we can. Tell DI Brennan to make sure the residents are all gathered, nobody must leave the house, and don't allow anybody to touch or move the dead man,' said the officer in clipped tones.

The dead man. Just hours ago, he'd been a person, vibrant and full of passion and poetic thought. I shuddered violently. Supposing whoever had killed Joyce and now Jean-Luc was determined to murder every resident of Athena House? I thought again of the villagers, how hated the artists were for their pacifism and 'loose morals', and of the missing Norman, last seen wandering nearby.

'Come on,' said Joan, seeing my face, 'may as well face the music. I know I didn't do it, but it does rather put the willies up one, knowing someone in the house might be a murderer.'

'Will you stay, after all this?'

She pulled a face. 'The real question is, where could I go?'

We could hear the shouting from the porch. Joan and I glanced at each other, alarmed.

'I don't know!' Aubrey was bellowing, while Theo's voice spiralled higher: 'Liar!' and '... always protected her', and Nora screamed, 'Stop it!'

Reluctantly, I followed Joan to the living room where Theo, Nora and Aubrey were all engaged in a stand-up row.

'Enough!' roared Joan, and they were shocked enough to fall silent.

'Our friend is lying upstairs,' she said, in a soft, trembling voice. 'Have you no respect?'

Theo looked up.

'Sabrina's gone,' Aubrey said.

'Gone?' I repeated faintly. In my confusion, I thought he meant she'd died, too.

'Her bed's not been slept in,' explained Nora. 'I went to get her, and her room was empty. There's no sign of her, but all her things are still here.'

'Does Lou – does DI Brennan know?' I asked.

'Not yet, he's still with... with Jean-Luc,' Nora said. 'We've only just found out – I don't know what to do, where can she have gone? Why has she run off?'

Joan caught my eye.

'Because she probably killed him,' she said flatly.

Theo gave a muffled cry and sank onto the couch, and Nora collapsed next to him.

'It's my fault,' she wailed. 'I knew Sabrina loved him, she always has – but when he was with her, and then Joyce, I thought he'd never look at me, and then he did, and... and now he's dead!' She dissolved into weeping.

'At least he looked at you,' Theo whispered. He was white, clutching the arm of the couch as if it were the reins of a galloping horse. There was a wheeze in his voice as he said, 'I feel terribly ill. I must lie down.'

'I'm so sorry, Theo, but the police want you all to stay put,' I said. 'They're on their way.'

'Surely if he's unwell...' Aubrey said.

'Even then,' I said. I hated myself, but if Theo was the murderer, after all... anyone could fake wheezing.

'Has anyone looked for Sabrina?' I asked. 'Outhouses, the studios, all the places she might be?' Or her body might have been hidden, I thought but didn't add.

'No,' said Nora. 'I didn't think. I can go and...'

'No, let Lou do it,' I said. 'I'll go and tell him the news. Joan, could you...'

She nodded. 'I'll stand guard over my pals,' she said with an icy weariness that chilled me. If she was a killer, of course, I was giving her the perfect chance to run – but I didn't think she was. Of them all, Joan was the only one who lacked a motive.

I ran up the stairs three at a time. 'Lou!' I yelled, though my voice died away as I stood on the threshold of Jean-Luc's room, confronted anew by the hushed solemnity of death. Lou was still where I'd left him.

'Sabrina's gone,' I said. 'It looks as though she's run away.'

'Well,' he said, 'we'd better try and find her then, hadn't we?' He looked down at the still body. 'Get some justice for you, old chap.'

The police car tore into the yard, spraying mud and terrified chickens, and three black-coated men climbed out. They were large, well-spoken, efficient.

'District Commissioner Ingrams,' said the tallest, as I hurried to greet them. 'You must be Miss York. An ambulance is on its way. Perhaps you could take me to DI Brennan while the others speak to the group inside. What can you tell us about them?'

I hardly knew where to start, but I tried to give the DC a potted history of Athena House's residents, and explain how Joyce had died, and that Sabrina was now missing.

'A tangled web indeed,' he said, when I'd finished. 'Thank you, Miss York – you may wait in the car.'

That was the last thing I wanted to do. If Lou had said it, I might have struck up the band and argued, but even I wasn't prepared to enter a debate with this man.

I waited until they'd trooped inside, hats held respectfully in their hands, then I drew my notebook from my bag. I scribbled a message which I stuck to the steering wheel with my hatpin, clipped on Marple's leather lead, and set off for the village.

Marple plunged into bushes and pranced through brambles. Just keeping him moving in a reasonably straight line was a challenge, like steering a sentient double decker bus, and I was glad of the distraction.

In Birchcroft, it was a normal Monday morning. Shoppers milled with baskets and ration books, children trailed after parents, and I saw Sally Corrin, the girl from the train, coming out of the chemist's. She had hated Joyce too... As I walked Marple past the shops and cottages, an ambulance raced by and turned up the lane. Several people turned to look, and one woman said, 'It'll be them sinners!'

There was tutting and head-shaking, and I was glad they didn't know what I knew – though they soon would.

I took the turning down to the station, trying to pretend it was an ordinary day, that I was a normal young woman out for a stroll with my dog, but my heart was like a lead weight in my chest. *Two dead and two missing,* I said to myself, and my steps marched to its repetitive rhythm until I felt I was going mad. It must all be connected, I felt certain, but for the life of me, I couldn't draw the strands together.

I was thinking of Jean-Luc's parents, innocently going about their morning in France and the dreadful call or telegram they would soon receive, when someone shouted, 'Hullo again!' and I looked up to see Rita walking up the lane towards me, carrying a small carpet bag.

'Back again? You must have a secret sweetheart here!' she called cheerfully.

'I'm afraid nothing that enjoyable,' I said. I told her what had happened, and she gasped.

'And Sabrina's missing,' I added. 'I don't suppose you saw anyone waiting at the station?'

'Nobody at all.'

'I was going to ask the stationmaster...'

'I wouldn't bother,' said Rita. 'He's just told me the trains out of Birchcroft are all cancelled this morning due to a UXB near Stockport. I wish the stupid bomb had exploded, then the trains might at least be running,' she added. 'My mother will wonder where I've got to. It really is the limit, she's been saving her rations up so she could make a cake for my visit, too.'

Sabrina couldn't have caught the first train out of

Birchcroft. She must still be in the area, unless someone had driven her away. I turned back, walking alongside Rita.

'You don't know if she's got any friends in the village, do you?' I asked.

'I don't think so,' Rita said, 'nobody's very fond of the sinners – that's what they call them, and rightly so.'

'Did you ever see Maggie with Aubrey?'

'That older one? Looks like a cartoon of a sailor, with a big beard?' I nodded, as Rita reached down to pat Marple's head. 'I did, yes. I was out with Dart, and we'd gone right up the hill behind Netherwood. I was hurrying as I was late meeting Sally and I saw them both, coming down. I passed close enough to hear what they were saying.'

My heart sped up. 'Can you tell me? It might be very important.'

'Oh, I'm sure it's not,' said Rita. 'It was freezing so he had his coat half over her, and he wanted to paint her portrait, that was all. He said something like "you do so remind me of my daughter" and was going on about how he wanted to capture her "spirit" – those were his very words – on canvas, while she wore a childish sort of dress – "nothing to suggest classical portraiture, rather a joyous depiction of youth" he said. You know the silly way he speaks.'

'What did she say?'

'She laughed and said she didn't think so,' said Rita, 'something like "I've seen those portraits you do, Mr Fagan, and I don't want to come out with a square face and triangles for eyes." That was all I heard, but she seemed quite happy, chatting away with him. More fool her,' she added darkly.

I gazed at her blankly.

'So it was innocent,' I said. 'It wasn't what we thought.'

'What did you think?' asked Rita beadily.

I ignored her.

Maggie missing. Joyce and Jean-Luc both dead.

'I'm sorry, Rita,' I said. 'I've got to go.'

I raced up the lane, Marple bounding ahead, my handbag jolting on my arm. It was vital that I reach Lou before he and Ingrams arrested Theo – or Aubrey.

The cars were still parked outside, though the ambulance had gone.

'Lou,' I shouted, my lungs burning. Marple followed me in, flanks heaving.

'Lou!'

I burst into the living room to find it empty. There was evidence of tea having been drunk, jerseys slung over chair-backs, a general air of the abandoned *Marie Celeste*.

'Hullo?' I called, to ringing silence. It occurred to me that the group could be in one of the studios, so I fetched Marple a pudding bowl of water from the kitchen, then hurried out again, my heart still thudding like galloping hooves.

As I stepped into the yard, I heard a raised voice, and traced the sound to Aubrey's studio. I shut Marple in the car again, then crept closer to listen.

'I barely knew Maggie Dawson!' Aubrey was shouting. 'Why would I harm her? I wanted to paint her portrait, that was all!'

I heard the low murmur of the DC's voice but couldn't make out the words. As I leaned further towards the side of the barn, a door banged shut across the yard, and to my horror, Lou came into view, frog-marching a weeping Theo towards the cars.

'Lou!' I shouted. 'It wasn't Theo or Aubrey!'

They both turned, and Lou saw me.

'Wait there,' he shouted.

'He didn't do it!' I yelled.

He pushed Theo into the back of his car, said, 'Guard him, Marple,' and slammed and locked the door.

Lou turned to me. 'For heaven's sake, Edie, come inside.'

Suddenly nervous, I followed him to the kitchen.

'Sit down,' he said, taking the seat opposite.

'What is it? You mustn't arrest Theo, he...'

'Will you be quiet!' snapped Lou. 'Edie, I have been extremely patient. I have heard out your theories, I have trusted you not to publish highly classified information, I have even accompanied you on your wild goose chases...'

'Just hold on a moment!' I said, furious.

Lou ignored me. 'I have done all of that,' he said, jabbing his forefinger into the table, 'because you're my friend, and you have good instincts about people, and I am, in fact, extremely fond...' He broke off. 'But do not' – his voice rose – 'do not *ever* challenge my authority as a Detective Inspector in the presence of a suspect. Do you hear?'

'But he didn't...'

'Do. You. Understand?'

'Yes,' I said. 'Sorry. But Lou, you must listen, I have to tell you something important about Sabrina...'

He closed his eyes, as if I had drained his patience to the last, trembling drop.

'Make it fast,' he said.

'Maggie and Sabrina were close friends.'

'Maggie's fourteen.'

'I know, but Sabrina's only twenty-one and she's not very grown up,' I said. 'She ran off with Jean-Luc when she was just eighteen and then he brought her here and dropped her for Joyce. We thought Theo had reason to hate Joyce because of his feelings for Jean-Luc, but so did Sabrina.'

'So did Nora, I don't doubt,' he said, lighting a cigarette without offering one to me. 'And probably Aubrey, too, and I expect Joan had an axe to grind for some reason or other –

they probably disagreed over a translation of Ovid or something.'

'Look, please listen,' I begged. 'Sabrina and Maggie used to go on walks and have tea together in the café. The last time Maggie was seen, she was arguing with Joyce, and "a blonde woman" was there – Sabrina knew all about the row, the night before Maggie vanished.'

'And what about Aubrey?' he demanded. 'The mysterious old goat with the penchant for very young "muses"?'

'I've just spoken to Rita!' I said. 'That's why I need you to listen – he said she was like his daughter, he wanted to paint her. Lou, I think Aubrey was drawn to young women because he missed his only daughter, and Maggie looks so like her. I think the photograph was of the daughter he left in Paris.'

Lou narrowed his eyes.

'There was nothing in Maggie's diary about Aubrey,' I insisted. 'Nothing to suggest she was in over her head with him. It was all about Joyce.'

I drew breath. Lou was still glowering at me. I was aware of time racing by, Theo trapped in the car, Aubrey on the verge of arrest, the search for Maggie not even begun.

'And,' I went on, 'if Sabrina lied about how often she saw Maggie, what else would she lie about? I think she might have killed Joyce,' I went on, 'and she's killed Jean-Luc, too. She stayed up talking with him last night – supposing she followed him up to bed to try and seduce him, and he rejected her?'

'Well, as a flight of fancy it has a certain drama,' Lou said flatly. 'Except it was Theo who sent Ethel the lilies to warn her off, which he's now admitted to, and Theo who was obsessed with Jean-Luc and was also painfully rejected by the Great Gallic Seducer of Netherwood. It's also Theo who is currently locked in my car waiting for Mancunian Miss Marple to finish her investigation.'

'Listen!' I cried. I wanted to smack him for his obstinacy.

'Theo can't walk as far as the others, he'd be half dead if he'd followed Joyce that morning. He was in bed ill that day when we arrived, and...'

'And he couldn't possibly pretend to have an asthma attack and take to his bed to avoid any awkward questions.'

I ignored him, even though I'd previously had the same thought. 'But if it was Sabrina, she walks all the time, she could have run back here and let herself in, as long as nobody spotted her. Then last night, if Jean-Luc rejected her...'

'Why did she wait till now to do away with him, then? Why not see off him and Joyce as a job lot?'

'With Joyce out of the picture, she hoped to get him back, and then found out he was with Nora,' I said. 'Maybe that's what pushed her over the edge. Or she was waiting for a chance all along. But more likely she didn't intend to kill him at all. All those broken sculptures – that wasn't planned, that was a fit of rage. And she stabbed him with one of his sculpting knives.'

I saw a vivid image of the little wooden-handled knife, dropped beside Jean-Luc's prone body. 'If she'd planned it, she'd surely have taken a proper knife with her.'

'And where's Maggie in all this?'

'Sabrina didn't get a train, and hardly anyone in Birchcroft has a car. So I think she's still somewhere nearby. I think there's a good chance she's been helping Maggie – and that she's gone to hide with her.'

'Or if Sabrina's as murderous as you claim, perhaps she's killed her, too,' said Lou. 'Why stop now, when she's so busy ending lives left, right and centre?'

'Because she cares about Maggie!' I said. 'She's no reason to harm her. The other two... well, she certainly has motive.'

'And yet little Nora remains unharmed.'

'Yes, because if Sabrina only found out about their affair last night, killed Jean-Luc by accident and ran, she wouldn't have planned a mass execution,' I said, with some bitterness. 'It all makes sense, you must know it does, Lou.'

'I might just as easily argue that it makes no sense at all,' he said. 'Aubrey showed Maggie round his studio, took her to his exhibition and wanted to paint her, claims to have forgotten he ever met her, adored Joyce, has been known to punch Jean-Luc. Joan – the quiet type, maybe her crush on Joyce masked unbearable jealousy. Nora – what's to say she didn't have a blazing row with her inamorata and smash all his badly glazed models of mutant Moby Dick?

'I've spoken to all of them separately,' he went on. 'It's obvious Nora was boiling with resentment about being treated as a skivvy by the lot of them, having run away from her deeply religious, slave-driving family. Aubrey's a pompous ass and quite happy to lie his way out of trouble – hardly surprising having abandoned several weeping families in his quest for artistic freedom. And Theo is a trembling inadequate who thought Joyce was his mother. What Freud would have to say about them all, I couldn't begin to guess.'

'Yes, they all have their troubles, of course,' I said, 'but Sabrina is the only one who had real cause to hate Joyce and Jean-Luc equally, and was definitely healthy enough to follow Joyce that day – if she was that close to Maggie, perhaps she was on her side about her father, too. I never thought she was as convinced by the pacifism as the others seemed to be.'

'So I should let them all go, free to prance about painting butterflies in the fields, while you and I hare off to find Maggie and Sabrina crouched in a foxhole?'

'That's what I'd do.' I glared at him.

'Then it's highly fortunate you're not a detective. Look, Edie, I can't let Theo go free just because you have a *feeling*.' Lou sighed. 'On the other hand, your argument does make some sense, at least, which is more than any of that bunch has managed. They're all alibied up to the hilt, merrily lying for each other – it's tighter than an illegal betting ring.'

'How do you know they're lying?'

'Like you, a strong feeling. Nora's in Joan's studio drinking tea that tastes of turps – we needed to put them somewhere while we talked to the men, so no doubt they had plenty of time to get their stories straight.'

'I think they're telling the truth,' I insisted. 'I don't think any of them knew about Sabrina being such great pals with Maggie.'

'That remains to be seen,' said Lou. 'I'm going to hand Theo to the DC for further questioning while you wait here. I'll mention this Maggie and Sabrina development, and I'll leave any further arrests to his discretion.'

'Then what?'

'Isn't that enough for one morning?' Lou sighed. 'Then I'll need a chat with your friend Rita, and finally, we might start the search for Maggie.'

'And Norman and Sabrina.'

'And Norman, Sabrina, the Wicked Witch of the West, the Cheshire Cat and Peter-flaming-Pan.'

But he rolled his eyes as he spoke, and despite my earlier irritation, I was relieved to discover that for now, at least, we were on friendly terms again.

By the time Lou came back, Nora and Joan had drifted back into the kitchen. Nora was weeping, and Joan pulled a kitchen chair alongside her and placed a comforting arm round her shoulders.

'They're going to arrest me!' she sobbed. 'Mam will die of shame, I know she will...'

'You ran away, Nora,' said Joan. 'They don't even know where you are.'

'But I'll go to prison!'

'Nora, you didn't kill him, so you won't be going to prison,' said Joan patiently.

'How do you know I didn't?' she wailed.

'I just do,' said Joan. 'Why weren't you with him last night?'

'I needed a bit of time to myself,' she said. 'I was so fond of him, you know, but he could be... quite intense. I'd told him earlier that I'd be sleeping by myself and he was a bit sulky.'

'And he stayed up talking with Sabrina?'

Nora nodded. 'I knew she still liked him, but he told me it was over between them. Then he said Sabrina was énervant – I didn't know what it meant, but it didn't sound very good.'

'Draining. Exhausting,' said Joan sadly. 'I suppose she can be, rather.'

I thought I might be draining and exhausting if I'd thrown over my entire life and family for a handsome sculptor, and he'd dragged me back to England then abandoned me for a string of other women under my nose.

'Poor Theo,' said Nora, through her tears. 'I know he had a little crush on Jean-Luc, but he would never have hurt him. He's a pacifist, for pity's sake.'

'Aren't all of you?' I asked.

Joan and Nora exchanged a glance.

'Sabrina's not, really,' said Joan quietly. 'She went to Joyce's talks to support her, but often they'd argue all the way home. She'd lost all her uncles in the Great War and she said her father was terribly sad, locked away in his study all through her childhood. She once said she couldn't bear to think all that sorrow was for nothing; she had to believe it was worth standing up for something and fighting if you had to.'

Almost exactly what Maggie had said to Joyce.

'If Sabrina was so upset about Jean-Luc and didn't agree about the pacifism,' I asked, 'why did she stay on here?'

Nora covered her face with her hands. Her shoulders heaved.

Joan looked up at me.

'She hoped he'd come back to her.'

I could see it clearly. Sabrina, anticipating that now Joyce was out of the picture, Jean-Luc would return. The discovery that he had, instead, chosen Nora. Last night, the chance, finally, to go and beg him to reconsider. His refusal, the row and then the knife in the neck, his body prone amongst the shards.

Leaving the house, stricken at what she'd done, and fleeing, through the night, to Maggie. Then what? I wondered. What was their plan? Maggie was a child, Sabrina a grown woman. Where did she think they could go, or hide indefinitely? How would they find food, in February, in the war?

I remembered Norman: his rabbit stews, his local knowledge, his sudden disappearance. He was a man well practised at remaining silent.

I stood up, but as I did so, Lou came back into the kitchen.

'Come on, York,' he said. 'Time's running away.'

'Is Aubrey...?'

'Off the hook, for now,' said Lou. 'He had another little snapshot of his daughter in his studio. This one was clearer, and it isn't Maggie. He showed us his "muse" paintings – they're all the spitting image of her.' I breathed out with relief that I'd been right. 'He corroborated what Rita told you about wanting to paint Maggie,' Lou added. 'Although there's no love lost there.'

'For Rita?' I asked, puzzled.

'He says it was her who sent the poison-pen letters,' said Lou. 'He caught her and her friend Sally leaving the yard very early one morning, says she had paint on her trousers and *Get Out Sinners* was written on the door. She claimed she'd just been painting the shed at Brackenfield, but...' He shrugged. 'The letters stopped after that.'

'Why didn't he tell Creech?'

'Thought there was no point.' Lou shook his head. 'He was probably right.'

'Where's Theo?' asked Nora, turning pink-rimmed eyes to him.

'Gone for a little chat with the DC,' said Lou. 'But all being well, unless there's very good reason to detain him, I imagine he'll be back later on, pending further inquiries. You might want to advise him that sending flowers as a threat isn't a particularly decent or sensible thing to do.'

'Oh, I shall,' said Joan grimly. 'Poor Ethel.'

I picked up my hat and followed Lou to the door. 'I'm so sorry about it all,' I said, inadequately. Joan shrugged.

'Hardly your fault, my dear,' she said.

Nora added, 'Come to Joyce's funeral. You found her, you and Ethel. You should be there to see her off.'

CHAPTER SIXTEEN

We found Rita in the vegetable garden, planting out her potato seedlings, and she seemed delighted to see us.

'Here I am, working away, instead of eating cake with Mum,' she said, extending a muddy hand, then thinking better of it. 'Glad to have a break. How can I help, Inspector?'

'Detective Inspector,' corrected Lou automatically. 'I need to know how friendly Maggie and Sabrina might be – and rather quickly if you can, as we haven't long.'

'Of course!' said Rita. She led us to a shed full of rusting garden forks and seed trays.

'Sorry it's a bit spidery,' she said, pulling out two moth-eaten deckchairs for us, while she perched on a ledge. A vast ginger cat uncoiled itself from a box marked PEABODY'S BEST COMPOST and jumped heavily onto Lou's lap, kneading his trousers with gleeful abandon. Lou stroked its head absently.

'Perhaps you could tell me, Miss Norton, how you came to know the people of Athena House?'

'I don't know them,' she said. 'Albert pointed them out to me round and about, and told me what they get up to.'

'And that upset you?'

'Well, yes!' Rita looked startled. 'It's not natural, is it? It's not British. It's sinful, what they do.'

'Do you know Sally Corrin?' I asked her.

'I do, as a matter of fact. She's been a good friend to me since I arrived here, has Sally.'

'I assume she's told you how she feels about them?'

'Well, of course. Everyone feels the same. Coming here with their pacifist rubbish—'

'Does she know you daubed cruel insults on their door?' Lou interrupted.

She froze. 'I... no, that wasn't me,' she said, her voice high with fright. 'I wouldn't do such a thing, Detective Inspector.'

'Miss Norton,' said Lou. 'None of us agree that they were right in their political convictions. But neither is it acceptable to intimidate householders, or deface property. On this occasion, I'll let it go. Don't do it again. And you might want to remind Miss Corrin that poison-pen letters are a thoroughly cowardly way of making your point. At least Joyce Reid stood up for her beliefs.'

Rita was scarlet-faced. 'I'm very sorry, sir,' she said. She glanced at me. 'I know it was stupid.'

'Now, perhaps you can be helpful for a change,' said Lou. 'What exactly do you recall about seeing Sabrina and Maggie together?'

'Well, let's think,' Rita said, relieved. She extracted a roll-up from the pocket of her cardigan. 'I remember seeing them before Christmas, because Sabrina had a shopping basket of parcels, and I wondered what the sinners did about Christmas, whether they'd go to church – they didn't as it happened.

'They were in the Singing Kettle and I was at the next table, they were talking about pacifism and I remember Maggie said that Joyce was very impressive and Sabrina said "not always" or "you'd be surprised" or something like that. It stuck with me because I thought they were all tight as ticks up there.

'Then another time, I went to hear Joyce talk, and Sabrina was with Maggie at the back, whispering to her... that was a few weeks ago.' She noticed the cat who had now curled into a ball, coating Lou's dark trousers in orange fur.

'Sorry if he smells of mice, he's had a bumper morning.'

'You're a fine fellow, aren't you?' Lou stroked its chin and the cat emitted a great, rumbling purr. It was oddly relaxing to be in the shed, with its smells of compost and creosote, its dusty striped deckchairs and trays of seedlings.

'Maggie's father was killed in action, soon after that,' I put in, hoping to steer Rita back to her recollections.

'Oh, how sad,' Rita said. 'I do hate hearing about these things, because of my brothers... I fret so much. Still, at least they're on a ship. I hear pilots have a much shorter life span.'

I thought of Clara. 'I hope not.'

'The next time I saw Maggie was when she rowed with Joyce after the talk. I'm sorry I can't help more.'

'You've helped a great deal,' Lou said. 'We must go, Rita – but I'll be in touch.'

As we headed back down the long drive, I spotted a woman and a boy walking up the drive.

'It's Spud!' I cried. 'With Mrs Dawson!'

'Oh, for heaven's sake,' said Lou, as we drew near and I rolled down the window, 'Edie, we need to hurry.'

'Spud!' I yelled, and his face lit up. 'Edie!' he called, and ran towards us.

'Hullo, Marple!' Spud thrust his head in through the window. 'He's a beast!' he said, admiringly. 'I'd love a dog like that, but Mum says it's not fair because of Pouncer, but when I'm grown up, I'm going to...'

'Spud!' called a tall woman in her thirties, hurrying up behind him. 'Whatever are you doing? Leave the lady and gentleman alone—'

'You must be Netta Dawson!' I cried. 'I'm Edie York.'

I climbed out of the car and shook her gloved hand.

'I'm so sorry about Maggie,' I said. 'I didn't know if I should write to you, but...'

'No, of course you did the right thing,' she said. 'I'm so grateful to you! How could it be that nobody thought to tell me? I've just arrived, and went straight to fetch Spud. I don't know where to begin looking...'

'I'm not at the Wrights' any more!' Spud almost shouted. 'I don't have to go back! Mum gave Mrs Wright what-for, and she said a swear-word, she said—'

'Yes, all right, Spud,' said Mrs Dawson hastily. 'Though it's true, I was angry. They were cruel to my children – and then they lost my daughter.' Her chin trembled. 'How can she have vanished into thin air?'

Lou emerged from the driving seat. 'Detective Inspector Brennan. I want to assure you, we're taking this very seriously, Mrs Dawson. We will do everything in our power to find your daughter.'

'Thank you.' She swallowed, her brown eyes glistening with tears. 'It's just not like her,' Netta whispered. 'If she's come to harm...' She pressed a handkerchief to her face and took a shuddering breath.

'Inspector Brennan's dog will find her, Mum,' said Spud, confidently.

'I'm so sorry to keep you, I can see you're busy,' Netta said to Lou. 'Perhaps we'll meet again later if you have any news for us – we're staying here at the Hall.'

'I thought you were staying at the pub,' I said, puzzled. 'Didn't Ned remember?'

'Oh, I'm so sorry,' she said. 'Lady Brackenfield sent a message via Mrs Wright to invite us to stay here, at Brackenfield. She's so very kind!'

I glanced suspiciously at Lou. His face remained impassive, but it was clear that he must have charmed Lady Brackenfield into hosting Spud and Netta while I was splashing about in my boiling bath earlier.

'We're about to go and loo—' I began and Lou cut across me.

'I fully intend to find her,' said Lou. 'And I'm terribly sorry about what you've suffered. Try to let the Brackenfield staff look after you now,' he added. 'They haven't got much else to do.'

She smiled as we clambered back into the car. Lou raised a hand as we pulled away and murmured, 'Lovely woman. Sweet kid. Those damnable people.'

'The Wrights?'

'Yes. Though I agree, that could apply to an awful lot of Birchcroft residents.' He checked his watch. 'Dear Lord, we need to hurry up.'

'Why didn't you tell Netta we were going to look for Maggie?'

'Oh now, let's see,' he said. 'Perhaps because she's a mother beside herself with worry who is desperate to do something practical to find her daughter, and the last thing I need is another impetuous woman running about all over top-secret Air Ministry property. Could it perhaps be that?'

'I'm not impetuous,' I muttered.

As we rattled back through the village, Lou heaved a vast sigh.

'What a mess,' he said, teeth clamped on a cigarette. 'It's hardly an advertisement for bohemianism, is it, all these miserable people, wracked with jealousy and rage? It makes me long for a cosy little wife baking pies, and a cottage with roses round the door.'

'I wonder what the cosy little wife would long for?' I said, rather sharply, thinking of my friends, and the long, thankless hours they now worked. But would Annie, or Clara, or even Ethel really be happier stuck in some rural idyll, rolling pastry?

I envisaged Suki, trapped in her own home, terrified of making a mistake.

'I don't know, but at least she wouldn't be stabbing her erstwhile lover in the neck,' said Lou. 'I hope you've got stout boots on.'

I looked at my feet. I was wearing my battered leather lace-ups as usual.

'I forgot,' I admitted. 'It was so early when we left, I...'

'Well, you needn't think you're taking part in a search, then.'

'I bloody well am!' I said. 'I'm the one who worked out where Sabrina is, I'm the one who...'

'We have no idea where Sabrina is,' said Lou. 'This is all your wild theory, which you've now decided is fact. As usual.'

'Well, either way, I'm coming with you,' I said. 'I'm not sitting in the car while you go off and terrify Maggie to death.'

'Assuming she's still alive,' said Lou flatly.

'She is,' I said. 'I'm sure she is.'

'Ah yes, Superintendent Hunch. Thank goodness for unsubstantiated feelings, just what we need on this tricky case.'

I rolled my eyes as we parked by the campsite gate – although with nobody there to camp, it was now just a field – and Marple bounded from the car.

'I'm officially stating now that you accompany us at your own risk,' Lou told me, lacing on his walking boots. 'You're not dressed properly for this, it'll be dark soon and you're probably still in shock after finding another body. I strongly recommend that you stay in the car.'

'I strongly recommend that you stop worrying,' I said. 'I'm coming to find Maggie and Sabrina.'

'That's a point,' murmured Lou to himself. 'Better bring the handcuffs.'

'Really?' I was shocked.

'Edie, Sabrina is a murder suspect. I'd now go so far as to say the chief murder suspect, of both Joyce and Jean-Luc,' said Lou, as Marple panted beside him, eager to set off. 'Do you think we're going to have a lovely chat and all back to Degenerate Towers for tea?'

'Oh, do stop being so damned sarky,' I snapped. 'Come on, let's go before it's dark. Couldn't any of the other policemen come with us?'

He sighed. 'They're still busy with the other bloody artists. And besides, I doubt they'd agree with our theory – as far as they're concerned, Maggie's just a young runaway, and Sabrina could be anywhere.'

Lou added a large torch to one capacious coat pocket, and produced a scarf from the other, like a magician.

'What's that?'

'Sabrina's scarf,' he said. 'Picked it up from her room. Maggie's trail will have faded by now. But Sabrina's won't.'

Marple sniffed the patterned silk, and we started up the field. A chill breeze had sprung up, battleship-grey clouds were gathering over the hills, and I buttoned my thin, WVS shop coat to the collar.

'I'm saying nothing about the inadequacy of that coat,' said Lou. 'Nothing at all.'

As we passed Norman's tent, Lou peered in, but nothing had changed. He had not been back.

'Here's hoping we find him with the others,' said Lou, 'though he may have gone for good.'

I felt sure that he hadn't – but given Lou's contempt for my 'vague hunches', I said nothing as we scrambled over the mossy stone wall and followed Marple's long, trembling nose back up the hill towards the woods.

As we trekked on, I noticed that the light was fading more quickly than I'd expected. Low clouds now filled the sky over the valley, and the breeze carried the chill dampness that precedes rain. Annie would soon be home from work, getting started on making our tea of corned beef hash, and Suki might be upstairs drinking tea with Agnes, I thought fondly. I longed to be home reading by the fire, this terrible day behind me.

'Come on, York!' shouted Lou. 'We need to hurry!'

Rain had begun to fall in earnest, the sharp, slanting kind that sets in, driven by a stiff breeze. We were close to the woods, and I ran, making for the cover of the trees. Marple was a dot in the distance, and Lou switched his torch on, waiting for me.

'This is far from ideal,' he said. 'I think we should go back, you can get the last train home, then I'll carry on looking with Marple.'

'Absolutely not,' I panted. 'I'm not giving up now.'

'Edie, it's not about *giving up*,' said Lou furiously. 'But you're dressed completely inadequately for an expedition like this, and I don't want you hurting yourself or becoming ill from exposure on the damned hillside.'

We were sheltering under an oak tree and rain was hammering onto the leaves above us.

'Well, let's go faster then!' I said. All I could think about was Maggie, frozen and terrified, Sabrina desperate and cornered.

'No, Edie, I can't let you...'

Lou gripped my arm painfully, yanking me back towards him as I tried to leave the shelter of the tree.

'You're not in charge of me!' I shouted. I was overwhelmed with fury. The horror of discovering Jean-Luc, the disappearance of Sabrina, the worry about Maggie, the dread in Mrs Dawson's eyes... I was not going to give up now and go home, like a child collected early from a party.

'I bloody well—' began Lou, and I said, 'If you won't go with me, I'll just go on my own. You don't own the hillside.'

'You stubborn little sod,' he said.

We glowered at each other.

'Fine. Come with me, then,' he said. 'I'm not leaving you to die of exposure. But rest assured, this is the last time I ever take you on police business. You're a damned liability.'

He turned, called to Marple, and stamped up through the wood. By the time we reached the perimeter of the fenced land, with its brutal barbed wire and warning signs, my coat was soaked through and my feet were like sodden lumps of mud, but I'd rather have died than complain. *Find Maggie. Find Sabrina.* It was all that mattered now.

'We're going to have to climb through the fence,' said Lou. 'I don't know where the gate is, and it could take hours to go round the edge.'

He pulled on leather gloves, and yanked at a wire stretched low to the ground. Beyond was an indeterminate murk, lost behind sheets of rain. It took him several minutes to stretch the taut wire far enough to let Marple writhe through, then he redoubled his efforts.

'How would Sabrina have got in?' I asked. 'Maggie must be tiny and could wriggle under, but Sabrina's quite tall.'

'God knows,' he said. 'We don't even know they're in here at all.'

But Marple was whining, nose low to the ground despite the rain, and I felt more certain than ever that we'd find them here.

Eventually, Lou's efforts created a gap just wide enough to climb through, and he held the barbed wire apart for me to go first. I managed to scramble in unharmed, and he followed, handing me his torch. I directed it ahead, and realised we needed to climb up a bank in order to see the area – though any sign of human occupation would be obscured by rain and encroaching dusk.

'Follow Marple,' Lou instructed me. 'Seek, boy!'

Marple set off at a trot, jumping up over the bank in a dark blur and disappearing from view. Slithering and scrambling after him, we saw that we'd come to a dip between the hills, and just visible in the torchlight, scattered over the rocky landscape, was what I could only describe as a half-town. It looked as though builders had begun to construct walls and sheds, outhouses and gables, then wandered off. Nothing formed a coherent structure, and in the rainy dusk the edifices looked abandoned as plague houses, a nameless warning from long ago.

Of course, I reminded myself, they had been built only recently and despite their initial resemblance to ghostly, collapsed crofts, in the distance were structures that resembled water towers, clad with scaffolding.

'It's not being used much at the moment,' Lou shouted over the rain and wind. 'They're probably redeploying the crew to the coastal airfields, because of the invasion threat.'

Clara was still training, but how long before she was soaring overhead, her tiny plane a moving target?

'Should we split up to look?'

'No, we've only one torch,' said Lou. 'We'll follow Marple, and just hope to God that Sabrina's somewhere here, and so is Maggie.'

As he spoke, a wave of horror washed over me, and I halted.

'What's wrong?'

'Lou,' I shouted into his ear, as freezing water dripped from the brim of his hat and straight down my collar. 'What if I was wrong? What if Sabrina wants to hurt Maggie? Or she already has? She's killed two people...'

'Why would she?'

'I don't know!' I cried, 'But she's obviously got a terrible temper – if Maggie finds out what she's done and threatens to tell the police...'

'All the more reason to find them quickly, then,' said Lou. 'Come on.'

. . .

As we trudged on, it became clear that the area was vast. The Ministry men had cleverly chosen a wide, isolated hillside, undulating and far from civilisation, where decoy buildings could be spaced out to imply the existence of an entire town. With each structure we came to, Lou would flash the torch inside, revealing only emptiness, tussocks of grass and bare brick. There was no sign of use, no wrappers, fires or blankets to suggest an occupant.

Marple led us onwards, my shoes sinking into fast-filling bog. The wind had picked up and was sweeping bolts of rain across the darkened landscape like theatre curtains, almost solid in the torchlight. It was hard to believe anyone could survive up here for almost three weeks, let alone a slight fourteen-year-old.

I battled to quell the panic that was rising in my chest – how were we to get back down the hill if the weather didn't let up, let alone find the runaways?

On we went, drenched and hunched against the battering of the rain, the wind too loud now for us to speak. Marple, a silhouette in the beam of the torch, turned to check we were following, then leapt up a series of rocky ledges. Dwarfing the ridge at the top was a bigger structure, with a flat roof, and a low brick tunnel leading to a door covered in corrugated iron. I felt hope flare.

'He thinks they're in there,' Lou shouted, pointing to Marple, who was standing still, barking at the tunnel mouth.

He grasped a tussock of wet grass and pulled himself up, swinging a leg up and rolling onto the ridge.

'Here,' he said, leaning down, a gloved hand outstretched to pull me up alongside him.

'I can manage,' I shouted. Perhaps I was still angry from earlier, perhaps I needed to prove to Lou, or myself, that I didn't need any help. I grasped a tuft of grass in both hands, and placed my right foot in a gap above a jutting rock, straining to pull myself up as Lou shone the torch downwards. At a foot or so shorter than him, and lacking Marple's four-legged elevation, I realised I'd struggle without help, but I couldn't bear to show weakness. If I gave in, I somehow felt the entire day's events would come crashing down on me, and I might collapse on the sodden earth and never get up again.

'Come on, Edie,' I whispered. I lifted my left leg from the ground, flailing for a foothold, and as I did so, I pulled hard on the grass to steady myself. I felt a sickening lurch, a dizzy moment of mid-air suspension, then I slammed backwards into the ground, right foot still trapped in the rock face, my ankle twisted like a corkscrew.

'Edie!' Lou was standing over me, patting my cheek alarmingly hard. 'Edie!'

For a moment, I wondered if I'd died. Nothing made sense – I was out in the open, yet it was dark, and water was pouring over both of us. I could barely see Lou, but Marple was next to me, barking wildly.

'What...' I began, then I tried to sit up and felt knuckle-whitening pain sear through my ankle.

'Don't move,' instructed Lou. 'I need to carry you.'

I was about to argue, but another wave of dizziness overcame me, and I let him work my foot from its mud-encrusted shoe, which was still stuck in the rock, breathing through clenched teeth as every small jolt sent new flashes of agony through my ankle.

'Did you hit your head?'

'No,' I said. 'My ankle...'

'I'm going to have to carry you back to the car and get you to the cottage hospital to see if it's broken.'

'I'm so sorry, Lou,' I said, but he didn't hear. Marple licked my face carefully, as Lou yanked my muddy shoe from the rock and stuffed it into his pocket.

'Can you hold on round my neck?' he said, and I reached up towards his comforting scent of tobacco and damp wool, as he slid an arm under my knees and stood up.

As he did so, the torch which he'd had jammed under his arm fell free and dropped to the ground. It hit a rock, blinked once, and was immediately extinguished. The night was black around us, and now it was impossible to see a thing.

Lou swore, laid me back on the ground, and snatched up the torch.

'Battery's fallen out,' he shouted. He patted the ground urgently, but after a few moments, he gave up. 'Lens is smashed anyway,' he said. 'I can't carry you down without a light, we'll break our necks.'

For the first time, I felt genuinely fearful.

'What can we do?' I asked him, eyes closed against the throbbing agony in my foot.

He glanced up at the looming structure. 'We'll have to get up there,' he said, 'and hope somebody's left the door unlocked. Then I'll strap up your ankle and we'll wait for first light.'

'I'm sorry,' I said again.

'Bit late for that,' said Lou shortly, and I wondered if this time, our friendship really was beyond saving.

He pulled me up the steep bank, almost dislocating my arms from their sockets, but this time, I didn't resist. I leaned on him and hopped, every step sending glass shards of pain through my ankle. One arm stretched before him, feeling for the bricks, and with Marple just ahead, we made it as far as the tunnel.

'Let's hope there are no crash-landed Germans lurking in there,' he said.

The rain on the corrugated roof sounded like a demented jazz orchestra, and as Lou lowered me to a sitting position against the tunnel's damp wall and went to try the door, I was so relieved to be out of the deluge I almost forgot the purpose of our expedition.

I heard him shouldering open the door, and Marple barking – then, dazzlingly, a light snapped on, illuminating Lou and a slice of the space behind him.

'Thank God for that,' he yelled. Then, 'Edie, somebody's been here.'

I tried to stand and fell back, whimpering with pain.

'What can you see?' I managed.

Now we were out of the rain and wind, it was easier to hear one another. 'Used dishes,' he said. 'There's a bucket, I think for washing-up...' I heard some clanking.

'I'm just round a corner – there's bedding and a Calor gas stove...'

'Help me up, please?' I called. Lou reappeared. Now the light was on, I could see he was filthy; coated in mud, soaked through, raindrops still clinging to his dark moustache – but he looked delighted.

'They've been staying here,' he said. 'They must have broken in somehow, it's just a basic officers' mess for the RAF when they're lighting the decoy fires, I think. Come on,' he added, bending low again and hauling me up. I hopped alongside him into the bunker-like, brick-walled room. There were desks, a huddle of sagging canvas chairs, some locked metal filing boxes, and no windows. Lou pointed round an L-shaped wall at the end, and I saw a pile of rugs and blankets, the gas bottle, a half-full pan of water, and a small pile of dirty crockery. He helped me to one of the canvas-covered chairs, then went over to look again, as Marple stood over the bedding pile, barking frantically.

'Sabrina, at least,' said Lou. 'And likely both of them, judging by the number of plates and cups.'

'But where are they?' I asked.

'Probably saw the torch or heard the barking, and ran,' said Lou. 'We can't go looking now, but they won't get far tonight in this weather.'

'What do we do?'

'Well,' said Lou. 'It doesn't look as though it'll clear up for a while. I suggest we sort your ankle out, and bed down here till first light, at which point, Marple and I will resume the search, and then we'll get you down to the cottage hospital somehow and have your injuries looked at.'

'But we know my theory was true, at least,' I said.

'Yes,' said Lou. He half smiled to himself. 'Your theory was true, York. Shame you almost had to kill us both to prove it.

There's some sort of ship's biscuits here,' he added, rummaging in a cardboard box. 'A whole tin of them. How on earth were they getting hold of this stuff?'

I looked at the little gas stove and remembered the first time I'd seen it, on a sunny day, outside a canvas tent.

'Norman,' I said.

We shared the dry, tasteless biscuits with a disgruntled Marple, and Lou boiled up a pan of rainwater and made us black tea, straining it into mugs through his clean handkerchief.

'Can't run to a toothbrush,' he said. 'But I suggest we hang our coats near the stove to dry out a bit, and wrap ourselves in the blankets. Though I can't speak for any fleas that might be in that pile of rags.'

'I really don't care,' I said. 'The more the merrier.'

I was so wet and cold I could no longer feel my limbs, beyond the consistent pain in my ankle, and I was starting to shiver.

'Come on,' said Lou. He wrestled me gently out of my coat, spread it over a chair back and placed a scratchy blanket round my shoulders, then he angled the gas stove towards me, and unlaced and removed my other shoe. My woollen stockings were so wet and dirty, I no longer had feet, just indeterminate clumps of mud.

'Can you roll them down please?' Lou asked.

'I beg your pardon?'

'You need to warm up, you idiot,' he said. 'If I were going to attempt a seduction – which I can assure you I'm not – it wouldn't be in a bunker lit like an operating theatre over a tin of ship's biscuits.'

I pulled my stockings off, shrieking in pain as I yanked the right leg over my swollen ankle.

'Let's have a look,' said Lou, taking my foot in his hands. The overhead light was bright enough for him to see it clearly, and he winced.

'What?'

'It looks as though you've been tap dancing through sledge-hammers,' he said. 'It's three times the size it should be, and a fetching royal purple.'

I leapt from the chair as he touched it.

'Sorry,' he said. 'Just trying to check if it's broken. Does it hurt here?'

He lightly pressed my ankle bone, and I grimaced. 'No more than before.'

'But here...?' He placed his fingers lower down on the foot and I almost passed out again.

'Dear Lord, you've gone white,' he said. 'Have another biscuit. I think it's a bad sprain, but I'd like a doctor to check to be certain. I'm going to bandage it; compression will help a bit. So you're going to have to be brave.'

I gripped the arms of the chair as he extracted Sabrina's silk scarf from his pocket and efficiently wrapped my ankle, tucking the ends in as neatly as a French plait, and propping my foot up on another chair.

'You're quite good at this.'

'Thanks to my ambulance-driver years,' said Lou. 'I learned a few things.'

'When you were fighting in Spain, did you...'

'I'd rather not talk about Spain,' said Lou. 'It was not a happy time.'

'No, of course.'

We fell silent, listening to the rain and Marple's gusty breathing as he pursued something delicious in his dream.

'We should try and get a bit of sleep,' said Lou. 'Do you want the rat's nest or would you rather sleep upright?'

'Upright, I think.'

'A sensible choice,' he said. 'If I'm bitten to death during the night, it's been lovely knowing you.'

'Has it?'

'No,' he said, and I laughed.

'Nor you.'

Lou clicked out the light and rolled himself into the blankets, and I sat in the dark, thinking of Maggie, Sabrina and Norman and wondering what on earth we should do and say if we found them.

CHAPTER SEVENTEEN

I woke with a wet nose pressed against my face. I'd fallen sideways in the chair, my legs were stiff as stepladders and my ankle was throbbing.

'Shh, Marple,' I whispered. 'Get down!' But Lou was already sitting up. He too had slept fully dressed, and we both resembled abandoned string puppets.

'What time is it?'

'Just before six,' he said. 'Listen.'

'I can't hear anything.'

'Exactly. The rain's stopped.'

Lou stood up and pulled on his boots. 'I'm going to look outside,' he said. 'Then we'll make a plan.'

Marple trotted after him to the entrance.

'Edie,' Lou called, after a moment, 'can you move?'

I flexed my working leg. 'I think so, if you give me a hand.'

'There's something I need to show you,' he said, returning. 'Because I might be hallucinating with tiredness.'

Puzzled, I leaned on him heavily and pulled on my almost-dry stockings as he chivalrously looked away. My remaining shoe was still heavy as a wet rugby ball, despite Lou having left it to dry by the gas stove, but I crammed it onto my left foot and shuffled to the entrance, gripping Lou's arm.

Outside, the sky was a clear ink-blue. The scattered half-buildings loomed black and uncanny, stretching into the distance.

'Look,' said Lou. He half turned me and pointed.

In the distance, beyond the scaffolded bulk of the water towers, an orange light glowed.

'Is it a torch?' I whispered.

'A fire, I think.'

I strained to see. 'It'll be dawn soon,' said Lou. 'I'll get the blankets, hold on.'

Wrapped in the scratchy wool, we stood concealed in the tunnel, waiting for the sky to lighten. We must have looked like ancient people at the cave entrance, a tamed wolf beside us.

Gradually, a strip of turquoise appeared on the horizon, and as it did so, the glow of orange became clearer – within minutes, it was evident that we were staring fixedly at a small fire.

'Can you tell how far away it is?' I asked quietly.

'No,' said Lou. 'But I need to go now.'

'I'm coming with you.'

'What are you talking about? You can't walk!'

'I can hobble,' I said.

Lou shook his head. 'There's determined and then there's demented,' he said. 'I can't arrest anyone if I'm holding you upright, can I?'

'I'll follow,' I said.

'I can't stop you, I suppose. But don't expect a medal for delaying an arrest.'

'I won't...' I began, but he was already climbing down the bank, gesturing for Marple to accompany him.

At the bottom, where I'd lain last night, Lou broke into a run, though he wasn't terribly fast – I remembered his injured lung. He might need help, I thought, if they fought back.

Sabrina was tall and strong, she had already murdered two people. Despite the pain, I lowered myself down the bank via my scraped hands and knees, and hobbled after him.

Lou was using the half-built walls to conceal his approach as best he could, though a weak sun was rising over the trees in the distance and lit his darting figure. I had lost sight of the fire now that we were lower down, but I followed, slowly and in pain, limping and reminding myself that thousands of soldiers were currently putting up with far worse than a sprained ankle.

As he drew nearer to where we had seen the fire, Lou ducked behind a high wall, put a hand on Marple's collar and gestured at me to stay on his left, out of sight.

He was now only about fifty feet from the fire, and as I inched nearer, bent low, I could see smoke rising in the sunlight. In the still air, a woman's voice was clearly audible from inside a small brick shed.

'You get the water from the stream,' she said, 'then we'll have to cook the porridge on the fire.'

A higher voice responded, and Sabrina said, 'No, I think they must have gone back last night.'

Lou turned to me, put a finger to his lips, then murmured something into Marple's pricked ear. The huge dog broke into a fusillade of barking, and leapt forward across the damp grass to the shed, Lou pelting after him. Somebody screamed, a high wail of terror, and there was a crash as something metallic fell to the cement floor.

'Police! Everybody in there, come outside now!' Lou bellowed. There was a second's pause and then Sabrina – muddy, frightened, her long, plaited hair wet as a ship's rope – stepped into the daylight.

'Do not move,' Lou said. He produced the handcuffs from his coat pocket and snapped them onto her wrists, calling,

'Maggie Dawson, step outside now – police orders! We know you're in there.'

I had managed to hobble as far as the wall where Lou had waited.

'Maggie!' I yelled, 'You're not in trouble! Come out, please!'

I saw that Sabrina was shaking violently.

'It's all right, Sabrina,' I called uselessly, as Lou said, 'Sabrina Chattock, you are under arrest for the murder of Jean-Luc Arsenault and the suspected murder of Joyce Reid.'

She began to sob, bending double in her grief.

'Maggie!' Lou yelled again, and keeping one hand clamped on Sabrina's handcuffs, he peered into the open doorway.

'Damn it to hell, she's run out the back!' he shouted, and I looked past him to see a small figure dashing through the trees.

'Guard, Marple,' he said, and the dog stood by Sabrina, gazing fixedly at her, as Lou gave chase. I hobbled as quickly as I could to her side.

'Oh, Sabrina,' I said. 'Whatever made you do it?'

But her sobs were too powerful for words, they racked her body – I had never seen such grief and guilt.

In the distance, there was a long, piercing scream. Seconds later, Lou came back into view, panting heavily and leading a young, bedraggled girl – one who was yelling, 'Don't take my friend! It isn't her fault!' and struggling viciously to be free.

Lou's mouth was set, and he had lost his hat in the struggle, but I felt a brief bubble of joy rise within me. Maggie Dawson was here, alive, and whatever else happened, she would soon be reunited with her family. For a second, I felt it had all been worth it.

'You need to come down with me and we'll drive to the police station,' said Lou. Maggie was skinny as a liquorice whip, panting from exertion, dark hair dripping down her back.

'We're not coming anywhere,' she snarled. 'Leave us alone.'

Through her shuddering tears, Sabrina said, 'Mags, we have to. Don't you see, darling? It's over, we've been caught.'

'But you didn't DO anything!' cried Maggie.

'She did, you know,' said Lou, quite kindly. 'Whatever she's told you, Maggie, I'm afraid she's now under arrest for murder.'

Maggie stared wildly at her. 'But you know you didn't, you...'

'I did. I killed them both.' She looked at Maggie. 'It was me. I killed Joyce and Jean-Luc.'

Maggie was about to speak, but we all heard the noise at the same time.

A throbbing, rumbling sound in the distance, and a high, piercing whistling...

Lou dug in his pocket and produced his police whistle, raising it to his lips. The sound was astonishingly loud.

'Here,' he shouted. 'Up here!'

An answering whistle came, and now we could hear shouts.

'Am I going to prison?' Maggie asked suddenly. Her bravado had crumbled now we were no longer alone.

'Maggie, no,' I said. 'Running away isn't a crime. You're going back to London with your mum, she's here in Birchcroft with Spud. They'll be so happy to see you.'

Maggie's face crumpled. 'I've missed them so,' she wailed. 'I'm such a wicked, awful girl, I never thought how worried they'd be. I never, ever thought.'

I put my arms round her, though she had no idea who I was, and she sobbed into my shoulder. She smelled of earth and rain, like a wild creature.

Another, closer whistle came, and a yell of 'Detective Inspector Brennan!' and then an ancient, sputtering tractor appeared over the brow of the hill, followed by a team of men. For a moment, I thought I must be hallucinating with pain and exhaustion, but as they approached us, it became clear that Harold Walker was driving the tractor, Constable Creech was bringing up the rear, and the rest of the party was made up of Albert Miller and several of the convalescing soldiers from Brackenfield.

'Everyone alive?' shouted Walker.

'All accounted for but Norman,' Lou called back.

'We'll find him, don't worry,' said one of the men. The tractor rumbled to a halt, and they surrounded us.

'Bloody good show that you've found them,' said Walker. 'What an upheaval you've caused, young lady,' he added to Maggie. 'Thought you were dead. Glad to see you're not.'

'Sorry,' whispered Maggie. 'Really I am, sir.'

'As for you,' he said to Sabrina. He seemed to be struggling to articulate quite what he felt, but his expression was one of baffled disgust. Creech was speaking to Lou.

'Vicar saw your parked car by the campsite when he got up for matins,' he told Lou. 'Raised the alarm. I cycled to fetch Harold, and then we went to Brackenfield to raise a search party. Robert Potter told us where to aim for, on the QT. We heard the shouting and knew it must be you.'

'How did you get through the fence?'

Harold looked slightly embarrassed. 'Pruning shears,' he said. 'Been cutting back my hydrangeas for spring, thought they might come in useful.'

'I'm sure the Air Ministry will forgive you,' said Lou. 'Under the circumstances. Now look, can you take Edie back? She's badly hurt her ankle.'

Walker glanced down.

'Good Lord,' he said. 'I'll take you straight down to the cottage hospital. But what about these two?'

'Could you cram Maggie on?' Lou asked. 'They're both small – and she needs to see her mother before I speak to her.'

'Hop up,' said Harold to Maggie, and I scrambled up behind her.

'You look for Norman,' Lou told the men. He turned to

Creech. 'The rest of us will bring Sabrina down, and go to the police station in my car.'

Sabrina was still sobbing. 'I didn't mean to do it,' she wailed. 'It was an accident.'

'Two accidents resulting in sudden deaths,' said Lou. 'What a terrible coincidence.'

Harold started the wheezing engine, and I held on tightly as the tractor bumped and jolted over the rocky ground, sending fresh pain shooting through my ankle.

Harold wanted to take me to the cottage hospital, but I insisted that we deliver Maggie to Brackenfield first – I couldn't bear to keep Mrs Dawson or Spud in a state of despair for any longer than was necessary. We juddered slowly up the drive, and Harold climbed down and pulled the rope that made a great bell clang somewhere within. Mr Magellan opened the door, and his bland expression fell away as he took in the sight of Maggie, looking like a netted mermaid in her wet clothes.

'My goodness,' he said, and cleared his throat. 'Do come in, Mr Walker, Miss York, Miss... I shall fetch Her Ladyship immediately.'

Lady Brackenfield came hurrying in, a skein of dogs waddling at her heels.

'Maggie Dawson!' she shrieked, as Maggie stood silent and expressionless on the polished parquet.

'Heavens above, child! The worry you've caused!'

'Sorry,' said Maggie in a voice so low it was barely audible. 'Could I see my mum, please?'

As she spoke, Netta rushed into the hall, her face radiating pure joy.

'Maggie!' she cried. 'Oh, my little girl!'

She enfolded her daughter in her arms, and gripped her so tightly I wondered how Maggie could breathe. When they finally pulled apart, tears shone on both their faces, though Maggie's expression remained oddly blank. I assumed that she was suffering delayed shock.

'Come and see Spud, he's upstairs,' said Netta, leading her by the hand.

'Oh, Maggie, my dear, darling girl, I thought we'd never see you again.' Her voice wavered. 'I should never have sent you away,' she went on. 'It's all my fault.'

'It's not, Mum,' Maggie said. 'It's all mine.'

'Well,' said Lady Brackenfield to us once they were out of earshot. 'This is all quite a surprise.'

I thought that however surprised she was, it was nothing compared to how Birchcroft would react when the news of Sabrina's arrest for double murder became public.

'Rather early for sherry,' she said regretfully. 'Tea in the drawing room, perhaps?' She glanced nervously at my muddy clothes and wild appearance. I must have looked like a child raised by wolves.

'I'm afraid we mustn't, Your Ladyship,' said Harold. 'I should get Miss York to the hospital, she's badly hurt her ankle.'

'Oh, how dreadful,' said Lady Brackenfield vaguely, with only a hint of relief. 'Then of course, you must go and get it looked at.'

I hauled myself onto the tractor again, grateful to Harold, who was proving himself quite a decent egg. At the small hospital, a kindly matron re-bandaged my ankle.

'Nasty sprain,' she said. 'I should think you'll need a crutch for a few days.'

She found a rather battered-looking wooden one in a broom cupboard marked MEDICAL SUPPLIES, and added, 'We can send the bill to your husband.'

'Oh no,' I said quickly, 'I'm not married.'

'I do apologise,' she said. 'I saw you with your young man

after church on Sunday, and you looked such a lovely couple, chatting away together.'

I swallowed, unable to summon a response.

'Still,' she added comfortably. 'No harm holding on a while for a proposal, what with the war on...'

I smiled weakly, and thanked her for her kindness. Outside, Harold waited on his grimy chariot.

'Where do you want dropping off?' he asked. 'No sign of that young man o' yours.'

'He's not...' I began, then tailed off. It was more complicated to explain what Lou was to me than to go along with it.

'I don't know,' I realised. 'Perhaps the police station? Though it's a long way on a tractor.'

'Tell you what,' said Harold, 'we'll drive by the campsite and see if the car's gone. If it has, we'll assume they're already back down with the other young lady. I say lady. "Murderess" more like.'

The engine throbbed into life, and I was grateful it was too loud to allow a reply.

The car had vanished, and Harold took me to the temporary police station in Lower Brackenfield, a mile away. The village was smaller than Birchcroft, only a huddle of cottages on the hillside and a couple of closed shops.

The door to the house that served as Creech's lair stood ajar, however, and to my relief, Lou's car was parked outside, Marple peering through the quarter-glass.

'Hello?' Harold called from the porch, and Creech appeared.

'DI Brennan here?' asked Harold.

'He's with a suspect,' said Creech, as if I didn't know who. 'I'm not to disturb him.'

'I'll wait,' I said quickly.

'I'd best return this tractor,' said Harold. 'Least Wright could do in the circumstances, mind.'

He raised a hand and stumped out, brushing off my thanks.

None of us had managed any breakfast, I realised, which, coupled with the lack of sleep and ongoing pain in my ankle, explained the feeling of light-headed unreality that was gradually stealing over me.

I must have gone white, as Creech said, 'Here, are you all right, miss?' He pulled out a wooden chair. 'Put your head between your knees,' he instructed.

The room resettled. I could hear the reassuring rumble of Lou's voice down the small corridor, and the plaintive answering mew of Sabrina's.

'Sorry,' I said. 'It's been quite the night.'

'I heard,' said Creech stiffly. He was obviously highly put out that nobody had rushed to find him.

'I'll get you some water,' he added, more generously. 'And I suppose I might have a couple of plain biscuits I can spare.'

I felt better once I'd eaten the biscuits, and I resigned myself to a long wait, but to my surprise, I heard a heavy door closing and Lou's voice coming nearer.

'... get the paperwork sorted out...' he was saying. They appeared in the doorway, Sabrina still in handcuffs, looking distraught.

'Ah, York!' said Lou. 'I thought you'd find us. I'm going to take Miss Chattock to Manchester now she's confessed to both murders, with Constable Creech as witness.' Creech looked delighted with himself. 'There are no suitable cells here where she can await a hearing.'

'She's confessed?' My blood fizzed unpleasantly. I realised I had somehow hoped it was all a terrible misunderstanding, that Joyce had fallen, that an intruder had killed Jean-Luc...

'Yes, I'm afraid so,' said Lou.

Would Sabrina be sentenced to death? I thought of her, so broken and bedraggled. Surely not – her terrible acts had been crimes of passion, sudden and unplanned – hadn't they?

I realised she would be driving back in the car with us, and felt a chill of horror, sharing the journey with someone doomed to such a terrible future. Would I have minded so much if it had been a man? Probably not, I admitted to myself. I thought of her flaxen glamour, her despair over Jean-Luc, her obsession with him – enough to cut off her family, to run away from finishing school, to give up all she knew to come and live in a strange, bohemian gaggle of artists; people who didn't acknowledge the normal rules of existence, who went to bed with whoever they liked every night, who refused to join the war effort.

Suddenly, I felt terribly angry with them all for their manufactured carelessness, their infantile convictions about right and wrong. If Sabrina had come home to her family, she might by now be married to a local landowner and overseeing a lavish nursery – or working for the home front, organising the sewing of haversacks for the troops in her parents' well-appointed drawing room.

But as she climbed into the back of Lou's car, trussed in handcuffs, Marple stiff and watchful beside her, those imagined versions of Sabrina's life fell away, and we drove out of Birchcroft once again, towards her dark and lonely future.

All the way back, she cried. Sometimes she'd murmur, 'I did it. I killed Joyce and Jean-Luc. I killed them both,' and break into a storm of weeping again. She reminded me of Lady Macbeth, wracked by unassuageable guilt after a bloody and terrible act – or in Sabrina's case, two acts.

I tried to talk to her – I asked, 'Sabrina, was it because you were in love with him? Is that why you killed Joyce?' She drew a shuddering breath to reply, but Lou said sharply, 'Do not question my suspect when she's in custody, York,' and I subsided.

'I'll take you home, then Miss Chattock and I are going to Newton Street,' he added as we neared Manchester. I thought of all the people at work, or sitting down over their midday dinners with the newspaper, blamelessly grumbling over petrol rations and food prices. Sabrina would never know normal, boring life again.

'I'm afraid the cells at Newton Street are rather Victorian,' said Lou, 'but we'll make sure you get something to eat and a cup of tea.'

Sabrina said nothing as I climbed out and Lou locked the car and helped me to the door, before driving away with his white-faced passenger. I felt suddenly exhausted as I hobbled upstairs, using the wooden crutch to haul myself onto every step.

Above me, our door opened.

'Is that you, Edie?' called Annie's anxious voice.

'Yes, it's me.'

'For crying out loud!' Her furious face appeared over the banister.

'Where on earth have you been? We've been worried sick! I thought you must have had a car accident or died of exposure, or...' She noticed my bandaged foot and my thoroughly bedraggled state.

'Whatever have you done?' she said. 'Let me help you, idiot – why are you trying to get upstairs on your own? Here, hold on to me,'

She ran down the remaining stairs and gripped my waist as I staggered onto the landing.

'You look as though you've been dug up,' she added. 'I thought you'd be back the other night! Don't say you and Lou finally...'

'No, nothing of the kind,' I said crossly. 'I'm sorry you were worried, but I found a dead body and...'

'What?' Annie stared at me. 'I thought you just said you found a dead body.'

I sighed. 'I barely know where to begin. Perhaps you could

make me a cup of tea and I'll tell you everything.'

I opened the door, expecting to see Suki in Annie's chair, and was startled to find Arnold in the chair facing hers instead.

'Hullo, Edie,' he said. 'Gosh you're hurt, come and sit down!' He stood up and gestured helplessly to the chair, into which I gratefully subsided.

'I was worried to death,' said Annie, 'so I rang up Arnold, to see if he'd heard from Lou, and he hadn't, but he *very kindly* said he'd come and wait with me.'

'I slept on the couch,' Arnold added hastily. 'We were both rather concerned...'

'Rather concerned!' shrieked Annie. 'I didn't sleep a wink! Edie, for goodness' sake, what happened?'

'Cup of tea,' I begged, 'and I'll tell you everything. Hold on, where's Suki?'

'Oh, that's the other news,' said Annie. She looked suddenly cheered.

'Suki's moving in with Agnes! Apparently, she's got a spare room going begging and Suki can have it for nothing until she's on her feet. They got chatting the other night, and discovered they both adore kippers and jazz,' she went on. 'They're quite the bosom friends – Suki said Agnes is like the mother she never had. She's up there now, discussing where to angle the mirror and the perfect cushion placement.'

'Oh, that's wonderful,' I said, astonished by this welcome turn of events. 'So she'll be our upstairs neighbour!'

'Looks like it,' said Annie. 'And well away from my Arnold.'

'Your...?'

She smiled at him, and he glanced shyly back, his face full of a quiet joy.

'We talked about things last night,' said Annie. 'And... well, it was Suki actually, who changed my mind.'

'What do you mean?'

'Oh, she was being as flirtatious as usual,' said Annie.

I tried to speak, but she held up a hand.

'No, I know, she's had a terrible time, it's all been awful,' she said. 'But she needn't be quite so eager to charm every man she meets. Anyway,' she said quickly, seeing my expression, 'she was worried about you, too, of course, but it was all *does Arnold think this*, and *does Arnold feel that...*'

'Annie...' protested Arnold feebly, but he was laughing.

'I couldn't get a word in,' Annie went on. 'And when she finally went up to Agnes's, I realised—'

'Or I made it clear, perhaps,' said Arnold.

'No, you were a perfect gentleman, as always. But I was so jealous at the idea of your liking Suki,' she added. 'It made me want to scream. And I thought if I felt like that, perhaps it was silly to push you away...'

They were smiling foolishly at each other, and I felt myself beaming, too, despite the past two days.

'So you're sweethearts again?'

'Well...' said Annie, as Arnold said, 'Looks like it!'

'Oh, I'm so pleased,' I said. 'You're made for each other.'

'I'll pop the kettle on,' said Annie, blushing.

Arnold turned to me. 'Now we've got our love life sorted out at last,' he said, 'are you going to tell us where you've been all night?'

It took me a good couple of hours to tell them everything. Annie kept interjecting: 'What? But you could have been killed!' and 'You might have caught your death of cold!' while Arnold shushed her, murmuring, 'Go on, Edie, do,' as I paused.

During the telling, Annie found some cold meat pie in the pantry, which I ate with onion pickle and nothing had ever tasted so wonderful. The pot of tea was refilled several times, rationing be damned, and I almost forgot the pain in my ankle as I recounted how we had finally discovered Sabrina and Maggie.

'But how did Sabrina know where to find her?' asked Annie, rapt.

'Maggie must have told her before she left,' I said. 'So Sabrina kept it a secret. Along with everything else.'

'And what about Norman?' Arnold asked.

I had completely forgotten about him.

'I don't know,' I admitted. 'But I think he was bringing Maggie food. And perhaps he was up there somewhere, keeping an eye on her.'

'Is Lou going to talk to Maggie?' asked Annie.

'Yes,' I said. 'He needs to know why she ran away, and what Sabrina told her. She may be in trouble for not reporting her for Joyce's death, if she knew. But she's too young to go to prison,' I added. 'I hope.'

'Oh, I doubt it would be that serious,' said Arnold. 'Surely some coercion was involved from the older girl. And Maggie may not have known anything – perhaps she just thought Sabrina was helping her.'

'Yes,' I said uneasily. 'Perhaps.'

As I spoke, I found myself yawning like the MGM lion.

'Righto,' said Annie. 'You're worn out. Quick bath for you Miss York – Mrs T's away again, so Arnold took the opportunity to sneak the boiler on. Then you can have a plate of my hash and a long sleep.'

'That sounds wonderful,' I said.

She helped me into my dressing gown. 'I'll leave you to it,' she said. 'Shout when you need help getting out, and try not to get your bandages damp.'

I lay back in the warm water, too tired to move. Steam rose around me, turning the bathroom mirror to silvery beads, and I thought of last night's mist dropping over the woods. How scared Maggie must have been, all alone for those long weeks, how cold and unhappy. Why had she really run away?

The Wrights were awful, of course, and she was desperately upset about her father. She had fallen out with Johnny. But to stay away for so long, in such a lonely and inhospitable place, to frighten her mother and abandon Spud... and Sabrina had known where she was and told nobody, except perhaps Norman.

The water turned cold around me, as I thought about Maggie, her heartfelt diary entries, what little I knew of her life. I remembered Sabrina in the back of the car earlier, crying, *I killed them both! I did it!*

I sat upright so fast, I banged my arm on the taps.

'Annie!' I called. 'Annie, come quickly!'

It was after teatime, I was exhausted and in pain, but I had no choice. I had to get to Newton Street Police Station and find Lou, before it was too late.

CHAPTER EIGHTEEN

As I shrugged on my still-damp coat, which now smelled like Marple after he'd rolled in something unspeakable, Arnold gave in. 'Come on, then,' he said. 'I'll not have you waiting for the bus.

As 'the death van' – as Arnold called his vehicle – motored sedately towards town, Annie's shouts were still ringing in my ears – 'fool to yourself' and 'die of exhaustion and it'll be your own fault' being the politer ones.

'What's the great rush?' he asked mildly, as we drove towards the garment district near Newton Street. Parts of the city were still blocked off by bomb damage, and it was taking far longer than I would have liked to get there.

'I've realised something vital,' I said. 'I can't believe it didn't occur to me before. But we were so sure she'd done it...'

'Who?'

'Sabrina. But now I see...'

'I'm glad you do, because I don't,' said Arnold, as we rattled past the huge new Daily Express building. 'Still, I'm sure our DI pal will make sense of it.'

'I hope so,' I said. 'Or there could be another death.'

. . .

Arnold helped me to the door of the police station and promised to wait in the van. The desk sergeant was sitting in his chair, smoking a pipe and reading a dog-eared copy of *The Code of the Woosters*. He set it aside when he saw me.

'Evening, miss,' he said. 'May I help you?'

'I need to see Detective Inspector Brennan, it's urgent.'

He shook his head. 'I'm afraid that's not possible, miss. He's conducting an interview, along with Sergeant O'Carroll. No knowing how long they'll be.' He tapped his nose. 'It's quite a serious one, between you and I,' he said.

Between you and me, said Mr Gorringe, sotto voce in my head.

'This is more serious,' I said. 'I have vital information about the murders – he's with Sabrina Chattock, isn't he? I need to see him to prevent a terrible miscarriage of justice.'

He laid his pipe on the ashtray. 'Now look, miss,' he said, 'I'm sure you mean well, but we can't have random members of the public wandering in, interrupting police business. So if you'll just—'

'You don't understand! She didn't do what she's supposed to have done!'

'I believe the lady has confessed,' said the desk sergeant. 'So I'm afraid you've been misinformed. I won't tell you again, miss.'

I had no choice. I could see a corridor beyond his desk, and an ominously closed door at the far end. It could have been a storage cupboard, but it was worth the risk. I hobbled as fast as I could manage past the end of his desk and towards the closed door.

'Hi! Get back here!' he yelled. 'Miss, I'm warning you!' It took him a moment to extract himself from the chair, and as I stumbled past empty rooms, I could hear voices coming from the far end. I put on an extra burst of speed, ignoring the searing pain in my ankle, and banged on the door with my fist.

'Come back here!' shouted the desk sergeant, as the door was thrown open and I almost fell into the room.

'Edie!' Lou was now wearing a clean suit, and Sabrina sat opposite him at a small wooden table. She and Sergeant O'Carroll were both staring at me in shock.

'Interview suspended at' – Lou checked the wall clock – 'a quarter past six.'

He turned back to me. 'What in *hell's name* are you doing here? How dare you interrupt a police interview?'

'Lou, I'm so sorry, but she's lying.'

'She's already confessed,' he said. I had never seen him so angry. 'This time you've gone too far, York. Get out of my interview room.'

'I can't!' I shouted. 'She's lying to protect her friend – you have to listen!'

'What are you talking about?'

I mouthed three words at him, and he blinked.

'In my office, now,' he said. 'And if you're wrong... if you'd wait there, Sergeant O'Carroll, I shan't be a moment.'

Outside, the desk sergeant was gaping.

Lou clamped a hand on my shoulder and steered me round a corner and down another short corridor decorated with lumpy brown gloss paint and the original gas fittings. It was rather like being inside a tin of mulligatawny soup. In the distance, I heard the echoing clang of a cell door.

His office was smaller than I'd imagined, with an oak desk and wooden carver chair, a towering filing cabinet and a hatstand. He had a telephone, a calendar, an ashtray and an anglepoise lamp neatly arranged around his blotter, and an in-tray of tidy paperwork, all overseen by a ticking wall clock and a nicotine-stained portrait of the King. It made my desk at work look like the bombed cathedral.

'Sit,' he said, indicating the chair opposite.

I felt like an unruly pupil called to the headmaster's office.

'You've got one minute to explain yourself.' His expression was stony.

'Lou, I'm sorry I barged in,' I began. 'I wouldn't have dreamed of it if it wasn't the different between Sabrina hanging for what she's done or just going to prison.'

'What are you talking about?' He lit a cigarette irritably.

'It was what she said earlier, when we were driving back. She kept saying "I did it... it was me... I killed them both."'

'Yes. That's what we call a confession,' snapped Lou. 'Very useful, avoids a lot of time wasting.'

'But she emphasised *both*,' I said, 'as if we might be in doubt. I was thinking about Maggie, and why she stayed away so long,' I added. 'And Lou, I think she was upset by Joyce's last talk, and meant to run away for a couple of days to get away – give everyone a fright and get her Mum to come back. I don't imagine she ever intended to stay away. But I think Maggie saw Joyce on the Saturday morning out walking – and I think they had an argument and she pushed her.' I repeated what I'd told him minutes earlier. 'Maggie killed Joyce. Though I don't suppose she ever meant to do it.'

Lou blew a stream of smoke out. 'Then why has Sabrina confessed?'

'To protect her!' I cried. 'Because Maggie is like her little sister, someone Sabrina thinks is pure and innocent, unsullied by all the bed-hopping and angst of Athena House. They have a tight bond.'

'And I suppose Maggie killed Jean-Luc, did she, with her satchel?'

'No! Sabrina did that – but it was a crime of passion, she lost her mind with jealousy and despair. Of course she'll go to prison, but she's less likely to get the death sentence – she's a woman and it's her first offence, it wasn't premeditated. Lou, this could save her life.'

'A fascinating theory,' said Lou. He still looked furious. 'But please explain to me – a simple man, who is only a humble Detective Inspector with a signed murder confession on my desk – why on earth Sabrina would risk hanging for two murders if she only committed one?'

'Because she believes there's nothing left to live for,' I said. 'She went to find Maggie to tell her she'd take the blame. That Maggie could be free. That's why Maggie ran away from us – because she couldn't bear to watch her friend arrested for something she hadn't done.'

'But you're convinced that Maggie had?'

'Yes. But accidentally. Do you remember how blank Maggie seemed when she saw her mother again? How flat? It wasn't just guilt at running away. It was the shame of never being able to tell her what she'd done.'

To my surprise, Lou sank his head into his hands and pressed his fingertips into his eye sockets.

'Bloody hell,' he muttered. 'Oh, bloody hell, Edie.'

'What?' I said eventually, when he hadn't spoken for several moments. 'Do you believe me?'

Reluctantly, he lifted his head. His face was pink from the pressure he'd exerted.

'Yes,' he said. 'It makes sense. I didn't understand why Sabrina was so eager to describe how she'd killed Jean-Luc – accidentally, as you say – but couldn't come up with anything beyond "I pushed her" for Joyce. She said she was jealous, which was true – but Theo said he'd seen Sabrina the morning Joyce died – in fact, they all did. He wasn't arrested for sending flowers to Ethel in a jealous pet, that's hardly a criminal offence

– we interviewed him under caution because he insisted he'd been with Sabrina all morning.'

Lou sighed. 'We initially assumed he was lying to protect her, but all of them claimed to have seen her about the place during those few hours. God, what a mess.'

I was so relieved that he believed me, I could barely form a sentence.

'What will you do?' I asked.

He took a long, shuddering drag on his cigarette and exhaled.

'Edie York, unlocking Pandora's box a speciality,' he said. 'I'll go back and put this to Sabrina. And if she changes her story as a result – which I suspect she will – then I'll have to go and interview Maggie. She's too young to stand trial, but she'll go to a juvenile court and then...' He trailed off.

'But Sabrina will avoid the death sentence?'

'If the jury agrees she didn't mean to kill him, yes.'

'Do you think she did?'

'I don't know. She claims they were arguing about Nora, and he came at her, she picked the tool up to protect herself, but he slipped on some of the clay she'd swept off the table and fell sideways onto the blade. There was a long smear of clay on the floor when I examined the area and some on the sole of his shoe, so it's just about possible she's telling the truth.'

'But we can't know?'

'That will be up to her defence in court,' he said heavily.

We looked at each other.

'Sorry I shouted at you,' said Lou. 'You did the right thing. Even if it is an unholy mess.'

'Sorry I burst in,' I offered. 'I didn't think you'd take a telephone call.'

'I wouldn't have. Look,' he added. 'Go home, get some sleep, and I'll keep you posted, when I've spoken to Maggie.'

'But...'

'Edie,' he said, 'your mind may be impressive in its workings, but you need to learn when to give up. Now go.'

At work the next day, I felt flattened, as though the Birchcroft bull had tossed me over a fence, and my wooden crutch caused quite a stir as I emerged from the ancient, clanging Victorian lift and hopped to my desk.

'Whatever have you done now?' asked Pat, as though I'd personally affronted her by being injured, and Gloria cried, 'Oh, Edie! Did you fall downstairs?' across the office, so everyone's heads turned to have a good look at me.

'Back to work, please,' Mr Gorringe called wearily, as he strode through the office.

'Are you quite all right, Miss York?' he added. 'Should you perhaps be resting at home?'

'I'm perfectly fine, thank you, Mr Gorringe,' I said, though my ankle twinged as though Harold's pruning shears were gripping it.

'I'm afraid I was out walking in the hills and I tripped.'

'Ah,' he said. 'The Peaks can be a cruel mistress to the unwary. Perhaps ask Miss Cooper to show you the ropes if you visit again.'

I hid a smile. 'I will.'

'It was a good obituary of Joyce Reid,' he added, unexpectedly. 'One rather feels one would have liked to know her.'

'Yes,' I said. 'She was a fascinating woman.'

'I imagine you're aware that there's been another death up at her home?'

'I'm afraid so.'

'I wouldn't bother with an obituary on that one,' said Mr Gorringe. 'Strange little foreign sculptors won't be of interest to our readers. Perhaps you could do some research on Sir Hugo Pickford, the barrister who died last week – quite eminent, and very supportive of the war effort. His widow is a friend of Mrs Gorringe, it might be a kindness.'

'Of course,' I said, thinking it might also be a relief.

I didn't hear anything from Lou. I was itching for information, wondering what had happened to Maggie, whether she was back in London with Netta, or – horribly – in a remand home, awaiting a hearing at the juvenile court. I thought of Sabrina in a cell, and the tragedy of her impulsiveness, and I thought, too, of Norman, and whether he had known the whole truth, or simply wanted to help somebody young and distressed.

I felt quite sunken in gloom, but I had lunch with Ethel again. I told her everything over a dried-up ham sandwich at the Cona, and she shed a tear over Jean-Luc into the deeply unpleasant ersatz coffee they served.

'It's so very sad,' she said. 'I know he probably wasn't awfully nice, but he didn't deserve that. Nobody does.'

I nodded.

'All of this, though,' she said. 'It's made me realise we none of us know how long we have ahead of us. I don't want to waste my remaining good years living with Mother and that blasted parrot any longer,' she went on. 'I earn enough now to afford my own little flat, and I could take a lodger. Mother's fit as a flea, she'll be furious, but she'll get over it.'

I smiled at her. 'I think that's a marvellous idea. Perhaps somewhere near us and we can all go dancing more often.'

'I should love that,' she said. 'Did Arnold and Annie get back together?'

'Yes, just!' I said. 'How did you know?'

'Oh, I can tell,' she said. 'That man had eyes for nobody else, and I could see she was violently jealous when he so much as spoke to me. They're made for one another.'

'Is there anyone...?' I ventured tentatively. Ethel leaned forward.

'Well,' she whispered, 'I went to visit my cousin Barnaby last weekend, over in Cheshire, while he was on leave. And he had a friend staying, too – Major Iain Carmichael. He's a Scot, and really, he has the most charming accent...'

Her cheeks looked rather warm, suddenly.

'At any rate, he's going to write to me. I suppose we shall see.'

'I suppose we shall,' I said, laughing. 'Does he like country walking?'

'Adores it,' she said. 'He was telling me all about the Pentland Hills. They sound marvellous.'

'September is nice in Edinburgh, I believe,' I said.

'What for?'

'A wedding, of course.'

'Oh, stop it,' she said, but now she was smiling into her tepid coffee.

That afternoon, I spent an hour or so dithering over *Sir Hugo loved Llandudno, and spent many happy holidays there with his family, enjoying the resort's sandy beaches and bathing huts* – could you enjoy a bathing hut, I wondered, or was it more of a practical matter? I could hardly say *regularly got changed in its bathing huts*, which conjured up alarming visions of a portly man struggling into a striped costume. Perhaps I'd leave out the bathing huts altogether. I knew I was procrastinating, as I always did when faced with something unpleasant, but as Parrot Paulson passed my desk on her way to the ladies' – or 'the girls' lavvy' as she called it – I beckoned her over.

'Janet,' I said, 'I'm awfully sorry to ask, but a friend of mine is looking for a job, and I wondered...'

'I am not a recruiting agency, Miss York,' she said. 'Perhaps she would do well to visit the Labour Exchange on Portland Street.'

'She's very efficient,' I said in a rush. 'She'd be an excellent receptionist, or a secretary, perhaps answering telephone calls on the switchboard...'

'She sounds quite the thing,' said Janet, raising her eyebrows. 'As far as I'm aware, unfortunately, we have no vacancies at present. Even if we had, they'd go to members of our troops who have been forced to return home due to injury. As I'm sure you're aware.'

'Yes,' I said, defeated. 'I just thought there was no harm in asking...'

'And no harm in accepting the answer,' she said tartly. 'We're all fortunate to have good jobs in this day and age, so think on.'

She marched off, and I sighed heavily enough to rattle the paper in my typewriter.

Now I'd have to tell Suki the bad news.

'No good deed goes unpunished,' Pat often said. For once, I wholeheartedly agreed with her.

It came as a great relief when my desk telephone rang on Thursday morning and Sally on the switchboard said, 'I've DI Brennan on the line for you, Miss York.'

She put him through. His voice was tinny and irritable.

'York?' he said. 'Look, can you get away at lunch? I can meet you at Bob's Caff at noon and tell you what's happened since Tuesday.'

'Try and stop me.'

I was already there when Lou arrived, despite my ankle, almost quivering with anticipation.

'Two specials, and a pot of your finest char,' Lou said to Bob, sliding into the seat opposite me.

There were a few other people in, eating cheap fried sausages and drinking tea, and their chat and the clatter of knives and forks covered our conversation.

'Firstly,' said Lou, 'it pains me to say it, but thanks.'

'What for?'

'For knowing about people.' He sighed. 'Sometimes I forget how complicated they can be. It's exhausting. That's why, after Lorna, I decided not to involve myself with anyone in particular. It's hard work.'

I felt sadness wash through me, but I couldn't have said why. I had often felt the same way. And after the fiasco of my brief fling with Charles Emerson, I didn't trust myself to choose anybody suitable.

'Do you mean me knowing about Maggie?' I asked, keen to return the conversation to a professional footing.

'Yes, of course Maggie. You were right.'

It was odd to feel both triumph and a terrible sorrow – for Maggie, for Sabrina, for the ruined futures of those two bright, passionate young women.

'Tell me what happened,' I said. Bob banged down two plates of sausages and fried bread. As he shovelled it in, Lou explained.

'I went back to Birchcroft yesterday. Maggie was still at Brackenfield, with Netta and Spud, in a terrible state. Netta said to me "She keeps crying, but she won't say why." I asked if I could have a word with Maggie alone, and we went into the late Lord Brackenfield's old study – what wouldn't I give for a room like that. Shelves of old books, overflowing cigar boxes, deer heads mounted on the walls, ancestral portraits peering down...' he sighed wistfully.

'Maggie?' I prompted.

'Right, yes, so I told her what Sabrina had said – that she'd killed both Joyce and Jean-Luc – and then I asked Maggie why she'd run away in the first place. She looked white with dread, I felt an absolute rotter. But I took down her statement – once she started, she couldn't stop, it was like turning on a tap.'

He reached into his pocket and pulled out a bundle of handwritten pages.

'I've typed it up more formally now, but I thought you might want to see it,' he added. 'I need hardly say, not a word of this must find its way into the newspaper. I'd lose my job.'

'No, I shan't do that,' I said. I took the papers from him, laid down my fork and began to read.

I had just been to Joyce Reid's talk and I felt very angry, I read, transcribed in Lou's neat copperplate. *I told her what I thought of her ideas, and ran back to the farm. I couldn't stand feeling so upset any more. I missed my dad every minute, and I couldn't sleep. I was awake all night and I heard someone in the yard before dawn the next morning. I looked out the window, and I saw Johnny leaving. I thought 'why should he leave when I'm stuck here?' I decided that I'd run away and give everyone a fright, and then after a few days I'd come back and my mum would know how upset I'd been and come and get us – I didn't want to worry her so I put up with it all, but I couldn't stand another minute.*

My heart ached for Maggie. I read on, my sausages cooling on the plate.

I didn't want to scare Spud, but I thought he'd understand that I would not be gone long, and I was doing it for both of us. I didn't dare leave him a note in case the Wrights found it.

I packed my bag and I set off in the very early morning, but because I had no money, I was not sure where to go. I passed the campsite and Norman was cooking his breakfast. He waved and I went to talk to him.

He asked where I was going, and I said I wasn't sure. He told me how to get to the place up in the hills, where the Ministry have the secret pretend city. He drew me a map and told me to burn it later. He said he understood why I wanted to get away from people, and that he'd help me out a bit – he said he would bring me food every evening and leave it by the fence until I was ready to come back.

'I knew it,' I muttered.

Lou looked up. He had finished and pushed his plate away. 'Brave kid,' he observed.

I nodded.

I climbed for ages and I got under the barbed wire. There didn't seem to be anyone about so I thought I was safe for a bit. I found a funny sort of building with some blankets and I decided to stay there. I was very lonely and quite scared, but I thought it was only for a couple of nights so I tried to be brave.

Norman left me a bit of food as he promised, but I didn't see him – it was always by the fence at five o'clock. By the Saturday morning, (Note: Saturday 15 Feb, 1941. DI Brennan) *I had had enough of sleeping in the strange building. I decided to come back while it was sunny and face the music and hope that Mum would come.*

I was walking back down, and I saw Sabrina, coming up the lane. She had been out for a walk. It was very early and she was by herself. I was pleased to see her – I liked her and I felt as if she listened to me. She had taken me to the café a few times, and we had chatted and even gone for walks together. She was kind. She once told me she was sad because she liked Jean-Luc and Joyce had taken him away. I told her I thought he must be an idiot and she laughed. That day, she said Joyce was going for a walk a bit later and it would be a relief to have her out of the house for the day. Then she said she had to get back for breakfast and that I should let everyone know I was back because they'd been worried.

I was frightened of going back to the Wrights, as I thought Mr Wright might beat me, the way he did Johnny.

I shuddered, and Lou said, 'The bit about Wright?' I nodded. 'It gets worse,' he said ominously, lighting a cigarette and offering me one. I took it absently, and continued to read.

I was still near Athena House, sitting in the sun and trying to be brave about returning, when I heard somebody shouting 'bye' and I realised it was Joyce Reid. When I saw her crossing the yard in her walking things, I felt very angry again, that she had said such awful things about soldiers like my dad, and I felt stupid that I had been taken in by her. I decided to follow her and ask her why she had said horrible things and try to make her understand that our dad was a hero.

Lou was now reading upside down from across the table.

'She began to cry at this point,' he said quietly. 'It was quite upsetting. I offered to get Mrs Dawson, but she said no, she wanted to "get to the end" – that was how she put it.'

I felt tears prick my eyes.

'Oh, Maggie,' I said. 'I do so wish she'd had the money for a train fare. If she hadn't bought that damned badger-hair brush for Johnny...'

'And him too spotty and callow to need it,' agreed Lou. 'Keep reading, I've got to get back soon.'

I went up the hill after her for about an hour. She was quite far ahead and I couldn't catch up. She did not look round, or seem to notice me. I was quite a way behind and there were rocks and trees between us. I just wanted to get near enough to talk to her.

In the end, at about ten o' clock, she climbed up along what I now know to be Nether Brow, and walked to the summit. She stopped there, looking over the hills, and I took my chance to catch up. She saw me when I was just beneath her. She seemed surprised, and she said 'Maggie! Whatever are you doing here?'

My neck was straining from looking up at her and the sun was in my eyes, so I climbed up the last bit to the summit to speak to her. I said, 'I want to talk to you,' and she said, 'All right, what about?' She did not sound angry, just puzzled, I suppose.'

My heart was thumping as I reached the next paragraph. I took a sip of tea to steady myself.

I said, 'My Dad, and why you think his death was pointless.' She said, 'Oh, my dear child, you can't be expected to understand the cruel theatre of war,' and I said, 'I am fourteen and I understand that we must all do our bit.' I told her, 'You're wrong to say it's a waste of time, we all have to fight the Nazis,' and she laughed at me and said, 'That's the naïve view, yes.'

I thought about my lovely, kind dad, and I remembered that Spud and I would never see him again, and Miss Reid had said he was as bad as the enemy, and that's when I lost my temper. I am very sorry to say this, and I have wished every minute since that I hadn't done it, and I could take it back. But I saw red, and I gave her a hard shove in the shoulder. I never meant to push her off, really I didn't – I was angry and I lashed out.

Miss Reid sort of staggered a bit, and I realised she was now right by the edge. She tried to steady herself, but a rock gave way under her boot and I saw her sway and stumble. I cried out and reached to catch her, but she fell backwards.

'Dear God,' I whispered. It was hard not to feel Maggie's horror as she described the scene. Lou nodded. 'Poor little kid.'

It was a horrible shock. I looked down, and saw her lying there. I thought she was just knocked out and would come round, but I was so frightened of what would happen to me and what my mum would think, and so ashamed, I ran away. I found my way back to the pretend town, and I stayed there. Norman kept leaving food and he even brought a gas stove and matches when the weather turned bad. I kept thinking I would be found, but Sabrina didn't tell anyone, because nobody came and the longer it carried on, the more frightened I was of going back. But a few days ago, he stopped bringing anything.

I was starving, and in the end, I went through the woods back to Athena House. I hid and waited for about three hours until I saw Sabrina come out to feed the chickens. I got her attention by saying 'ssss!' as that was a signal my brother and I had used, and I had told Sabrina about it. She came over, and I asked if she had anything to eat. She went and brought me some pie that Nora had made. I told her where I had been, and she said I should go back home to London and she would give me some money to get the train. She asked why I had run away again, as she had thought I was going home. At this point, I did not know that Joyce had died. I thought she must have recovered and be inside the house. I told Sabrina about going after Joyce that morning, and I confessed what I had done.

Sabrina looked very shocked. She said, 'Maggie, Joyce passed away.'

I felt very faint, and she gave me some water to bring me round, and then I panicked. I ran and ran, I thought I would be hung for murder if anyone found me, and the shame I had brought to my family and the terrible thing I had done was too much to bear. I did not know what to do, so I hid up in the strange buildings again, and I ate dry biscuits from a tin I found and drank water from the stream and that was the last I knew until Sabrina found me in the early hours of Monday.

She was crying and shaking, and she said she needed to

stay with me for a day or so to 'think about what to do', but she would not tell me what had happened. I shared my blankets and biscuits with her and she slept most of the day, then that night we saw a light on the hill and realised someone was looking for us, and she said we should hide. We took a blanket and a pan and some oats and we stayed in the little shed until dawn. It was very cold and in the morning, she thought it would be safe to light a fire.

Then we heard voices, and I ran, but you caught me.

I do not know where Norman went. I am very sorry and I accept whatever happens to me. If I am going to prison, or am for the rope, please tell Mum, Nanna, Spud and Pouncer that I am more sorry than I can ever say.

I promise that this is all true and accurate.

Signed: Margaret Antoinette Dawson (14)

I realised there were tears on my cheeks, and I rubbed at them with my palms. Lou passed over a laundered handkerchief.

'Lord,' I said into its comforting folds. 'What a tragedy. Does she know what Sabrina's done now?'

'Yes. She was horrified that Sabrina had confessed to both murders. Sabrina has retracted her statement now, and admitted that she was covering up for Maggie. She said, "I did kill Jean-Luc, so I thought I may as well say I'd killed Joyce as I was going to prison anyway. That way Maggie would be off the hook."'

'But she says Jean-Luc was an accident?'

Lou nodded. 'She went up to confront him about Nora, she says, and they had a row. I tend to believe her, but whether a jury will, I don't know. Her trial date hasn't yet been set. One good thing, though, has come of it all.'

'What?'

'Her parents are with her. She wrote and told them, and

they've come to see her. I spoke to them briefly and they were so grateful to have their daughter back, I think they'd forgive her anything. They thought Jean-Luc was the devil incarnate – he made her cut off all contact, apparently. They've had a private detective looking for her.'

He looked at his watch. 'I must get back to work.'

I handed back Maggie's statement.

'Joyce's funeral is on Saturday morning,' he added, as he paid the bill. 'Will you come? I thought I'd go, take a last look at the Bohemians of Birchcroft,' he said. 'Jean-Luc's family are trying to get his body repatriated. Best of luck with that in occupied France in the middle of a war.'

'Yes, I'll come,' I said. 'I think Ethel will, too.'

I thought of my friend, eating breakfast eggs with Joyce in the kitchen at Athena House, talking about art and philosophy till the early hours, daring to get a little tipsy and kissing a handsome Frenchman.

'She'll want to say goodbye.'

EPILOGUE

'Take these,' Annie said, thrusting a packet of sandwiches into my hand. 'Knowing those bohemians, there'll be no funeral tea. You'll be offered a carafe of red wine that tastes like vinegar, and they'll expect the glory of creative genius to fill you up better than a Bakewell tart.'

I laughed. Suki, who had come down to see me off, said, 'You do look nice, Edie. What a pretty hat.'

I had borrowed it from Clara. 'Wore it to grandfather's send-off a few years back,' she had said of the little black silk pill-box. 'Only because Mother made me put a dress on. I felt such a fool, I can't tell you.'

She had spent the night with her family, and had dropped in on the way back to the airbase with the hat.

'How's the aeroplane training?' I asked, and her face shone.

'Oh it's wonderful!' she said. 'Of course, one wishes there wasn't a war on, but without it, how could I have known the sensation of soaring above the clouds? It's the most alive you'll ever feel.'

'The most sick I'll ever feel, more like,' said Annie. 'I can't imagine how queasy-making it must be, swooping about...'

'We don't *swoop*,' Clara corrected her. 'We fly on a carefully charted course, straight as an arrow. And besides, I'm only delivering planes to airfields, I'm hardly battling Messerschmitts. If only one could,' she added wistfully. 'Perhaps if there's an invasion...'

'Oh, don't say it!' cried Suki. 'Just as I'm free of that awful man, the very idea of finding Nazis hiding under the bed...'

'Don't you worry,' said Clara. 'We'll see them off before they get near you.'

Suki smiled at her. 'I'll be all right,' she said. 'Agnes is rather stout, I'm sure she'll protect me. And Madame Faye is quite fierce too. She told me her real name is Freda Fishwick and she can knock a grown man down with her right hook. She's marvellous.'

Annie and I glanced at each other. My news from the *Chronicle* had badly disappointed her, but it had also galvanised Suki into action and propelled her to visit Madame Faye at her salon, who had, long ago, promised her a job. It seemed Suki had charmed her way back, eight years later – and since being taken on at the salon as a receptionist earlier in the week, Suki had been full of admiring tales of 'Madame'.

'Ta-ta,' said Clara, as she left. 'I'll see you all soon. I hope the funeral is... well, as it should be.'

'So do I,' I said. 'Though I'm not sure anybody agrees on quite what that is.'

After the burial, the little knot of mourners drifted away from the freshly dug grave. The sun was shining, and the vicar squinted from the porch as he waved us off. The service had been quiet and respectful, and Aubrey had not thrown himself onto the coffin shrieking with anguish, as Lou had suggested he might, though he had blown his nose with a muffled honk several times.

Nora laid a wreath of wild spring flowers on the newly dug earth, and Theo stood apart, lost in contemplation.

Joan broke away from the others and came over to us. She was wearing a fitted black jacket and trousers and looked both imposing and rather handsome.

'Thank you for coming,' she said. She looked at Lou. 'And for finding out the truth about what happened to her.'

'It was Edie, really,' he said. 'She had a hunch.' He caught my eye and smiled.

'What will happen to Maggie?' she asked him. 'I believe she's back in London for now?'

'Yes,' Lou said. 'No more running away. She's waiting for a juvenile court date, but I suspect they won't be too harsh. She may get three months in a remand home, or a conditional discharge, if she's lucky.'

'And Sabrina?' Joan looked worried.

'Hard to say,' said Lou. 'But she won't hang, I'm pretty sure of that. There's too much evidence that it was an accident. Perhaps prison... but her parents will write and visit, and they'll take her in when she's released. She's still young.'

Joan sighed. 'What a ghastly mess,' she said, lighting a roll-up.

'What will you do, Joan?' I asked. 'Will you stay on at Athena House?'

'No,' she said. 'The will reading took place last week. It seems Joyce never had any intention of leaving her house to us. It's all going to some distant nephew. What a joke, eh?'

Ethel looked astonished. 'But you were all so close!'

Joan shook her head wearily. 'I'm not so sure we were. Look, I'm leaving on Monday – I'm going to lodge in Manchester with some friends for a bit, and rent a studio, so this may be the last chance of a walk while the sun's out. Will you come with me, and say a final farewell to Birchcroft?'

'Of course,' I said. I glanced down. 'Though my ankle's still playing up a bit...'

'Oh, we won't go far,' said Joan. 'We'll just take the path up to the viewpoint. You can see quite far enough from there on a clear day.'

Ethel, Lou and I followed her slowly up the dry little path, a stream tumbling alongside it. After fifteen minutes, we emerged from the trees, which were just coming into leaf, and saw the vista of hills and valleys spread before us.

Joan hitched herself onto a rock, and we lowered ourselves to the grass. Below us, the first lambs skipped alongside their mothers, and smoke drifted from distant chimneys.

'Goodbye Joyce,' said Joan quietly. 'You lived freely. And there was nobody like you.'

Lou produced a hip flask of brandy and handed it round.

'A toast to the memory of Joyce Reid,' he said. 'I didn't agree with her, but I'd like to have met her.'

We were silent for a moment. High above us, a small plane droned, its shadow chasing along the valley floor.

'Perhaps it's Clara,' I said, and all of us looked up, tracking its progress across the blue and white sky.

'Hard to believe the war's still happening,' said Joan. 'Living here, it's been easy to forget.'

I thought of Maggie and Sabrina, and what they'd lost – innocence, and freedom. I thought of Theo's bitterness and Nora's frustration, Aubrey's grief. I thought of Norman – he'd simply gone, vanishing like a ghost into the landscape. I thought of Annie and Arnold, and Suki's escape from her violent husband.

I thought of Lou and how much he longed to be on the front line, and the injured soldiers, trapped in the gilded cage of Brackenfield Hall.

'Come on,' said Lou. 'Let's see if Ned will open up early for us. I'll buy you all a drink.'

'Not much to celebrate,' said Joan.

'We're alive,' I said. 'That's worth something, these days.'

We turned and followed Lou down the winding path, as overhead, the aeroplane shrank to a gleaming dot in the sunlight, and disappeared over the distant hills.

A LETTER FROM F.L. EVERETT

Hello,

I'd love to hear what you thought of the book – it would be wonderful to hear your views. The good news is, Edie and her friends (and Lou – is he just a friend... or a bit more?) will be back soon in a third novel, so to keep up-to-date with my latest releases, just sign up at the following link. Your email address will never be shared and you can unsubscribe at any time.

www.bookouture.com/f-l-everett

Thank you again for reading *Murder in a Country Village*. I truly hope you enjoyed it and, if so, I would be extremely grateful if you could write a review. It makes a huge difference in helping new readers to discover my books.

I love hearing from my readers, wherever in the world you may be – you can get in touch on my Facebook page, through Twitter, Goodreads or my website.

If you've got this far, you've almost certainly read *Murder in a Country Village* (unless you're the type of reader who checks the ending first) and I do so hope you've enjoyed it. Writing about my much-loved hometown, Manchester, comes very easily to me. I was born there and lived in the city for over forty years, and while it's changed enormously since Edie's time, there's also plenty that's recognisable, from ghost signs reading

Fire Warden's Bell in the Northern Quarter to the grand Victorian architecture and the rebuilt cathedral.

In this book, however, Edie and Lou venture further afield, to Birchcroft, a village in Lancashire which doesn't exactly exist, but in its layout and position owes a significant debt to Edale in the Peak District. I went up there alone one day in January, seeking inspiration, and was struck by its beauty, the sudden changes in weather from sunshine to sweeping rain, and the almost theatrical fall of light on the hills. It all helped me to envisage Athena House, the Wrights' bleak hillside farm and the Black Horse pub.

Decoy cities were real, too, and though there's very little concrete evidence left of these cunning examples of misdirection, some photographs exist, showing the eerie half-buildings and scaffolding that confused the Luftwaffe.

During the war, my grandpa was briefly in the Home Guard, patrolling the hills around Manchester, so I have borrowed a little from his experiences too. As those long, cold nights have largely faded from living memory, I'm immensely grateful to the people who wrote and talked about their wartime experiences, so we can at least try to understand how it might have felt to be shivering on a winter hillside, worrying about invasion.

Of course, those who lived through the war didn't just worry about the big dangers – bombing, their loved ones away fighting or the threat of a German victory. They worried about coupons and the sugar ration, or how they'd get to work through the rubble, why prices had suddenly gone up, or whether their young man would ever propose. Reading diaries and letters of the time, it's notable how much people thought about day to day life – finding their way home in the blackout, or a cake that didn't rise and wasted the margarine ration. Even those away fighting dreamed of sleeping in a comfortable bed, and going dancing again.

They were, of course, ordinary people, caught up for almost six years in something extraordinary. Writing about Edie and her friends brings the war to life for me – and reminds me that while we have the historical privilege of knowing the outcome, the people simply getting on with life in 1941 had no idea. I admire those past generations enormously, and I feel very lucky to be able to write about them with the benefit of hindsight.

Thanks again for reading,

Flic x

fliceverett.com

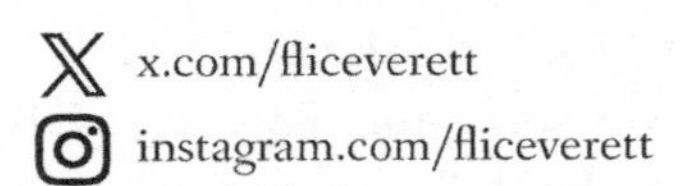

ACKNOWLEDGEMENTS

I try to be as accurate as possible when it comes to describing Edie's world – so first of all, I must thank the amazing historian Catherine Pitt. She's my friend and she's also a powerhouse of knowledge. There's not many people you could message with the question 'what did a district commissioner wear in 1941?' and have an answer pinging into your inbox five minutes later. Thank you so much, Catherine, for your tireless help and support.

Thank you, as ever, to my brilliant editor, Susannah Hamilton, who was right about so many things, particularly the things I really didn't want to lose from the book. It's far better for it. And enormous thanks to the whole Bookouture team, particularly Jess, Kim, and everyone else who works so hard to make my books as good as they can possibly be. Any mistakes are entirely down to me playing with my new kitten when I should have been focussing, so thanks also to Kit Marlowe. Keen readers may notice that several cats have wound their way into these pages, quite possibly inspired by her presence on the kitchen table as I typed.

I am also extremely grateful to my novel-writing friends on and offline, for quotes, advice, support and generally making me laugh. Thank you Erin Kelly, Mhairi McFarlane, Clare Swatman, Rowan Coleman, Catherine Cooper and Andreina Cordani.

Thank you to my dear husband, Andy, for taking the dogs

out when I needed to concentrate and listening to me bang on endlessly about bombs and rationing.

Lastly, thank you to my beloved family of fellow writers – particularly my mum, Janey, il miglior fabbro.